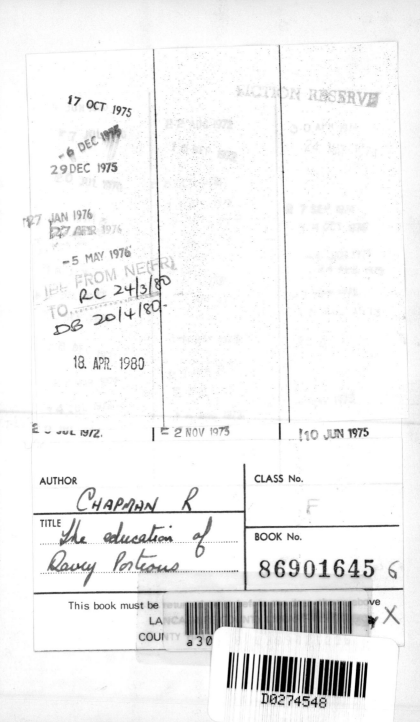

AUTHOR	CLASS No.
CHAPMAN R	F
TITLE The education of Revay Portious	**BOOK No.** 86901645 6

THE EDUCATION
OF DAVEY PORTEOUS

The betrayal of love is the hardest education of all. For Davey Porteous, such a betrayal marks a crucial moment in his childhood. Brought up alone in his grandmother's house, he knows only the companionship of his nanny, the servants and his tutor – until the day when his beautiful and flamboyant mother bursts into his world and sweeps him away to a life he has only dreamed of – a house by the sea for the summer. But slowly, imperceptibly, his intoxication with her gives way to a sickening sense of disillusion, then betrayal, as he becomes the victim of his mother's cynical abuse of her child's innocence.

For appearances, as Davey learns, can be deceptive. The refuge of the calm Victorian house, the happiness of the pretty seaside cottage, even the warmth of a mother's love, are an illusion. Trying to complete the mysterious and tantalising fragments of adult life that he hears and sees, he wanders into a dangerous world of passion, of squalid intrigue, perversion and a madness that leads to suicide.

Set in the early Twenties, this is a fascinating and dramatic account of a child discovering an uncomfortable reality, as Davey is drawn irrevocably and at times unwillingly out of childhood.

By the same author

The Laurel and the Thorn (*Faber and Faber*)
Father Faber (*Burns and Oates*)

RONALD CHAPMAN

The Education
of Davey Porteous

COLLINS
St James's Place, London
1969

WHALLEY

Printed in Great Britain by
Northumberland Press Limited
Gateshead

CHAPTER ONE

My first and deepest memories are of a house and not of a person. The Firs had been built in the '80s by a successful painter. It lay on a little knoll of green-sand at the foot of a chalk down. The knoll was covered with a dense wood. Tall, melancholy firs crowned its summit and surrounded the house on all sides except to the south where there had been a clearing which had been turned into a lawn. In places the trees grew right up to the walls. Even in the height of summer the breeze whispered in the blue-green branches. At the bottom of the hill, at the edge of the wood, there were great, primordial trees, beeches, oaks, acacias and an occasional holly.

It had been built, as was so often the case with Victorian houses in Surrey, as a country cottage, and had then been added to, bit by bit. There were three great studios which made the house look bigger than it was. It had a sloping, red tiled roof, stone and half-timbered walls in the Surrey style, leaded light windows and huge chimneys which towered up among the Scotch firs.

My grandfather, George Porteous, a famous poet of his time, but now no more than a name in a single text-book, had altered the house very little when he bought it after his marriage. One studio became a drawing-room, the other a study, while the third was used for various purposes and eventually became a study for myself. More land had been purchased, including an old farm house, and was laid out in shrubberies, orchards, rose and kitchen gardens. It became a small residential estate.

My grandfather had married, when he was sixty-five, an admirer of forty. It had come as something of a surprise when a son was born. Giorgio, as the poet was called by all his

5

friends, died at the age of eighty-eight in 1910. My father was then in his teens. He was killed at the end of the Great War soon after a romantic marriage to a Belgian girl, my mother. My mother was very young and it was decided that it would be to everyone's interest that I should be brought up at The Firs. My mother was therefore a notional rather than a real figure, whom I saw only infrequently.

The melancholy of the wood and the great fir trees bending over the house mingled with Grandma's melancholy. Death had taken her husband and her son. We always seemed to be in mourning. Grandma had adored her Giorgio. His study, one of the studios, was preserved as he had left it the day before his death. The pen which he had been using still lay on the blotting pad. In Grandma's eyes he was one of England's great poets. She cherished his memory like a wonderful dream. Giorgio came first for her in everything. She had loved my father but the love was in part due to the fact that he was Giorgio's only child.

It was a haunted place. The past seemed more real than the present. It was not so much that time had stood still and the world went its way all around the little estate; it was rather that the past had invaded it and made it its own. Everywhere in the garden there were memories of Giorgio. This clump of laurels on the lower lawn had been planted by Grandma to shield him from the east wind. This seat, under a great elm, and modelled from local clay by Grandma herself, had been placed so that he could see a favourite view. This summer-house was where he had written his poem on *Demeter*. This clump of brambles showed the place where there had once stood a lightning-riven acacia he had refused to cut down. Here in a ride in the woods was a terra-cotta cross, a work of Grandma's, of course, to commemorate the passage of pilgrims on their way to Canterbury. Giorgio had written a poem on the subject. In this door, next to the stoke-hole, was the old photographic dark-room, for Giorgio had been a keen photographer. The wood was left as wild as it could be, with its

6

tangles of brambles and bracken. This was how Giorgio had liked it. As a disciple of Tolstoi and Ruskin he felt it was an offence to trim or alter it. The only concession to humanity was a network of little paths along which he had wandered meditatively, dressed in his Inverness cape. Two capes, one a faded green and the other blue, still hung in the hall. It would have been no feat of imagination to have seen his small but impressive figure at the turn of one of the overgrown tracks.

Inside the house there were portraits and photographs of him everywhere; as a young man, romantic and melancholy; middle aged, tired and melancholy; in old age, grand and melancholy. In the later photographs he sat at his desk writing, or out in a little arbour in front of a splendid Della Robbia, dressed in his doctor's robes. The staircase was made unnecessarily dark by overlapping photographs in dark frames of the Sistine chapel. Giorgio liked to pause on his way up and downstairs to see these great forms, with their magnificent, nebulous evocations. To be magnificent, evocative, nebulous – that was the aim of his poetry.

Giorgio's shadow pervaded everything. There was no action in the household, if you went into it, which did not emanate from some order or other of his. He ruled us from his grave on the hill outside the village. His sad, melancholy, finely modelled features brooded over the place, brooded over it with his greatness and aspirations. He had aspired to greatness and in his lifetime achieved it. Somehow we, and I in particular, as his grandson, were the poorer for it. For what, after all, could we do to emulate him? In the darker paths at the edge of the wood, or when darkness was falling on a winter afternoon, before the lamps had been brought in, his spirit seemed to suck our very life. While he was alive the place had been an object of pilgrimage. Admirers had come to see the grand old man and listen to his views on life. Now that he was dead it was a shrine, still filled with his presence, but without worshippers. The war had scattered them like dust before an angry wind.

7

But for me The Firs was home. I drank in its melancholy from the first and therefore did not find it depressing. I loved it deeply and there was no place in my mind for rancour at the spirit that brooded over me. On the contrary, what I heard of Giorgio I loved. I was told that he was a great man and I believed it. Even the little criticisms that he could be irritable and unreasonable only made him seem more human in my eyes. He was to me, what he was to Grandma, a god who lived among gods. The names of Browning, Tennyson, Thackeray, Millais and Ruskin – all of whom he had known – were often mentioned by Grandma. I looked on them as on a race of giants departed from the earth. The thought of them even now brings a nostalgia into my mind which I can scarcely control.

I knew less of my father. Of course, Grandma told me of him but somehow her stories lacked the vividness of the anecdotes about Giorgio and his friends. I heard a little about him, too, from the servants, particularly from Mr Courtenay, the chauffeur, who had once been groom and coachman. My father was a remote person to me, fine, sensitive, gallant, a hero who had died for his country, but indistinct, whose character I never grasped, perhaps because he had died so young. To me, prompted by Grandma's romantic imagination, he was simply one of the mighty fallen. I then had no knowledge of the cynicism and disillusion which he must have experienced in the trenches. At the roots of consciousness I irrationally feared and envied him. Giorgio was too great to emulate, but in my father's case I felt I should try to be like him. And in my heart I knew I could not. Whenever I thought of him playing as a child along the woodland paths I played on, I made a comparison – a comparison which was to my detriment.

As for myself I was as normal as an only child in such circumstances could be. I suppose I was what is called sensitive and delicate. I had no friends of my own age, partly because I did not meet many other children, partly because I did not want to meet them. I read early and was content with my own company and that of adults. Besides, I had become prone to a mysterious illness at about the age of eight which was never satisfactorily diagnosed. After exertion or excitement I had terrible dreams which, on waking, led to temporary unconsciousness. Occasionally I had fits when awake. It was the fear of having one of these when with other children that made me misanthropic. I do not know to this day whether I suffered from some sort of epilepsy or whether it was an illness with nervous origins. As it happened, to be truthful, it did not play a great part in my life, except that it delayed my departure to boarding school. In any case Grandma had no love of the boarding system and did not see much harm in my being without the company of my contemporaries. I was eight before I had any real lessons, though I read early. It was at this age that what I can only call full consciousness began to dawn for me. I was much older in some ways than boys of my own age. I knew and understood adult states of mind. I was precociously interested in what interested them. But I had no knowledge of children, of games or companionship.

I was playing one morning in the nursery and Grandma sat by the little coal fire. The canary's cage hung in the high window and caught a gleam of scattered sunlight. The bird sang a few intermittent bars and relapsed into silence. Grandma was dressed, as usual, in a long black dress. She wore a black velvet band on her head trimmed with lace to match that at her neck and throat. Her silver hair, tinged with streaks of gold, like raw silk, was tied back in a bun. She always carried a little velvet pouch containing a rubber, a Royal Sovereign pencil, and a pen knife. She was an amateur artist of talent, and delighted in sketching bramble shoots, bracken fronds and details of Gothic or Celtic tracery. Her fine, sensitive face with its thin aquiline nose and thin lips, was particularly melancholy that day, as she gazed into the crackling coal fire. It was not usual for her to come to the nursery. She was a busy woman who always had some project in hand and seldom had time to waste. But that morning, as the fog lay about the leafless branches, dripped in the silence and the sun, ghostly and luminous, appeared from time to time through the trees, Grandma was lonely. She sighed and pinched the bridge of her nose. I left what I was doing and went over to her. I stood in front of her and looked into her sad, pale-blue eyes.

'Grandma,' I said, 'I wonder if it could be that Daddy will return?'

She reached out her light old hand, which had the texture of silk, and put it on mine.

'But, Davey, he can't.'

'Why not?'

'He's dead, darling.' And she shook her head resignedly.

'But they didn't find his body'

She shook her head again.

'Mightn't he be a prisoner or something? Or, perhaps he's been ill.'

Grandma sighed. 'He won't come back now.'

'But he might,' I persisted, swinging one of my legs, still holding Grandma's hand, and at the same time looking at the fog-laden trees, which I could just see through the high window, 'I think he will.' I glanced back at Grandma since she did not reply. She was looking into the fire. A pale gleam of sunlight fell on the window-sill.

I turned back to the world outside. The sun was breaking through. The canary fluttered, cheeped and gave a fragment of song. 'I think he will,' I repeated, my mind distracted by the things I had been looking at. As I said it, I thought I had brought it into being.

I stood there and the vision of my father's return flashed through my mind. A knock at the back door. I opened it all unsuspecting. There in the doorway stood the hero, saddened by sorrow, as if the grave had given him up, dressed in khaki. He lifted me into his arms and gave me a long kiss on the forehead. He walked with me past the servants' hall and through to the drawing-room. Grandma wept, tears began to flow down his cheeks. He said: 'It's hard to return to life.'

Later that evening he took me on his back to bed. I felt the rough uniform on the back of my knees.

'No,' Grandma said, without looking up. 'No, he'll not come now.'

As she spoke I realised, obscurely, without understanding it, that I did not want him to return. Perhaps nor did she. Life had dealt its unkind blows. She had made her dispositions accordingly. And she would not have had it otherwise.

She wrote innumerable letters to the dwindling admirers of the old, half-forgotten poet. She stuck letters he had written, fragments of poems, photographs, into albums, ready for the time when he would once more be recognised. She realised sadly that it would not be in her time. But posterity would recognise that her love and confidence had been justified. She wanted to write his life, but she felt it beyond her, and contented herself with collecting the material which someone else would use. I often came across her in the Red room, surrounded by papers, vexed by their complexity, racking her memory to find a clue to a correspondent's identity, or an obscure allusion.

At other times she would model in clay – crosses, plaques, reliefs covered with angels and obscure Celtic symbols. These would mostly be for memorials to her friends who had died. But they were sometimes used in the house. The niche in the Red room, where Giorgio had lain on a couch to compose, had been decorated by her in tow and plaster and heavily painted in gold, silver and dark blue. The high ceiling in the drawing-room was filled with plaster panels decorated with strong, simple symbols in relief.

But, of course, Nanna was the centre of my life. I loved her with the serenest and the most untroubled love. As I gradually grew up my dependence on her diminished, but not my love. It was just that my attention became diverted from the world of dreams to a more defined world which I found around me. She was all, or almost all, that mattered. I called her when I was frightened or hurt myself or dirtied myself. I vented my feelings on her when I was tired. I slept in her room and crept into her bed when I needed comfort. The warmth of her breasts cradled me to sleep when I was anxious. She was a black-haired woman of thirty. She had a simple handsome face, a healthy, fresh complexion. She was always lively and energetic, always kind and protective. Gentle, never sentimental, except over love songs, high-spirited, energetic and serious – she was the rock of my existence. She was also, as I came to discover, weak.

At night, when she came to bed, she would undo her bun and let her long hair fall down her back over her pink wool dressing gown. She would often sit pensively awhile as she brushed her hair. She would smear her hands with cream, rub it in, blow out the little paraffin lamp. The scent of extinguished lamp and the cream on her hands would mingle in the darkness as she climbed into bed. She would fall almost immediately into a tranquil sleep, snoring and grunting to herself.

Nanna was as tractable as she was even-tempered. But she was also possessed of a streak of obstinacy, which was responsible for her bossiness. This ruined her relationships with men over and over again. She was far from plain, indeed rather handsome and attractive, but the poor fools never saw beyond the bossy manner. She had one or two serious affairs but they did not go very deep. She was slapdash, energetic, inaccurate, a great lover of change, games, of a good laugh and little jokes. At bath-time she would watch me as I slid down the soapy back of the bath and splashed about in the water. It must have given her a great deal of trouble clearing up the mess but she never complained. In fact she and Cook only laughed when one day the bathwater went through the bathroom ceiling into the kitchen.

She came of a large London family and was never quite reconciled to country things. She had a great fear of cows and horses but she loved dogs and cats. She did not have a cockney accent and did not drop her hs, which was, apparently, a

12

great thing in her favour. I once heard Grandma say to a visitor: 'But, after all, she *speaks* so nicely.'

She often slapped my buttocks to make me hurry, to get me out of the bath, and, sometimes, simply out of good spirits. Grandma could never get used to this and found it vulgar and offensive. She was devoid of vanity, and, deprived as she was of male companionship, devoted herself wholeheartedly to women friends. She would sit for hours at a time with Cook, either in the servants' hall, stirring a cup of tea on her knee, or in the nursery, quietly sewing and as quietly talking. She never played the dominant role. I am sure she loved me as I loved her, but her tranquil nature in its unselfishness never wished me more dependent than I was. Moreover her friendships meant more to her than I did.

At one time her delight was to tell me the rhyme:

> *Adam and Eve and Pinchme*
> *Went down to the river to bathe.*
> *Adam and Eve were drowned.*
> *Who do you think was saved?*

Of course, when I answered 'Pinch-me' she would pinch me and laugh.

But there was a flaw in the trick, which I eventually discovered. When she sang out the first line and mentioned 'Pinch-me', I then pinched her. I was triumphant at my cleverness. But I almost regretted it. Her face fell as if I had cheated her. She tried the rhyme two or three times more and each time I pinched her. And then, a little puzzled, a frown on her simple face, she gave up and never played it again. It was the first step of independence, or of such illusory independence as I ever possessed.

Nanna had no great expectations from life. She looked at it with tranquil realism. Her father and mother had struggled hard to bring up their family. That was what real life was like, she knew, and not the sheltered life of The Firs. Her love of sentimental songs was fantasy and she realised it as such. Her patience grew from this realism. Once, when I had been ill with bronchitis, she had been kept awake all night by my coughing. Next morning, to make a change of scene, as she called it, I was placed on a sofa in the day-nursery. Nanna sat on a low, nursing-chair by the fire and sewed. The conversation between us grew desultory and then stopped. I saw she had fallen asleep. Her face was as calm as an angel's. I grew restive and then annoyed. If I was awake why then shouldn't she be? I began to speak and woke her up. I did this three times. When she fell asleep again, I demanded a glass of barley water. She did not complain but simply went and fetched it with a sigh.

She was normally a very healthy woman but from time to time she would get what she called 'bilious attacks'. These would take some days to come on, and then one morning she would get up, her face pale and pinched. The bridge of her nose would be white, almost transparent. By the middle of the morning she would have to lie down. Usually by the evening, after being violently sick, she would slowly recover. She kept large bottles of lavender water in her bedroom and after an attack the place would reek of it. To prevent the occurrence she would take heavy doses of salts in the morning. During these attacks, and as they came on, she would be sharp tempered, unlike her normal self.

One summer day, when it was raining, I went out to what was called the shelter. This was the undercroft of one of the studios. It was a dark and dismal place. The wood came right up to it and was there composed of evergreens. No sunlight ever penetrated it. A big yew blocked the light from the front lawn. It seemed like a different world, a Hades of chill grimness. Strangely enough, Giorgio's myrtle sent from Greece had been planted here and tried to grow, and did a little, in this most inhospitable part of the garden. Next to the shelter was the stoke-hole and the photographic dark-room. Beyond was a mysterious store, carefully locked, filled with bits of furniture in various stages of decay. You could just see through the grimy windows a place of ghosts and desolation.

I was that day under the shelter, partly to prove that I could stand up to the ghosts of the place without being too frightened, and partly because I was waiting for Mr Courtenay to come to the stoke-hole. The rain fell steadily on the leaves with a patter of sound. A skylight in the studio above me produced the noise of distant clapping, as though the great poet was receiving an ovation. It was warm and damp. The wood seemed to be growing in that pattering fecundity before my eyes.

I suddenly thought of my mother, the slim, elusive, well-dressed woman who flitted through my life like a ghost. Why was it, I asked myself, and the question, strangely enough, had never arisen before, or at least not so sharply, that she and I were parted? How was it, why did Providence require it, that I had no father, and that my mother lived away from me? And then, why should I have had no brothers and sisters? As I thought it, I saw that it was right, that it could not be otherwise, that it had grown as it was, from a seed in eternity.

Mr Courtenay did not come to the boiler house, but from the back door I heard the bell ring. This was for me, and meant that Cook had prepared the lemonade and biscuits. I ran through the rain to the back door. Nanna was standing there with a tray as I came up.

'Nanna,' I asked, 'why is it Mother doesn't live here?' I could not think of the idea of living with her elsewhere.

Nanna looked pale, as if she was in pain. 'Well,' she said wearily, and without thinking, 'your mother did live here for a time.'

I stood stock-still in astonishment. 'When?' I demanded.

'When you were very young.' Nanna spoke snappishly. 'Now,' she went on briskly, pulling herself together, 'don't think any more about it.'

'And, Nanna,' I said, with guileful simplicity, sensing that this was a time for revelations, 'how was it that Grandma was so much younger than Grandfather?'

'Well, because when she married him he was already old.'

'But why didn't he get married when he was young?'

'He had been married before,' she said incautiously, like someone falling into a trap. She looked confused and turned away. I opened my eyes very wide.

'Why so many questions?' Cook's voice came from the half-opened back door. She gave me a shrewd glance and looked meaningfully at Nanna. 'You're all wet, Davey, come in and get those clothes off. Nanna isn't feeling well today.' Cook had a shrill, common, penetrating voice. When something was afoot she stared with all her might, as if to put you down. She was a large, fat, shrewd woman, uncommonly intelligent and very prejudiced. She loved children and would produce from the store-cupboard jelly cubes, sugared cherries, lemonade-powder and chocolate biscuits. But no-one took liberties with her, not even her best friends or employers.

Next day, when I was sitting in the drawing-room, I asked Grandma to tell me of Giorgio's first wife. As there was nothing more she liked talking about than Giorgio, I was amazed at her reaction. There was silence in the great dim room after I had spoken. It was one of the big studios, built to the north of the house, its skylight disguised by tattered yellow silk curtains. On one side it was lined with books in white *art nouveau* cases above which there were pictures in gilt frames by Watts, Burne Jones, and Holman Hunt. On the other side of the room, hung with faded green canvas, there were copies of studio paintings of the Venetian school, which Giorgio loved. The room was so big that the furniture was unimportant. There was a grand piano near the window, an ornate, ivory-inlaid table, covered with vases of flowers, two decrepit sofas covered by pieces of brocade to hide holes where the stuffing was coming out. These stood in front of the huge chimney piece Grandma herself had modelled from the local clay.

Grandma and Giorgio believed in the simple life and disapproved of ostentation of any kind. There were two plain arm chairs with antimacassars over their backs provided with rickety side tables for coffee cups. It was a room in which high seriousness in pursuit of beauty, truth and goodness was taken for granted. A tall Chinese screen by the door, to eliminate or dissipate draughts from the front door beyond the lobby outside, excluded much of the west light from the window. In the evening, rays of sunlight, weakened by the presence of the trees outside, especially when they were in leaf, shyly penetrated into the room. Otherwise it got no sun. The window-sill was filled with plants from the greenhouse, colourful, exotic, gay, but also consumers of light and scarcely visible at the other end of the room. Coming into it for the first time one hardly noticed all this. The eye was conscious only of the great size, the cloudy glory of the gold framed pictures, and the immense Pre-Raphaelite chimney-piece with its ornamented tiers rising up under the yellow silk curtains of the skylight.

In front of the bank of flowers, by the door and the Chinese screen, there stood a little inlaid table, its top decorated by the figure of a shell and some flowers. It was in the eighteenth-century style but was probably made at the end of the nineteenth, when Gosse and Austin were reviving classical taste. On the lower shelf of the table stood a piece of William De Morgan pottery, a beautiful jar, decorated with gold and a pink as delicate as that of an old-fashioned rose but with a faint touch of raspberry which I have never seen since. On the top shelf there was a little notebook bound in silver, two Japanese daggers in cases and a filigree bowl of pot pourri. The scent of the withered petals, nostalgic and redolent of death, pervaded the green room, mingling, as it were, with the golden lights from the pictures. It was a scent of autumn and disenchantment.

Grandma sat in one of the arm chairs, I sat in the other. A brass tray set with brass coffee pots stood on a tripod occasional table between us. I sucked pieces of coffee sugar. Grandma put her cup down with a crash on to its saucer. Her face was vexed. Little patches of red appeared in the centre of her cheeks. She drew her lips together.

'Who told you that?'

'Nanna,' I said, frightened.

'It was not a happy marriage.' And with that she swept out of the room, pulling her little gold watch from her pocket as she did so, feigning to have an appointment.

I was left to the drumming of the rain on the skylight with a feeling of desolation in my heart. I had broken a beautiful image. I realised dimly that it was not my fault. But that did not make it any better. I realised, too, unconsciously, where the trouble lay. Grandma was as possessive of Giorgio's memory as she had been of the living person. She wanted to believe that she had shared him with no-one, that he had not been married before, that his reputation had not been sullied by a vulgar divorce case. To her his life was her life, it was indivisible. I, of all people, should not know the factual truth, which in her eyes was not the real truth, the truth of how things had really been. There had been no children of the first marriage, it had been a short, unhappy episode, and was better forgotten. He had not then married for love, had been tricked into it....

That night Nanna's eyes were red. When it came to bed-time she said: 'What ever made you tell Grandma about the first Mrs Porteous?'

I hung my head. Really it was sheer curiosity. 'I don't know,' I said.

Nanna wiped a tear from her eye with the corner of her apron. 'I nearly got dismissed,' she said.

'Dismissed?' I exclaimed, thunderstruck.

Nanna sat down on the bed and nodded her head. 'I shouldn't have said it, I know.'

With a bound I jumped out of bed on to her lap. I hugged her, pressing my head against her breasts for comfort in an agony of remorse. 'You could never go, you could never go, could you?' I repeated again and again. It was a light summer night. Everything was very quiet. Nanna rocked me to and fro, to and fro, till I was quieted. And then, without a word, she lifted me into bed. She sat beside me in the very slowly gathering dusk till I fell asleep.

CHAPTER TWO

Grandma took some time to forgive me, or, at least, to forget. But she was a reasonable woman, and, by way of a peace offering, she produced from a cupboard in what she called her 'mess room', an adventure story written at the time of the Boer War. It was about a band of boys who rode round tracking suspicious agents of foreign powers. She read this for hours on end and it inflamed my imagination. I longed to be a tracker, too.

Mr Courtenay (coachman promoted to chauffeur), who, I suppose, had had enough of horses in his life, could never be persuaded to look after a pony. So I tracked on foot. I crept about the garden and tried to get as near people as I could without being discovered. Mr Evans, the head gardener, was my main quarry. I watched him from the shadow of the laurels as he watered his plants. If he saw me, he pretended he had not done so. In this way I overheard conversations which were not intended for my ears – none of them of any interest.

One morning I crept up the steep back-stairs. I stood in the shadows and listened to the hiss of the primus at the end of the passage. It was Monday and the pantry was, as usual, in a turmoil. Steam and the smell of washing-soap filled the end of the house. Nanna and Fanny, the head housemaid, gossiped as they worked. They had to talk at the tops of their voices to be heard over the roar of the stove. I slipped past Grandma's room and the bathroom. I leant behind the pantry door and listened, my heart filled with guilt and excitement. I could see inside through the crack.

'Did he so?' Fanny was saying in her squeaky, half-cracked voice. I could hear Nanna dabbling in the galvanised bath in the window. Little eddies of steam drifted past the window and disappeared into the air outside. The place itself was dark and steamy. Fanny was standing with her back to me, her arms akimbo, and her hair, as usual, beginning to fall down her neck from under her cap. Nanna stood at the far side of the room by the window, so I could not hear what she replied.

Then Fanny resumed: 'He's a lovely child, a caution. Puts me in mind of a love child.'

Nanna, who was intent on the stirring, did not appear to take in what she said. 'No,' she replied at last, turning round, 'there's nothing of that.'

'I don't know so much.' Fanny leant forward to make sure she was heard and gave the primus a professional look. 'I 'eard Madam and the missus at it one morning. That was when she was 'ere and Davey was little.'

Nanna put down the long wooden spoon with which she had been stirring the clothes. 'No, it wasn't like that. It was a real wedding, I've seen the photos.'

'It may be as you say,' Fanny answered reluctantly. 'But I still 'ave me doubts. Old Fanny's learnt a thing or two in 'er time. I knows a love child when I sees one. Why don't she live 'ere?'

Nanna turned from the sink and pumped the primus. Their voices became inaudible and I went down to the kitchen. This was a large high-ceilinged room. Saucepans were puffing comfortably on the black range. Cook riddled the fire with a pointed poker and tasted the contents of pans with a wooden cooking-spoon. From the scullery came the sound of rain water being pumped and then the noise of the coffee grinder. The grinding of coffee was a job I liked doing for Cook. But that day I wasn't interested.

'What do you want?' Cook looked up from her stove, wrinkling her forehead in a kindly but penetrating smile. 'You'll 'ave to wait a minute and then you can 'ave a bit of jelly again, if that's what you're after.' She went to the table and began chopping parsely swiftly, rhythmically, with a butcher's knife. Through the open door of the scullery I could see Catherine, the kitchen maid, pass to the larder to fetch more coffee beans. She was an upright, plump girl with rimless spectacles. Her white, fat face was, as usual, expressionless. She looked as if she were deep in thought and that her thoughts pleased her. I knew very little about her and to the end she was a mystery. I had heard that she was a Methodist – that was all.

'Well,' Cook said a little sharply, 'are you coming?' She had the knife in her left hand and the key of the store cupboard in the other. We went outside into the passage. The door of the cupboard under the stairs was opened and the scent of cake, candy peel and raisins gently wafted out. Cook took a slab of crimson gellatine and cut off a piece with the knife.

'There you are, then,' she said handing it to me.

'Thank you very much.'

'That's right,' she said appreciatively, leaning forward with a good-humoured expression on her face. I nibbled the gellatine and shuffled my feet on the brick floor of the passage. She watched me with her shrewd, brown eyes, her hands on her hips, though she was still holding the knife.

'What's a love child, Cook?' I asked.

She gave me a sharp, penetrating glance. 'Whatever made you ask that?'

'I just wanted to know.'

'Well,' she said, swiftly considering whether she should answer me or not, 'it's a child whose parents aren't married.'

'Does it matter if you're a love child?'

'Course it do.' Cook looked indignant. 'Course it do, if there ain't no wedding.'

'Are love children different to other children?'

'Course not. They're just the same.'

'But . . .'

Cook wrinkled her forehead. 'They're not different in themselves, but they are different as they 'as no father and mother.'

'Well, then,' I said with a note of triumph in my voice, 'I must be a love child, because I've got no father and my mother doesn't live here.'

Cook looked at me very sharply. 'Don't act so stupid. The captain was married to your Mummy and you've got a Mummy like everyone else. You're no love child and I don't know 'ow you got the idea into your 'ead.'

'Then why doesn't Mother live here?'

'That's 'er business and your Grandma's.' She said this very swiftly and then added more slowly. 'I expect she thought Grandma would be able to look after you better. Besides, Grandma wanted to 'ave you 'ere with 'er.'

I said no more and slowly ate the piece of gellatine.

Cook looked at me menacingly, holding the kitchen knife in her hand. I was reminded of the farmer's wife in *Three blind mice*.

'I knows what it is,' she said, leaning over me, 'all this 'ere silly creeping around and listening to what people are saying. Heavesdroppers never 'ear good said of 'emselves. It's just silly gossip, that's what it is. Silly gossip.' As she turned away : 'Drat these silly girls. What will they be saying next?' She made for the kitchen, ponderous, vexed, aggressive. And then she turned back to me. 'Now run along with you. You get into the fresh air and don't go listenin' to what doesn't 'ave no concern of yours.'

I ran the length of the drive and seated myself on the terracotta sun dial in the barn garden. It was a small secluded place. On one side was the great tiled barn behind which was Mr Evans's house; on another there was a row of cowsheds which had been converted into stores for garden produce; the other two sides consisted of high stone walls, one of which was pierced by a little Pre-Raphaelite wrought iron gate decorated with a motif of hearts. There were straggly beds of flowers, patches of lawn, brick paths up to the sun dial, terracotta pergolas and chains hung with roses. In front of the sheds were several fine fig trees and three free-standing magnolias. Between the barn and the sheds there was an oak gate which led into the kitchen garden. It was a different world to that of the house.

I drew two dusty chocolate fingers, which I had secreted, from my pocket and slowly ate them in the sunlight. I regretted that I was not a love child. An intuition of fate, of the merciless either-or of destiny, passed through my mind. Life imposed a pattern which could not be ignored. I was as I was and could be no other. Great white clouds, majestic, as sad and detached as what had made them, passed slowly across the sky above my head. A faint breeze rustled the roses on the pergola. From the kitchen garden came the tack tack of a hoe as it struck at flints. A speckled thrush hopped from the tangle of the fig trees, began to sing, thought better of it, and its notes died away.

Mr Evans, the head gardener, and I were great friends. He had been in the Great War and had brought back from the Near East an Arab costume. On my birthday and for treats he would dress up in it and there would be elaborate games of hide and seek in the wood at dusk. He enjoyed these games as much as I did. He crept from tree to tree, from shadow to shadow, with the cunning and skill of a real Arab.

He was a small, lean, dark-haired man with keen eyes and active intelligence. He was, I suppose, almost middle-aged but he always seemed young to me. He was full of nervous energy and could not bear to be idle. He was a first-rate gardener. Grandma, being old, left everything about the garden in his hands. Sometimes he would let me come with him pigeon shooting in the early hours of the morning. This was more or less a secret, as Grandma didn't like the pigeons being killed.

Oh yes, Mr Evans was a hero to me. I admired his vitality and independence. When there was a football match between

Wales and England he would sing 'Men of Harlech' and I would reply with 'Rule Britannia'. He sang in a low, lilting and provocative voice. He treated me as an equal. When I first wore my best suit for a party, long trousers, waistcoat and all, he had disapproved. 'All dressed up and no-where to go,' he commented. I was hurt and pretended not to understand. I suppose he thought I was growing away from him. I quickly changed into old clothes and he was his old self again.

I was flattered that he had an entirely different attitude to his own sons. He treated them with a sort of contempt and demanded instant obedience. They were older than myself and I enjoyed playing with them. But Mr Evans discouraged it. It was as if he wanted me to be with him rather than them. And I don't think he got tired of me trotting behind him as he went about the garden. In fact in some obscure way he seemed to have the same admiration for me as I had for him.

He thought I ought to be tough, self-reliant, self-assured. He hated any sign of weakness. It gave him pleasure to see me drag my handcart through the brambles till my legs ran with blood. He implanted in my heart high ideals of courage. Courage was to him the supreme, almost the only, virtue.

Mr Evans was, I knew, something of a ladies man. His wife was a small, white-faced, untidy woman running to fat, who kept her hair tied up in a handkerchief. She had an anxious, scared expression as if life had not turned out as she had expected. I hardly knew her and Mr Evans placed a barrier between us. His manner implied that I could not be friendly with both of them. And, in fact, Mrs Evans made no overtures. I only entered his cottage a few times. Somehow I did not find this strange. I had been appalled by the disorder, the coldness and the lack of comfort. The earth closet in the wood-shed at the bottom of the garden especially shocked me. Mr Evans was clearly not at his best at home.

He *was* at his best in the servants' hall up at the house. This room, hidden away behind the baize door or approached from the felted back stairs, was the most cheerful place in the house. Gusts of laughter and guffaws resounded from it – never more loudly than when Mr Evans appeared with his wooden trug full of vegetables. It was a pleasant, square room overlooking the front lawn. It contained a circular table around which the maids sat, presided over by Cook. In winter there was a bright coal fire burning in the grate which lit up a brown plaster bust of Edward VII. This bust was decorated with a paper hat at Christmas and was known familiarly as 'Teddy'. The maids sat in hierarchical order, so far as this was possible at a round table. On the right next to Cook, who sat with her back to the window, was the parlour-maid, a large melancholy woman in cap and apron – much preoccupied with her health. She smiled but did not laugh. Next to her sat Fanny, the head house-maid, a cheerful, rather cracked person, always laughing and making unintelligible jokes. On her right was the under house-maid, Kitty, aged sixteen, whom I greatly admired. She was attractively ugly, her face almost negroid in its happy coarseness. Her neighbour was the kitchen maid, Catherine. Her eyes behind her rimless spectacles were dark brown and her chestnut hair was drawn back from her face. Next to her sat Nanna on Cook's left. And that completed the circle.

When Mr Evans appeared at the door a chair would be drawn up and placed between Nanna and Catherine. He would be given a cup of tea and the sallies would begin. The maids would stir their teacups vigorously, expectantly. I did not fully understand the jokes and I knew the best were reserved for the time when I was not there. I was never made to feel unwanted but I did undoubtedly damp down the fun. After I left the guffaws would grow louder, and more frequent.

One day, I took them by surprise and saw Mr Evans give the kitchen maid, Catherine, a kiss on her cheek. He had got up from his chair, lent forward as if to whisper something in her ear and then kissed her in a spontaneous gesture. He did it so naturally I was not even surprised. He then returned to his seat and as he did so brushed Nanna's cheek with his lips. Nanna was as good-natured as she was handsome in her fresh direct way. I, therefore, did not expect her to blush angrily. I knew she liked Mr Evans and I decided there must have been something awkward in his manner which I had not noticed. Some time before this I had seen Nanna come from behind a tree, very red in the face. I had spotted Mr Evans walking away in the opposite direction. And then Nanna had often shaken her head with a serious look on her kind face: 'Mrs Evans doesn't look after him. She's a bit of a slut. Look at his clothes.' I wondered what Catherine, the kitchen maid, thought of the kiss. Her plump, white face expressed no emotion that I could make out except what I can only describe as a sort of receptivity.

After that I took more notice of Catherine. I used to watch her walking down the drive on Sundays, an upright self-contained figure, her clothes as plain as her face, on her way to the village Methodist chapel. She always carried a well-bound prayer book in her hand. It puzzled me that there had been no disapproval on her face when Mr Evans had kissed her. I didn't know much about Methodists but what I had heard from Nanna and Cook made me think she ought to have been shocked. That she wasn't, strangely enough, made me dislike, almost fear, her. She had accepted Mr Evans's kiss, as if by right, but had in no way responded to it. It seemed to indicate an unnatural pride.

It was a small enough incident but it did seem to make things change, slowly at first. There were fewer laughs and guffaws from the servants' hall. Nanna looked preoccupied and sad. Once I heard Cook say: 'I've nothing to complain of. She does her work well. But I don't like it.' Now Mr Evans only occasionally sat down for his cup of tea. And then ceased to do so at all.

I half expected that Mr Courtenay, the chauffeur, would take his place. But he was not asked in. Mr Courtenay cut the wood and stoked the furnace as well as drove the car. He was a stocky, handsome man with bushy, black eyebrows and beautiful white hair. He was always very tidily dressed. His shoes shone like mirrors. When he went out in the car he wore shining gaiters. I was very fond of him and used to help him with the wood. But, of course, he was not quite like Mr Evans. He had not fought in the war. He had been a special constable. This lowered him in my eyes. He had a majestic childless wife who was scarcely ever to be seen outside her spotless cottage. Mr Courtenay was very respectable and very respected.

Mr Courtenay's domain lay round the old stables by the lane. Here he had a large, tiled garage and a wood shed concealed in the trees, where he cut the logs. The most mysterious place was the harness room behind the stable block. It was a long, narrow place, lit by skylights and built into the side of the hill, therefore considerably damp, especially as it was also overshadowed by trees. The harness was, of course, never used, but Mr Courtenay kept it bright and polished as if, at any time, the horses, who had all been shot in September 1914, might return. Mr Courtenay was the most unsentimental of men and sentiment was not the reason for carrying out this useless duty. Nor, I think, had Grandma ever issued orders on the subject. It was simply that the harness had been entrusted to him and it was right that he should keep it in good condition. The door was kept locked but from time to time I was allowed to go inside, look at the harness hanging from its hooks and smell the mingled scents of decay. When Mr Courtenay cleaned the car he whistled and hissed as he had done when washing down the horses. The stable itself was clean and bare but still faintly smelt of dung, horseflesh, straw and hay.

One day I was mooching about on my bicycle and, hearing the familiar sound of stoking, made my way to the stoke-hole. The great firs round the house stood out dark green, almost blue, and red and brown against the light blue of the sky. Beneath them the brambles and the thickets of small trees were green with the first luxuriance of the year. The Big Wood, the other side of the road, owned by Grandma but not often visited, seemed, from where I stood, more mysterious than ever. I had parked my bicycle by the stoke-hole door and looked inside. Mr Courtenay had stopped shovelling and was looking at some photographs, frowning and pursing his lips as he did so. I watched him for a few moments as he turned the photographs over and over in his hands.

I knew Mr Evans was a keen photographer who developed his own films and made his own prints. In fact he had taught me how to do it. From the door I said: 'Aren't those Mr Evans's photographs?'

Mr Courtenay jumped. A startled look came into his face. 'By Job's I didn't hear you,' he said hurriedly trying to conceal the photographs in his hand, 'No, they're just trash I picked up.'

I knew he was lying by the smooth tone he had assumed. 'They are on just the same paper as Mr Evans uses,' I said innocently. I felt sure some trick was being played on my friend and wanted to save him. I was outraged by Mr Courtenay's duplicity. 'I'll tell Mr Evans,' I said on the spur of the moment.

Mr Courtenay's manner suddenly altered. 'By Job's you won't,' he exclaimed. I was aware that there were layers in his character I had never experienced before. He threw the photographs into the furnace and I ran forward. But I stopped dead. I had seen one of the photographs before it was consumed. It was of a naked woman posed before a tree. The impassive face was vaguely familiar, but I couldn't place it. In any case Mr Courtenay slammed the furnace door.

There was an awkward silence as we stared at each other. Then Mr Courtenay began sweeping up some coke in front of the furnace and I realised he did not know what I had seen.

CHAPTER THREE

The Firs was a self-contained community. Nevertheless it had its relationships with the outside world. There was, first of all, Uncle John, Grandma's half-brother, who lived on a solid Victorian estate some forty miles away at the foot of the South Downs. He paid us occasional visits but always without his wife. Grandma disliked her because she was a divorcee, (Uncle John had met her on a cruise), and because she had been an actress of sorts. The combination spelt vulgarity. Aunt Joan might have been forgiven her background, her profession, and her humour, which smacked faintly of the Music Hall. After all, Giorgio was the son of a piano tuner, the great George Eliot had not been married, and Grandma considered Ellen Terry a great woman. But someone who considered art, religion and thought, as only part of existence – such a person was not to be countenanced. In a word she was not serious and, moreover, had no other qualities or status to balance this almost hopeless defect. It was the defect from which Edward VII had also suffered and was presumably the reason why his bust was relegated to the servants' hall.

Uncle John was a short well-set man with a veined red face, strongly hooked nose and neat, white hair. He looked like Mr Punch and behaved like a hunting squire. He had, in fact, been a stockbroker. The highlights in his life had been the hunting field and the Boer War. He would come into the drawing-room at The Firs, stand with his back to the fire, raise his coat tails, look round at the pictures with his darting, shrewd eyes and talk in a loud, extroverted voice. I can see him now in this attitude talking to the Mayor of the local town, who had been for some reason asked to lunch. To the Mayor's visible surprise Uncle John described the Boer war

29

as 'a very pleasant little campaign'. I was a little in awe of him and his masculine ways. But he always behaved kindly to me and never left without giving me a tip.

He was not, I think, quite the man he pretended to be. He suffered from asthma. He had had a delicate and unhappy childhood clouded by the tantrums of his mother, Grandma's hated step-mother. He loved Grandma as a superior being, living in a superior world. If he did not understand poetry and the poetic life he nonetheless revered it. When Grandma had married Giorgio he had whispered, before he gave her away: 'I'm giving you to the Nation!' Or that's the story Grandma used to tell me. The atmosphere at The Firs made him more positive than he was elsewhere. At his home, which we seldom visited, he was quieter and drier in his manner. On those occasions he would take me out to see the horses while Grandma and Aunt Joan exchanged frosty remarks in the drawing-room – either out of embarrassment or in the vain hope that the two women would, if left alone, become friends.

He bought Grandma's wine. He knew a good deal about vintages but never bought her anything but the sweet, white wine she liked. He was also her business adviser. There would be conferences in the drawing-room or the Red room. He would talk pessimistically, as if the good old days had gone for ever, with a relish which other men reserve for the discussion of food. Grandma would listen deferentially, which was her way with men, and interrupt him from time to time with remarks such as: 'Do you really think so, John? Dear me, I didn't think things could be so bad.'

And Uncle John would reply: 'Ah, but that's not the worst. It's the waste. And can we keep the fellows out?'

'The Liberals are no good?' This timidly from Grandma.

'Led by that Welsh preacher?' he would exclaim, fill his cheeks and then let out the air with a deflationary sound.

'I always voted Liberal when Giorgio was alive.'

'I know. But then it was different. Now we're up against it.

And what,' he would ask, looking round for someone else to convince, 'can you expect? Before the war, whichever party it was, did its best for the country. Now it's every man for himself. Every man for himself.'

I think Uncle John enjoyed the slump although he lost a lot of money. It confirmed what he had prophesied all along. From what he said I understood that Lloyd George was actually mad and that the Labour leaders were devils perversely intent on the country's destruction. They would ruin the stock market, destroy the country house, subvert the servants and do away with hunting. And what could be worse than that?

He was my nearest male relative, and as such was delegated by Grandma to tell me the facts of a boy's existence. He would do this from time to time with a pomposity which hid his distaste of the task. Much of what he said was incomprehensible to me and applied to the period of *Tom Brown's Schooldays*. This was not surprising. I afterwards discovered that he had only been one half at Eton.

Aunt Emma's true relationship with Grandma and myself escapes me, but I suppose she was in reality a cousin. She was a very short, red-faced old woman, ugly, energetic, irascible, rich. Though a Liberal and interested in new ideas, socially she was a conservative. One day, after visiting us, she was setting out homewards. Her great, green limousine was drawn up at the front door. The chauffeur, in green livery, hovered with a rug on his arm. Nanna incautiously said to me: 'Now say good-bye to Aunt Emma.' Aunt Emma stopped in her tracks, her ugly red face, just visible under a squashed black hat, stuck about with a dozen pins, blazed with anger. 'I was not aware,' she pronounced to Nanna, 'that I was *your* aunt.' Poor Nanna mumbled an apology but Aunt Emma took no notice, stumped across the steps and thumped herself down on the back seat. I could see her through the window tapping with her stick on the glass panel which separated her from the chauffeur. It is said that she dismissed a kitchen maid for daring to go to church with a rose in her hat.

She lived in a large, comfortable but unattractive house half a dozen miles from The Firs. It was copied from the black and white houses one sees in Cheshire. The grounds were famous for their rhododendrons which were grown among fir trees at the edge of a heath. There were also oriental-style green houses in whose warm and damp interiors orchids and exotic fruits flourished. There was a peach house and a grape house. After a visit we always returned with a basket of fruit.

It was all on a more lavish scale than at The Firs. The old butler had died and was replaced, as at The Firs by a parlour-maid. But Aunt Emma retained her lady's maid whom she called Hall but whom I was taught to call *Miss* Hall. A tall, prim spinster with very large false teeth and steel-rimmed spectacles, she lived in a little room fitted up with a sewing machine and life-size tailor's dummy which was supposed to resemble Aunt Emma's figure. The house had an eastern flavour. All Aunt Emma's relatives, including her brother, from whom she had inherited the property, had been in India. The rhododendrons came from the Himalayas. There were Indian swords and daggers, Indian silks behind glass, Indian chests, pictures and, of course, everywhere lovely Indian rugs. The hall and the living-rooms were filled with exotic azaleas in pots. There were bowls of sweet-smelling, but somehow, saddening pot-pourri. Their scent was the first thing you noticed when you came in at the front door.

The rooms were spacious, everything breathed comfort and ample means. But I never liked it or felt at home there. I resented the greater opulence, the better and more numerous servants. It lacked the dedication and the austerity to which I was used. Aunt Emma never bothered herself with art or reflection. She knew what she liked and thought it her duty to get what she wanted. I did not know her well and I fancy she was very different from what she appeared to be. She had been the ugly duckling of the family and a sense of inferiority made her assertive. She wanted people to love her and from nervousness rebuffed them.

On one visit I found a frog hopping about the borders near the front door. Miss Hall found me a jar and I was stepping into the car with it, delighted at the thought of taking back a foreign visitor. My mind was filled with the imaginary difficulties the frog would have in adapting himself to life at The Firs. Suddenly Aunt Emma's little eyes, as small and sharp as a pig's, caught sight of the jar.

'Who told you that you could take that creature?' she demanded.

I quailed. 'Miss Hall fetched the jar.'

'Did she?' She turned to Hall who was standing in the background among the stained glass in the lobby, and who now began to look upset. 'Well,' she went on, returning to me, '*I* didn't give it you. And you can put it back where it came from.'

I stared at her. 'It's mine,' I said.

'It isn't.' And she tapped the red, inlaid tile step with the end of her walking stick.

Nanna, who was witnessing all this from the back seat of the car, opened her mouth and shut it again. She shrank modestly into the corner as if she had no right to be there. Mr Courtenay, who was standing by the door of the car, creaked in his leather gaiters and pursed his lips.

'I *will* have him,' I said on the verge of tears.

'You won't.'

'I will.' But as I said it I threw the jar on to the grass and the frog hopped out. Then I burst into tears. Aunt Emma turned and stumped into the house.

On the way home Nanna tried to comfort me by explaining that the frog had not been mine and that I should have asked permission. But she said it without much conviction and anyway I was not to be comforted. At bedtime I told Grandma the whole story but she made no comment.

Next day Aunt Emma's green car drew up at the door of

33

The Firs. The chauffeur got out with a basket of fruit. On top of the fruit, and tied with a piece of green ribbon, was a bronze frog.

Another neighbour was the village squire who called only occasionally, but whom I saw every Sunday in church reading the lesson. He and his wife lived in an Elizabethan manor house two miles or so away up the Sandy Way and about a mile from the village. He was a small, slight, vague man who had been a general in the war. I was acutely aware that he lacked a finger on his right hand, and could not help thinking of it when talking to him or seeing him at the lectern. He had lost it in the trenches and this made him a hero to me.

His attitude to us was mixed. He was friendly enough but he could not place us. A poet should be poor, but Giorgio had made money. He expected a well-to-do neighbour to be a landed man. Yet we lived in what would now be called a suburban way. In his eyes people who lived as we did should be rich and vulgar. Grandma was not. She was the daughter of a Scotch laird with an old name, almost as old as his own – and his family had been squires of Brimpton since the sixteenth century.

What is more, Grandma knew much more of the aristocracy, through her connection with Giorgio, than he did. This intimacy with the aristocracy was on the wane, as Giorgio's fame died away like an evening's twilight. Nevertheless old Lady This and old Lord That would pay us a visit from time to time to see the relics of the once famous old poet. Of course their sons and daughters, more worldly wise and with differing tastes, did not come in their turn. Unbeknown to me it was now the world of D. H. Lawrence and Aldous Huxley. The name of George Porteous had become a joke in literary circles.

There were a pair of terracotta coronets on the gate posts which led to the stable yard. The General, passing one day with a friend had said with a laugh: 'Don't know what they're doing with coronets!' – Mr Courtenay had overheard him and

34

innocently relayed the remark to me. Of course to me the terracotta coronets were simply ornaments – as they were to Grandma.

Mr and Mrs Thoroughgood were more frequent visitors. They rented a cottage from the General which they used for weekends and holidays. Their permanent house was in London and they had another holiday cottage in Wales. They had married late in life and had no children. Mr Thoroughgood was a tiny ingratiating man with a bald head and a rich, pompous voice. Because of his size, or because of his wife, he was incurably diffident. Always eager to do the right thing he hated the eccentric in politics, manners, cooking or anything else. To have been to Eton, to Christ Church, or to have a title was the summit of achievement. Where he had been to school, why he had not gone to a University (which he would have called the 'varsity'), who his parents were, or how he had come by his money, I never enquired.

Mrs Thoroughgood was a very thin, tall, sallow-faced woman who wore necklaces round her scraggy neck and chains of beads to her waist. Her expression was alert, intelligent, impish, as if conscious of her superiority to other people. In different circumstances she would have been an intellectual. She had a reedy voice and was prone to witticisms at the expense of those not present at which she would laugh in a high falsetto and tinkle all over. She was rich in her own right, came of an almost aristocratic landed family, was well read and a minor poetess. As such she was an admirer of Giorgio whom she imitated, so I discovered later, with not a little skill. Having known the great man she thought it her duty to protect his memory and promote his fame.

In summer she used to walk over with her husband from their cottage along the Sandy Way for tea. In winter they drove over by car. Sitting bolt upright at the wheel she did the driving and little Mr Thoroughgood sat beside her, ready to jump out to open gates, or to remove any other obstacles they might encounter. At tea Grandma and Mrs Thorough-

35

good would talk of poetry and poets. Mr Thoroughgood and I would have desultory conversations which were very polite, seemed always to lead nowhere, and ended in no bond of contact. In the middle of these exchanges Mrs Thoroughgood would break off her talk with Grandma and dart a glance at me. 'His name,' she would say, now fixing her eyes on Grandma, 'is down for Eton, isn't it?' 'Oh yes, yes it is,' Grandma would reply in an undertone. Mr Thoroughgood, who realised I must have heard, would beam at me and then, after a few seconds, continue our pointless talk. His beaming smile, strangely enough, did not make me like him better or think him a nicer man. It was not a spontaneous expression of pleasure at my golden future. It was rather an automatic reaction to the prospect of success and the deference it engendered. Then, when we had finished the neat piles of tiny sandwiches and eaten all we could of the shortcake biscuits, characteristically Cook's, hard with fretted edges, dusted with castor sugar, and always surmounted by a cherry withered in the oven, we would move from the tea-scented dining-room to the drawing-room.

Mrs Thoroughgood's malicious laugh rings in my ears as she said, crossing the hall one Sunday afternoon in summer after tea: 'But the Vicar has probably never *heard* of Browning or Swinburne. He and his wife are entangled in the "poetry" of this man Eliot or whatever his name is – all about eggs and anaesthetics. Poof!' And she swept modern poetry away with a wave of her chiffon handkerchief.

Grandma had one sister, the widow of a canon, a tragic version of herself, always dressed in deep black. But she lived far away and I had only seen her twice. Other relatives lived on estates in Scotland and appeared infrequently at The Firs. I heard about them but did not know them. I never came across any relative of Giorgio's.

All around us the world had changed and was changing. But we did not change. The Thoroughgoods were constantly moving from one house to another as people do today. The

General was introducing modern methods into his farms. Aunt Emma, having been one of the first women to own a motor car, had a wireless set. Even Uncle John was at least in contact with the modern world through the stock exchange. But at The Firs everything remained as it had been, symbolised by Giorgio's pen laid out on the blotter where he had put it down the day before his death. And I thought the world of The Firs was the real world. The world outside was to me unreal because unknown.

CHAPTER FOUR

Grandma was a religious woman. She had been brought up an Episcopalian in the Highlands. This made her into a Tractarian with a deep but sorrowful attachment to Newman. She told me about his conversion as an event of great and tragic consequence. The Church of England, its hierarchy, sacraments and liturgy meant a good deal to her – as did Herbert, Vaughan and Traherne whom she read constantly. But there was another side to her religion. Her husband, whom she adored as a great prophet, had been a liberal and a Romantic. It is difficult to discover from his lofty but nebulous poetry what his beliefs really were. He seems to have possessed the impulse and the spirit of religion without a form into which he could satisfactorily express it. It therefore ran to waste and became merely aspirational, vague. He revered Jesus but rejected the dogmas and institutions of Christianity. He put no philosophy in their place and formed no philosophy of his own.

In another woman these two contradictory tendencies, the dogmatic and the liberal, would have produced a tension. I do not know whether they had done so in the past. When I knew her there was no tension and I doubt if there ever had been. She managed to infuse into her Christianity an ardent Romanticism which simply eliminated dogmatic or philosophical difficulties. She was content – and this was her humility – to leave dogma a cloudy mystery.

The day started with morning prayers and, when I was promoted from the nursery, I always attended. I went down early and stood with Grandma in the dining-room before they commenced. She would be standing with her back to the circular mahogany table looking out over the lawn. The low sill of the window had been fitted with a zinc tray and was always filled with flowers from the greenhouse. The pots were concealed by layers of moss, so one had the impression they were somehow growing out of the wall. A terracotta birdbath was placed outside the window. We would stand, Grandma and I, to watch the birds drink and fight over it. A wrought iron erection stood beside the bath hung with coconuts and bits of fat dangling at the end of pieces of string. The lawn stretched away to the wood which lay round the house on every side. In spring and summer it was gay and speckled with sunlight, in autumn and winter sombre and shadowy. Over everything towered the great Scotch pines whose dark green foliage cast a melancholy spell. The biggest at the edge of the wood was a veritable giant. I could see it from the nursery window and could make out in its branches strange and sombre features. We said nothing or very little, as this was a time for recollection.

And then there would be a tap on the door which led to the kitchen quarters and the maids would file in. Grandma and I knelt down at Chippendale chairs at the table. The maids knelt before plain chairs at the side of the room, placed there for the purpose. Grandma opened a tattered scrap-book into which she had pasted favourite prayers. Silver and red silk markers hung from it. Peeping through my fingers I could see Grandma's noble profile against the light from the window. She had china-blue eyes, edged with the wrinkles of old age which made them appear sad. And, in fact, they often had a far-off, wistful expression in them. She had a thin, slightly hooked nose with sensitive nostrils. When she read poetry, looked at a picture which she found ennobling, or, as now, read the prayers, she seemed to catch the scent of beauty as though it hung on the air. Nanna prayed with simple attention like a child asleep. What or whom was she thinking of? Of her elder brother whom she had admired and who had been killed in the war, her younger brother whom she loved? Her face suggested that she was far away, reposing in tranquil pools of recollection. Otherwise I could only see the long line of the maids' shoes, soles and heels uppermost, in various states of disrepair. Grandma read the prayers in a clear, intense voice. When she came to the Lord's prayer she always read 'leave us not in temptation' for 'lead us not into temptation', the original, in her eyes, being incompatible with omnipotent goodness.

After prayers we again went to the window. Grandma would sometimes sigh at the beauty of the scene. She would raise her eyebrows and wrinkle her forehead as if she found it too poignant to bear. I knew she was thinking of Giorgio. 'Ah me!' she would exclaim and it was only later I found it old-fashioned and funny. I once asked her why she sighed and she replied: 'Because I have altered so much and nature remains as beautiful as ever.'

I looked puzzled. But she was unable or unwilling to formulate the problem more precisely. She patted me on the head and turned away.

It seemed strange to me then that the sparkle of the sunlight on the grass should make you sad.

'Beauty is always sad, Giorgio used to say,' she explained.

'But why?'

'I suppose,' she said, not looking at me, 'life should always be a little sad.' That was her profound conviction and paradoxically the reason why she was, as people go, a happy woman.

At that moment the parlour-maid entered with the salmon

kedjeree and the oatcakes wrapped in their warm napkin. I deserted metaphysics for my breakfast.

But, of course, neither Grandma's nor my own religion revolved round the dining-room table. Its centre, insofar as it had an external centre, was the little Norman parish church. It was here that I first tasted the rich, sweet wine which was said to be the blood of God. It was a beautiful little church with thick rounded pillars and arches. Above and behind the altar was a gallery with an old oak rail. This made the place especially interesting to the antiquarian and it did produce an intimate, restful effect. Owing to the gallery above it, the east window was very small. It was filled with fragments of ancient yellowish green glass which cast a faint, supernatural light on the altar. The church was, of course, dominated by the well-to-do middle class. The village was mostly chapel. But nothing – neither the respectability of the rich nor the absence of the poor – could rob it of mystery. It was haunted by the righteousness of God, by His wrath and perfection. It was haunted, too, by the strivings of Christians, Catholic and Protestant, to be perfect as He was perfect.

When I think of Christian perfection a picture of that little church comes into my mind. I also think of Mr Brailes. The church had been served by a succession of vicars whom I do not remember. And then, when I was about eight or nine, Mr Brailes arrived. I happened to be in the drawing-room when he called.

He was a slight, rather diffident man of middle height with sandy hair and spectacles. He appeared to be thirty or so. He was dressed in black with a clean clerical collar. His expression was keen, intelligent, enquiring, as though used to the dissection of problems in his mind.

'Ah, Mrs Porteous,' he said with a sing-song drawl in his voice, as he came self-consciously, hand out-stretched, across the long drawing-room carpet. He might have been, at first glance, a Jane Austen clergyman. That, at any rate, seemed the part he wanted to play on this our first meeting. When I come to think of it, he often played this role with a faint air of disbelief, especially when embarrassed. 'Ah, Mrs Porteous, I am so pleased to meet you,' he said shaking Grandma by the hand.

'And I you,' Grandma replied shyly, taken a little by surprise. She twisted her hands uncomfortably and then plumped up a cushion in one of the chairs.

Mr Brailes looked at me and back at Grandma. 'This is Davey, my grandson,' Grandma explained.

'How do you do, David,' Mr Brailes said extending his hand to me. His hand was light and dry, an intellectual's, like an old woman's. He never called me Davey and this correctness typified the frostiness which touched our friendship from the start.

'Would you like the boy to go?' Grandma asked.

'On the contrary,' he replied, as if outraged at the idea and seating himself in the chair Grandma had drawn up to the hearth for him, 'I would like him to stay.' He paused a little awkwardly. 'That is, if he would like to stay.'

I could see them both from where I was making a Meccano model. He peered in my direction. 'Ah,' he exclaimed with a sort of flourish in his voice, 'you have some Meccano!' I expected him to make a further comment, thinking that perhaps he knew something special about Meccano. But he continued to smile reminiscently without saying any more. I stared at him expectantly for a moment or two and then went on with my building. 'Meccano!' he repeated, as if he was talking of gold ingots.

'I suppose,' Grandma enquired politely, 'you came on foot through the woods?'

'I do not own a motor car,' he replied precisely, 'and, yes, I made my way through the wood, happily for me. It is very beautiful.'

'Whenever you want a walk, I hope you will go in the wood.'

'That,' Mr Brailes said with a smile and raising his eyebrows, 'is uncommonly kind of you.'

41

As I built my model under the inlaid Chinese table I was struck even then by his stilted literary manner, but I think I also understood that it was not the whole man.

'I have heard,' Grandma remarked, 'of your success at Cambridge. I have just bought your book on suffering.' Mr Brailes made a little noise like pooh, shrugged his shoulders and made a depreciatory gesture with his hands. 'It is a great honour for this little parish to have as its vicar a rising theologian.'

'I'm really more of a philosopher than a theologian as yet. But I hope my parish work here will make me more of a theologian than a philosopher.' The antithesis pleased him and he gave a laugh.

'There are,' Grandma said, misunderstanding his meaning, 'a great many chapel-goers in the parish.'

Mr Brailes snorted contemptuously but at what I did not know – at the chapel-goers, at the stupid divisions of Christendom, or, perhaps, at the failure of the Church of England.

'I had,' he changed the subject, 'to choose between teaching at Cambridge and the cure of souls.' I had never heard this last phrase and was puzzled by it. I did not connect anyone I met at church with having such an insubstantial thing as a soul. Anyway how could it be cured?

'You did quite right,' Gandma exclaimed enthusiastically.

'Not,' Mr Brailes said, as if he were making a fine intellectual distinction, 'not that I shall be giving up philosophy altogether. I shall write when I have the leisure.'

Mr Brailes turned to the fireplace as if suddenly surprised at its presence. It had pillars and tiers of niches decorated with Pre-Raphaelite angel heads. 'What a splendid fireplace!' he exclaimed, putting his head back on the antimacassar and looking up at it critically. There was a touch of sarcasm in his voice. The Pre-Raphaelites were not fashionable at that time. I had known the fireplace all my life and was nettled by his tone.

'It was modelled by boys from the village,' Grandma

explained not noticing the criticism. She glanced at it sadly, thinking, no doubt, of happier times.

'Ah!' Mr Brailes commented, as if he had found a clue in a cross word puzzle, 'Ruskin and the Arts and Crafts Movement.'

'The Home Arts' Movement,' Grandma corrected. 'You see Mr Ruskin was a great friend of my husband. When you come again perhaps you would like to see the Ruskin letters? I have them in this little show case with my husband's decorations.' She pointed to a glass topped cabinet which stood at the side of the fireplace.

'*The Stones of Venice!*' Mr Brailes said for want of anything better. He belonged to the new post-war world and knew nothing of Giorgio, the nineties or Pre-Raphaelitism.

'Of course,' Grandma said, at last noticing he was ignorant of and condescending to her gods, 'everybody's reputation goes down after their death. But in time.... I suppose not many people now read *The Stones of Venice* for pleasure?'

Mr Brailes shrugged his shoulders. 'But,' he said kindly, 'I expect our grandsons will. For instance, David here.'

This remark came as a small shock to me. I did not know there were fashions in art. I thought a thing was beautiful or not. Strange that Mr Brailes, of all people, should have made me perceive for the first time the uncertainty at the heart of things.

When Mr Brailes had gone, Grandma sat in the armchair which had been for so long Giorgio's and stared in front of her into the fire. She sighed and whispered his name. I did not know then what she was thinking. I know now. In Giorgio's day, to come to The Firs had been a sort of pilgrimage.

'Grandma,' I said, 'what did he mean by "cure of souls"?'

Grandma frowned. 'Oh, he meant he wanted to talk to ordinary people about religion and not about ideas to learned men.'

'Then shouldn't we have asked him a religious question?'

Grandma gave me a loving look but did not reply.

'We didn't say anything about religion at all.' I saw that the new vicar was a clever man, even a very clever man, and I was disappointed.

Mr Brailes married, Grandma called and then the newly married couple came to tea.

Eva Brailes had vivid china-blue eyes and a perpetual smile on her lips as though she had just discovered how amusing life was, and was pleased at her perception. She had a high colouring and her cheeks were weather-beaten, or looked as if they were, which gave her a homeliness she would not otherwise have possessed. Altogether she looked like a pretty clergyman's wife who wanted to be something more. She had a drawling, slightly slurred voice. It was sometimes difficult to catch what she said because she often spoke as if only for the benefit of herself or her husband.

When she came into the drawing-room her eyes fell on the great mantelpiece and she exclaimed: 'Mark, how delightfully Pre-Raphaelite!' Grandma, who was shy, and already a little deaf, did not hear and looked at her enquiringly.

'I was saying,' Eva Brailes explained in the voice of one used to the old and the deaf, 'how strongly Pre-Raphaelite this room is.'

'Ah, yes, my husband knew all the Pre-Raphaelites and most of them sat in these chairs. But now nobody knows anything about them.'

'Mark had a pupil who was doing a thesis on the Pre-Raphaelites.'

The conversation came to a standstill with this remark. Mrs Brailes leant forward to me. 'Ah, David, what have you there? A train!' she simpered. I said nothing, of course, because there was nothing to say. Mr Brailes leant forward, too, and smiled, but made no remark. I now noticed that Mrs Brailes had a kinder expression at close quarters than I had expected. But there was something lifeless about her eyes and they seemed to look inward rather than outward. This did not accord with her sprightly manner.

'It must be nice for you, Mrs Porteous,' she said turning back to Grandma, 'to have your grandson.'

'Oh yes, for me,' Grandma replied, pinching the bridge of her nose and sighing, 'but things might have been different, very different had my son lived. There it is, that awful war. And it's not good for a young boy to be with an old woman. He really only has the servants.'

'I'm not lonely, Grandma,' I said defensively from under the Chinese table. I had a dread of any other life.

'He must,' Eva Brailes exclaimed, 'come down whenever he likes to the Vicarage. And, who knows, perhaps before long we shall have some very much younger child for him to play with.'

All this time Mr Brailes had not uttered a word. He had sat watching his wife with an expression of loving interest. He listened intently to everything she said. 'Certainly,' he chimed in at last, looking at me, 'You must come down whenever you like and we shall give a children's party or something of the kind.'

I hated parties and wanted to say so.

'What do you say?' Grandma put in quickly before I had time to speak.

'Thank you very much,' I replied dutifully, irresolutely standing up and looking from Mrs to Mr Brailes.

'Oh yes,' Mrs Brailes went on, turning back to the fireplace but first throwing me a kind glance, 'you see, Mrs Porteous, we intend to have masses of children. Mark is an intellectual and he needs something other than his work. We want,' she went on enthusiastically with childish simplicity, 'to live in the real world. It's so easy for an intellectual to live in his own little world.'

I glanced at Mr Brailes to see what she meant. I understood immediately. He was smiling, but he fiddled nervously with his fingers.

'Intellectual? But, of course. . . .' Grandma said, bewildered.

'For the intellectual the natural life is a necessity.'

45

'I'm told,' Grandma said at a tangent, 'your husband has a great career in front of him.'

'Oh yes,' Eva Brailes responded, 'I'm afraid we won't be at the Vicarage all that long.'

They had been talking in rather low voices out of politeness to Mr Brailes. But he now intervened. 'I don't know about that,' he said in case Grandma had taken offence.

Mrs Brailes ignored her husband. 'Oh yes,' she responded, as if he had not spoken, 'he's intended for high places. His Principal told me so. Wasn't it nice of him? He said: "Eva, it's up to you!"'

Mr Brailes was embarrassed, but not very. He looked round the room, then at me. Finding nothing to say he gazed vaguely at the ceiling. The gong sounded for tea. Grandma led Mrs Brailes to the dining-room and I asked Mr Brailes the religious question I had prepared.

'Is it true, Sir,' I asked when we were alone, 'that I could move a mountain if I prayed hard enough?'

Mr Brailes looked startled and gave a little laugh. 'What makes you ask, David?'

'Because it's in the Bible and I wanted to know whether it was true.'

'So you're asking me to tell you whether the Bible is true or not.'

'Yes.'

'But who am I to be a judge of the Bible?'

'I thought you might tell me what you really believed.'

'You could,' he replied with a little smile of amusement and gratification playing round his lips, 'you could do greater things, such as being holy, by praying hard. But, no, you couldn't move a real mountain.'

'I thought so,' I said in a disappointed voice, 'I knew it wouldn't work.'

'You tried, then?' He asked the question seriously and I answered him seriously.

'Well, only a hill.'

46

A look of incredulous delight flashed across Mr Brailes's face and vanished. 'You should only pray for good things,' he said.

'I prayed that Nanna's cousin's mother would get better and she died.'

Mr Brailes looked at me through the side of his spectacles and said: 'It isn't automatic. We pray God's will shall be carried out. Either it is through us or, if it isn't, then He carries it out in some other way. In the end it must be, because God is perfectly good and absolutely powerful.'

From that moment I liked Mr Brailes. He had taken my question seriously and answered it seriously. Of course I did not understand why the death of Nanna's cousin's mother had been God's will but I didn't like to press it. Besides, we had lingered long enough in the drawing-room.

Tea was something of a ceremony at The Firs. A large brass tray was placed on the polished mahogany table and on it stood a wrought iron contraption which contained a spirit lamp under a copper kettle. Although the kettle was filled with hot water from the kitchen range, it took some time before it boiled. The curtains were drawn, a lamp stood on the sideboard, the Valor Perfection glowed beside Grandma in the gloom, the copper kettle sang its impersonal melody.

'I've been telling Mrs Porteous how fascinated I am with her kettle,' Eva Brailes remarked as we entered the dining-room.

'Certainly,' Mr Brailes replied and he stood looking at it for a moment before sitting down with the air of approval which an adult might give to a child's steam engine. As I slowly munched through the tiny sandwiches and then the rather hard shortcake biscuits, I wondered at the change in his attitude. He had reverted to his social manner, which seemed to express him less well than the serious tone he had adopted in the drawing-room.

When the Brailes's had left I pondered about it as a fatherless

47

boy will about an older man. I decided that Mr Brailes was good and I liked him. There was a link between us. As for his wife I did not know.

The next time I saw Mr Brailes was at a morning service on a Sunday in Lent. Grandma and I were driven down to church in the highly polished, upright Austin by Mr Courtenay. Mr Courtenay attended neither church nor chapel. He was a materialist who considered religion to be a matter of taste and all ministers of religion hypocrites. He therefore dropped us at the war memorial and drove home to await the end of the service. The memorial, modelled by Grandma from local clay, was in the form of a tall lamp on a plinth. The lamp was kept alight day and night as a sign of remembrance. On the plinth were carved the names of the fallen, my father's name being at the head of the list. The place always made me feel uneasy, partly because I had to doff my cap, which I noticed other people did not do, and partly because I felt expected to be a hero which I had no opportunity of being.

People in their Sunday best were arriving by car and on foot. Grandma made little bows to those she knew. But they were now not many, as she seldom called or went out. We paused at the memorial as usual. I doffed my cap in honour of the dead and Grandma sighed as she read her son's name. We then made our way up the little, tidy, stone-pitched path, through the old church-yard, past the two vast yews, to the church door. Mr Brailes was standing there in his surplice, chatting in an agreeable way as the congregation entered. 'Do you now?' he was saying. 'Ah really? Certainly! Very nice to see you.' And so on. His eyes sparkled behind his spectacles. His face creased and uncreased as he smiled. His voice was high and shallow. He looked lost in his surplice. As we approached he polished his spectacles and his eyes looked tired. Grandma bowed to him but he did not take particular notice of us. I smiled but he only gave me a vague look in return. I wondered if he had recognised me.

All around, the trees were bursting into bud. The grass in

the graveyard was a light green. Over the wall, by the half ruined manor, came the chatter, gossip, and quarrelling of the rooks as they flew about the old cedars. A soft breeze, impalpable, deceptive, stirred the dead leaves of the previous year in little scurries of excitement, as if it could bring to them the resurrection it promised. I had seen a hare that morning before breakfast drinking at the bird bath. He had limped away and then risen on his hind legs before loping back into the wood. I thought of him as I entered the subdued bustle of the church.

There was a rustle of new clothes, the shifting of well polished shoes on the floor, the riffling of the pages of prayer books, the thump of the organ bellows, now and again a hoarse bass note. The muffled caw of the rooks penetrated through a half-opened window. The old sexton, grave, wrinkled, bespectacled, dressed in a black cassock, led us to our pew near the lectern.

There is nothing, I now know, in the Mattins of the Church of England which can compare with the enchanted moment of consecration in the old Roman rite. But the little church absorbed and transformed the boisterous singing, the ragged tunes from the loud, wheezing organ, the half-distracted attention of the areligious congregation, into mysterious communication with an inner world. It was a world at the root of things, quiet, but not with the quiet of repose, ancient and awful, absorbing, living. It was perceptible in the same way as a great hidden fire might be perceived at one remove by the tiny chink of falling ash.

The text of the sermon was: 'Be ye perfect as your Father in heaven is perfect.' It disappointed me because it did not call up an image into my mind. I do not remember the beginning, but I think it was in what I had come to call in my mind Mr Brailes's social manner. His cleverness went over the heads of his congregation. No-one was amused except Eva Brailes who sat smiling, almost laughing, in the front pew under the pulpit. Towards the end his manner changed. He looked up at the old wooden roof and seemed to be speaking to it.

'Do not be deceived, my dear brethren. Do not presume to think you know what is best for you. You cannot bandy words with the creator of the universe, and that universe of heaven which lies beyond it, far vaster than all the fields of stars. The only attitude you can take is that you know nothing, nothing about this world, nothing or next to nothing about the hereafter. God holds us in the hollow of his hand and we work out his purposes. It is for us to tremble and not to argue. Our most cherished ideas of what is good for us or our neighbours are as chaff before the wind. The all-perfect, all-penetrating eye of God is upon you from the day of your birth to the day when you shall come before the throne of judgement with Jesus Christ at your side. Perfection belongs to God alone, we can but reflect it. He sets us an ideal which we must, whether we like it or not, follow. The path to heaven leads inevitably to Golgotha, to the foot of the cross.'

He paused. It was the voice of one crying in the wilderness. The congregation felt it and did not stir. Outside there was a momentary silence in the rookery. The soft, spring wind, redolent of rising sap, fluttered at the half-opened window. A flash of sunlight gleamed in the old yellow glass above the altar. A dog barked, the handle of a pail clinked in a farm-yard. And then, far away in the woods, sounded briefly but distinctly, the mocking voice of the cuckoo. It was the voice of nature, of renewal, of utter indifference to the Christian God.

'Jesus Christ,' Mr Brailes ended, 'taught us love. Love demands perfection, which is a mirror of God's terrible righteousness. Righteousness is a burning fire into which we must plunge, if we are to cleanse ourselves of defilement. My dear brethren, turn your backs on the world, fly from the city of wrath. "Be ye perfect as your father in heaven is perfect."'

CHAPTER FIVE

The little property of The Firs, which only amounted to some twenty acres in all, was divided by a deep and narrow lane. There was not much traffic on it, but at regular intervals a small private bus came down the hill from the market town to the village and then returned. Mr Courtenay used the passing of the bus as a means of telling the time.

I found a more superstitious use for it. When I heard the bus stop at the top gate, I would run as hard as I could through the wood to the stable gate. If I got there before the bus, things would go well for me. But if I arrived late, things would go badly. It was absurd, I knew, but there was a sort of inner truth about it. God knew I was taking on the bet and he therefore regulated the speed of the bus. I realised, of course, that the driver actually determined the pace of the bus. But then, God knew what it would be, indeed might have influenced the driver. In any case, God had worked it out in advance and then inspired me to test the omens. It, therefore, appeared to me not unlikely that I had discovered a way of looking into the future.

It was a secret between God and myself. Once divulged it might well dissolve and I kept it to myself. Moreover I tested it. Sure enough, when the omens were bad, things did go wrong. And usually, but not so certainly, when the omens were good, things went well. If it did not work out I would find on reflection that I had omitted to carry out some part of the ritual. I would have started too near the stables to ensure a good omen or I would not have run as fast as I should have done. This, I felt, was the great temptation: to try and regulate the future instead of trying to discern what was to be.

One day, Mr Courtenay, who was sawing logs in the wood

shed, saw me come tearing down through the wood – once when the bus came down the lane, and again when it returned. I was too late on both occasions. I returned from the stables puffed and put out.

'And what,' he called out from the wood-shed as I passed on my way back to the house, 'do you think you was doing?' He was leaning on his saw taking a rest. 'You went by like a flyin' machine.' He was dressed in old clothes, very shabby and patched, but neat and clean. He wore a dark blue apron. There was a pleasant smell of sawdust, half pine but mixed with the scent of oak and elm. He leant there watching me, his turned-up eyebrows cocked, a smile of interrogation on his lips. He gave a little laugh that was half a chuckle, but so habitual to him I did not notice.

I explained that I tried to beat the bus.

'That's a funny sort of a game,' he said, wiping his forehead with a coloured handkerchief.

The disappointment of missing the bus twice tempted me into thinking that the whole thing was ridiculous. I wanted someone to confide in so I told him what my game really consisted of. He gave me a long, hard look from under his eyebrows and brushed his stubbly chin with the back of his hand. He had his sleeves rolled up and his arms were covered with thick brown hair. Some hair, tinged with grey and white, escaped from his unfastened shirt.

'Well,' he said at last, 'I don't think much of that, Master Davey, and that's the truth on it. If I was you, I'd think of some other sort of game.'

'It wasn't exactly a game.'

He pursed his lips, and sucking in his cheeks, blew as if expelling air from his lungs. It was a sign of disapproval. 'If I was you, I'd think no more on it.' He said this gravely. He had unexpectedly seen something he ought not to have seen, something he did not like, which he would expel from his mind. The disordered complexity of life, its irrationality and power, made him uneasy. What I had told him was like the vision of a poisonous snake in a trim garden – a thing to be crushed and forgotten.

'Well,' he said, taking the big saw from the log and carefully greasing it from a tin, 'I be goin' 'ome. Come along with me and say a word or two to Gertrude.'

He would not say anything more about what I had told him. He wrapped a piece of cloth round the saw and carried it under his arm. 'There we are, then,' he said, making his way to the cottage. ''ave to be careful. There was a fellow leanin' over the gate this morning asking for work. But I rumbled 'im, I did. Told 'im to be off, I did. There's no work 'ere for the likes of 'im.' The chuckle had come back into his voice.

When we came to the porch of the cottage he called out: 'Gertrude, my dear, 'ere's Master Davey.'

There was a shrill but low response from inside. This was followed by the sound of moving furniture, as if things were being prepared for me. Mrs Courtenay received me with a smile and shook me by the hand. We entered the kitchen, a chair was drawn up, dusted and placed in front of the fire. Mr Courtenay went through to the outhouse at the back of the cottage where he could be heard washing himself.

Gertrude was a tall, portly woman with a figure as ample and as upright as Queen Mary's. Her face shone as if it had been polished, placid as the figure on the large cameo pinned to her blouse. Her skin was milk-coloured like a plant kept too long indoors. And, in fact, I had hardly ever seen her outside her dark little kitchen. From the kitchen window, hung with white lace, she could see the tiny patch of the garden, the gate into the lane, but no further. Everywhere else there were tall, dark trees, casting shadows. She had been, a long time before, parlour-maid at the house. And that was the extent of her experience. After she had got married, she had, as Mr Courtenay put it, 'stopped at 'ome'. There were no children and Mr Courtenay, who was very careful with money, would allow no pets. The one exception was a canary he had found in the lane. He had gone so far as to buy it a cage and it now hung

53

in the window, looking out on the same view as Gertrude.

I sat in the spick and span little kitchen and watched the fire burning briskly behind its bars in the range.

'How are you then, Master Davey?' Gertrude enquired in her musical, silver voice.

'Very well, thank you,' I replied politely. It was as difficult to talk to Gertrude as it was to a hospital patient.

Mr Courtenay raised his voice from the outhouse. 'Give Master Davey a sponge finger, Gertrude,' he ordered.

She brushed back her white hair from her face with her hand. It was in fact very neat and the bun might have been that of a prize doll. It was a mechanical gesture of exasperation. Whether she wanted to give me more than one sponge finger, or whether she resented the tone of command in Mr Courtenay's voice, I did not know. But I noticed that her fingers trembled as she nervously patted at her hair. Her face took on an expression of stony indifference as she glanced at the outhouse door. She fetched a sponge finger from the store-cupboard and placed it on a highly patterned, gleaming plate which she handed to me.

'Do you like sponge fingers, then?' she asked as I began to eat it. She watched me with a sweet, very kind smile on her placid face.

I nodded, trying to think of something to say. 'Did you know,' I asked at length, elegantly putting down the sponge finger on the plate, 'that a great bough has fallen off an elm in the Sandy Way?'

'Mr Courtenay did mention it. 'E says a couple were nearly 'urt. They were lying quite near when it fell.' She noted this piece of information without emotion and placidly looked out of the window.

'Why don't you go and have a look at it?'

But Gertrude shook her head. 'Mr Courtenay doesn't like me going up the Sandy Way,' She turned to the range and looked into the fire. Her fingers quivered as she arranged her apron in little folds.

Mr Courtenay entered, his face glowing from the ablutions he had performed. 'Yes 'm,' he said, blowing out his cheeks, 'that there bough near killed a couple. Serve 'em right, if it 'ad. Up there at that time of night.'

'Can't think what they was doing that time of night,' Gertrude said rather shrilly with a touch of malice in her tone.

Mr Courtenay sat down on a Windsor chair and drew it up to the fire. It was cold in the kitchen, although there was bright sunlight outside. He blew out his cheeks again. 'You'd be surprised, me dear, surprised at the goin's on. Luckily,' he continued, turned to me, 'Gertrude doesn't go out much, not much now.'

'Can't think what they was doing at that time of night,' Gertrude repeated, 'it must 'ave been well gone eleven.'

'It was nearer midnight,' and Mr Courtenay shook his head, taking a little pipe from his pocket.

'No it wasn't,' Gertrude said unexpectedly in a shrill voice, 'it was just turned the quarter past.'

'Nearer midnight than that, me dear.' Mr Courtenay pressed the tobacco in the bowl of his pipe with a great splayed thumb.

'You was asleep and snoring,' Gertrude remarked, determined to gain her point, 'I was awake. I 'eard the crash and looked at the clock. There was a bit of a moon so I could see the dial.'

'They say,' Mr Courtenay resumed, ignoring his wife and beginning to puff at his pipe, 'they say she 'ad 'er skirt clean swep off 'er.'

'They 'ad to pass through the village like that?' Gertrude asked, 'there was a bit of a moon too. I expect she was bruised.'

'A good few stripes. More'n a few, I dare say, with the briars and that.' He contemplated the scene in his mind thoughtfully. 'It was a sight, they say, to see 'er without her skirt or stockings or shoes in the moonlight.' He chuckled into his pipe. 'They won't do more of that in a hurry.'

Mr Courtenay took his pipe out of his mouth and pointed

it at me. 'Did I ever tells you,' he asked, almost without pausing between sentences, 'of the time when I went down to Cambridge with Madam?' He had a far away look in his eyes.

'Course you did,' Gertrude said shrilly.

Mr Courtenay ignored the interruption. 'It was like this. . . .'

'But Master Davey's 'eard it already.'

'We was bowlin' along with a big trunk at the back. By Job's, the pace . . .'

Gertrude sat down on a very upright chair and placidly watched the canary as it darted backwards and forwards in its confined cage.

I got away at last and went up through the wood. It was full of sound. The birds were chattering and chirping in the trees. Overhead came the caw of rooks as they circled, far away, invisible.

I ran back to the house, fearing I would be late for lunch. An old blackbird chattered with fright as I caught him at the bird-bath and scuttled away into the laurels. Bees were humming about the south border. The rosemary at the foot of the steps was in flower. A pale blue morning glory, very delicate in colour and appearance, had come out in the sunshine. I paused on the steps, for inside I could hear voices.

A deep, slow voice was saying: 'The trouble is I don't like Giorgio's work.'

Another male voice, higher in pitch, and with something that was not quite unction nor relish in it – but something between the two – replied: 'O come, now, George, that's not the point.' I recognised the voice of Mr Treet, a clergyman who had come to breakfast from time to time after taking the services.

I hesitated a moment on the step and then entered the Red room through the glass door. Although it looked south over the lawn, it was dark inside because of the red coloured walls hung with Pre-Raphaelite pictures in heavy gold frames. I was blinded for a moment and then I made out Mr Treet's white hair and pink, somewhat puckish face. He was a small, spare, persuasive man, obsequious in his manner. He had little rat-like teeth, sharp and efficient. His had been a late vocation, and perhaps because of this he was always immaculate in a well pressed grey suit and a spotless clerical collar.

'Ah,' he exclaimed breezily, raising his hand to greet me, 'here's young Davey.'

He motioned me towards his companion. They were both standing with their backs to the empty grate. 'This,' Mr Treet said with a flourish, 'is David Porteous, and this is Mr George Oldacre, who has come down to see the Porteous papers.' I looked puzzled and he explained: 'Your grandfather's papers, which have not yet been sorted. Your Grandmother thinks they should be. Mr Oldacre may perhaps help her to do it.'

I now shook Mr Oldacre's hand. He was a tall, heavy man in his early forties, dressed in grey flannels and a sports jacket. He had a large round face and the dome of his head was growing very bald. Round his ears and neck the hair was thick and brown and he wore sideboards which gave a Victorian flavour to his appearance. He was not indeed unlike Dante Gabriel Rosetti whose photograph I had seen. He had a short moustache, turning a little grey; brown, thoughtful eyes; heavy cheeks. He looked comfortable, self-sufficient, relaxed. He was slowly smoking a pipe with a curved stem which he took from his mouth when he shook me by the hand. He gave me an interested smile.

He did not speak and I did not know whether I should make conversation or not. I hesitated a moment or two and then said: 'I think I ought to go and wash.'

'You don't look very dirty,' Mr Oldacre remarked, sending a thin whiff of pipe smoke to the ceiling and examining me closely. 'Anyway, your hair has actually got a parting.' He took the pipe from his mouth and turned to Mr Treet. 'When I was a boy,' he continued, 'my hair was never tidy.'

I glanced at his bald head. He noticed and half giggled, half guffawed. 'Yes,' he said ruefully, smoothing his head with his hand, 'now I don't have to worry. Well, never mind, there must be a few compensations for growing old.'

When I came back Grandma was talking to Mr Treet.

'This is David,' she said as I entered, a little vexed at being interrupted.

'We have,' said Mr Oldacre, taking the pipe for a moment from his mouth, and making a gesture as if to rise from his chair, 'been introduced.'

Grandma continued her conversation with Mr Treet and I sat down on a small stool near Mr Oldacre.

'You were saying, Mr Treet?' Grandma enquired.

'George Oldacre and I were discussing the cataloguing and indexing of your husband's papers. In fact,' he went on animatedly, raising his forefinger in the air as if to prevent any interruption, 'to tell you the truth, Mrs Porteous, I was saying that this place could be a centre for late nineteenth century literary studies.'

Grandma looked thoughtful but she said slowly, pinching the bridge of her nose: 'I'm too old to manage the papers myself. There are so many of them.'

'Ah, but Mrs Porteous, that's a simple matter. George here, for instance...'

Mr Oldacre who had been listening to this conversation as he puffed at his pipe and watched the thin curls of smoke ascend into the air, now turned to me. 'And what do you do with yourself, Davey?'

When I hesitated he said: 'Do you fish, for instance?'

I shook my head.

'Or shoot?'

'Grandma doesn't like the pigeons shot. And,' I added modestly, 'I'm too young.'

Mr. Oldacre removed his pipe and gave a slow, almost inaudible titter. He ignored the latter part of my remark. 'But there must be rabbits in all this bracken and brambles.' He looked vaguely in the direction of the window.

'I sometimes go out with Mr Evans the gardener.'

'There must be rivers and ponds round here,' he remarked meditatively.

'I have a bicycle. And I've a train in the nursery,' I said defensively.

And then the gong rang for lunch.

During the meal the conversation turned on Mr Brailes.

'Oh, yes, Mrs Porteous, I'm afraid you'll lose him.' Mr Treet looked up with a knowing expression from his plate. 'He's the most brilliant man in the diocese. I would go as far as saying there hasn't been as brilliant for many, many years.'

'His sermons,' Grandma remarked, 'are very fine. If he goes, there won't be anyone to replace him.' She turned to Mr Oldacre and said: 'We were talking of our new clergyman,' and added: 'Perhaps you know him.'

'Oh, George,' Mr Treet explained, 'takes no interest in ecclesiastical affairs, so he wouldn't know what you were talking about.' He gave a little laugh. 'You see, Mrs Porteous,' he added slyly, 'he's the son of a clergyman.'

Grandma looked at Mr Oldacre with a mixture of timidity, reproach and respect. 'They say Mr Brailes may become archdeacon.'

'I have heard his name,' Mr Oldacre said non-committally.

'Oh yes,' Mr Treet remarked, putting down his knife and fork and finishing his mouthful, 'Brailes is a name to be reckoned with. He could remodel the theology of the poor old Church of England.'

A look of disapproval passed over Grandma's face which Mr Treet did not notice.

'I suppose,' Mr Oldacre interposed, 'he's high church.'

'Oh no, not at all,' Mr Treet replied in his lively, faintly common voice, 'that's the interesting thing. In spite of Eliot and so on, he has a strong affinity to the Evangelicals, and through them, to the Puritans.'

'I suppose Eliot has as well – not that I've read much of him. Couldn't understand what I did.' Mr Oldacre looked across the table as he finished his sentence.

'But liturgically Brailes is low. No,' Mr Treet continued, turning back to Grandma, 'I'm afraid he won't stay here long. Everyone is canvassing for him. Anyway, who else is there except old Canon Barker and he's well over sixty?'

'But wouldn't Mr Brailes be rather young?' Grandma suggested.

Mr Treet shook his head. 'We want somebody young and vigorous to bring us into the twentieth century.'

'It's not often,' Mr Oldacre remarked, eating his pudding with a table spoon which he had somehow managed to get hold of and masticating with little nibbles like a rabbit, 'that a theologian is a good administrator.' He looked up from his plate and exclaimed: 'What a good pudding this is!'

After lunch we had coffee and then I walked up and down in the sunshine with Mr Oldacre. As we passed the Red room door I could hear fragments of Grandma's conversation with Mr Treet. 'It would be a great contribution to scholarship,' Mr Treet said.

'To poetry,' Grandma corrected him.

'I wonder,' Mr Oldacre suggested ruminatively, 'if you could get some snares?'

'What for?' I asked.

'For rabbits, of course.'

'He's worked in the public record office,' came Mr Treet's voice.

'Well, no doubt, it would be a great comfort.' Grandma's voice was uncertain.

I saw Nanna looking for me at the end of the path, hastily said good-bye, and went after her. Mr Evans had found a frog and had put it in a galvanised bath for me.

A month later at breakfast, as she methodically slit the envelopes of her letters with a silver paper knife, Grandma told me that Mr Oldacre was coming to sort Giorgio's papers.

'Where will he live, Grandma?' I asked.

'Not here, Davey. He'll be at Kiln Cottage with a housekeeper. I'll send the papers down to him. I'm getting old,' and she pinched the bridge of her nose. She looked out on to the mist-filled wood with melancholy dissatisfaction. A fat wood pigeon was drinking at the bird bath but she did not notice. 'Yes,' she continued, 'I'm getting too old for anything and I hope he'll help me with some of the business.'

CHAPTER SIX

Mr Oldacre arrived and a new chapter in my life opened. As it turned out his main job was not editing the papers. He paid the wages of the outdoor servants. He interviewed prospective employees. He talked to the gardeners about flowers for the house. He soon became, though not in name, Grandma's secretary. As time went on, he became a substitute son.

Their relationship was strange. Grandma respected and liked him, but, I think, never grew to love him. He was too detached a man, too independent, too rational for her turn of mind. On his side he despised many of the things she most cared about and he was determined not to lose his identity in her service. She had a powerful personality and he knew that he was entirely in her hands. He had no private income. He was at a time of life when it would have been difficult, almost impossible, to find another job. He was self-indulgent, not very competent, and knew it. He also knew when he was well placed. Not that his salary was high but he could do almost as he wished. He could go fishing, for instance, whenever he liked. He disliked what he considered Grandma's sentimentality. But he had fought and suffered in the war. He would put up with it for a safe billet. He sometimes dropped in to lunch and often came up in the evening to read aloud to Grandma.

On the first Sunday after his arrival he agreed to come with us to church. He was silent in the car and said nothing as he helped Grandma up the churchyard path. For some reason or other, I forget what, he did not sit with us but was in a pew at the back of the church. I looked at him from time to time and saw his bored, critical face droop. The congregation, as usual, was in its best clothes, the men in black. But he had arrived in brown plus fours. Grandma had said nothing but I am sure she had noticed. That day, with George Oldacre sitting behind me, the little church seemed to have less power to move my heart.

The sermon was about the resurrection. Mr Brailes in his high-pitched voice said: 'There is one single fact in history that matters. It stands like a great tree in a desert. But it is not a tree. It is the cross. The crucifixion is the one fact we need to know, for by the crucifixion we are given as from a spring of everlasting life, – resurrection. The resurrection is a fact as the spring is a fact after the coldness of winter. And,' he continued, looking obliquely at the old roof, 'the cross is the one fact we need to understand in life, because by the cross we come to resurrection. Without the cross there is no resurrection, no meaning to our lives. Without the cross there is no understanding of history.'

When we were driving back Grandma began:

'Well, what did you think of the sermon?'

Mr Oldacre fidgeted and looked out of the window. 'I'm afraid I was disappointed. You see, I can't agree with what he says about the crucifixion.'

'Why not?'

'Because I don't think the crucifixion is the central event of history, nor,' he continued, his placidity shaken by what he was saying, 'is it unique in itself. Many other men than Jesus were crucified and in more appalling ways. During the war I saw worse crucifixions than He had to bear.' He got out his pipe and slowly filled it.

'Surely', Grandma replied after a pause, 'it's not so much the amount of suffering but who suffered it.'

'But,' Mr Oldacre responded, 'if you make the cross the

central point of history – then bang goes art, literature, music, culture, all that makes life worth living. The trouble,' he went on in his deep voice, and, as he lit his pipe, regained his composure, 'with a sermon is that one can't answer back. That's why I always get so annoyed. The truth is it's all an exaggeration. Everybody knows it's not true in the way other things are true. If it was, things would be very different. We should be living like St Francis of Assissi or Tolstoi.'

'Then you don't approve of Mr Brailes?'

'No, I don't think I do. I don't like,' he said puffing smoke all through the car, 'prophets dressed up as clergymen.' There was a silence and then he said: 'Besides, he's not all prophet. You can tell that by his voice.'

'But I've always thought,' Grandma said with simple dignity but also with a little timidity, 'that priests should have the touch of prophets.'

'Oh no,' George Oldacre rumbled over his pipe, as if talking to himself, 'the two things are clean contrary. When you try to put them together you get Puritanism. Poetry and art come first, then religion.'

Mr Oldacre was not asked to accompany us to church again. But Grandma esteemed him for having opinions of his own and for having the integrity to oppose them to her own.

Kiln Cottage was a low, long building, which had been used in the days when Grandma had had her pottery classes. It was built under a bank to conceal its presence. Grandma did not set herself up as a rival to nature. Luckily it was built on sand, and though dark and overshadowed by trees, it was at least dry. Mr Oldacre had good taste and a lot of knowledge, perhaps a little too much for his purse. He loved Baroque and florid art. On his meagre salary he rummaged from junk shops, old pictures, china, dishes, porcelain, silver, ornaments, and, of course, splendid but odd pieces of furniture. There were, I noticed on my first visit, many nudes, some by Etty. Mr Oldacre spent his working day in a dark study that overlooked a wretched piece of sandy, moss-grown lawn which lay in front of the Big Wood. He worked away there, seated on a frail Hepplewhite chair at a round wobbly pedestal table, writing notes in an indecipherable handwriting, smoking his pipe, reading the letters.

It became a habit for me to tap on a window pane. He would always good-naturedly let me in. I would sit on the book-laden sofa and look out of the window. He would sometimes exclaim to himself as he read a document: 'Awful! God, what a sentiment!' He would never tell me what occasioned these outbursts but I guessed one day when he dropped a book and a photograph of Giorgio fell out. When he picked it up, he said: 'Ah, the great man himself!' He put the photograph down and turned to me with a wicked smile of complicity on his face. He began to speak, thought better of it and smirked. Instead he simply lit his pipe. A few moments later he left the room and returned with two halves of an orange, a sugar lump stuck in the centre of each of them. He handed them both to me and when I offered him one of the halves he shook his head, sat down in an easy chair and watched with pleasure as I ate them.

'Mucky pup!' he said admiringly as I got the sticky juice all over my face. 'Now,' he went on, 'wipe your face with your hanky and I'll let you hear a story.'

He walked to the study door and called: 'Mrs Farmer! Mrs Farmer!'

A few moments later there was a shuffle of feet on the quarry tiles and the housekeeper entered. She was a wizened, frail, old woman, bent and thin. Her grey hair straggled about her face. She had beautifully moulded features, as if she had once been a beauty. But she was now witch-like and this characteristic was intensified by her sharp little brown eyes which darted from Mr Oldacre's face to mine as she entered the room.

'Well, Mrs Farmer,' Mr Oldacre said, taking his pipe for a few moments from his lips, 'this is Master Davey.'

Mrs Farmer wiped her skinny hands on her apron and

extended one of them to me. She made a sort of little bow or curtsy and looked hard into my face. 'Very pleased to meet you,' she exclaimed.

Mr Oldacre was not in the mood for the niceties of introductions and said immediately: 'Now, Mrs Farmer, tell Master Davey about the woman in your village when you were a girl.' He threw her a long, shrewd glance.

Mrs Farmer pursed her lips and looked from one to the other of us. Her face was very lined and seemed to possess immemorial wisdom.

'Ah, well, Mr Oldacre,' she said, 'is it you's be wantin' it or Mr Davey? 'E,' she said turning to me, 'don't believe a word I say.' She gave a girlish giggle. 'But,' she continued, the smile disappearing from her face, 'it's true what I'm goin' to tell you.' She looked seriously round, again pursed her lips and began before Mr Oldacre could interrupt her.

'It was, Master Davey, like this. At the edge of the village there was a great big house all overgrown with weeds and bushes. Dark trees right up to the windows and you couldn't get in at the gate 'cause it was all broken. It had belonged to a very rich corn merchant years ago and 'e'd lived there in style with 'is wife who was the daughter of an earl. They had lots of servants, wine and money, as much as you like. They 'ad a daughter and when they dies all the money goes to 'er, see. The strange thing was nobody 'ad ever seen 'er, never so much as by a glance. When I was a girl there were only two servants, the old footman and 'is wife who was the cook. They lived there with the daughter all alone.

'There were tales in the village, I can tell you. They said she was all right in every way – except she 'ad a pig's 'ead on 'er, see, a pig's face all complete. You don't believe me do you? As sure as I'm 'ere she 'ad a pig's face, snout, little nostrils, piggy eyes and 'airy ears, just like a pig. You see in the village it leaked out. She was rich, very rich, but that didn't make no difference. They used to feed 'er on pig's food for that was what she liked, from a golden trough set on the polished dinin' room table. One of the boy's in the village 'ad glanced through the window one summer evening after 'e'd been fishing and he saw 'er gulpin' down 'er swill from the trough.'

Mrs Farmer paused and looked keenly with her shrewd eyes into my face to see how I had taken it. 'Yes, Master, that's 'ow it was,' she said, nodding her head. 'Yes, that's 'ow it was. Strange thing wasn't it?' She pursed her lips seriously and smiled a faint, faded smile which brought something youthful into her old face.

'And what happened?' I asked.

'She died and was buried in the churchyard,' Mrs Farmer replied, 'and you can see 'er stone to this day.'

George Oldacre took the curved stem of his pipe out of his mouth and guffawed. 'And now,' he commanded good-naturedly, 'get back to your kitchen.'

Mrs Farmer took no notice and said to me: 'Mr Oldacre don't believe me. But you do, don't you, dear?' Without waiting for my reply she turned on her employer like an angry bird, hunching her shoulders into an even more pronounced stoop. Her eyes blazed and she looked as if she might attack him.

Then it all suddenly passed and she said: 'Now, Mr Oldacre, don't forget the blood when you fetch that 'are from the poulterer.' She paused and licked her lips, sucking her toothless gums. 'You must 'ave the blood for the gravy.'

'All right,' George Oldacre muttered, 'I haven't forgotten. Have you a bottle?'

'It's out there in the 'all. It's been there all the time. I told you so.'

'Oh did you?' he asked vaguely.

'Yes I did,' Mrs Farmer responded shrilly, casting a sharp look of maternal admonition at him. 'Now mind you don't forget 'cause if you do it won't be as you likes it.'

She now turned to me and with a little bow made for the door. 'You see 'ow it is, Master Davey, 'e don't believe nothink.'

I had begun to have some vague lessons in reading and writing from a retired schoolmistress in the village. These were now supplemented by others on painting from Mr Oldacre. But they were not a success as he was an impatient teacher. He tried to teach me to fish. But instead of taking me straight to a pond or river he made me learn to cast for hours on the lawn. When I did get to the water, at last, the only thing which bored me was the fishing itself. I loved the sound of the river, the eddying pools, the breeze through the willows, the flowers in the grass on the banks.

We used to pass through a large, dark-green, sloping field in which rough cattle were tearing at the grass round the buttercups. We sat on camp stools on the bank and watched the water ripple and whisper its way through trailing willow boughs and shrubs. There were moorhens, fussy and self-important, there were intent water rats hurrying by on important errands. But it was mostly the wind on the surface of the water, the broken image of the sky reflected on it, which delighted me. The fishing with its tiresome, intricate apparatus, which always seemed to tangle itself in a tree, was an unpleasant irrelevance. I became content to leave well alone. I wandered about while George Oldacre slowly fished and smoked his pipe.

One summer evening when it was warm, and the daylight seemed unwilling, or unable, to ebb quite away, George persuaded Grandma and Nanna to let me go mothing. We painted the trees round the house with sugary gum and hung lanterns in them. The moths flew on to the gum and stuck there. Many of them flew away but we captured a fair number and mounted them next day. The wood, mysterious and solemn, shuddering now and then in the night wind, seemed enchanted by the light of the flickering candles in the lanterns. In the course of the proceedings George, who was sentimental but quite unromantic, suddenly said: 'Pump ship!' and went behind a tree. I heard the patter of urine in the pine needles above the sough of the breeze in the great pines. I studiously

67

followed the outline of the chimneys against the skyline. We found no rare moths and the mothing was never repeated.

I often followed him as he went shooting in the big wood. His old black and brown spaniel bitch would snuffle around in the undergrowth. She was only half trained and would try and catch the rabbit. George would shout: 'Damn the dog, get out of it!' as time and again he was in danger of shooting her as well as the rabbit. At home she was a docile, loving animal who spent her time in the hall devoutly licking the butt of the gun. But when it came to shooting she was too excitable to be managed. It was my task to pick up and carry the twitching corpses.

Despite George's kindness, in spite of his affection for me, at first I somehow distrusted him. He was an interloper into my world, an alien influence which disturbed and changed it. I could not understand his mixture of intellect and impulse, his devotion to ideas and his indolent self-indulgence. He would pursue an object so far, but then an invisible rein – boredom or self-interest – would jerk him backwards. I came to see later that he feared involvement, responsibility, or as he put it 'giving hostages to fortune'. Life was a predicament that necessitated caution.

One morning that summer, after lessons, I went down to the lower lawn where Mr Evans had placed a galvanized bath for a frog he had found. The poor frog was allowed to go hopping round the lawn when I was there. But the rest of the time he was confined to the galvanized prison which was in the deep shade of a clump of laurels. This morning I sauntered down through the wood with an easy feeling that the disagreeable part of the day had passed. Sunlight played through the gently moving leaves. I walked by the holly I loved climbing and made my way to the gap in the laurels. There in the deep shade lay the galvanized bath.

And then I saw it. My frog had turned into a great upturned corpse, floating like a plucked chicken, and almost as big, on the surface of the water. It lay on its back, white, bloated, monstrous. Its belly was hugely inflated and its legs stuck up in the air. And then I saw it was not the frog. He was swimming peacefully round the blown up piece of flesh as if he had not noticed it. I looked at the corpse more closely, shuddering as I did so. The blotchy skin was lumpy, irregular. It was a toad which had jumped in during the night and had drowned, or was drowning.

I dared not rescue it, or even touch the bath. The movements of the little lively frog, oblivious of its awful companion, filled me with horror. I ran as fast as I could for Mr Courtenay whom I thought would be more sympathetic in my trouble than Mr Evans. Mr Courtenay fetched a bucket and the drowning toad was unceremoniously tipped out in the wood.

'But how, why?' I demanded. An injustice had been committed against the toad, and also against the frog whose water had been polluted.

' 'E'll probably be all right if a bird or a rat don't get 'im,' Mr Courtenay said comfortingly, walking away with the empty bucket. 'The water will come out and 'e'll go down to 'is size.'

After that I decided not to go near the galvanized bath. I could not bear to put my hands in the contaminated water. I played instead with some cast-iron guttering which Mr Evans had put out for me. I placed them in a line from the garden tap on the low wooden water butt and made an irrigation scheme. There were difficulties. The water would not always flow down the right gutter and overflowed the sides. Some of the gutters leaked and made pools on the cinder path which I knew would annoy Mr Evans. I was very busy with all this when I heard the bell from the house. This meant it was lunchtime. I ignored it and threw a stone I was using into the tub with a great splash, I *would* not be disturbed at this critical moment.

Nanna appeared from the wood, her apron fluttering in the breeze. I watched her out of the corner of my eye but refused to look up.

'Davey,' she shouted, 'come along or you'll be late for lunch.'

I took no notice.

'Come along, Davey,' she shouted in a slow wearied voice to emphasise she meant what she said.

'I'll come when I've finished what I'm doing,' I answered rudely, addressing the water butt.

'Now then, Davey,' Nanna said, approaching me, 'you're not to talk like that and you're to come immediately.'

'I'll come when I want to.'

'You'll come now.'

'I won't.'

Nanna changed her tactics. 'You'll be late for lunch and Mr Oldacre is coming.'

A blind irrational hatred for Nanna possessed me. I hated all the things I loved about her, her neat white apron, her fresh face, her comfortable walk.

'I don't care who's coming for lunch,' I said defiantly.

She had now come close to me and grabbed my hand to drag me away. I hit her as hard as I could and darted away.

'Davey!' A loud, masculine voice shouted behind me. It was Mr Oldacre. He stood by the cordon apple trees and glared at us. For all I knew he had witnessed the whole scene. 'Davey,' he repeated, 'you're a very naughty little boy.' And he began to advance on me.

I had turned round but as he approached I broke away from Nanna. 'It's nothing to do with you,' I shouted, bursting into tears. 'It's nothing to do with you.'

George Oldacre had a stick in his hand and he ran forward to catch me. But I was too quick for him. 'You little devil!' he muttered as he tripped on the edge of the lawn.

'You're not my father,' I shouted as I ran to the wood. There was lead in my heart as I ran. I sped to the back door, kicked off my shoes and tore up to the night-nursery. The key was in the door. I turned it and threw myself on the bed.

I then gave vent to my feelings in a series of howls. I tore at my hair, scratched at my pillow and sobbed uncontrollably. All the time I was thinking: 'This is strange. Why am I doing it?' The occasion was too trivial. It was a storm which had blown up from nothing. I wandered round the room with a tear-stained face, in my stockinged feet, moaning to myself.

Nothing happened. No-one tried the door. Why had no-one come to see where I was? The house was very still. Were they looking for me? I peered cautiously out of the window but there was nothing unusual to be seen. Had nobody noticed that I had had no lunch? I realised I was hungry, very hungry. Lunchtime had come and long since gone. George Oldacre must have sipped his coffee in the drawing-room long ago. I wished I had been there. Had Grandma and he discussed me together and shaken their heads? I wailed resentfully, hoping that someone would hear and pity me. Nobody came. The two grandfather clocks, one in the hall and the other in the big studio, whose cases had been painted by Grandma in Pre-Raphaelite colours, chimed their silvery chimes, one after the other.

And then my resentment turned again into hatred. I again roamed round the room thinking of revenge. On Nanna's dressing-table stood the photograph of her brother who had died in the war. He stood there, upright and gallant, dressed in his sergeant's uniform. Here was the chink in Nanna's armour. I took the photograph out of its frame and was about to tear it in pieces when I heard the soft turning of the lock. I sat on the bed perfectly still. Perhaps they would think I was dead. At last I heard Nanna's voice, very calm, aloof: 'Davey, do you want anything to eat?'

I could not open the door while I had the photograph in my hand. 'No!' I said defiantly, 'I don't want anything to eat.'

'Davey, are you going to unlock the door?'

'No!'

I heard her footsteps die away on the stairs.

I was in a ridiculous situation. They held all the cards. I had none. And I had no-one but myself to blame. A cold rage possessed me. I caught sight of a pot of hand cream on the dressing table. I ran over to it and deliberately daubed the photograph.

When I had finished I was left with a feeling of emptiness. Hot tears again began to flow, tears from the depths. I lay on the bed and kicked. What had I gained? Nothing but remorse. The photograph, Nanna's dearest possession, was ruined. I could not put it right. There was only one thing left – the humiliation of surrender. I waited for the inevitable, I stood on a chair by the window and looked outside. Sunlight filled the scene. A blackbird hopped from the bushes and then scurried away for no apparent reason with a peal of shrill, frightened laughter. A thrush warbled for a moment in the shade, perched on a low bough, and then his song died away into the long, monotonous summer silence. The silence was oppressive, like a sub-conscious, everlasting hum. Why had I done what could not be undone?

I waited a long time measured by the far off chimes of the clocks. When teatime had come and gone the door was tried again. It was Nanna. With a wail, which really expressed my feelings, but which was at the same time calculated to move her heart, I rushed to her, clung to her apron.

'Oh Nanna,' I cried, rubbing my head against her and glancing up to gauge her expression, 'I'm sorry, very sorry.'

Nanna shook her head sadly but said nothing. At least she did not push me away. 'But Davey,' she said at last, 'how could you have been so rude, you who've always been such a good, polite boy?'

I hung my head, miserably dejected. I had fallen low, but as yet she did not know how low. 'Your photograph of Cyril,' I burst out and the tears flowed, 'your photograph, I've covered it with cold cream.'

Nanna stiffened, looked at the photograph lying on the dressing table, and then at me.

'Oh Nanna,' I went on, 'I don't know how I did it. I feel so wrong, so wrong.'

Nanna picked up the photograph, examined it, saw that it was indeed ruined, and calmly put it on the window-sill. There was a look more of surprise than anger on her face. She was even a little startled.

'Well, are you sorry?' she asked calmly.

'Oh yes,' I mumbled.

And then she put me on her lap and gently hugged me. There could have been no worse punishment than this comfort. 'I don't know what came over you, I really don't. No I don't.' She rocked me to and fro. Later she fetched me a cup of hot milk and unbuttered bread. She watched me eat it, pondering on what had happened. When I had finished she said: 'You may go downstairs.' She left the room so that I should go down by myself.

I crept downstairs to the bathroom to wipe my tear-stained face. I had gone no further than the first flight of the back stairs when I met Grandma. I had tiptoed in my stockinged feet over the dark green felt and it was just bad luck that we met. I stood back in the shadows hoping she would not see me. Her usually kind and sweet face became severe. She drew herself up to her full height, gave me a look of scorn and then passed me by without a word. Her black skirt swept along the passage with a swish of contempt.

I wiped my face and softly descended the back stairs. I passed through the servants' entrance, past the larder and Cook's room, to the back door. Here I put on my shoes and entered the wood. The fresh air, and the indifference of nature to my behaviour, soothed me. Plans of running away and of revenge passed through my mind and vanished. A wood pigeon in the pine trees cooed with the luxuriant, liquid notes of summer, remote, wrapped in a mysterious melody of his own. The toad had disappeared. It seemed all one that he had been eaten or had recovered. I shrugged my shoulders.

I now had Grandma to face. The drawing-room with its green walls and high ceiling was dim. The refraction of light from the glasses of the great pictures and their heavily carved

73

gold frames did not dispel the gloom. As I stood at the screen by the door I thought obscurely: There is no time here. It has always been like this and always will be. Giorgio in his skull cap at the books, Giorgio sipping his Turkish coffee, telling Grandma about his thoughts; the reflection of the firelight in winter, of sunlight again and again strained by green leaves, in the brass coffee pots on the little mahogany table; Giorgio's aspirations soaring, dissolving, reforming and disappearing in the plaster panels of the ceiling – all this had always been and would surely continue to be. I had never seen Giorgio, but his presence was as real to me as that of a living person.

Grandma was standing very erect in front of the fireplace. She still looked grim and unfriendly. I realised she was waiting for me.

'Grandma,' I said timidly, 'I am very sorry.' I went up to her and slipped my hand into hers, which was dry and smooth. She looked down on me with an expression of reproach and sorrow.

'I didn't expect it of you,' she said, and then to soften it she added, 'Davey.'

The reproach died away and she just seemed sad. But now it was not so much with me as with life itself. She gently stroked my hand with one of her fingers and looked out of the window at the far end of the room. The declining sun, its splendour weakened, shot rays of light through the wood and on to the red trunks of the motionless pines. Melancholy, and with it inertia, seeped from the pale green sky on the horizon, just visible, in part, through the trees. To rise in quivering vigour in the quiet of the dew, to ride godlike at noon, to sink slowly as the evening breeze arose, the whole cycle, was all one. And so was my temper, my shame, my punishment.

'How could you be so rude, when you say you love Nanna?' she asked, but gently, as though applying a standard alien to her feelings.

I hung my head and thought: 'How did it happen?' Incredibly it had happened to me. I feared the depths from which my anger had sprung, which was me and was not me.

Grandma looked at me sharply. 'You do love Nanna, don't you?'

'Oh yes, oh yes I do.' I said fervently.

Grandma seemed relieved. 'Then why did you do it?' It was talking of love in the language of mathematics.

'I don't know,' I replied.

'If you love somebody,' Grandma said with a sigh, looking past me, over the hot house plants, out of the window, her eyes fixed on the melancholy pines, 'you will do anything for that person.' I knew it was true of her. But was it true of me? I had defaced Nanna's photograph. Grandma did not know about that. If she was so serious, without knowing, what would she think when she did?

'I'll try and be good,' I said.

She bent down to kiss me and her watch on the thin gold chain swung out and then hit her spectacle case. She again looked out of the window. Her eyes had the expression of the very old, without hope, and with the acceptance of despair. There is the same stark acceptance in the grey lifeless boughs of an ancient tree. The boughs are raised on high but there is no expectation that there will be any response from the beautiful, pitiless skies.

That night, after I had said my prayers, I asked Nanna if she could forgive me.

'Yes,' she replied, 'but you must never do such a thing again. Otherwise your temper will master you, and then you might do anything.'

'I know,' I said, 'I know. But is there another photo of your brother?'

Nanna shook her head. 'It was the only one that was taken.'

I knew this already but I wanted to be sure. A chill of despair ran through me. I had done something which could not be undone. The image of her brother had been obliterated by me. How would anyone remember him now? I had, as it

75

were, murdered his memory. I did not cry. I somehow could not. Now was not the time for relief.

When Nanna had gone I lay and tossed in the gloom. Grey light filtered through the faded chintz curtains and filled the night nursery with disenchantment and guilt. I could hear the caw of a last, few rooks as they winged their way homeward. I imagined them outlined against the broken, darkening clouds, specks of movement, like dust in an eddy of wind.

I was still awake when Nanna looked in before coming to bed. The cold water storage tank in the attic began to hiss. At the end of the passage I could hear the swish of water as the maids filled jugs of water to take to their rooms. The two grandfather clocks chimed one after the other in their treble voices. Downstairs a curtain was drawn with a muffled rumble. Night, the mysterious, warm night of summer, had closed in.

'Aren't you asleep?' Nanna asked.

She had a hand lamp in her hand and peered down at me. 'What's the matter?'

I shook my head.

She tried to settle me down by fluffing up the pillows and tucking up the bedclothes.

I said suddenly: 'Did you tell Grandma about the photo?'

'No,' Nanna said and went on with the tidying of the bed.

'And Cook?'

'I told Cook.' She was now tucking in the bottom of the bed. 'But,' she went on, 'I've told no-one else, and I won't.'

'I feel very sorry.'

'Now,' said Nanna practically, 'settle down and think no more about it.' She was tucking up the bottom of the bed. 'We all do things we shouldn't do. And,' she went on, 'we shouldn't do them. But once they're done there's no more to be said.'

A few moments later I was asleep.

Next morning I tapped on George Oldacre's window. It was half open and he was reading a volume of letters at the circular mahogany table. He looked up and told me to come in. When I got to the study door, I said my set piece which I had made up on my way through the wood.

'I'm very sorry, Mr Oldacre, that I was so rude yesterday.'

George Oldacre stood up and began to fill his pipe from a pouch, watching me with a quizzical expression as I stood in the doorway. 'Come in, Davey,' he said, 'and sit down. Yes, you were very rude. But you punished yourself by going without your lunch. And do you know, I had bought you some peppermints from the post office. And now,' he went on, 'I've eaten them, or –' he paused to light the now filled bowl of his pipe, 'or almost all of them.'

'I'm so sorry,' I said again, moving a pile of books to one side and seating myself on the sofa.

He went over to the chimney piece and handed me a bag of sweets. They had not been opened.

'Thank you very much,' I said gratefully and made no comment about the unopened bag.

'That's all right, Davey,' he replied, in a vague voice looking back at his papers. He puffed little clouds of smoke from his pipe. This seemed to indicate that he wanted to think no more of the subject.

'But, Mr Oldacre,' I said as I opened the bag, 'these aren't peppermint, they're bullseyes.'

'Are they?' he asked more vaguely than ever. 'Try one.' And then in the silence which followed, while he read the letters and scratched notes on a pad, I sucked a bullseye.

CHAPTER SEVEN

I met the Brailes's some weeks later as I was making my way through the wood to Kiln Cottage for a painting lesson. They were walking happily together up the uneven root-filled path.

Sunlight and green patches of shadow passed across their faces. They seemed to be telling each other amusing anecdotes, for every now and again I could hear Mr Brailes's high, intellectual laugh.

'Ah, David!' Mr Brailes exclaimed, catching sight of me and looking obliquely at me through his spectacles. 'And where are you off to?'

Before I could reply Mrs Brailes said: 'Oh, how nice to see you, David! You look very important with that satchel.'

I explained where I was going and Eva glanced at her husband. 'We were half thinking of calling on Mr Oldacre ourselves. We ought to have done so ages ago. If we walked along with you, we wouldn't stay long and disturb your lesson.'

We came to an intersection in the way where an old holly grew over the path. One had to walk here in single file and Mr Brailes made way for his wife. But, with a little smile, she waved him forward.

'You go ahead, Archdeacon Grantley,' she exclaimed playfully.

I did not understand that they were continuing the game they had been playing before they met me and I said: 'Are you ...?' looking into Mr Brailes's face.

He seemed a little vexed and embarrassed. There was something bleak, withdrawn, shadowy, about his face, as he stood there in the luxuriant undergrowth. I noticed the pallor of his cheeks, the thin lips, the scraggy neck above the clean clerical collar. Thick, green fronds of bracken, tender and sweet as summer herself stood all around him.

'Certainly not,' he said in his high pitched, jaunty voice, but quickly, like a man dextrously killing an insect. 'Certainly not, if it's what I think you mean. It was just a little joke.'

He walked ahead and Mrs Brailes followed him. I walked as near her side as I could.

'We'll come along slowly,' she said to me, 'he loves walking fast. But now, of course, I can't do it.' Her pleasant pink face was relaxed. Her blue eyes were sultry, a little withdrawn, receptive. A smile of pleasure hovered round her lips. She looked as pretty and as ordinary as a dog-rose in the hedge.

I looked at her enquiringly and she said to herself in her slurred way, which was unintelligible to me: 'It will be an autumn cherub.' I thought this was some classical allusion and did not reply. I do not think she meant me to understand.

When we reached Kiln Cottage I tapped on the window as usual. But there was no answer. The jasmine at the door stirred in the faint, summer breeze. The air was hot, scented with the sweet smell. There were pink geraniums in large terracotta pots, yellow and brown snapdragons in the beds, visited again and again by bees. Their hum seemed part of the heat. There was no other sound. Everything in the Big Wood, the other side of the sandy lawn, had fallen into a drowsy sleep. I jangled the bell through the silent house again and again.

After a long time Mrs Farmer appeared. Her face was pink and crumpled as if she had been asleep. She sucked her gums and looked suspiciously at us through the half open door.

'Ah, it's you, Master Davey,' she said, recollecting herself, 'and the vicar and his wife.' She blinked and plucked the front of her faded chintz overall.

'What a shame we've disturbed you,' Eva Brailes said with an engaging but conscious smile which seemed to annoy Mrs Farmer.

'I've come for a lesson,' I explained, glancing at my satchel.

'Fact is, Master Davey,' Mrs Farmer said, a sweet conspiratorial smile lighting her old face, 'fact is 'e's out. 'E went for a stroll after lunch.' She looked up ingratiatingly into Mr Brailes's face. 'I'll go after 'im, that's what I'll do.'

'Oh no,' he replied, 'we couldn't put you to that trouble.'

But Mrs Farmer had darted on her bird-like legs behind us and was calling in her shrill voice: 'Mr Oldacre! Mr Oldacre!' She ran about in little circles towards the wood.

'It's no use, Mrs Farmer,' Eva Brailes said sweetly, 'there's no reply. We were going for a little walk in the wood, anyway.

We'll see if we can find him.' And, in fact, Mr Brailes was half way across the lawn already, making for the gate into the wood.

Mrs Farmer shook her head. 'The wood's very thick this time ayear.' She sucked in her cheeks. 'I shouldn't go if I was you.'

But Eva only smiled. 'I shall have David with me, so I shall be all right.' And with that she also made for the gate.

Mrs Farmer hovered about uncertainly before returning to the cottage. She muttered to herself as she went, put out that they were not taking her advice.

At the gate we joined up together and entered the wood. In fact it was not so overgrown as the home wood. Under the trees there were open spaces and there were not many brambles. It was leafy and warm. Flies buzzed about the bracken in the drowsy silence. We walked without speaking, subdued by the tranquillity of the great trees.

And then I heard the healthy cockney voice of a girl: 'Don't do that.' It was sulky, sensual, defiant. 'It tickles.' Through a ragged path in the bracken I saw them. George Oldacre was lying full length, his arm round the girl's waist. He had his back to us and was whispering something to her. She was a tall, black-haired girl, her hair tied with a crimson ribbon. I could not see her face for it was buried in his shoulder. She lay there seemingly half asleep. Her black and white frock was pulled up revealing her thigh and part of her buttocks. Her high-heeled shoes had been kicked into the bracken. George Oldacre began to fumble at the front of her frock.

We saw them simultaneously and stopped in our tracks. We scarcely breathed. And then, after a pause, we stealthily turned round and retraced our steps. A bird chirped faintly in the distance. Otherwise silence. Even our footfalls were deadened by the moss and damp brown leaves.

At the gate we stopped. Eva Brailes glanced at her husband. He glanced at me. He began to speak and then thought better of it. Instead he looked obliquely through his spectacles into the distance.

'Well,' Eva Brailes said at length, 'as we've got to be back for tea, we shall have to be going.' And regaining something of her old manner: 'You can come along, if you like.' I shook my head politely. 'In that case,' she continued, 'we shall be off. I hope we shall meet again soon. And –' an astringent quality entered her voice – 'tell Mr Oldacre we did call.'

I watched them as they made their way across the lawn down to the lane. They did not talk but Eva took her husband's arm and leant on it.

I found the front door of Kiln Cottage open and slipped into the study. The girl had left her bag behind and there hung about the room a smell of scent, pervasive, disturbing. I sat on the sofa and drew doodles in my painting book. I waited patiently, hoping, or at least half hoping, I should see the girl's face when she returned.

After a long time Mrs Farmer put her head round the door. 'Oh it's you, Master Davey,' she exclaimed, 'fancy you being 'ere. So you didn't find 'm, then?'

'No,' I lied.

Mrs Farmer shook her head. 'I thought you wouldn't,' she said thoughtfully. 'Well now,' she continued more brightly, 'it's tea-time and you must come along with me, eh? I've made some scones, there's fresh butter and some blackcurrant jam from last year. There now, you'd like that wouldn't you?'

I smiled appreciatively and followed her out of the room. The kitchen was dark and smelt of washing up, of the recently baked scones, and grease from the joint. The little black range hummed and there was a fine show of red coal between the bars. A large kettle hissed on the hob, occasionally overflowing with a cloud of steam. Its lid rattled merrily. Mrs Farmer hurried round getting out the best cup and plate. She wiped the kitchen table with an old dishcloth.

'There now, Master Davey,' she fussed around me, 'this will be a grand occasion for me, and we shall enjoy it won't we?'

She gave a little cackle of laughter. 'Now take this.' She produced a toasting fork from the side of the range and handed it to me. 'We shall 'ave some toast for tea. We shall be ever so cosy and we shall 'ave eat everything up before Mr Oldacre comes in. Not that I'm expecting 'im now, not now. 'E's got 'imself involved some'ow and there won't be no tea for 'im left. We'll see to that, won't we?'

She laid the table and placed before my seat a starched napkin. Then, taking an embroidered cloth, poured some boiling water into the teapot, ran into the scullery and made the tea. She placed the great brown teapot on a cool part of the range, gave it several vigorous stirs, sniffed it appreciatively and replaced the lid.

'You see,' she said in her shrill voice, shooting a piercing glance at me as I made the toast, ''ow it is that I looks after Mr Oldacre. I love making other people comfortable. There's nothing in life like a bit of comfort.' She sucked in her cheeks at the thought of what she had said and looked into the fire. 'There,' she continued pointing at the hearth, 'are 'is slippers, always warm whenever 'e wants them. And when the paper arrives in the mornin' I warm it for 'im. 'E likes it that way, you don't want to be touching cold paper early in the mornin'.'

She darted like an old bent bird to the door and listened, her head cocked on one side. 'I thought I 'eard 'em, that is Mr Oldacre,' she whispered but raised her voice as she came away from the door. 'I'm a farmer's daughter, that's what I am. You can always remember that because of me name, see, that bein' my 'usband's name of course, and 'e was no farmer I assure you, else I wouldn't be 'ere, would I? A farmer's daughter knows what comfort is, she 'as to. When we was small and Father was strugglin', we didn't 'ave any butter on our bread except on a Sunday. Think of that.' She straightened up and looked me full in the face. 'Here I go,' she said with a giggle, her manner changing, 'and I've forgotten them scones. Why you needn't 'ave made the toast. Whatever was I thinking of? Well, we'll 'ave both, shan't we?' She buttered

the scones with a wicked looking kitchen knife which she
dipped into a bowl in front of the range. Then she started
cutting and buttering thin slices of bread.

'Mrs Farmer,' I pointed out seriously, trying not to giggle,
'we've now got bread as well as scones and toast.'

'Ah, but see,' she replied, 'this is for them when they comes
in. Mr Oldacre will have a great appetite, you see if 'e don't.
'E loves an anchovy sandwich.' She cackled to herself. She
cocked her head on one side and listened. But there was no
sound but the regular ticking of the old grandfather clock
and the chink of ash from the range. The window was open
and from the wood I could hear the soft liquid notes of a wood
pigeon in the tree tops, dreaming, perhaps, of an eternal
summer.

'Don't you get very hot at the range in summer?' I asked,
seating myself at the table and feeling hot myself.

'Never, me dear, old Mrs Farmer's never too 'ot.' And she
spread her hands in front of the coals. 'Feel me. See.' And
her smooth old hands, it was true, were cold.' Cold 'ands, kind
'eart, they say.' She pursed her lips into a reminiscent smile.
'But me blood wasn't cold once upon a time, when I was a
girl, I can tell you.' Her eyes sparkled at the thought.

After the scones and toast we had some of the blackcurrant
jam on thin slices of bread and butter. Then there was Madeira
cake and, finally, she brought me red currants covered with
caster sugar. These were served with thick, slightly sour cream.
For the first time in my life I was given strong, sugary tea
straight from the brown teapot on the range. When I had
drunk it, she darted over to the window to read the leaves left
in the cup.

'Ah, yes, Master, there's a woman, a beautiful woman, in
your life. Beware of 'er and you'll be all right. And there's the
mark of danger and some ill 'ealth. There'll be a dark woman
who loves you and you won't love 'er. A stranger crosses your
path, casting 'is shadow upon you. But,' she went on more
cheerfully, 'you'll always be prosperous but not rich, if you

understand my meanin'. No, the money's not for you. And in the end it'll be all successful. You'll live to a ripe old age.'

She replaced the teacup back on its saucer with a little crash. 'There now, what do you think of that?'

'Thank you very much. And do you tell your own tea leaves?' I asked, looking at the mysterious patterns in her own cup.

She drew in her lips and looked at me darkly. 'Oh no,' and she shook her head, 'you must never tell your own fortune. It would bring bad luck.'

After the tea things had been cleared away we sat down on an old settle covered by a rug. Mrs Farmer leant forward and lit a cigarette from the glowing coals in the grate. She puffed away at it as if it might go out like a damp pipe. 'I always 'ave me smoke after tea,' she explained and she settled back. The smoke drifted into her eyes and was wafted towards the grate. 'I'm old and I don't think I should stint meself.' Flies flew about the room over the range and sometimes alighted on a yellow fly paper which hung from the middle of the ceiling where they hissed and perished. There was a long silence as we sat there like old friends. Then she fixed her dark, brown eyes on my face.

'You remember the story of the woman with the pig's face?'

'Oh yes.'

'Well, it's true. All of it's true, let me tell you.' She puffed a pall of smoke in my direction. 'What's more I say so, whatever Mr Oldacre likes to think.'

'I believe it,' I said.

'Listen to this then. I'll tell you another. In that village there was a girl, long before I was born, in the bad days when things were 'ard for the poor. She was a tall black 'aired girl with dark eyes like me own, thin-faced she was, but with full lips. You see I've seen a picture of 'er. A young gipsy made love to 'er one summer evening. The gipsies came in their vans and in the morning they were no more to be seen. And

84

the shame of it was that this girl, whose name was Rose, was left to carry the cost and the shame of it.' She paused and looked at me to see if I had understood. 'You see, she was soon 'eavy with child. No-one would 'elp 'er, nor stir a finger to be good to 'er, see?'

'And what,' I interrupted, 'happened to the young gipsy?'

''E was off into the night and wasn't seen no more, never no more,' Mrs Farmer emphasized, a little vexed at having to tell her story in a different way than she had proposed, 'Oh yes that's the way with the travellin' folk.' She lit another cigarette and began puffing the smoke in front of her. ''E didn't want no more children. 'E couldn't be bothered. It was all left to poor Rose. When 'er father came to 'ear of it 'e turned 'er out one wild night as a shame to the family. 'E was respectable, a farmer, see? "Well," she said, "be it on your 'ead, father," she said. And she went straight out to the great hay barn, fixed a rope round a beam and there and then 'anged 'erself.'

Mrs Farmer puffed meditatively at the end of her cigarette. She watched me closely to see whether I had taken in the full tragedy of the scene she had described. She shook her head and said reminiscently: 'Many a time I've seen that old beam and thought of poor Rose.' She paused again and then continued. 'But just at that moment, in the nick of time, a labouring lad came in with 'is lantern, saw somethin' danglin' from the beam and cut 'er down. She was still just breathing, 'eavy in child though she was. And do you know, Master Davey, not long after she gave birth to splendid twin boys.' She leant forward and looked reflectively into the grate. 'One of them twins was me father. That's 'ow I know it. The labourer what cut 'er down married Rose and brought them up as 'is own. In the end he got a farm of 'is own. 'E was a good 'ard working man and loved Rose none the less because of the gipsy.'

When I got back to the house I told Cook what had happened.

'You 'ad tea with Mrs Farmer?' she asked sharply, her arms akimbo, giving me a piercing glance.

'Yes,' I said, 'and she told my teacup.'

Cook gave me another look as sharp as a knife. 'You did that, did you? Well you 'ad no business to 'ave done. You should 'ave nothink to do with that woman.'

'Why not?'

'You're best 'aving your tea up 'ere where you belongs. I'd 'ave given you as good a tea, I dare say, in the servants' 'all along of the rest of us. I suppose Mr Oldacre was out, eh? You should 'ave come back 'ere where you belongs.'

'I didn't mean any harm,' I said, a little frightened by Cook's vehemence, and intrigued at her dislike of Mrs Farmer. 'I don't see what's wrong with Mrs Farmer. Why . . .'

I began but Cook did not let me finish. 'For why,' she exclaimed, and drew hard, dry, wrinkled fingers across her mouth, in a gesture of impatience, 'for why? Because the woman tells lies. That's why.'

Mr Treet, the parson, was now more often a visitor than before. But although he had introduced George Oldacre to Grandma, he and George did not get on well. I did not discover the cause of their disagreements. It may have been George's theological opinions, it may have been Mr Treet's brash manner, or it may simply have been a clash of temperaments. Perhaps, more simply, George felt under a disagreeable sense of obligation. Whatever it was, George was not at his best with Mr Treet.

One morning, before lunch, Mr Oldacre and I were sitting in the drawing-room waiting for the gong. I was dangling my legs over the arm of a chair, lying back on it, looking up at the skylight, hidden by the tattered yellow silk curtains. I could just see a jackdaw hopping about on one of the tall chimneys. The door opened with a click and Mr Treet entered.

'Hello, you old sybarite,' he said addressing George and not seeing me, 'how are you getting on with your Giorgio stuff?'

He came forward, neat as ever, a bright smile on his pink face. He gurgled with pleasure as he spoke. Then he noticed me and said: 'Hello old fellow, I didn't see you. You don't know what a sybarite is, do you?' He spoke with a relish, partly as if he enjoyed talking and partly as if he had taken lessons in elocution.

I shook my head.

'A sybarite,' said Mr Treet with a little guffaw as he looked slyly at George, 'is a man who loves his comfort too much.' He turned back to me. 'It means having pies and cakes and wonderful home-made jam crammed into him by that old witch – what's her name? George,' he went on, smiling and showing his little white teeth, 'you're getting fat on it.'

George Oldacre stiffened. 'How,' he asked, slowly lifting the stem of his pipe from his mouth and raising his eyebrows, 'is the ecclesiastical front with all its chatter and excitement?'

'There,' Mr Treet said, his face falling, and becoming serious, 'you have me, old boy. The fact is there's been a bit of a blunder and I was coming to tell Mrs Porteous.'

'Oh?' George enquired without interest and replaced the pipe in his mouth. He watched the smoke rise into the high ceiling.

Mr Treet lowered his voice. 'The truth is,' he said, as if someone might overhear him, 'and I've just heard it, Mark Brailes has been turned down for archdeacon. Old Canon Barker has got it after all.'

'Why do you think that was?' George asked, frowning a little.

'Well,' Mr Treet pondered the matter, 'Mark's all right but I don't think his wife does. She's apt to make awkward remarks and somehow she upsets the clergy's wives.'

Grandma entered and what had happened was explained to her. She had come straight in from the garden and she slowly pulled the pins from her hat before replying. 'I'm sorry to hear that for Mr Brailes,' she said gently and placed her straw hat on a chair by the door, 'and it may be bad for the church. But

87

for us it's a good thing. We have had so few good clergymen here.'

'But, Mrs Porteous,' Mr Treet said seriously, 'you see it's a blow against all the new forces. Mark Brailes stands for a new re-vitalized attitude. There is now, thanks to him, a way between Rome and disbelief which just wasn't there before. He has managed to join Catholicism with the old Puritanism.'

'Well,' Grandma said comfortably, 'I don't know about that, but I do know he's a great comfort to us here. Perhaps he'll write all the better for being in a small country vicarage. After all, as an archdeacon, would he have had much time for theology?'

'I quite agree,' George said ruminatively, 'and anyway I don't think he was made to be an archdeacon.'

The gong was sounded and we went into lunch. In the dining-room the conversation turned to general topics and I did not listen. When I did Mr Treet was saying: 'The man's a saint. When I told him about it and saw his reaction I said: "Your vocation is not to be an archdeacon but a saint, Mark." ' Mr Treet ate his food with relish and looked across the table at George with a sort of amused defiance. 'Yes,' he continued, 'although you may not think so, George, he is a saint. It must have been a blow for him but all he replies: "Just as I thought. I knew it would never be. It was not God's will and that's the end of it." I said: "Canon Barker is an old man, you're young and your chance will be greater next time." He shrugged his shoulders. "My work, given to me by God, is in this parish." '

George was eating his food with a rabbit-like motion of his jaws. 'And do you think he *is* a successful parish clergyman?' he asked.

Mr Treet opened his mouth to speak and then said nothing. He waited till the parlour-maid had left the room. 'Who am I to question what God intends for another human being?' he asked in a voice that was almost apologetic and did not ring true.

George smiled broadly and looked into Mr Treet's face. He

seemed to be enjoying the spectacle of the clergyman's silver grey hair, his long pink nose, the thin pink lips which revealed the little white teeth, the clean white clerical collar, the very black worsted coat. 'In fact,' George said, 'you've heard, as I have, that he's too clever by far to be a success as a parish clergyman?'

'Do they really say that?' Grandma asked in dismay. 'You can never please everybody in a village. I suppose he's not so good at the social side, but then what is the bishop to do with an intellectual clergyman?'

'He could teach,' George said, nibbling at a water biscuit.

'But he feels,' Mr Treet said, breaking silence, 'that it is God's will for him to be here.'

'And I suppose he may be mistaken?' George asked ironically.

'If,' Grandma said, 'he feels it's God's will then he must do it, cost what it will.'

'But that means,' George said, 'you may do the most idiotic things under a mistaken impression. Also, you may torture yourself all your life in order to do something you should never have attempted.' He paused, holding the water biscuit in the air. 'It's like that awful story of the husband and wife. The husband ate the fat because he thought his wife disliked it. The wife ate the lean because she thought her husband hated it. It was only in their old age they found out they had both been making unnecessary sacrifices.'

'Ah well,' Mr Treet laughed, 'it was probably very good for them.'

'I entirely disagree. It was very bad for them and most likely made them bad tempered. It was also,' George added, 'extremely stupid.'

'It's always defeated me,' Mr Treet said brightly, cocking his head on one side and giving George an impudent look, 'how you ever came out of a country rectory.'

'I had enough of this stupid self-sacrifice at home to last me a life-time,' George replied.

89

Grandma looked wistfully at the two men and then a little anxiously at me. She pulled back her chair. The meal was over.

CHAPTER EIGHT

I made slow progress with my lessons. My handwriting was large and awkward, my reading desultory. I could see no point in these difficult activities. Grandma read me fairy tales before bed or told me what she called 'accident stories'. These accident stories were far better than what books could provide for the simple reason that they were what had really happened to Grandma or her friends. They were authentic in a way that the stories I was told to read were not. Grandma also took a delight in reading out tragedies from the newspapers – which, of course, made it unnecessary for me to do so. 'Alas!' she would exclaim at the picture of a derailed engine or a sinking ship. She would then read out the story. And at the end I would say avidly: 'Did they die?' She would put back her spectacles on her nose and return to the paper. 'Ah, yes, it says "fatally" injured. That means they died, Davey.'

Mrs Cork, who came up most mornings from the village to teach me, was a short, fat, quiet old lady, as lazy as she was kind. A large part of lesson time was taken up in sharpening pencils and laying out sheets of paper. I spent twenty minutes every lesson copying words on to these sheets. I would read a little to her and I soon noticed that her attention wandered from the dull book out at the trees beyond the window. I did a very little simple arithmetic and for geography learnt by heart the counties and their county towns. I also memorized insipid and largely unintelligible poems about Jack Frost and the like.

It was not long before I discovered a way of doing nothing at all. I would casually mention her son. She would look at me gravely and say: 'I'll tell you about his doings another time, Davey.' And then looking at her little silver wristwatch which he had given her, she would place the books and papers in a neat pile and say: 'Well, as there isn't much time now ... I think, perhaps...' Cyril Cork was purser in a ship which sailed to and fro from the Far East. I never met Cyril and he never came to life for me. His adventures, such as they were, were very dull or, at any rate, Mrs Cork made them seem so. But, then, Mrs Cork did not have an heroic or romantic outlook on life. I was bored with her son but I was more bored with her lessons.

One morning, at breakfast, Grandma slit open an envelope with her silver book marker. As she read the letter a vexed and puzzled expression came over her face.

'What is it, Grandma?' I asked.

'Oh,' she said, pinching the bridge of her nose as if to dispel the irritation, 'it's rather a worrying letter from St George's' – this was the prep school I was going to when I was well enough in Grandma's eyes – 'and Mr Gordon, the headmaster, says you must be able to read and write well and have started Latin.' She gave me a look of concern and perplexity.

'*Latin?*' I echoed.

Grandma shook her head. 'Mrs Cork doesn't know any Latin and Mr Oldacre must have forgotten it.' She paused. 'The only person I can think of is Mr Brailes and he's far too busy. But he might know of somebody....'

'Mrs Brailes,' I suggested.

Grandma shook her head. 'Not now....'

That morning, as fate would have it, Mrs Cork was in a particularly lazy mood. Cyril Cork was in Hong Kong. She told me that he was staying in a Y.M.C.A. hostel.

During her recital I noticed the door slowly open and Grandma appeared. She looked grim and annoyed.

'Davey,' she said, looking at Mrs Cork but addressing me, 'I wish to speak to Mrs Cork, will you please leave the room?'

I did not linger but I did not quite close the schoolroom door.

'Mrs Cork,' I heard Grandma say icily, 'I do not think Davey will profit by what you have been telling him about your son.'

Mrs Cork coughed apologetically. Then, after a pause she said: 'Davey is very inattentive, you must understand, Mrs Porteous. It's difficult to get him to concentrate. I tell him about my son to interest him in geography.'

There was a silence as if awaiting a reply from Grandma which did not come. 'So,' Mrs Cork continued, emboldened by her cleverness, 'we follow, Davey and I, Cyril's passage round the world and learn our geography that way.'

'I see,' I heard Grandma say more coldly than ever.

And then with a little click the door was tightly closed and I heard no more.

That Friday I said good-bye to Mrs Cork for ever. We parted without emotion or regrets on either side.

The following Sunday, before lunch, I found a man I had never seen before, standing in front of the fireplace talking to Grandma. As I entered, Grandma was saying: 'You see, Mr Range, he has now got to an age when he needs a man to influence him. . . .'

The young man had a slim figure, a thin, rather red face and fine curling black hair. He had about him an air of Romanticism which was not, somehow, dispelled by the crookedness of his nose.

'Ah,' he said, looking me up and down as I entered the room, 'so this is Davey. We were just talking about you. I hear you've got to learn some Latin.'

I nodded my head and shook him by the hand. His dark, brown eyes, which seemed to smoulder with a sort of poetry, searched my face. His grip was firm, masculine.

'But,' he said in a well modulated voice, like an actor's, 'it won't all be Latin by any means. You may find my methods a little unusual,' – he was now speaking to Gandma – 'I believe so much in poetry and drama.' He pronounced the word drama as if it was a talisman. 'We shall start with a few short poems,' he said, returning to me, 'with a few short poems of your grandfather's. I shall teach Davey, Mrs Porteous, to read them with expression, so that he really begins to understand them.'

He looked down at me from his position in front of the chimney piece and jingled coins and a key in his pocket. He was smartly dressed with rather tight, well-creased trousers, a well-fitting jacket, and a coloured waistcoat. He placed his hand on my shoulder in a protective, but at the same time a possessive, way. Already I liked and admired him.

'As you know, Mrs Porteous, I am a schoolmaster....' He looked down at me with professional interest, assessing my worth. 'So I know boys, what is to be made of them, and what is not.' He jangled his hands in his pockets again. 'Do you mind if I smoke?'

'By all means,' Grandma said, hurrying forward with an ash tray, a little overwhelmed by Mr Range. 'I like to see a man smoke.'

He fetched a gold cigarette case from his pocket, selected a cigarette, gently tapped the tip on the case, still looking at me with a critical eye.

I had taken my lessons with Mrs Cork in the smallest studio, a dark room behind the drawing-room, which was called for courtesy's sake, the 'schoolroom'. Mr Range and I were now promoted to the great studio which had been Giorgio's study. It seemed only right that Mr Range, with his Oxford degree, his signet ring, his gold watch and chain, should have the best room in the house. It was two stories high with great windows to the south over the lawn. A long refectory table ran the length of it and we sat at the southern end in the sunlight. Giorgio's desk was not, of course, disturbed.

Lessons with Mr Range were very different to those I had known. He put enormous energy into them. He made it seem an adventure to learn anything. Admittedly he was not impressed by my knowledge or intelligence, in fact seemed rather cast down after the first lesson. But he made these difficulties into a challenge, both for himself and for me. Everything was now bright and dynamic. I began to improve.

When I had become, one day, a little depressed by my lack of knowledge, I told him I knew all the counties and the county towns. He looked down at me with an air of indifference. 'Oh yes, why?'

'Why?' I stammered. 'Because Mrs Cork taught me them.'

He did not reply. I was under a very different sort of tuition now.

There was poetry to be declaimed at length, and parts learnt by heart in the evenings. For geography he described regions of England he had visited. I had vivid impressions of the Yorkshire dales, the Cotswolds, the Chilterns, and, of course, Oxford. Oxford appeared to be a dream city. He told me of night climbers, debates in the union, sconces, hockey matches, and dinners with his tutor. It was the place that really mattered to him.

He was a religious man and I would see his dark, well-cut features in a surplice as he sang in the choir on Sundays. Mr Courtenay told me as a strange fact that he visited the church every morning on his way up to the house from his cottage in the village. He read Old Testament stories to me, the calling of Samuel, David and Saul, above all the story of David and Jonathan. David became a hero to me, so associated with Mr Range that I could not think of the one without the other. His religion was poetic, romantic, dramatic.

Latin was the lesson I disliked most. Mr Range was a fair classical scholar. Teaching the rudiments of grammar to a dull, unwilling boy was irksome. When I made stupid mistakes which I frequently did, his face would twitch with irritation. He was not a patient man and I feared these spasms of anger. It was fine weather when he commenced teaching me and he took it into his head to go for walks during the Latin lessons to alleviate the tedium. We would stroll down to the swing in

94

the middle of the wood. He would carry on a plate the two pieces of cake Cook had provided for eleven o'clock. Then I would sit on the swing and recite the declensions I was learning. As I swung to and fro under the bough of the great oak, surrounded on all sides by the quivering life of the wood, I learnt what he told me, slowly, painfully, uncomprehendingly.

'Mensa, mensa, mensam,' I swung backwards and forwards in the sunlight and shadow. 'Mensae, mensae, mensa.'

If I was successful he gave me my piece of cake immediately, and we sat on the leaf strewn ground through which fine shoots of grass pierced upwards. We sat together in the encircling green like two friends. He told me about the preparatory school he had taught in.

'It's a hard life, Davey,' he said, 'you have to be tough and manly. You must do what you are told. Discipline is the thing. Most of the boys were going into the Navy. When they pass out at fourteen they go to Dartmouth and then take up difficult posts of command in ships. Discipline at the school is hard. If a boy disobeys an order or makes a foolish mistake at drill. . . .' He mused, studying the end of his cigarette.

'Drill?'

'That's the most important thing in the school. The boys get up to the sound of a bugle. Then comes a cold shower. Then breakfast, then the parade. And woe betide any boy who is slovenly or whose hands are dirty.'

I looked shyly at my grimy hands. Mr Range smoked in silence and then continued: 'That, Davey, would mean a beating.'

'And who,' I asked, 'did the beatings?'

'Sometimes the headmaster who had been a naval captain, sometimes myself.'

'Did you beat hard, sir?'

'That depended on the boy.'

'You mean whether he was weak or strong?'

'Partly that,' Mr Range said casually, blowing some smoke

up into the shady air. 'Partly whether it was deserved or not.'

'So you had a cane?' But the words 'deserved *or not*' rang through my head.

'Yes, indeed. I've got it at the cottage now.' He gave me a little mocking look and raised his eyebrows. 'Would you like me to bring it along?'

'I would like to see it.'

'Mind you, if I did, I might be tempted to use it during Latin lessons.' And he gave me a long uncomfortable look.

I felt confused, did not know what to reply and giggled instead.

'The will and discipline of the master is the first thing in teaching,' he said meditatively, 'but it should always be enforced by the cane. It's a short and sharp correction, and leaves no ill feelings. Boys respond to it.'

'And where, sir, did you beat the boys?' I asked innocently.

'It was on the bare buttocks at St James's.'

'Then they took down their shorts?' I asked, blushing.

He threw his half-smoked cigarette into the bushes and got to his feet.

'They took down their shorts, as you say,' he answered grimly.

Next day he showed me the cane, a short, knotted piece of wood with a handle.

'Does it hurt a lot?' I enquired.

'It can tickle a bit,' he said with a little laugh as he opened the dreaded Latin Grammar.

That morning I was particularly bad at my work.

Mr Range tapped irritably on the table with an unsharpened pencil. This distracted me and my answers became more erratic than ever.

'Now, look here, Davey, you're not trying. You knew all these cases yesterday. Why is it you can't get them today?' His voice was strained with suppressed anger. He got up and went over to the fireplace, standing in front of it, cane in hand. As I gave my answers he looked at the floor and swished the cane against his trousers. 'The truth is you're not making any progress at all.' He swished the cane again. 'I don't like to have to do it but you'll have to stay in this evening and go through it all again.'

I looked up and saw that his swarthy face was twitching with impatience. He was still looking at the floor. I glanced out of the window and saw the pale blue, radiant sky, the dark blue firs gently swaying in the summer breeze. A little cloud coquettishly passed across my vision and disappeared. I had planned to take my bicycle on to the down behind the house.

'Well?' he asked, and I saw he was watching me.

'It will take a long time,' I muttered.

'Yes,' he answered grimly, 'it will.' His manner altered and he looked into my face. 'You can choose. Either you have three up with the cane or you stay in this evening.' He paused and raised an eyebrow quizzically at me. 'It's up to you.' He stood there in front of the fireplace, swishing his cane, his deep, brown eyes smouldering like coals about to leap into flame. He passed his long fingers again and again through his black, curling hair and then brushed from his coloured waistcoat any hairs that might have fallen. There was something aggressive in the tight, well-creased trousers, the nonchalantly fitting sports jacket, the gold signet ring on his little finger.

The palms of my hands sweated. I shifted uneasily in my chair. My face was damp. My mouth was dry and I did not know what to reply. A dread of the unknown, not a fear of pain, gripped me.

'Well?' he demanded. 'Make up your mind.' He struck the palm of his left hand with the end of the cane. It made a hollow thud.

I knew what was expected of me. If I shied away from this thing I should never be a man – never. It was like jumping into an ice-cold river at the dead of night. I said: 'Yes, please, the cane, sir.'

'Well,' he replied, bending the cane into a half circle, 'if that's what you want, so be it.' He smiled a little, thin smile. 'But remember it's your choice.'

I nodded and got up awkwardly.

'We'll go into the lavatory,' he said as if he was talking of an indifferent subject.

At the end of the studio was a minstrel's gallery. Under it was a door which led into a dark corridor off which was a tiny cloakroom. He led the way till we got to the dark corridor. Then he pushed me in front of him and opened the lavatory door as if I might escape him. He held me by the sleeve and I noticed his hand was trembling.

When we were inside he bolted the door. It was a dismal place, for its window looked out on to the evergreens near the shelter. It was furnished with a small basin and an old-fashioned mahogany box lavatory.

'Close the lid,' he commanded in a low voice as if the lavatory pan offended him. I obeyed. 'Now,' he went on in an urgent whisper, 'take your trousers down.'

I undid my belt. The shorts and pants fell to my ankles.

'Bend over the lid.'

I did so and felt the rush of wind as he raised the cane. There was a pause as he lifted the tail of my shirt. He stood back and poised the cane again. I could hear the whistle of birds outside in the wood. Some starlings were quarrelling in the jasmine at the side of the window. A crate, or something heavy, was dropped from a cart in the lane with a hollow crash.

Then it came. One. Two. Three. The sting took me by surprise. I let out a little sigh of pain. And then Mr Range was pulling me towards him. I felt the rough material of his trousers against my bare legs.

'Wasn't too bad, was it, old chap?' he asked in a hoarse whisper as if we might be overheard.

I shook my head. I was frightened that if I spoke I might burst into tears. The tingling began to ache.

'Shouldn't tell your Granny or your nurse if I were you. They wouldn't understand.' He was pressing me close to him and pulling up my shorts with the tenderness of a woman. 'No hard feelings, old fellow, eh? You took it like a man. That's the way. Now let's get back to some work.'

I looked up into his face and saw there were beads of sweat on his forehead.

When we got back to the studio he put away the Latin grammar. 'It's geography now,' he said, drawing up his chair close to mine. And then he told me about an expedition he had made to Burford when he was an undergraduate. It had been a dream morning with winter at the brink of spring. The keen bright sun had played on the grey stone walls. There were lambs on the early grass....

There was a bond between us – or was it that we were sharers of the same secret?

CHAPTER NINE

Mr Range, who was a newcomer to the district, soon became popular. He was energetic and sociable. He reorganised the choir, started rehearsals for a pageant, and became scout master. He was asked everywhere and soon was a force in the village.

One evening, that lovely summer, Grandma told me to go to bed early. She would not be able to tell me a story as she had some friends coming to dinner. This was an unusual event as she lived very quietly. Mr Range, Mr Oldacre and Mr Treet were expected and there was to be a discussion about Giorgio's papers.

I duly went to bed earlier than usual and Nanna took Grandma's place as the storyteller. It was an exceptionally warm night. Darkness came with imperceptible slowness. When I was left alone in the night-nursery, I tossed in my bed listening to every sound. I thought of the duckling, white wine, and the raspberries and cream which I had been allowed to taste for my supper. The clocks in the hall chimed, water was drawn with a faint hiss from the tank in the attic.

The night-nursery overlooked the front door. I tiptoed to a chair by the dormer window and looked out. Mr Treet arrived first in new, very black clothes and an even whiter dog collar than usual. He waited at the door swinging his arms and looking about him like a mouse that smells a piece of cheese. His silver hair, and in one so young for it too, commanded respect. But his alert expression, his pink cheeks, his inquisitive nose were brash and vulgar. He went in with a smile on his face to the parlour-maid that was condescending and conciliatory.

The two other men came round the path from the wood on to the drive talking.

'The trouble I find with teaching,' Mr Oldacre was saying, 'is quite simply I've got very little patience. I last so long and then my energy fades away. I get bored.'

'Impatience with imperfection', Mr Range replied, 'is right and proper.'

'I get bored so easily,' George Oldacre said with a sigh, as they reached the front door. They were dressed in dinner jackets. Mr Range wore his clothes well with a subtle air of indifference that they suited him. The black and white set off his dark, handsome face. His long fingers plucked at the silk handkerchief in his pocket. George Oldacre's dinner jacket was tight and shiny. It bulged in unexpected creases in unexpected places. He tapped his pipe on the jamb of the door.

'And what,' he asked, 'do you think of this scheme about Giorgio's papers?'

'I know very little about it,' Mr Range responded in an off-hand way.

'But from what I've told you?'

'To have the house as a museum of later nineteenth century studies?'

'That's Treet's idea.'

Mr Range considered. 'I'm not sure at all. What demand will there be? The good hasn't yet been sorted from the bad. We're too near it. Personally I prefer the early twentieth century – but am I right? Time hasn't made its judgement. I'm only a schoolmaster. Besides....'

'Besides,' George said slowly, 'there's the boy.'

Mr Range examined his nails. 'I suppose he'll have to make his own way once his education is provided.'

'Some are better at that than others,' George Oldacre said dryly.

'He's all right. He'll get on. He's appreciative....'

George Oldacre gave a bitter little laugh. 'Appreciative! What good will that do him? Look at this place.' He swung his arm round at the house and the melancholy firs. 'A boy brought up in a place like this – what will he make of life? What will life make of him? Mincemeat. He won't begin to understand what earning one's living means. If he's no money....' He shrugged his shoulders and blew down the stem of his pipe. 'It's dispossessing the grandson for the memory of the husband.'

'For poetry,' Mr Range corrected him thoughtfully.

'Life versus literature. I'm all for life.' He paused and then added heavily: 'Literature has got the upper hand here. That was the trouble with Giorgio. All this will simply perpetuate a mistake.'

'You think so? You may be right. But some things *are* more important than life. Religion, for instance. And art, too, which is a sort of religion.'

George Oldacre gave his little cough which was always accompanied by a smile. 'Great art is one thing and very rare incidentally. Another sort of art is a substitute for life....' He opened the door and the two men entered the house.

I stood for a few more minutes at the window and looked

at the fading woodland. It seemed in that light as if it had a life of its own, disconnected with any other, in which it was absorbed. It reflected on its cares like an introspective woman, sad and nostalgic. Its cares were not mine and I crept back to my bed.

It was very quiet. Melancholy hung on the air, as if it was part of it. There was from time to time the clatter of a dish, the jingle of a dropped fork, the chime of the grandfather clocks. Outside silence like a blanket. When the first course was finished, there was a renewed clatter as the washing up began. The usual gusts of laughter from the kitchen followed.

I was wakened by footsteps outside and the sound of voices. I tiptoed to the chair by the window. It was Mr Range and George Oldacre pacing round the house after dinner.

'If you want to know,' Mr Range was saying with more animation than usual, 'anything else is simply hedonism.'

'And what,' George Oldacre asked, 'is wrong with that?'

'Simply this. It explains nothing. It does not explain why man is moral as well as pleasure loving. It does not,' and he gestured to the wood now shrouded in dusk, 'throw any light on Nature which is controlled by laws other than pleasure.'

'You mean,' George asked with an air of deep interest, 'Nature is cruel?'

'I mean that Nature is without morals. Nature does not exist, nor do we, for our own happiness. We exist to express what I can only describe as the divinity which lies at the root of things.' He paused and then continued: 'And, perhaps, you are right. There is a streak of cruelty, as we see it, woven into the stuff of life.'

'Well, then what of your discipline, your morality, your laws?'

The two men were standing near the front door. They were growing more and more indistinct in the dusk. I could see the tips of their cigars glowing as they drew at them.

'All that,' Mr Range responded with wilful detachment in his voice, 'belongs to man as an intelligent being. He does not merely express beauty and strength but also goodness. A man is not truly human unless he is moral. God expresses himself in man through the moral law. That is why man is the crown of creation.'

'And where,' George Oldacre asked with a hint of amusement in his voice, 'does your discipline you are so fond of, come in?'

Mr Range reflected for a moment or two before replying. 'Discipline,' he said at last, and then faltered. 'Morality,' he began again, 'cannot exist without discipline. Discipline cannot exist without courage.'

George drew at his cigar. 'Ah well,' he responded after a pause, 'we see things very differently. Your view is bleak, rather terrible. To me life is a predicament. The art of living is to shrug one's shoulders and make the best of it. I think you make too much of discipline and morality. Nature makes fools of us all. The best one can hope for is to hang on with the minimum pain. And then there are the great pleasures of life – women, laughter, art.'

Mr Range scraped his shoes on the stones of the drive. 'If there is good there's also evil. And,' he went on slowly, 'the great evil for man is pleasure.' He paused. 'Besides,' he continued, 'pleasures collide. In one's own life one has to choose between one pleasure and another. And what is that if it's not morality?'

'That's precisely what it is,' George replied, 'exactly that – and nothing more. Where you go wrong is to make it absolute, divine and unchangeable. That way, if I may say so, leads to the breaking up of one's own life. If defied, Nature takes its revenge.'

A lamp stood in the pantry window near where they were standing. A bat fluttered in an unsteady, erratic motion to the pale yellow light.

'See that?' George enquired. 'Aspiration, or pleasure?' He threw away the gleaming end of his cigar and they walked on round the house in silence.

Next morning, after breakfast, I stood with Grandma at the dining-room window and looked out on the sunlit lawn. The air, which came into the room from an open casement, was fresh with that dew-laden purity which portended a long, hot summer's day. Already there were the buzz and thump of flies at the window. Bees hummed among the flowers in the bed outside. A wood pigeon glided gracefully from the wood down to the bird bath. The sunlight shone on its irridescent feathers.

'Grandma,' I said, catching her old hand in mine, and recalling her from a reverie, 'when I'm grown up I should like to earn my own living. Like Giorgio did,' I added.

'Yes,' she said absently, her sad eyes withdrawing from the green of the wood and resting on me, 'he started with nothing, nothing at all. He was a poor boy.'

'I'd like to start like he did. He made all the money to buy this house?'

'Yes, that's right. Except the little I gave him when we married. But why do you ask?'

'I just wanted to know that it was his house.'

She gave me a puzzled look and I ran into the garden. I looked over my shoulder as I went through the hall. Her noble, sorrowful profile was outlined against the light of the window. I could see she was no longer thinking of me. She was thinking of Giorgio, of the irrevocable past, of summers long ago with Giorgio, days that had faded, as this one would fade, like a poor photograph. The present hour, which meant so much to me, was to her but a means of recollection. She stood there for a moment as I passed, seeming to snuff the air with her sensitive nostrils, resigned, almost tragic, yet at the same time resolute.

I met Cook on the drive. She had a wooden yoke on her shoulders from which hung two buckets filled with scraps and corn for the chickens.

'It was such a lovely morning,' she said as I ran up, 'I thought I'd feed early. Will you collect the eggs?'

The chickens ran eagerly towards us as we entered the orchard, pushing their way through the tall grass. They stalked on the tips of their claws and peered at the buckets.

'I'll have hundreds of chickens when I'm grown up,' I said as I undid the padlock of the next box.

''Undreds will you?' she asked as she threw the scraps on to the ground. 'Then you'll 'ave to 'ave a bigger orchard. And 'ow will you do that?'

I laid the big brown warm eggs one by one in the pail. 'It won't be here, probably,' I replied in an important tone.

'And where will it be, then?'

'I don't know.'

'I thought you loved it 'ere?'

'I do, but when I'm grown up this will be a museum or something.'

Cook opened her eyes very wide, looked scandalized at the idea, and watched me intently. 'Oh,' was all she said. And then added: 'Is that so?'

'I think it is,' I said gravely. 'It will be a museum for Grandfather's papers. Nobody has told me, but I think I'm right.'

'I quite thought as 'ow...' Cook began and then thought better of it. I realised she knew as much as I did.

'It will belong to the nation,' I said in a superior voice to impress upon her the significance of poetry and how much could rightfully be sacrificed to it.

'All this learning's a lot of rubbish,' she muttered under her breath. She began scattering the corn with an irritable gesture. ''Ere you 'ave a go.'

I took the bucket but before I could start there was a peal from the bell at the house.

'That'll be Mr Range. You'd better be goin'.' And off I went.

Lessons passed uneventfully. But I watched Mr Range with renewed interest. His conversation of the night before had impressed me. I did not, of course, understand all he had said but I had understood something. I knew his view of life was heroic, romantic, fatalistic. His swarthy complexion, his hard mouth, the smouldering brown eyes, the elegant clothes were the embodiment of an aristocracy of the spirit. As he sat on his chair in front of the empty hearth in the great studio running his long fingers through his black curly hair, one leg crossed over the other, his expression as of one brooding on a great wrong and yet never faltering in his attention to the lesson in hand, he seemed tragic, even great. At least he appeared so to me. As I gathered up the books at the end of the afternoon lesson he suggested I go to his cottage for tea. I told Grandma and we set out together.

On the way we passed the village church and he took me inside. The interior was dim, shadowy, staid with age. Not a ray of sunlight was to be seen. The clang of the heavy door shut out the world. The rough tick-tock of the steeple clock was the only sound and drowned the soundless voices in the shadows. Time seemed to have stopped. Or was it that this was the only time?

Mr Range knew a lot about church architecture and was something of an expert on St Nicholas's. He showed me that what I had always thought was a patch of damp was, in fact, a wall painting of St Sebastian, his body pierced by a dozen arrows.

'But why,' I asked, 'was there a picture of such a horrid thing?'

He hesitated a moment, and then running his long fingers through his curly hair he said: 'Because St Sebastian was like Our Lord, He suffered for his faith. That's what Christianity means. We must all suffer like him.' His face was creased into an expression of what seemed like a mixture of cruelty, pain and exaltation. 'You see, Davey,' he continued, 'the altar is not just a table where we eat and drink bread and wine. Nor is it only a place where we eat mystical flesh. It is much more. It's a place where a real sacrifice takes place. You remember the sacrifice of Isaac? Well, this is where that sacrifice goes on to this day.'

He gave me a searching glance, for my attention had been diverted by the strange quiet of the place. Mr Range made me uneasy, a little afraid, and I wanted once more to be in the open air. His terrible words came with a force that seemed to be of nature, not of man, pumped, as it were, from the depth of his being. He talked to me as he might have done to a doubting shadow.

'The cross,' he went on, intense, compulsive, 'means sacrifice. Sacrifice means pain because the sacrifice is ourselves. It is a propitiation to God for our sins.' His eyes smouldered. A fire burned behind them.

He then took me to the leper window which was inside the chancel. 'You see, Davey,' he explained, 'this was where the poor leper, the outcast, stood to see the Mass. He could not be with the congregation so he stood in this little room by himself. He would realise that the sacrifice of leprosy God had called on him to make, was one and the same sacrifice as the priest was re-enacting at the altar. Do you understand?'

How it was I do not know, but I did. I could not express what I felt and said instead: 'Why didn't you become a clergyman?'

Mr Range gave me a strange twisted smile. 'For the same reason that the leper did not become a priest. I was not good enough.'

We were standing in the enclosed space very near together. I looked up into his unhappy face and said: 'I'm not tall enough to look through the window.'

He lifted me up. A swift, momentary pleasure ran through my body as he held me. He bent down with his cheek to mine. It was rough and bristly.

'There now,' he asked, 'now you can see, can't you?' He shifted me in his arms. His long fingers grasped me. I half expected to see the priest at the altar. But there was nothing – just the altar cloth, the brass cross, some dying flowers, all redolent of the commonplace Sunday services. A bluebottle was bumping against the stained glass window. As he lifted

me down his fingers brushed my thighs. It was only for a
moment.

And then we were outside again. The village dozed in the
sunlight but behind every curtain there seemed to be a watch-
ful eye. There was the sound of a trowel cutting bricks, the
whine of a dog.

The cottage was small and thatched. It stood down a side
lane by itself, half-timbered, untidy, picturesque. Mr Range
opened the front door and I stood in the living-room. A crude
beam traversed the low uneven ceiling. At one end there was
a wide hearth half filled with paper, cigarette ends and pieces
of wood. It smelt of tobacco smoke, damp and cooking. The
remains of a meal lay on a deal table in the centre of the
stone flagged floor.

'Don't you have anyone to do the washing up?' I asked in
surprise.

Mr Range coughed. 'I prefer,' he said coldly, 'to do as much
of my own work as I can. You see,' he continued, piling up
the crockery, 'I don't care for women about the house. They
disturb everything.'

'Not even for the cleaning?' I looked round. The room was
shabby but it was not dirty.

'An old woman does come in for that. But I prefer to do the
washing up and make my bed.' He placed the crockery on a
tray and went into the kitchen. 'Make yourself at home and
have a look at the pictures,' he called out.

The room was furnished with rickety Windsor chairs. Two
wicker arm chairs stood in front of the hearth, covered with
faded chintz. There was an old oak bureau under one of
the diamond paned windows. On the walls there were coloured
reproductions and photographs of Greek statues. There was a
small crucifix over the chimney piece. A silver framed photograph of an elderly woman with a predatory expression stood
on a little table by itself.

'That's my mother,' Mr Range explained as he came in
with a cloth and the tea-things. 'Over by the door is St

Sebastian,' and he pointed to the reproduction of an Italian painting. 'Next to him is Richard Coeur de Lion in armour, and then there is my patron saint Dominic.'

I examined them one by one and then the photograph of a Greek piece of sculpture. It was the torso of a nude boy. To me they seemed as shabby as the room. I had not expected that Mr Range would live in this way. I had imagined a different picture as I had watched him lounging, faultlessly dressed, in front of the hearth in the studio. I did not think less of him but I felt that I had not understood him.

The kettle began to sing. A few moments later he entered with the teapot in one hand and a cake tin in the other. He stood with them in his hands and looked at the picture of St Dominic. 'I once wanted to be a monk,' he said reminiscently. 'But now,' he shrugged his shoulders and put the tea things on the table, 'now I see it wouldn't have done and I go on as I am.' He went out again and returned with the cups and saucers.

'I think,' I said deliberately, 'you should have been a clergy-man, a priest, sir.'

He looked up as he was pouring the tea but said nothing. For a while we ate our tea in silence. I stirred my cup noisily and drank the warm sweet liquid.

'And what,' he asked, 'do you want to be when you grow up?'

It was the tedious question they all asked but Mr Range was looking at me carefully. 'I don't know at all,' I replied. 'But I do know,' I added swiftly, 'that I want to make my own money – do it myself.'

'I suppose you think you want to be a soldier like your father?'

I reddened, partly because the tea had heated me, partly because he had read my mind. 'I would like to be a soldier,' I said, 'but . . .'

'But you're really a dreamer,' he finished the sentence for me.

'I'm not,' I answered indignantly, 'and I wasn't going to say that.'

He took a cigarette from his case and tapped it gently on the lid. 'There's nothing wrong in being a dreamer provided you dream the right dreams.' He looked at me thoughtfully. 'You'll be a writer like your grandfather.'

'But I don't have dreams,' I said obstinately.

'You've dreamt up your life,' he answered with a smile I could not interpret. 'Besides,' he went on, lighting the cigarette, 'you have passion and detachment. Ah, but will it, can it, last? Should it last? That is for you and life to decide.'

I had never seen Mr Range, or anyone else, in a mood like this and I did not know what to reply. I drank down my tea in silence and then my eye fell on a cane propped against the bureau. He saw what I was looking at and raised his eyebrows.

'Yes,' he said, 'you see I have another.' And he was again the Mr Range I had known before.

'What do you want it for?'

He smiled sardonically. 'I might want it.'

'But who for?'

'You, for instance. Besides, I am the scoutmaster.'

'I didn't know that scouts got beaten.'

'They do in my troop if they need it.' He blew out a cloud of cigarette smoke. 'By the way,' he asked in an offhand way, 'how are your weals?'

'Weals?'

'The marks made by the cane.'

'Oh, they're all right,' I said carelessly.

'Has anyone seen them?' he asked like a doctor.

'No, no-one at all.'

'Well, then, perhaps I ought to have a look.'

'But,' I prevaricated, 'you told me not to tell anyone.'

'Quite right, but I think you should show me. We don't want anything to go wrong, do we?' He again spoke like a doctor but there was a gleam in his eyes.

'All right,' I said uncertainly, 'but I don't think there's much to be seen.'

'How do you know if you can't see them yourself?' he laughed. He got up from his chair and motioned me to the door by the fireplace. We mounted a dark flight of stairs which led to the bedroom.

It was a tiny attic with a dormer window. He drew the faded chintz curtains. 'We don't want the whole village to see,' he said with a little laugh, 'now bend over the bed and get the trousers down.'

I did what he told me and he lifted the tail of my shirt. His long fingers passed over the places where the weals had been.

But he suddenly straightened up. 'Drat!' he exclaimed, 'there's someone at the door.'

I could now hear, when I lifted my head, a gentle tapping.

'Hurry,' he ordered, 'get yourself dressed. The weals are quite all right. We'll go downstairs.'

In a few moments I was following him downstairs.

A pale-faced, lanky boy with sandy hair was standing on the threshold. 'Mr Range, sir,' he said in a half whine, 'I thought there might be somethink in the garden, somethink or other I could do for yer.'

'No, Reggie,' Mr Range replied firmly, 'there's nothing in the garden.'

'Then ain't there nothink in the 'ouse?'

'No, I don't think so, thank you, Reggie.'

There was a pause. 'I was wonderin',' Reggie said slowly, 'whether you was goin' down to the river to show me them fish.'

'Well....'

'It's an 'ot evenin' like you said..' he broke off, catching sight of me for the first time. 'I didn't see 'im,' he stated bluntly.

'That's all right, Reggie,' Mr Range said stepping aside, 'it's only David Porteous. Perhaps,' he continued for a moment undecided, 'we could all go down to the river.' He turned to me. 'Would you like to go?'

I nodded my head. Meantime Reggie looked me up and down with a menacing expression. 'Cor,' he said contemptuously, 'bet 'e can't swim.'

'I don't know,' Mr Range replied. 'Can you?' he asked, turning to me.

'A bit,' I said.

The three of us made our way through a beechwood down to the river, which was, in fact, not much more than a stream. The wood slept in the heat. A few birds whistled sleepily in the distance. The beechnuts crackled beneath our feet. Reggie trailed behind Mr Range like a dog at heel. From time to time I looked up and saw his wary eyes on my face. He was a boy of about twelve, dressed in long trousers and boots. He slouched rather than walked and seemed proud of the holes and patches in his jacket. I dimly recollected that he was the son of a poor widow at the other end of the village. His eyes were pale blue and his face thin. His complexion was smooth like a baby's or an angel's.

The river meandered through a lush meadow. Woodland rose on either side. The water, therefore, passed across the almost flat basin of a little valley as hidden as a stream in fairyland. Kingcups grew at the water's edge. There was a faint hum of gnats swarming above mirrors of sunlight on the rippling surface. A dragonfly droned by like an ungainly, ancient aeroplane. Cabbage Whites trembled among the flowers and reeds.

Reggie suddenly threw off his clothes and plunged into the water. I was startled by the whiteness, the delicacy, the smoothness of his body. What I had seen before was a bundle of old clothes and a rustic voice. But for a moment he was transformed into a white, flashing thing of beauty outlined against the lush grass and bathed in sunlight.

'What about you, Davey?' Mr Range enquired.

I hesitated. I wanted to say that I had not got my bathing

trunks. Then I thought better of it. 'All right,' I said and began to undress.

I looked round apprehensively. But Mr Range said reassuringly: 'No-one ever comes down here.' He watched me with an amused smile.

I ran quickly to the water and plunged in with a great splash. I had hardly recovered from the shock of the green, cold river and was wiping the water from my eyes when Reggie seized me from behind and ducked me. He had me by the head and shoulders in a grip of iron. I seized his legs with all my strength and nearly overturned him. He let me go and I came to the surface again. I saw his face, hard and cold, as he stood near me.

'Sissy, you!' he whispered hoarsely so that Mr Range should not hear.

Before I had time to reply Mr Range had joined us. He swam to a deeper part of the river and shouted: 'Let's have some races!'

I raced against Reggie but he was much faster and splashed water into my face as he passed me. Then there were handicap races with Mr Range. As I swam ahead upstream I saw him overtake Reggie from the corner of my eye. He passed right over the boy, who lay for a moment or two beneath him. Then it was my turn. Mr Range ducked me as he passed. To prevent me sinking he held me for a while to his cold, shining body. And then he was after Reggie. So it went on till I was tired and sat on the bank. The others followed.

We sat in the sun watching the flowing stream, its surface broken here and there by eddies and ripples like cold, enigmatic smiles. There was a plop upstream and a water rat cautiously swam by on the current and disappeared in the rushes on the far bank. A hidden bird let out a monotonous cry again and again, a single note of despair from the depth of nature.

Mr Range lay in the thick grass on his back. I had never seen a naked man before and glanced furtively at his genitals.

I noticed Reggie's pale eyes on me. Mr Range looked like one of the pictures of Greek statues I had seen in his cottage. His body was olive colour, as if used to air and sunlight. He rolled on to his front and remarked that it was his way of getting dry. Beads of water lay in the arch of his back and the nape of his neck. Reggie followed suit and I noticed that there were weals on his buttocks. I rolled over and lay with my face in a new world of green grasses through which passed tiny insects like travellers through a great forest. A little gust of wind whispered over the stream and ruffled the grasses. The day was waning. It was growing colder.

We dressed in silence and returned to the cottage. A chill of satiety, disappointment, or, perhaps, just disappointment, had damped our spirits. At the door Mr Range glanced at his watch and said it was time for me to get home.

'I won't come with you, Davey,' he said, 'but Reggie will go as far as the wood.'

The boy nodded his head, expressionless. 'I'll get along of 'im,' he answered sullenly.

We said good-bye to Mr Range and set off in silence. We passed through the village. There were more people about now. Reggie nodded greetings to them but did not speak. When we got to the wood he took my arm and said: 'Get in 'ere.'

'Why?' I asked.

'Yer does what I tells you, see.' And he gave me a push which sent me reeling into the ditch at the side of the lane. It was dry but full of nettles which stung my hands and legs. He seized the shoulder of my coat and heaved me out on the other side. He dragged me into the wood till we were out of earshot of the lane. Then he said: 'I wants to ask yer some questions.'

'Oh. . . .'

'Oh,' he mimicked my accent and twisted my arm behind my back. 'Now then, Master Davey, you answers and I gives the questions, see?'

'And if I don't?'

'I'll break yer bloody arm.'

'Well?'

'Tell me the truth.' And he gave my arm a twist so that I jumped forward.

''As 'e tanned yer?'

'Tanned?'

'Yus, tanned yer 'ide. Beaten yer?'

'Yes,' I answered unwillingly.

''As 'e?'

'Yes, I told you so.'

''Ow many times?'

'Once. He gave me three.'

'Three,' he repeated. ''As 'e beat yer with 'is 'and yet?'

'No, with the cane.'

He said something which sounded like: 'Oh, ah.' He paused, still holding my arm behind my back. 'I believes yer,' he said at last letting my arm go slack for a moment.

With a sudden jerk I freed myself. My shoulder came in contact with his face and he reeled back. I ran towards the lane. But he was soon in pursuit and grabbed me again.

''Ere,' he said breathlessly, 'I didn't mean no 'arm. We could be friends corse you told me the truth, didn't yer?'

I nodded. Looking up I noticed his lip was bleeding. 'Did I do that?' I asked.

'Yer did,' he said and shrugged his shoulders.

'I'm sorry,' I said, 'I didn't mean to hurt you.'

He looked down at me for a moment or two and let go of me. 'I likes yer,' he said simply.

'I've got to get home.' And I turned to the lane.

'Jest a mo,' and he paused as if unable to express what he wanted to say. 'Ain't it lovely afterwards when 'e's so kind?' There was a look of reminiscent pleasure in his face.

I nodded, not knowing what to say.

'I'll come along of yer,' he said and we made our way to the lane. 'Yer see,' he added, 'I told 'im as 'ow I would. I does what 'e says. 'E's taught me that in the troop. I'm 'is special one, see?'

We crossed the ditch into the lane and soon the house was visible on top of the little pine-topped hill. 'I ain't goin' no farther,' he said, turned round, and without another word slouched off into the shadows.

I saw Reggie from time to time after that, but never alone. He sometimes came up to the house with notes for Mr Range. Sometimes he was waiting by the front door for the lesson to end. He never showed by any alteration in his expression when we met that we had had that conversation in the wood. He was now no longer hostile. He was simply indifferent.

CHAPTER TEN

From this time Mr Range treated me more as a friend and less as a pupil – a friend to whom, shall we say, he had confided a secret, but to whom he intended to confide no more. It was an easier relationship than before and it flattered my vanity. A disagreeable, even if exciting, tension had been released. There was now more poetry and less grammar. I felt at times that I was almost his confidant, though what he confided would be difficult to say – a mood, a manner, a part of his mind hitherto hidden, rather than anything specific. In any case I was too young to follow his meaning all the time.

One day after describing a Norse saga he walked over to the big south window. He stood on the little dais formed by the bow of the window. Sunlight fell on the back of his head and I noticed for the first time how much auburn there was in the black of his hair.

'You see, Davey,' he said, 'it's the fight that matters. It's not whether you win or lose. The hero fights even when he knows he can't win.' He paused and stroked his chin with his long fingers. His face, half in shade, half in the glare of the sunlight, was now not so romantic as it had always seemed before. It was heavy with a sense of failure and defiance, of what seemed to me to be a sort of tragic fatality. 'When you're older, Davey, you, too, have got to fight against overwhelming odds. When there's nothing we can do about it, we still have to fight on.'

There was a good deal of the actor in the man and he let his hands fall to his side with a dramatic gesture of despair.

When the class was over I opened the studio door for Mr Range to go. Mr and Mrs Thoroughgood were in the hall.

'Of course,' Mrs Thoroughgood was saying in her thin, penetrating voice to Grandma, leaning forward as she crossed the hall, her beads jangling, her hand outstretched and her expression a concentration of disappointment and sincerity, like the conductor of an orchestra attempting to get a reluctant musician to co-operate, '*Of course* we wanted to come to your dinner party. But we were away and only got your letter today.'

Grandma was leading the way to the Red room, a little shyly, as though embarrassed at having provoked an emotion which might overwhelm her. 'Never mind,' she murmured, pulling aside the heavy oak sliding doors which moved with a little rumble. Mr Thoroughgood, who had been watching the scene with a deferential grin on his face, looked from one woman to the other with the absorption of a lip reader.

'Alfred!' Mrs Thoroughgood said suddenly.

Mr Thoroughgood started.

'The doors, Alfred!' He leapt forward to help Grandma with the doors.

'Ah,' Mrs Thoroughgood exclaimed, catching sight of me and turning round, 'it's Davey and Mr Range isn't it?' She was suddenly, charmingly at ease. She smiled and she shook us by the hand and cleared her throat as though to show that the former scene was at an end. 'I have seen you in your surplice in the choir,' she went on to Mr Range almost coquettishly, 'and I wondered, didn't I, Alfred' – she turned for a moment to her husband and Grandma – 'if you were not one of the Shropshire Ranges. I knew them as a girl.'

117

'No, I'm afraid not,' and Mr Range inclined his head.

'These things never work out! What a pity! Never mind. But,' she added graciously, 'I hear such wonderful things about the scouts.'

'And I hear,' Mr Thoroughgood said in his deep, manly voice, coming across the room, 'we are to have a pageant!' He smiled ingratiatingly and shook Mr Range by the hand, raising his own in the air at shoulder height, like a child, owing to his shortness.

'Well, we mustn't keep you, must we!' Mrs Thoroughgood said after a careful examination of Mr Range's features, and seeing that the latter had made a movement towards the lobby, 'I expect, living by yourself, you have no end of things to do.'

Mr Range bowed slightly and, followed by me, made for the door.

When I returned I could hear the Thoroughgoods through the half-closed doors of the Red room discussing Mr Range.

'Such a good looking, mysterious man!' Mrs Thoroughgood was saying. 'We don't know a thing about him. He says so little.... One wonders.'

'He was at the Varsity,' Mr Thoroughgood interjected.

'At some minor college perhaps?' she asked with a little tinkling laugh.

'I believe it was Hertford,' Mr Thoroughgood responded gravely.

'Alfred knows everything,' Mrs Thoroughgood proclaimed, her tone of voice a blend of triumph and malice. 'But *I* know that he was at that naval preparatory school in Sussex, I forget its name, the place where they have whistles and bugles instead of bells.'

'But we do not know,' Mr Thoroughgood said gravely, pessimistically like a man who has lost a coin in a dark room, 'where he was at school himself.' His voice was as if in deliberate contrast to hers. His was bass, deliberate, humourless, hers high, reedy, tinkling with sudden laughter.

I closed the studio door and sat down to my homework. When I came out the Thoroughgoods were still in the Red room but preparing to leave.

'I *am* so thankful,' Mrs Thoroughgood was saying emphatically, 'you consulted us. You know we wouldn't have been left out for anything.'

'No, no, not for anything.' From her husband.

'I remember,' she went on with a little girlish laugh, 'when The Firs was a place of pilgrimage. It will become one again, I'm sure of it. I remember coming to see Giorgio when he was ill. "Miss Isabella," he said – he always called me Miss Isabella – "you think they'll go on remembering me? You think so? I don't. I shall be as forgotten as a pail of water emptied into the ocean!" "But," I said, "you'd like to be remembered?" "Oh yes," he replied, "that is what I've worked for." "You shall be," I said, and took his hands in mine, "you shall! I'm sure of it." He smiled at me and said : "Perhaps you're right." '

'There are always times after a writer's death,' Grandma remarked pensively, 'when his reputation goes right down. Giorgio will be recognised again.'

'When this Eliot is forgotten.' Mr Thoroughgood spoke with unction as though willing the oblivion of the young poet.

There was a rattle and tinkle which was the sign that Mrs Thoroughgood had moved to the doors. 'But remember,' she said archly, 'there is one provision to my "consent". Davey must go to St George's and to Eton.'

'And to the Varsity,' Mr Thoroughgood added.

The word 'consent' in Mrs Thoroughgood's remarks seemed to have been misunderstood by Grandma, which was apparent, I suppose, from a gesture or her expression. Mrs Thoroughgood added quickly : 'I only meant that the boy should have a good education.'

There was a pause, broken by Mr Thoroughgood's voice. 'I see Oldacre from time to time in London.'

'I did not know he was often in London.'

'He did not say he had seen me?' he asked inquisitively.

'Ah,' said Mrs Thoroughgood, 'Alfred often sees him walking down Piccadilly.'

'I suppose,' Mr Thoroughgood said heavily, 'he has to go to the Public Record Office.' And then he pulled aside the rumbling oak doors.

Uncle John also visited us at this time. I met him in the lobby on his arrival. He had placed his bowler hat on a chair and was being helped out of his velvet-collared black overcoat by the parlour-maid. When she had gone he fumbled in his pocket for the usual tip.

'Here, Davey, you'd better have it now as I'm not staying. I'm on my way to London.'

He paused, looked at me hard, and sniffed through his heavily veined nostrils, wrinkling them like a man who has just taken a pinch of snuff. He seemed about to speak and then thought better of it.

I thanked him and was moving away. 'No,' he said, 'I'd like you to come in with me just for a moment.' And he pushed me to the drawing-room door.

When we entered Grandma was standing in front of the fireplace with a tense expression on her face. She was fiddling with the broad wedding ring on her finger. She looked up with a wisp of a smile at Uncle John and then gave a little frown in my direction.

But before she could say anything Uncle John wagged his index finger at her: 'Mary, I don't like what you're doing. I don't think Giorgio would have liked it.'

Grandma gently rubbed the bridge of her nose and I noticed warning red spots of anger on her cheeks.

'Well,' she said stiffly, pecking Uncle John's cheeks, one after the other, as if she could not bring herself to kiss him in her accustomed way, 'when Davey runs along we can discuss it.'

'I realise,' Uncle John replied, ignoring the last part of her remark, 'that the money is yours. . . .'

Grandma tossed her head. 'I don't regard it as my own, nor my family's. I regard it as a trust. . . .'

Uncle John shrugged his shoulders and stood beside her in front of the fireplace. 'People usually regard money left to them by their husbands as their own.' He swayed on his toes and leant forward looking at his well polished shoes.

'This,' Grandma exclaimed with an irritable look at me, 'is not a usual situation.'

There was a pause as Uncle John slowly swayed backwards and forwards. 'No, Mary,' he said emphatically, 'you can't make me approve.' He looked up at me as if to impress his words on my mind. 'Well, Davey, run along while your grandmother and I have a little talk.'

And so I left the room.

CHAPTER ELEVEN

Nanna went for her fortnight's holiday. For me this had been in the past a time of uncertainty and upheaval. But this year there was to be no temporary Nanny. I was thought to have outgrown such a thing. I was therefore placed in the care of Kitty, the under-housemaid. She was a short, slim, strong girl of sixteen. She had a mischievous face, lined like a satyr's. I suppose it would have been ugly in repose but I hardly ever saw it anything but animated, mostly brimful of laughter. Her black hair was thick and curled with the vigour of a southern vine. Her eyes were quick, brown, intelligent, her lips, full and red. She always wore a well-fitting, black frock which set off the slimness of her figure, her large adolescent breasts, her trim legs and feet. She was neat, deft, practical. Her apron was spotlessly white in the afternoons as if she had spent the morning starching it.

The afternoon of Nanna's departure was spent in carrying some of Kitty's things into the night-nursery. She normally shared a room, not very far from mine, with the kitchen maid.

It was a bleak place, partitioned off from the attic, with a window, so high that you could not look out of it even on tip-toe, giving on to the wood. Once you got up to it – and I had to put a chair on a chest of drawers – you seemed to be part of the wood. A great red and blue branch of a fir swung almost into it, indeed brushing it on stormy nights with a feathery hissing sound, so Kitty told me. It contained two iron bed-steads, two deal chests of drawers and a double wash-stand, complete with ewers, basins, slop-pails and chamber-pots.

'I shall like bein' on me own,' Kitty told me, 'Catherine ain't much company.' She looked disparagingly at Catherine's bed. 'She's like a clam. It takes two to make a friendship,' she observed.

She emptied the contents of a drawer on to the bed and I carried the garments to the night-nursery. They were old and patched but they had for me a mysterious attraction I could not understand. I fingered them lingeringly as I put them away – the white, much washed brassiere, the thin knickers, the suspender belt, the black stockings. They were impregnated with the litheness, the agility, the otherness of Kitty's body. They came from a world that lay all around me but which I had never penetrated – a bewitching, frightening fairyland.

'Yer see, Davey,' Kitty said prosaically when I returned, 'I ain't ever 'ad a room of me own.'

'What about at home?' I asked.

She shook her head. 'I shares,' she said laconically, 'with Elsie when she's 'ome.'

'But,' I pointed out, 'you won't be alone with me.'

'No, but we'll 'ave some fun.'

She handed me a painted wooden bowl. I looked inside. 'Do you use powder?' I asked, surprised.

'When I goes out with Clive.'

A feeling of dislike, compounded of Puritanism and jealousy overcame me. 'I think your face is nice as it is.'

Kitty shrugged her shoulders and tossed her black hair. A smile flitted across her primitive, impudent face. 'Ain't yer gallant?' she said.

'I don't like the smell of it.'

'Well, take a sniff at this.' She took a small bottle from the drawer of the rickety looking glass and uncorked it. 'What d'yer think of that?' And she held it under my nose. It was sweet, pervasive, exciting and repellent. I knew it well, mingled as it usually was, with the heavy scent of sweat. It recalled an evening in summer when I had passed the village hall. It recaptured the sulky atmosphere, the sound of a waltz and laughter drifting among the leaves of the old elm trees. It, too, belonged to a world I had not, perhaps could not, penetrate.

'I don't like it,' I said, blushing at my rudeness and the strained emotions the scent evoked.

At last everything Kitty wanted was carried through. The bowl of powder, the scent bottle stood in the place of Nanna's hand cream on the dressing table in the night-nursery. The room took on another air. It was transformed. It, and I, no longer belonged to Nanna but to Kitty.

It was a warm and sultry evening when I went to bed. Birds whistled in a desultory way in the trees, oppressed by the warmth and the melancholy. Kitty tucked me up with her long deft fingers. I had said my prayers at her knee as usual but I was overcome by a sense of loss, of excitement and guilt that I did not miss Nanna more. The accustomed chink of crockery and the rattle of cutlery from the kitchen only made me feel the more uneasy. Kitty had not drawn the curtains and I watched the light slowly ebbing like a retreating tide. I thought of George Oldacre reading in his deep voice to Grandma in the drawing-room by the light of the Aladdin lamp. I thought of Nanna with her mother at the bungalow on the outskirts of the London suburbs, in almost unbelievably alien circumstances. Her life at The Firs was her real life, and I resented it that she could so easily go off and lead another.

These thoughts, passing through my mind like clouds across

a windswept sky, would not allow me to sleep. I went to the window and looked out on the darkening, featureless scene. The moon was rising behind the trees, huge, top-heavy, yellow, but as yet unable to compete with the lingering daylight. I went to the chest of drawers, fiddled with the scent bottle and the powder, looked into the drawers, fumbled, by what impulse I do not know, among the youthful clothes. Outside an owl shrieked in eerie anger as though awakening to a sense of deprivation. At the window again I could see a white shimmering mist below the moon, stealthily moving through the trees towards the house. A cloud, huge, majestic, many-towered, floated, self-absorbed, across the face of the moon. It was as if a great hand had been placed in front of God's splendour, and in a moment, obliterated it. I turned in the darkness to the comfort of my bed.

I awoke with a start. Moonlight, now cold and silver, poured into the room through the uncurtained windows. It was as pale and mysterious as light reflected from an immemoriably old looking-glass. And then I saw Kitty. She had undressed and was standing motionless by the window. She was naked and her clothes lay in a pile beside her. She was so intent she did not notice me stir. She seemed like a statue bathed in moonshine. A strange, sweet smell, the exhalation of earth, carried on the warm mist, pervaded the room.

She stood there a full minute. Then she stretched and yawned. She ran her fingers through her thick, black hair. She bent down to scratch her thigh and, as she did so, her breasts fell to one side, large and voluptuous, one in the bright moonlight, the other hidden in the dark shadow. I watched her with half-closed eyelids, awed and a little frightened.

She turned to my bed, bent over me for a moment, yawned, stretched, sighed and got into her bed. Her freckled face, with its snub nose, its lines of humour, its full lips, lay on the pillow, looking up at the ceiling. It was the first time I had seen her in repose.

I stirred as if I had just woken. She made no response. I thought for a moment she had fallen asleep.

'Kitty!' I whispered, 'what are you doing?'

'Are you awake?' she asked unnecessarily.

'Yes, it's the moonlight.' I sat up.

She raised herself on her elbow. 'I'll draw the curtains,' she whispered. We kept our voices low in the silence of the house, like conspirators.

She flitted across to the window, her body flashing in the moonlight, and then flitted back to her bed in the darkness that followed. 'It's too 'ot for me to wear me night dress. I've only a wool one. Besides, at 'ome we never wear 'em.'

'Don't you?' I whispered back. I could no longer see her.

' 'Ere,' she said suddenly, 'would yer like to move in along of me? It might make you go to sleep.'

I often went into Nanna's bed in the morning. But that night I felt shy and hesitated.

'I've got somethin' for yer if yer come,' she said coaxingly.

'What?'

'Wait and see.'

I scrambled out of bed and went to hers. She pulled back the bedclothes and I wriggled inside beside her.

Her body was warm and a little moist. It smelt of perspiration. It was a sugary, not unpleasant smell.

'Comfy? I 'ope we don't get too 'ot.'

'What have you got under the pillow?' I felt something hard under my head.

'Look and see.'

I fumbled about and drew out a torch. I switched it on and found it had green, red, and white discs of glass which could be slid over the bulb.

'Can I try it down the bed?' I asked, delighted.

But she was fumbling at the other side of the pillow. There was a rustle of paper and she handed me a toffee. We sucked comfortingly, not speaking. 'I uses the torch when

Catherine's asleep for readin' under the bedclothes,' she said at last with a tone of luxury in her voice.

I wriggled under the bedclothes and switched on the green light. I was in a warm green cave insulated from the real world. On one side was the green wall of the sheets, on the other the outline of Kitty's green body. She was lying on her back. Her thighs, the flat plateau of her stomach, one breast with its dark nipple, all green, lay beside me. The smell of her body was strong, and suddenly seemed overpowering. I switched off the light and put my head out of the bedclothes like a diver coming up for air.

'Yer do wriggle,' she said good-naturedly, loudly sucking her toffee.

- 'Kitty,' I said seriously in the darkness, which seemed complete after I had switched off the torch, 'why do grown-ups have hair between their legs?'

Kitty considered the question, as she sucked at her toffee. 'Funny thing, I dunno,' she said at last with a giggle.

'Nanna won't let me eat a toffee in bed,' I remarked.

'Don't tell 'er,' Kitty said easily.

There was a long pause. Then I asked: 'Kitty, do you say your prayers?'

'Sometimes I do and sometimes I don't.'

'Nanna always says hers.'

'She's on 'oliday now so I expect she's forgot.'

I thought this unlikely but did not say so. 'Kitty, do you think it's a good thing to pray?'

'Clive says God's cruel.'

'Clive?'

Kitty stretched herself luxuriously. 'We're walkin' out together. 'E's a labourer on Skindle's farm and 'e's going to be a farmer hisself one day. 'E knows 'ow to work. 'E'll get on. 'E knows all about animals. 'E's clever, yer see.'

'Why does he say God is cruel?' The idea struck me as bizarre.

' 'E's on the sheep and 'e's seen crows pluck out the eyes of dyin' ewes – before they be dead, yer see? 'E can't allus save the little lambs. 'E says,' she confided as if it was a secret, 'we're kinder than what God is.' She paused and then continued: 'We 'ave to be cruel to live but we ain't so cruel as God. Course,' she went on irrelevantly, 'Clive's an orphan so 'e knows what life is.'

I yawned suddenly and unexpectedly. Kitty drew me to her and a moment later I was asleep.

When I awoke she had already dressed, tidied the room and started her work. This happened for several mornings. And then I began to wake up earlier. One morning as I sleepily watched her dress my eye caught sight of a blood-stained napkin on the floor. I looked at it for some time without speaking and then I said: 'Kitty, what's that?'

'I thought you was asleep,' she replied irritably. Then she bent down, picked it up and took it out of the room.

When she returned I was sitting up in bed. 'Are you ill, Kitty?' I asked. 'Do tell me.'

'Only as ill as all women are,' she said sulkily.

I looked puzzled and she explained with rather bad grace.

'Does every girl have it on the same day?' I asked in surprise.

Kitty laughed and became more like herself again. 'Course not, silly.'

'And does it hurt?'

'There's the pains. Yer jest feels miserable. That's nature's way.' She began tucking up her bed. 'Mind don't yer tell nobody I told yer. It's not thought,' she explained with an unexpected piece of bourgeois sentiment, 'nice – to know at yer age and with the way's you've been brought up.' She gave me a hard, long look. 'At yer age yer shouldn't know nothink about it,' she repeated. 'Besides it's 'orrible, ain't it?'

I did not reply and she smiled a little smile of triumph. 'Yes yer do. But, as mother says, it's nature and there's an end on it.'

She left the room to start her work. Water, pumped from

below the hill, gushed and roared through the pipes and fell with a rhythmic splash into the great tank in the attic. I could hear the pop pop of the engine in the pump house the other side of the lane. Starlings quarrelled in the eaves like angry women. Mr Courtenay was clearing up in the boiler house, his boots crunching the fragments of coke as he walked backwards and forwards. At the back door someone was chopping wood for the range. Curtains were being drawn downstairs with little roars as they rustled across their rods. Life, another day, was starting.

CHAPTER TWELVE

There was a patter of rain drops in the leaves, which gradually grew to intensity, slowed down, and settled into a steady downpour. Water dripped from the trees, hissed on the ground and was swallowed by the earth. It tinkled prettily in the rain-water pipes.

Mr Range arrived late that morning. He was wet and out of sorts. He seemed unable to concentrate on the lessons and, for the first time, indifferent to my performance. The rain tapped on the north skylights of the studio like an impatient finger. Mr Range kept drawing his hand across his forehead. Grandma, too, was out of sorts, vexed by the loss of a paper she wanted. We could hear her in the room above and behind the studio's minstrel's gallery, muttering to herself as if in a dream.

'Aren't you well, sir?' I asked Mr Range at last.

He looked at me in surprise. Then, collecting himself, he replied: 'I've a headache, Davey. After our elevenses I had better go home. In any case I've a great deal to do.' He spoke as if excusing himself. It was the first sign of weakness he had shown. 'When I've gone get on with the declensions so that you know them backwards and forwards. But, of course,' he went on with seeming irrelevance, 'poetry is the really important thing.' He ran his thin, white fingers through his hair. 'Poetry is the way we learn to look at life and understand it.'

'Shall I fetch the tray?' I asked.

He looked at his watch and nodded his head.

Cook greeted me a little sharply with: 'Aren't you early?' for she had not yet prepared the tray. She stood at the range stirring a sauce with a long wooden spoon.

'Mr Range isn't feeling well,' I explained, 'and he's leaving early.'

'Don't wonder at it with this weather,' Cook remarked morosely looking out of the window at a dripping fir tree. 'Still,' she went on, tasting the sauce inelegantly, 'they say it'll clear up this afternoon.' She again tasted the sauce appreciatively and smacked her lips. 'So you'll be at a loose end by yourself?'

'I suppose so.'

She moved ponderously across the kitchen to the store-cupboard in the passage. 'Kitty's going 'ome for tea,' she remarked, picking the sugar-coated biscuits, one by one, out of the tin and laying them on a plate. ' 'Ow would you like to go along with 'er?'

'I think I would,' I said uncertainly.

'No need to be shy. It's a 'omely sort of place. And there are pigs and chickens and geese. You'll enjoy it.'

She smiled encouragingly with an appreciative look to indicate it was the sort of place she would like herself. And so it was agreed.

I returned with the tray to the studio. Mr Range was not to be seen. I waited but he did not come. I looked into the lavatory and ran down the path in the wood he would take on his way home. But he was not there either.

I returned to the studio and sat with legs outstretched on the window-sill, drinking lemonade and chewing a biscuit. The rain still came down, pattering on to the leaves, and rolling off them in heavy droplets. The vine, outside the window, was bowed with the wet and every now and again let fall from its branches little cascades, which trickled down the panes. A thrush sat under the laurels and whistled plaintively, melodiously.

After lunch the clouds cleared away and rode buoyantly in the air, like balloons on invisible strings. Sunlight sparkled on the trees and shrubs. Kitty and I, hand in hand, made our way across the drenched fields to Kinglinton. The corn turning from green to pale brown, bowed on its tall stalks, swelled almost before our eyes as we passed. 'One more shower,' Kitty remarked 'an' it'll be ready for cuttin'.' She wore a rain-coat and wellington boots. In one hand she carried a basket filled with presents from Cook. The other firmly grasped mine. We did not talk much as Kitty had brought with her a bag of toffee which we munched and rolled in our mouths.

At one point the footpath passed through a narrow field, little more than a strip of cultivated ground, enclosed on both sides by woodland. Sunlight filtered through the branches but hardly penetrated to the path. As we walked through the shadows I thought of Mr Range.

'Kitty,' I said, pushing my toffee to one side with my tongue, 'don't you think it's funny the way Mr Range didn't wait for me at elevenses?' I had already explained to her what had happened.

She walked on for a while without responding. Then she said: ''E's a rum un, 'e is.' There was a cruel, hard look in her face.

'Why do you say that?'

''E ain't normal, that's all.' She withdrew her hand from mine and dislodged a toffee from her teeth with her forefinger. 'It ain't normal to live alone.'

'But,' I objected, 'why shouldn't he?'

'Ain't natural.' Kitty paused as she sucked a piece of toffee off her finger. 'A man in 'is position don't live in a little tumble down cottage by hisself. And why,' she asked, clinching the argument, 'ain't 'e in a school? Besides,' she continued darkly, 'it's all over the village about the scout troop the way 'e treats 'em. It ain't right.'

'It's only the way of doing things in prep schools for the Navy,' I said stoutly and incautiously.

Kitty was looking at me closely with a scrutiny I did not like. ' 'Ere,' she pounced, ' 'e didn't touch yer did 'e?'

I blushed and knew I had revealed my secret.

'Yer ought to 'ave told Madam.'

'He only did it once,' I stammered.

She gave me a frankly curious look as though she had read my thoughts and was reassured by them. 'Shut yer eyes and open yer mouth,' and she popped a toffee between my teeth.

A shaft of sunlight shone across the glade through which we were walking. It fell on Kitty's thick, black, curls and on to her strong, coarse features making her look like a satyr. I saw she had decided not to mention the subject again. I put my hand again in hers and we walked slowly on through the wood. The place was full of noises – the tiny crackle of dead leaves stirred by unseen feet, the curious attention of bright eyes among the trees.

Before long we were in sight of the village. It was a straggling, uninteresting place. The houses seemed to have been built without consideration of their neighbours so the general impression was one of untidiness.

But Kitty's cottage, part of an old, long farm house, lay in a dip by itself. The house had mullion windows and shaky, diamond-paned leaded-lights. It was partly covered with ivy which in some cases had crept over the drip-stones into the windows. The thin, pink, weathered brick on a thick course of brown stone, seemed to have absorbed the sunlight. The roof was tiled, half-red, half-green with moss, and had an irregular, twisted ridge which gave the place an air of antiquity. A great chimney, in need of pointing, with a fanciful course of bricks at its tip, rose in the centre of the house. Wisps of blue smoke lazily drifted from it.

'It's not all yours?' I asked in surprise.

'Course not, silly. All the labourers live 'ere. We're in number four.'

We entered a wicket directly on the road. It led into a well-tended cottage garden, carefully laid out with neat rows of vegetables, interspersed with flowers and soft fruit. At the end of the garden was a large apple tree covered with green apples. We turned a corner and knocked at a peeling door. The walls here were covered in a prolific winter jasmine cut with the severity of a hedge. There was no answer from inside and Kitty knocked again.

From upstairs, a voice, frowsty and querulous called: 'Comin'! Comin'! Yer'll knock the door down.'

Steps could be heard descending a creaking staircase. And then the door was unbolted. A little woman with cheeks like ripe apples stood on the threshold. She wore a dirty apron and her grey hair hung about her face in untidy wisps, which she endeavoured to draw back from her eyes. She looked as if she had been disturbed at her rest for her little brown eyes were bleary. She blinked at us for a few moments in surprise and then said, brightening: 'Oh, it's you Kitty is it? I didn't know you was coming.' She rubbed her knuckles in her eyes and looked at me. 'And 'oo's this?' she added in a kindly, sentimental voice, evidently designed for children. Without waiting for a reply her sharp eyes fell on the basket Kitty was carrying. 'It must be young Master Davey, that's 'oo it is.'

'Davey's come along of me as 'is tutor ain't well,' Kitty explained. She embraced her mother and gave a perfunctory kiss with her large lips on the elder woman's cheek.

'Yer look well, Kitty, that's a fact.'

'Yer don't look so bad yerself.'

Kitty's mother then turned to me and began to bustle about in the doorway. She shook me by the hand, smoothed her apron, began to untie it, thought better of it, patted her hair, darted in and out of the house like a hen that has unexpectedly found a chick. 'You're very welcome, I'm sure, Master Davey,' she said rapidly with a roundness and courtesy in her tone which she suddenly assumed, 'It's only a simple 'ouse. It's a poor place but then we're simple folk. You're welcome, very welcome. If only I'd a'known....' She gave Kitty a vexed look, which vanished and turned into a smile when she looked again at me. At last, as if postponing it for as long as possible, she ushered me into a room with a half-curtsy. Kitty watched all this with a little smile, amused, derisive.

The room, which gave directly on to the garden, was dark. Heavy white lace, none too clean, hung at the windows. Shrubs outside, and pot plants inside, cast green shadows so that the place seemed to be filled with a green light. It was a long low room with fine beams and carved joists. At one end there was a great stone fireplace in which a small fire was smouldering. This was evidently used for at least some of the cooking, for inside the hearth there was a rough grate of bricks, to the side of which stood a heavy black kettle. The mantel-shelf was draped in rusty-green serge, its fringes done into little green balls. It was ranged with pieces of old china, crammed with odds and ends such as spills of paper, twigs and pieces of cardboard. At one end there was a large pipe rack.

The floor was paved with large, honey-coloured flag stones, many uneven and broken, especially around the hearth. A deal table covered with the same material that hung at the mantel-shelf stood in the centre of the room. Various pieces of furniture, Victorian in origin, upholstered in dark colours and fitted with buttons, stood about in an easy-going way. Among them, quite at home, were mahogany and oak pieces of an earlier period. But the table was accommodated with cheap Windsor chairs. The place smelt of damp, mutton fat, wood smoke, soot and paraffin. The last came from a small stove on a side table by a cupboard near the fireplace.

'Now come along and sit yer by the fire,' Kitty's mother

said to me. 'I'll put some chips of wood on so it burns up a bit. And I don't know,' she rambled on and turned to Kitty enquiringly, 'do yer drink tea? If so I'll put the kettle on. Otherwise I've some elderflower in the larder.'

'I think,' I said politely, seating myself on a rickety chair, 'I would like to try the wine.'

'Yer would, would yer? Well then yer mustn't 'ave too much of it.' She wagged her finger at me and again gave the mirthless chuckle.

'I think,' I added a little embarrassed, 'this is a lovely place.'

Kitty's mother put her hands on her lips and laughed again. 'Yer do, do yer? Yer do, do yer? 'Ark to 'im. I'll 'ave to tell Welcome, I shall.'

'Welcome?'

'Me 'usband. Fancy yer not knowin' Kitty's surname. Don't 'e ever 'ear yer name, Kit?'

'Don't suppose 'e ever 'eard it,' Kitty said with indifference as though she was talking of another species. She took up the basket from the table where she had placed it and carried it out of the room.

Mrs Welcome followed her and I could hear them whispering together as they unpacked the foodstuffs.

I was left alone in the strange, dim room. Suddenly with a start I noticed that I was not alone. On the other side of the fireplace an old woman was sitting motionless in her chair. She was dressed in rusty black clothes, she was very thin and had a thin, pale face, with a hooked nose. Her skin had the transparent appearance of a plant which has had insufficient light. I shifted uncomfortably in my chair. There was no sign of life about her except the movement of her eyes. They were small and dark and seemed to watch me with amused curiosity. Her thin, blue veined hands grasped the arms of her chair. On one finger there was a simple gold wedding ring.

'Oh,' I gulped, startled and embarrassed, 'I didn't see you at first. . . .'

The old woman did not reply and made no sign of recognition except a faint flutter of her eyelids.

I got up from my chair, thinking I should have greeted her. I put out my hand but hers still held the arms of her chair. I hesitated a moment and then covered one of the ice-cold claws with my hand. The thought passed through my mind with a thrill of horror that she was dead.

'Don't mind Grandma,' Kitty's voice came from behind me, 'she's paralysed.' I turned round. Her face was indifferent. She placed a small tray she was carrying on the table. 'There yer are,' she went on comfortably, 'there's the wine and ginger bread.'

I sat down at the table and glanced furtively at the old lady. Her little eyes were still on me as I ate. The ginger bread was moist and heartening. The elderflower wine tasted of summer flowers. It was as cool as if it had been just drawn from a well.

'When Father comes in,' Kitty announced from the pantry door, ignoring her grandmother as if indeed she was dead, ''e'll take you out to the pigs. 'E's keen on 'is pigs is dad.'

'Yes,' Mrs Welcome called, invisible in the larder, 'it's 'is life, them pigs. I often says,' she continued with a chuckle, ''e thinks more of them pigs than 'e does of us – don't 'e, Kitty?'

Kitty picked up a shining bucket which stood by the outer door and went out.

When she had gone Mrs Welcome bustled over to me. 'Well, 'ow d'yer like me elderflower wine? And 'ow,' she continued inquisitively, 'd'yer find Kitty as a Nanny, eh?'

'We had a midnight feast,' I said as if that was recommendation enough.

'Oh, did yer?' Mrs Welcome did not seem very pleased.

'It wasn't really at midnight,' I added.

'Yer real Nanny wouldn't 'ave liked that.'

'I don't know,' I temporized.

'I suppose yer miss yer real Nan?'

'Oh, yes, but I like Kitty, too.'

'Welcome and me were thinking Kitty might become a Nanny 'erself. What would yer say to that?'

'She'd be a very good Nanny, I'm sure,' I said politely. My glance fell for a moment on the old lady in the chair.

Mrs Welcome noticed it and said, raising her voice: ''E says she'd make a very good Nanny, our Kit.'

'Is she deaf?' I whispered.

'Welcome reckons she is sometimes, and sometimes,' she went on with a little chuckle,' 'e reckons she ain't.' She bustled over to the apparently lifeless figure in the chair, plumped up the pillow behind her head. 'Yer always letting yer pillow fall down,' she said in a loud, complaining voice. 'It only makes yer uncomfortable. I've told yer so again and again. But it makes no difference. No one listens to what I 'as to say.'

She turned to me. 'We're not brought into the world to please ourselves.' Mrs Welcome smiled a smile compounded of sentimentality and hypocrisy. She picked a crude plaster cast of three monkeys off the mantel-shelf. 'I say: See no evil, 'ear no evil, say no evil. That's my motto....'

There was a step on the road outside and the click of the gate. The door was thrown open and a tall, thin man, wearing a battered Trilby hat entered. He blinked for a moment in the gloom, took the pipe he was smoking, out of his mouth, and then pointed it at me. 'Who's the visitor, Ma?' he stared at me with keen blue eyes and raised his bushy eyebrows interrogatively. He had a spare, strained face, tanned but faded. As he stood in the doorway the nails of his boots grated on the stone floor and his gaiters creaked with the movement of his legs. He had a straggling grey and dun moustache which gave him an air of authority. There was, in fact, an alertness in his manner which almost amounted to a swagger.

'I didn't think it was you. It didn't seem it was yer step,' Mrs Welcome said with a thin wail of complaint in her voice, as if she resented her husband's return. She glanced at me. ''E come along with Kitty. I wonder yer didn't see 'er.' She spoke defensively. 'It's young Davey Porteous from The Firs.'

Mr Welcome made a sound which appeared to be 'Ah Um', and eyed me up and down with critical attention. 'Well boy,' he said at length with a smile, 'yer've come on the right day. How old are you?' I was about to reply but he went on: 'Yer'll do, yer'll do. Yer a big lad I can see. There's a lot to be done tonight and yer can give me a 'and. It'll pay for your tea,' he added with a laugh.

Mrs Welcome gave a cackle of dismay at this rudeness. 'Yer should 'ave seen the basket Kitty brought from Cook. It were a reglar 'amper.'

'I'll see it soon enough, Ma. And,' he pronounced, 'there's plenty more where that came from. Now,' he said in a commanding tone, 'let's 'ave tea later than usual. There's work to be done tonight. Yer come along of me. This will be a useful day's work for yer. Perhaps there won't be all that more useful ones in yer life.'

I followed Mr Welcome outside where we were joined by Kitty. The three of us trudged through the little garden. Mr Welcome walked with a rolling gait as if his knees were weak. He puffed at his pipe and let fall complacent glances at the neat rows of vegetables. In the corner of the garden there was a wire pen in which half a dozen chickens scratched fitfully at the bare surface of their yard, softly chuckling to themselves.

'I 'ates fowl.' Mr Welcome commented as we passed. 'Smelly things best in the pot.'

'But,' Kitty said shrilly, 'you likes the eggs all right, Dad.'

'Dirty things,' Mr Welcome growled, 'women's business.'

We had now passed through the garden and entered, through a wicket, an enclosed yard from which arose the smell of pig dung and an agreeable medley of grunts, squeals, snuffles, and rustles. At one end of the yard there was a long, low shed roofed with rusty corrugated iron on to which a line of dunging yards had been added.

'Now take a look at that,' Mr Welcome exclaimed, clutching

my shoulder with his hand and turning me to a pond at the edge of the enclosure. 'Look at them geese. Now they be another thing altogether to the chickens.' Four geese and an old angry-eyed gander were circling sedately on the little pond every now and again hidden by the dark shadows of the willows. When they saw Mr Welcome they made little winnying sounds of pleasure and anticipation. Mr Welcome stopped in his tracks and looked at them appraisingly. 'They're beautiful fat, beautiful fat,' he said in a low voice. 'But,' he went on severely, as if he were reprimanding me, 'we can't stand 'ere all day lookin' at the geese. There's work to be done.'

When we reached the pig shed he stood for a moment in front of the door with his hand on the latch. 'It's only a rough 'ole place. I made it with me own 'ands from odds and ends. But,' he took a pull at his pipe and winked, 'pigs do better 'ere than in many a better sty on a rich man's farm. I tell you what, Davey, what they say round 'ere and that is – there's no better place for a pig to fatten in than down Joe Welcome's.'

He opened the door and we went inside. It was dim and moist, filled with the smell of pigs and clean straw. Happy grunts, turning to wails of anticipation, rose on all sides as the door clicked to. Sty doors were rattled impatiently and the wailing rose to a crescendo. Mr Welcome picked up two buckets of scraps and swill. Then he put them down.

'No,' he shouted above the din, 'better wait while I show yer me beauties. Waitin' does 'em no 'arm. It sharpens the appetite and they fatten best that way. Now, look 'ere,' and he caught hold of my shoulder, 'these are the 'ilts with the boar.'

Four sleek, young but grown pigs were circling round in the dim light. I stood on tiptoe and looked over the door which the boar was rattling with his snout.

' 'E bain't be mine,' Mr Welcome explained, ' 'e's been lent for this business.'

The boar looked up at me with an enquiring expression on his bewhiskered face. He looked genial enough but there was a glint of danger in his eye. A yellow tusk protruded from each cheek. He recalled to my mind pictures of Indian army colonels.

'He doesn't look very fierce,' I remarked.

Mr Welcome chuckled. 'Not now perhaps,' he said sardonically and leant over the door and gave the boar an affectionate scratch on his neck, 'but that's because 'e's got what 'e wants.' He pointed the stem of his pipe in the direction of the shining-coated hilts and winked. 'Yer've got what yer want, ain't yer ole boy?' The hilts, realising they were not going to be fed immediately, snuffed demurely in the clean straw.

We moved to the next sty. A huge sow scrambled to her feet and upset a dozen piglings as she did so. She gave them an impatient look and then smiled up at Mr Welcome. She gave a great yawn and grunted yearningly. 'There ye are me beauty,' Mr Welcome crooned and softly scratched the creature's ears. 'Ye'll be gettin' yer grub soon, me dear.'

The next sty contained a sow with a litter of larger piglets. She lay resolutely on her stomach with a wary, ill-tempered expression on her face while the hungry piglets nuzzled at her flanks. 'Yer see, Davey,' Mr Welcome explained, 'she's 'ad enough. She's fed 'em long enough and she knows it. If she went on that sow would go straight down'ill. That's why we're goin' to take 'er out presently, get 'er into a clean sty of 'er own, and 'ave them piglin's cut.'

'Cut?'

'Carstrated,' he explained laconically. 'Otherwise yer see some of them, the males, would grow into boars and be no use for fattenin'.'

'So they'll be eaten?' I asked, looking curiously at the young pigs, so happily unconscious of their fate. Mr Welcome nodded.

We moved to the last sty which contained a large pig with a thoughtful, wary expression on his face. He lay on the straw with his snout between his trotters, motionless, but his eyes followed every movement. The eyes reminded me of the old lady's in the cottage.

'Ah, this one,' Mr Welcome told me, ''e knows 'is number's up. 'E's come to the end of 'is time, see? There's nothin' left for 'im but the table. And a nice bit of pork 'e'll make, too.' His manner changed with that bewildering rapidity which seemed to be characteristic. 'Now, we can't 'ang about all day showin' yer these things. First thing to do is to get that sow out of 'er sty on to a bit of grass. Kitty, go around to the front with them pails and feed 'em up. But, mind, not the sow with the grown litter.' He gave his orders like a general.

I helped with the distasteful task of castrating the piglings, holding the sweating males as they were cut. Mr Welcome placed the testicles in his pocket with the remark: 'Mustn't lose they, Davey. They be the best part of a young pigling!'

When we came out, it was that indeterminate time in summer when it is not still the afternoon but is also not the dusk. The air was filled with strange, rich smells. Gnats, as if performing sacred dances, hung in the air. Downy moths fluttered at the thin light. A great white cloud, attended by smaller ones, trailed across the sun, so slowly it scarcely seemed to move. There was not even a whisper of wind. Across and beyond the yard I could see a little wood. In a bottom far away a faint haze, like wood smoke, was beginning to form. But soon it drifted away into the trees and disappeared. It seemed as if time had stopped and the evening would go on for ever. Birds chattered in the trees, their voices magnified by the stillness. They flew in and out under the time-bleached eaves of the old house. The geese on the little pond made little noises to each other like old men talking through toothless gums. Every now and then there was the sound of disturbed water and the drip of it from one of the bird's beaks. Flies hummed and buzzed in the manure. An old cat, striped and ginger, blinked sleepily on a wall and pretended not to listen to the liquid song of a thrush perched on a mossy apple tree.

As we stood for a few moments in front of the shed door

Mrs Welcome appeared at the gate followed by a stout, red-faced man in a butcher's apron.

' 'Ere's Tom Stranger, Joe,' Mrs Welcome said in a querulous voice, 'I thought as 'ow yer said 'e was comin' tomorrer.'

'Ah, Tom,' Mr Welcome exclaimed, coming forward and shaking him by the hand, 'yer've come ternight, then?' He ignored his wife who watched the two men with a sharp expression of disapproval on her face.

'Well, Joe,' Mr Stranger said in a genial voice, his dark little eyes buzzing with amusement, 'if it's all the same to you, and you ain't frightened of yer missus' – he chuckled and glanced at Mrs Welcome – 'then tonight would suit me well for our little business.'

'Course, Tom, course, Tom. Tonight's the same to me. Mary,' he went on, 'supper will be late. We're killing the pig.'

'But, Joe, think of Kitty and the lad. They've to get back. They can't stay the night.'

'Who's the boy, Joe?' Tom asked. This was explained to him. He wiped his hand on his apron and proffered it to me. 'Oh ah,' he said, ' 'ow do?' He greeted me with genial curiosity, mixed with a little suspicion, reserved for those who live in the country but do not derive their livelihood from it.

' 'E'll be so late to bed,' Mrs Welcome wailed, 'there'll be no end of trouble.' But she had already given up and went back to the cottage muttering to herself. 'Besides,' she said, turning round for a last fling, 'it ain't right for a boy like that to see an animal killed, is it, Kitty?'

Kitty did not reply, Tom Stranger chuckled, and Mr Welcome made a noise like 'pshah' in the back of his throat. 'Yer'll see the day out, Davey boy, if yer want to,' he said reassuringly, 'yer ain't seen a pig killed afore, I suppose?'

I shook my head.

'And yer'd like to?'

I nodded. The truth was I did and I didn't.

'Then yer shall,' Mr Welcome said triumphantly.

Kitty, who had followed her mother, now appeared with dishes and bowls. It was warm and windless. Imperceptibly dusk had begun to fall. The rays of the declining sun seemed to wither away. The moon, round, cloudless, mysterious, rose and shone faintly on the green-blue horizon. Stars, here and there, glittered in the pale grey sky. Rooks, flying high and swiftly, passed cawing overhead, eager to reach their nests before the end of the day. Smaller birds in the trees chirruped softly and sleepily or were silent. The activity of the village was conveyed on the warm air as a low murmur, like the motion of a hive, the sound of a dropped bucket or a shout or a laugh momentarily raised above it.

'I dunno's that yer ought to be 'ere,' Kitty whispered, 'but yer sees 'ow Father is. Yer needn't look if yer doesn't want to.'

I shook my head vigorously and thought of the condemned pig in the sty with his snout between his trotters. Did he know that his wary little eyes would see the evening sky once more, but only once?

Mr Welcome had got through the back of the sty. There was a short squeal and the sound of a scuffle. A moment later the pig appeared through the pop hole, slow, suspicious, marking every movement. Mr Stranger, large, portentous, red faced, stood in the yard. He seemed hardly to notice the pig. He carefully took off his cap and placed it in his apron. He then drew from his pocket a thin noose of rope. 'Come along, Jack,' he coaxed comfortably. 'Come along, Jack. That's a good fellow. There yer are.' It had the softness of an incantation. Then with a sudden movement, surprising in so stout a man, he slipped the rope into the pig's mouth and drew tight the knot. The pig grunted and backed away. Mr Stranger followed him for a minute or two as the animal tried to find the pop hole which had been closed. The two circled, Mr Stranger talking all the while in a low voice. As they passed the yard door for the second time Mr Stranger opened it. The dance went on. They reached the door for the third time. The pig, sensing freedom, walked through it and they were outside. Little by little Mr Stranger shortened the rope.

Meanwhile Mr Welcome had placed a heap of fresh straw, very yellow in the fading light, in front of the sty yards. Beside it was a heavy wood bench, stained, and worked with holes and notches. Kitty stood beside me, motionless, still holding the bowls in her hands, watching the drama as the pig was drawn closer and closer to the bench. The pig's eyes glittered in the dying light as he looked warily round for a way of escape. Mr Stranger's passivity confused him. Shadows were falling everywhere. Minute by minute the blue of the sky grew deeper. Stars, immeasurably far away, became visible like meaningless beacons. The duck-egg blue of the horizon was swallowed into the evening sky and disappeared.

The pig was on the straw beside the bench. Mr Welcome approached and stood between me and the bench, so I could not see what was happening. But suddenly, and unexpectedly in the silence, there was a shriek of despair and terror as the animal was dexterously tied to the bench. It all seemed to happen in a moment. The great body, glistening with sweat, writhed and floundered, tilting the bench this way and that, its great strength impotent before the cunning of the men. The squealing continued and I looked away at the placid pond round which the geese were still circling, scarcely disturbed by the terrible cries that rose to the evening sky. The water was pale silver, as if all the light that remained had been emptied into it. Little ripples moved on the tranquil surface disturbed by the movement of the geese.

I looked back at the shrieking pig. As I did so Mr Stranger drew a large bladed knife from the pocket of his apron, poised it for a moment, and brought it down and round in a curving motion to the pig's throat. The screams rose for a moment in a jagged liquid crescendo and then slowly died away into the silence. A spurt of blood, as if squirted from a pump, fell on to the clean, yellow straw and made a rich red patch upon it. The cords were untied, as if by magic, and the dead pig rolled on to the straw. Kitty put down her bowls, ran forward and moved the bench to one side. A moment later there was a crackle and the straw burst into lurid flames round the body of the pig.

There was a short lull as the straw crackled skyward. The men had relaxed and chatted to each other as they rolled the pig over and over in the flames with long poles. There was a faint smell of burnt bristles in the smoke as it eddied about for a minute or two and then vanished into the thin night air. The flames died down and went out. Kitty fetched two pails of water and the men scraped and scrubbed at the blackened body with broom heads dipped in the cold well-water. It was then rolled clear of the ashes on its back and the bowls placed round it.

The butcher raised his knife again and slit down the soft under belly of the pig. He inserted a piece of wood the shape of a coat hanger into the slit to keep it open. Steam from the warm entrails rose into the air. And then he was quickly cutting, slicing and plunging his arms up to the elbows into the intestines. The bowls were quickly filled, carried off and returned. At last the cleaned carcass was carried into the house and hung up by the two men in the larder.

There was a little altercation between Mr and Mrs Welcome when the two men came back into the living-room. 'Yer needn't think,' Mrs Welcome announced with an aggressive sniff, 'that I'll do them faggits tonight. That's it.'

To my surprise Mr Welcome answered mildly enough: 'Keep 'em in the pail then. They can stop there till the mornin'.'

'That's right, missus,' Tom Stranger said over his shoulder as he made for the door, 'don't 'e be 'urried.' There was a gleam of malice in his little eyes.

We all went out again to tidy up, Mr Stranger to pick up his jacket and Mr Welcome to have a last look at the pigs. He was in high humour and whistled as he went down the garden path.

'Fine pig, Tom,' he remarked.
'Fine pig, Joe,' Mr Stranger responded.

CHAPTER THIRTEEN

The moon had now come up and was beginning to cast its
pale eerie light over the landscape. The village was full of
sounds – the clink of hobnailed boots on the street, a hoarse
murmur from the pub, the sound of a quarrel suddenly
quelled, the rumble of cart wheels, the sound of a lorry drawing away in the distance. A sweet smell, seemingly compounded of honey and dung, hung about on the air. The
house, blanched in the silver light of the moon, looked like
the home of a witch in a fairy tale.

I visited the earth closet at the bottom of the garden,
attended by Kitty, and sampled its atmosphere of intimacy
and satisfaction. It smelt of lime and the sickly scent of human
dung. As we came out and extinguished the candle I could
hear the happy grunts and snores of the pigs, interspersed
now and again by an outraged squeal from a pigling
momentarily deprived of his happiness. The two men were
talking in undertones, evidently settling the account.

The curtains of the living-room were tightly drawn. An oil
lamp with a white china shade threw a circle of pale yellow
light round the room, bright at its centre but quickly
diminishing in intensity at its circumference. The corners of
the room were shadowy and mysterious. A bright little fire
now burnt up contentedly in the hearth, licking at some green,
hissing logs. The table was spread with a clean white cloth
on which were laid the appurtenances of high tea. A tea
cosy, from which sprouted the large cracked spout of a dark
brown teapot, stood importantly at the end of it. The tea
cosy was embroidered with the picture of a winking cow. The

door into the garden had been left open and Mr Welcome and Mr Stranger could be heard still talking under the winter jasmine over the garden gate. The pale light of the moon shone onto the threshold and cast eerie shadows from the overgrown shrubs outside.

'I dunno, I'm sure,' Mrs Welcome grumbled, coming out of the larder, a dish in her hand, and looking at me, 'I dunno what Cook will think. She'll think yer've been murdered. But there yer are,' she continued, lighting the paraffin cooker and fetching a frying pan from a cupboard, 'ther's no goin' against Mr Welcome's will. I should know after all these years.' She placed floured pieces of meat in the pan and they began to fry. 'I've written yer a note, Kitty.' She raised her voice so Kitty could hear her in the larder. 'I only 'opes yer doesn't lose yer place. It says 'ow yer come to be so be'ind. And mind yer don't 'ang about after supper.' She stopped and looked critically at me. 'What are yer thinkin' about, Kitty? Yer'll make no Nanny. Look at that boy's face.'

Kitty popped her ugly, earthy face round the larder door. 'Come on, then,' she called to me with a grin.

I followed her through the makeshift larder which in reality was the foot of a narrow newel stair. It was lit with a small hand lamp on a shelf. The pig hung head downwards from a hook attached to the back of a stair tread – neat, cold, clean, so dead that it looked as if it had never been alive. A hare, its head in a tin pot, hung from another hook. At the top of the stairs there was a small landing with a little camp bed made up in it. 'Grandma's' Kitty said laconically. She picked up a night light and entered her own room, which was long and narrow and contained three iron bedsteads. She poured out a jug of water into a ewer that stood on a washstand and I did my best to make myself clean with the aid of a damp piece of towelling.

As we paused on the landing again she pushed open another door and shone the light inside. 'Dad's room,' she explained. At the far end there was a huge four poster bed. Its mahogany posts reached the ceiling and it was almost as wide as the room. It still had curtains but they were in tatters.

'Belonged to Grandpa,' Kitty explained proudly, 'Grandma's 'usband. 'Is father was a farmer. They say 'e owned all these cottages.'

'Did he?' I whispered, impressed.

When we got downstairs, Mr Welcome was sitting at the far end of the table. Mrs Welcome presided at the other. The old grandmother still sat in her chair by the fire but she had a bib round her chin and was very slowly chewing at something with her toothless gums. The soup had already been poured out and it lay steaming in the plates. Mr Welcome was drinking his with great pieces of bread.

'Well,' he asked with his mouth full and drawing the back of his hand across his untidy moustache, 'what d'yer think of it 'ere, then?'

'I think it's very nice,' I replied politely, 'but –'

He looked up from his soup and his eyes twinkled. 'But yer wouldn't want to live 'ere?'

'No,' I said defensively, 'I was going to say that Mrs Welcome says it's damp.'

'It's that right enough.'

'And 'ow,' Mrs Welcome chimed in, swallowing a large piece of sodden bread awkwardly and noisily. Her red rimmed eyes gazed round the room and a look of defeat came over her face. ''Ow can yer keep a broken floor tidy? There's no way to do it.'

'I told yer years ago,' Mr Welcome replied aggressively, 'yer'd crack the flags if yer chopped the wood in 'ere instead of the shed. It was makin' work for yerself.'

'Yer knew I 'ad a bad chest them days. Yer didn't offer to do it yerself did yer? Besides,' she went on more amicably, daintily putting another piece of bread in her plate, 'it ain't only the flagstones. It's everythink.' She gave her head a little toss and a wisp of grey hair fell onto her nose. 'Truth is the place ought to be pulled down. It ain't fit for 'uman 'abitation.'

Mr Welcome snorted. ''Ark to what she says about me 'ome!

I was born 'ere. Me father was born 'ere and so was Grandpa – weren't 'e, Mum?' He jerked his head towards the motionless figure in the chair. I couldn't see from her eyes whether she had understood or not. 'She understands what I say,' Mr Welcome pursued, apparently having read my thoughts, 'and she knows what I says is true.'

Kitty collected the soup plates and Mrs Welcome dished up the meat which had been quietly sizzling on the paraffin stove. Meanwhile Mr Welcome poured out the tea which was the colour of blood. The meat was the tenderest and sweetest I had ever tasted.

'Would yer believe it,' Mr Welcome asked me, looking at me from under his bushy eyebrows, 'that this was part of a living pig not fifty minutes gone?' And he waved a piece of the meat on the end of his fork. 'That poor old fellow certainly is very good. 'E didn't come into the world for nothink.' He ate the meat for a moment or two in silence. Then he said: 'It ain't so bad a death after all. I've seen men in the trenches whom it would 'ave been a kindness to slit their throats.' He paused reflectively either at his reminiscences or at the intractable grammar of his sentence.

I put my knife and fork down with a little clatter. I remembered the shrieks to the pitiless evening sky.

'No good mentionin' now,' Mrs Welcome said in an audible whisper and glancing at me, 'that it was tonight's pig. It's upsetting,' she added comfortably.

Mr Welcome who was polishing his plate with a piece of bread, growled out: 'It don't matter when the pig was killed. It's if yer eats it at all!' He sucked his teeth noisily as if that would prevent her stupidity.

At last it was time to go. I had grown so sleepy that the room, the old lady in the chair by the fire, and the killing of the pig seemed parts of a dream. Mr Welcome accompanied Kitty and me through the wood. The moon was full with an exuberant life of its own. It cast long, dark shadows among the trees, grotesque and motionless. The wood was full of little, mysterious sounds, perceived rather than heard. Where the path widened, a white owl as quiet as a ghost, floated in front of us. Here Mr Welcome left us.

'Perhaps,' he said as he shook me by the hand, having listened to my thanks with detached amusement, 'yer'll come again and give me a 'and.'

He searched in his pocket and produced an apple which he gave me. He briefly kissed Kitty on the forehead and turned back into the shadows.

Kitty and I made our way through the enchanted moonshine, hand in hand. As we passed through the field, a herd of mischievous, inquisitive heifers ran up to us, lowered their heads and snorted. They blew through their nostrils, backed away, lifted their hooves in the air. It was a sort of game mixed with fear and curiosity. We walked on. Kitty seemed as much in a dream as I was, and appeared not to notice. The cattle were disappointed, but followed, snorting a little, and every now and again lowered their heads for a tuft of grass which they tore up with a sound like the crumpling of paper. Bunches of thistles in full bloom glittered in the moonlight.

Cook met us on the back door verandah. Directly she saw us she placed her hands on her hips and pursed her lips. I was hurried off to bed with the warning that I was not to tell anyone how late I had come in – especially Grandma. As I made my way up the green baize-covered back-stairs, my shoes in my hand, I could hear Cook's sharp voice interrogating Kitty. 'You shouldn't 'ave done it!' she kept repeating, 'you shouldn't 'ave done it, that's all!'

Next morning I waited for Mr Range in the studio. He was usually punctual and after half an hour I went to tell Grandma that he had not come. She was sitting in the Red room at the bureau. She looked up through her gold rimmed reading glasses with a vexed expression as I entered.

'Well, Davey, what is it?' she asked, looking down again at the mass of papers in front of her.

I explained.

'He's probably ill.'

'But what should I do, Grandma?'

My question annoyed her. 'You can do what you like,' she answered shortly. She turned back to the papers, and then, seeing that I had not gone: 'You're now old enough to decide things like that for yourself. There are more important matters to be dealt with.'

This was very unlike Grandma and I left the room without another word. For the first time I felt in the way.

The weather had changed in the night. It was warm but cloudy and it looked as if it might rain. I mooched about and then began cleaning the silver for the parlour-maid in the pantry. This, and grinding the coffee in the scullery, was an occupation for wet days.

I was idly looking out of the window, waiting for the polish to dry, when there was a ring at the back door. A ring at the back door was unusual as most people walked in and called out. I peeped out to see who it was. I was in time to see a country woman in an old overcoat talking in low tones to Cook.

'Mrs Wollacombe?' Cook asked in a sharp surprised voice.

Mrs Wollacombe was a tall gaunt woman. Light from the open door fell on her face which was lined, resolute, worried. She said something in a low voice I could not hear.

'Reggie's mother? Ah, yes.' Cook was still aggressive, put out that she had been disturbed at her cooking by a village woman.

'Reggie's got fits,' I heard the woman say. Then I caught: 'the scoutmaster, Mr Range, scout practice. I thought it was for the best.' Then there was a lot I could not hear ending with: 'Me duty to tell Mrs Porteous.'

Cook stiffened. She had her back to me but I could see she was looking into Mrs Wollacombe's face. And then the two women entered Cook's bedroom, which was on the ground floor, and shut the door behind them.

They were in there ten minutes or more. I polished the

spoons and forks and thought of Mr Range. My only comment on what had happened was a sensation of loss and disappointment. I would never see him again and he had not even said good-bye.

The parlour-maid went rustling by in the passage with Mrs Wollacombe at her heels. I did not move. I knew all there was to know. I didn't care to hear it all over again, even if I had been able to. Then Mrs Wollacombe passed back to the kitchen, there was a whispered conversation with Cook at the back door. It was all over.

In the afternoon a note was despatched by Mr Courtenay which said, I suppose, that Mr Range's services would no longer be required. Mr Courtenay returned with an enigmatic expression on his face. He would tell nothing of what had happened but squeaked his way in his leather gaiters to report to Grandma. He met her in the hall.

'Beg pardon, madam,' he said, his chauffeur's cap held across his stomach, 'I could not deliver the note.' He drew it importantly out of his pocket and handed it to Grandma.

'Why not, Courtenay?' she asked sharply, glancing at me. I was drawing myself up the bannister rail at the foot of the stairs.

'Mr Range 'as left.' He gave me a look as much as to say: 'I told you so' although he had hardly ever talked to me of Mr Range.

'Left?'

''E left early this mornin', madam, and no-one knows 'is address. I took the liberty of enquiring at the Vicarage and the Post Office.' He pursed his lips but looked satisfied. He bent his knees in a gesture of self-importance and his gaiters squeaked.

Grandma plucked irritably at the lace front of her blouse. 'That's all, Courtenay, then. There's nothing more to be done.'

Mr Treet appeared unexpectedly for tea. I had mine in the servants' hall but went into the drawing-room afterwards.

He was sitting in an armchair in front of the empty hearth talking to Grandma.

'Oh,' he was saying as I entered, 'I thought you would have heard. Poor Canon Barker passed away last night.'

Grandma clucked sympathetically and shook her head. 'It was a mistake from the beginning appointing so old a man to be archdeacon,' she remarked after a pause. 'It's a heavy job and it must have been too much for him.'

'Very heavy work,' Mr Treet echoed, looking at me with interest, and giving me a faint smile. He turned back to Grandma and shrugged his shoulders. 'But, what in the circumstances, as they then were, was to be done?'

'But what, Mr Treet,' she asked in a puzzled tone, 'will be the position of Mr Brailes now?'

Mr Treet gazed up into the skylight over his head as though examining the yellow silk curtain which hung across it. 'Frankly, I don't know. Mark would be my candidate. But,' he continued after a pause, 'there are obstacles, yes, obstacles. A defeated candidate, so soon after the contest, doesn't stand the same chance as he did in the first place.'

'No,' Grandma said uncertainly, 'but Mr Brailes is an exception, surely....' She caught sight of me for the first time and added awkwardly: 'But here's Davey.'

'Yes, indeed,' said Mr Treet jovially, 'and I was going to suggest, Davey, that you showed me how well you rode your bicycle.'

I looked, I suppose, very surprised. 'It was only an idea,' he said cautiously.

'Oh no, I should like to show you,' I said.

We walked through the Red room and I rode round on the lawn doing as many tricks as I knew how. Mr Treet watched with more interest than I had expected which flattered me. At length he beckoned to me and I dismounted, leaning my machine against a garden pot.

'Young fellow, I want a word with you,' Mr Treet began, leading me to the centre of the lawn, and not mentioning bicycling at all, 'I just want to make a few enquiries about . . . er . . . your tutor, Mr Range.'

He paused but I made no response.

'Well, now,' he asked, putting his long nose into the air to catch a scent, 'how did you like him?'

'Very much,' I said noncommittally, and then added: 'I'm sorry he has gone.'

'Quite so.' Mr Treet suddenly became very clerical. 'Of course. And,' he mused, 'you know he has gone.'

'Grandma's note was returned.'

He nodded, thinking of something else. 'Did you know this boy Reggie Wollacombe?'

I nodded.

'Would you say he was an excitable boy?'

I nodded again.

'Do you think,' Mr Treet enquired looking up at the chimneys of the house as he paced across the lawn, 'do you think Mr Range would have been – er – unkind to Reggie?'

I shook my head.

'Do you think Reggie thought he was?'

'No,' I said definitely.

'And you, Davey –' Mr Treet lowered himself so that his face almost touched mine – 'was he kind to you?'

'Yes, always.'

'Always?'

'Always.'

'Did he smack you or beat you?'

'No,' I lied.

'Was he ever –' Mr Treet seemed to be picking his way down a precipitous path – 'ever too – er – too kind?'

'I don't understand what you mean.'

Mr Treet reconsidered what he had said. 'Was he ever, perhaps, a little over-affectionate?'

'I don't understand what you mean, sir,' I said intensely.

'Did Mr Range ever, for instance, kiss you or press you to him?' Mr Treet tried to look away but could not forbear darting a glance at me to see how his question went home.

'No, never.'

'He didn't for instance, er, unfasten your trousers?'

I stared at Mr Treet and looked amazed. But Mr Treet was not to be deflected. His thin, pink nose was quivering on the trail.

'He did not...' he began and then thought better of it. 'Davey,' he began again, 'you know what your private parts are?'

'I think so.'

'Now answer me exactly. Did he ever touch you...?'

'Never.'

'Not even,' he said suddenly and cunningly, 'when he took you bathing?'

'No.'

'Then he did take you bathing?'

'Only once,' I replied sullenly.

'And he never did any of these things I have mentioned?'

I shook my head.

'And what,' Mr Treet darted a last question at me, 'what sort of cane did he use to punish you?'

I had been caught once and I was not to be caught again. 'He didn't cane me,' I lied and hoped that Reggie and Kitty would never tell what I had told them.

Mr Treet looked me carefully up and down as if I might, after all, have committed a crime. Then he fetched half-a-crown from his pocket, held it up for a moment, and gave it to me.

'You're a good boy, I'm sure,' he said, 'and you're a good cyclist. Will you be taking your bicycle to school?'

'I don't know whether I shall be allowed to,' I answered, a feeling of apprehension taking hold of me at the thought of what lay ahead.

Later I heard him on the doorstep saying good-bye to Grandma. 'Not to worry,' he was saying heartily, 'there's nothing wrong and nothing to worry about. It was unfortunate but luckily no harm's done. As to the other matter, you're thinking in old-fashioned terms. No child has any right to expect more than his education. And from what I can see of him he's all right. He can look after himself.'

George Oldacre also questioned me. But it was characteristic that he chose to take me shooting as a pretext.

We had trudged along the Sandy Way under the over-arching trees of the Big wood and had come to the side of a chalk down. He had put down two crudely painted decoy pigeons in the thin grass and we crouched in some straggling bushes. A little pond, where the pigeons came to drink in the evening, lay in front of us, its surface rippled by a gentle breeze. We waited expectantly. But either the pigeons saw us, were suspicious of the decoys, or most probably it was too early in the evening – at any rate no pigeon appeared, though they could be heard fluttering in the wood.

'Well, Davey,' George began, looking round at the magnificent rolling landscape which terminated in a line of deep blue on the horizon, 'how d'you like having no more work to do?'

I did not answer at first. Then I said: 'I hope Mr Range hasn't got into any trouble.'

George looked at me thoughtfully, drew out his tobacco pouch and began to fill his curved stemmed pipe. 'Matter of fact,' he said, 'I don't think anything has been heard of him. You see,' he went on, watching my face through the light of the match flame, 'this isn't the first time it's happened.'

'But...'

'He frightened young Reggie Wollacombe,' George remarked, again looking round the sky.

'I know.'

George raised his eyebrows and wrinkled his great brow. He nodded to himself and then asked: 'He didn't frighten you?'

'No.' I paused. Then I went on. 'I liked Mr Range very much. But, you see, he liked Reggie better than me.'

George looked startled for a moment and his pipe went out.

'Ah well,' he commented at last, 'it's just as well there's no harm done.' He lit his pipe again and smoked meditatively, looking out at the view. The thin, fine, chalk grasses rustled around us.

'But what,' I asked seriously, 'will they do to him?'

'Oh Reggie will be all right. It was nothing but a little fright.'

'No, I mean Mr Range – if he's caught.'

'Well,' George said slowly, taking the stem of his pipe out of his mouth, 'there could be trouble, but I don't suppose there will be. He'll become an outcast, of course.' He puffed meditatively at his pipe. Eddies of smoke, sweetly-scented, drifted past and vanished into the air. 'There was a funny little pink faced chap at my prep school. He had very thick lenses and when he read the prayers he used to make silly mistakes.'

'Was he a clergyman, then?' I asked in surprise.

'Oh yes,' George answered meditatively, a faint smile playing round his large face. 'After choir practice he used to pounce on the boys a bit and ruffle their surplices. I don't think,' he ruminated throwing me a look of curiosity, 'it did anyone any harm, and, to tell you the truth, nobody thought much about it in those days. He used to give us bags of sweets, and we thought most about them.'

George cautiously looked around, raised the butt of his gun to his shoulder, and a moment later, fired, right and left. I had been thinking of Mr Range and my eyes had been dreamily fixed on the distant skyline. But I saw the right hand pigeon topple from the sky and fall with a thud near the two decoys. The other pigeon escaped and made off in a zig-zag flight, with a great beating of wings. George's spaniel bitch which I had been fondling, bounded forward and seized the quivering bird. She carried it triumphantly in her mouth and tossed her head up and down. But instead of returning to the hideout she made for the wood. No amount of whispered cajolment would divert her and we had to break cover and catch her. This meant that any more pigeon shooting was out of the question for that evening. George scolded her but gently and with affection as if he well understood that she wanted the bird for herself.

As we made our way back along the sandy track George muttered: 'Poor Range, poor fellow.'

We drew near Kiln Cottage and were about to turn off the track when we came on Eva Brailes. She was sauntering along by herself, a dreamy expression on her rather flushed face. She looked strained and tired. I noticed subconsciously that she had grown fat.

'Ah,' she exclaimed – and this was the invariable greeting given by husband and wife with a look of surprise – 'you, Mr Oldacre, and David, as well!' It was too bright for the occasion. There was something unusual in her manner which I sensed but could not grasp – a heightened dignity and condescension, which was as ridiculous as it was faintly annoying. 'Delicious evening! The breeze is so soft, enchanting!' She looked about her with a dreamy, self-conscious expression.

Birds whistled and chattered, but sleepily, moodily, in the trees. A wood pigeon began to croon compulsively, was disturbed, made off deeper into the wood where it could be heard faintly, like a distant incantation.

'Perhaps,' George ventured, 'you would like to come in?'

But she shook her head. 'Thank you, no. Mark is with old Mrs Fowler who's dying.' She said this brightly, amused, as if saying that Mrs Fowler was out on a coach trip.

'I'm sorry to hear that,' George murmured, shifting from one foot to another.

'The villagers,' she pursued, still smiling which she did most of the time, 'take death so philosophically. To them the death of an old woman is like the fall of an old tree.'

'But,' George interposed, 'isn't that how it should be?'

Eva Brailes smiled to herself. 'I don't think so,' she said, putting her head on one side and self-consciously reflecting, 'it's so unchristian.'

'You think there should be more to it, then?'

'Yes, indeed. It's the most important moment in life.' She

smiled flatly, with a look in her eyes which implied certainty, superiority, and thus detachment. 'There is a great deal more to it than that – the return of the created human spirit to its creator, a sort of return home. Really.' she went on brightly, looking into George's face, 'the villagers are still pagan. The Christian rites are an irrelevence, a little finery. That's all.'

'I don't know,' George began, but she interrupted him.

'You've heard, I suppose, that Archdeacon Barker has died?'

George nodded sympathetically.

'Oh,' she interposed, 'he was very old. Besides the business of the diocese was getting very muddled.'

'I suppose so.'

'Oh yes,' she responded, 'it is so. There will be no end of work for his successor.' She glanced at her watch. 'But look at the time. I must be getting back to Mark. He will have said everything there is to be said by this time.'

She sauntered along with us for a while and, then, giving us a little smile and nod, she went down the track to the lane.

'Poor Mrs Fowler,' George muttered to himself as he mounted the steps which led up the side of the track into his garden. 'I only hope,' he added, glancing at me, as if he had previously forgotten my presence, 'Mr Brailes was some consolation to her.' His eye fell on the dead pigeon in my hand and he shrugged.

CHAPTER FOURTEEN

The next days were spent in preparation for my birthday. There was paper, rubbish and hedge clippings to be carried in my cart to the bonfire in the field. A pile of boughs, branches and logs was already in position. There were a few fireworks to be bought. And, above all, there were the paper bags to be filled with flour to be used as bombs in the 'attack'. The 'attack' was a war game in the wood after dark played by myself, Mr Evans and his sons. It was very occasionally played on days other than my birthday, but it always took place on my birthday and was its highlight.

At last the great day dawned. After prayers, and before breakfast, the presents were brought in and I opened them. There were a few books from distant relatives whom I hardly knew, a catapult from Uncle John, a new set of Meccano from Grandma, a torch from Nanna, and most exciting of all, a set of carpentry tools in a wooden box given by Aunt Emma. When I had finished with the string and the rustling paper, which was placed in a corner to be removed after breakfast, Grandma and I stood hand in hand looking out across the lawn. It had rained in the night but the sun was bright and hot. Everything was green and lush. One could see down green valleys into the wood and they terminated in mysterious shadows almost as blue as green. Birds were hopping round their bath whisking the water about as they washed and drank.

I looked up into Grandma's face. She was frowning slightly and I had seen her eyes thoughtfully watching my face as I undid the parcels. All around us life was pushing forward and upward, impelled by the mysterious forces of nature. But she, at her age, was now a spectator. A thrush, her speckled breast shining in the sunlight, hopped from the bath and glanced curiously at the dining-room windows where we stood. She was the embodiment of nature, of an existence different to our own, perhaps a symbol of life itself.

Grandma gripped my hand in hers and squeezed it affectionately. She ran her fingers over the back of my hand and sighed. She gave me a look compounded of puzzlement and something like sorrow.

'Grandma,' I said, 'there's nothing from Mother this time.' I glanced appreciatively at the cardboard box of coloured

Meccano and the shining tools. On the top of them lay a saw, George's present.

'No,' she answered briefly, 'but perhaps it will come by the next post.'

'I don't think so,' I said flatly, 'I think she's forgotten.'

A feeling of dejection passed over me, like a gust of cold wind on a summer's day. The vision of my mother, bright, gay, distant and enchanting, as one might think of a fairy princess, trembled in the cool wind of criticism, trembled and became more remote. She had forgotten me and there was no more to be said. I had put my face forward to be kissed and there was nobody there. A fly buzzed ineffectively at the window pane and fell back discouraged among the flower pots on the window-sill. A rose, so crimson it was almost black, dropped its petals, one by one, in the sunlight, as if disenchanted with life.

'How dark it is in here!' Grandma remarked with a little sniff as she turned away from the sunlit window to serve the breakfast.

Lunchtime came. As I ran through the hall to wash my hands I noticed the doors of the Red room were half-open. Grandma was silhouetted against the window. She was motionless, thoughtful, looking at the floor. Her face was stony. Mr Brailes stood by the hearth, as usual dressed in his very black, pressed clerical clothes. He was saying in his thin, intellectual voice: 'Since you ask me, Mrs Porteous, I must tell you what I think. You are disinheriting your flesh and blood for an idea.'

Grandma remained immobile at the window. I did not hear what she replied, if she replied at all. The scene was flashed like a fragment of film upon my mind.

When I returned Mr Brailes was standing in the same position by the fireplace. Grandma with two small spots of red on her cheekbones was still at the window. I looked round for Mrs Brailes. He shook his head and extended his hand: 'Many happy returns, David. Mrs Brailes sends her love. But she isn't feeling well. She'll be here for tea.' He produced a parcel from behind his back and gave it to me. It was a xylophone and in the awkward silence that followed my thanks, I played with it.

Through its meaningless tinkle I heard the clang of the front door. A few moments later George Oldacre arrived.

'Hello, Brailes,' he said in his deep voice, and then turned to me: 'You know, Davey,' he said, smiling affectionately down at me, 'you already look older. I thought so when you came down this morning. I hope Mrs Farmer didn't make you sick with that piece of cake. I think she must have made it for you, because she knows I don't like it.'

At lunch my health was drunk in the sweet white wine Grandma kept for important occasions. Grandma was cold and thoughtful. She barely spoke to Mr Brailes and addressed her remarks to George who noticed nothing amiss. I knew she was not feeling well because several times during the meal she told me to hold my knife correctly and was visibly irritated when I relapsed. Mr Brailes was ill at ease, smiling brightly but thinly like a cold sun in a wintry sky. George had two helpings of duckling and then two platefuls of raspberries and cream. He, alone of us, enjoyed himself.

While the grown-ups had their coffee, I made what I called in my mind 'a reconnaissance' to see if everything was in order for the evening. It was, of course, as I knew it would be. The bonfire looked imposingly large. The bell tent was filled with chairs, a trestle table in pieces, cases of lemonade and beer, a packet of fireworks, some matches, and, lying on the floor, Mr Evans's Arab costume.

Satisfied, I bicycled slowly back to the wood. The air was drowsy and the leaves hung limply from their boughs. Sunlight, almost an enemy, penetrated the hidden recesses of the wood. As I free-wheeled slowly down a path, I saw the panamas of George and Mr Brailes bobbing about ahead of me. They were deep in conversation.

'You would think from what you say,' George said in a voice

unusually tense, 'that there was nothing to be said on the other side.'

Mr Brailes looked obliquely through his spectacles at the sky, which appeared serene, blue, here and there dotted with little white clouds, through the green of the trees: 'There *is* something, of course,' he replied in a tone of voice which sounded reedy and remote in the sylvan scene, 'there always is. But in this case there's very little.'

'It would, at least,' George said irritably, 'be a contribution to literary history.'

Mr Brailes laughed a laugh that was thin, unexpected and derisive. 'Oh, I see that.'

They walked on in silence for a few moments. George was clenching and unclenching his hands. 'You seem to think,' he burst out suddenly, 'or at least imply, that I am only interested in it for myself. What d'you expect me to do? Resign? Cut my own throat? I went through the war,' he continued, his voice quivering and his hand shaking, 'and I had enough of hardship then. Where was I when this job turned up? Living in an attic in Pimlico. You in the church have your vicarages ... I know, because I was the son of a clergyman.'

They had not heard the tyres of my bicycle behind them. I could not very well turn round without being discovered and I did not wish to be found out.

'I would not,' Mr Brailes said, again looking obliquely at the sky, as if by this process he might be able to stand back impartially from the question, 'I would not suggest that you resign. Why should you? It would be foolish. But there is the consideration. ... ' His voice implied irritation that he had been misunderstood, that George had exasperated him by missing an obvious distinction.

But I had put on my brakes and they were now drawing away from me. I turned back and went down another path but came on them again at the gate which led out of the wood into the lane.

'Oh no,' Mr Brailes was saying in his detached voice, as if

162

speaking of something which did not concern him, 'it's really nothing, simply nerves. It's good of you to enquire, Oldacre, but everything will be all right when the baby's born.'

George was relaxed once again. 'I thought,' he murmured courteously, 'that she seemed not quite herself the other night.'

This seemed to irritate Mr Brailes. 'Of course,' he said, catching sight of me and inclining his head to show that he had done so, 'she isn't well. She's far from well. But it's only a temporary thing, something that will pass. Eva will be herself again as soon as we have our new arrival.' And then, as if feeling he had said too much, he turned with a wave of his hand to each of us and walked away down the lane.

It was a hot, sultry summer afternoon and tea was laid on the lawn outside the dining-room window. A table had been set up for the food, chairs for the guests, and a large rug for myself. It had been thought proper to ask at least one child. But Grandma knew few people and there were only two eligible families in the district. Happily for me, as I did not take to other children, one family was away and the little girl from the other fell ill. So I found myself in my usual position, a child alone among adults. Mrs Brailes felt well enough to come, but not alone and was therefore accompanied by her husband. Aunt Emma was away at the sea.

Grandma sat in a great black straw hat tied with a ribbon under her chin, looking round at the scene before us with an appreciative but disenchanted air. She had had a sleep in the afternoon and had recovered from her ill-humour. George slowly puffed at his pipe and vaguely smiled at me from time to time. The sun was too much for his balding head and he went to fetch his Panama which he had left in the hall. Mr Brailes sat in a wicker chair occasionally glancing anxiously at his wife, patting her hand, making an inaudible witticism to her, or listening to one of hers, also inaudible. He laughed in a high pitched but loud way, as if he had a sense of the ridiculous, but not humour. Eva Brailes seemed in a busy dream. She once or twice bent down to the rug on which I was sitting and said something in a simpering voice which I could not understand. The rest of the time she spoke very fast and in a low voice to her husband or stared dreamily in front of her, a smile on her face.

The parlour-maid, trailing ribbons and lace from her apron, passed to and fro from the house with the tea things, preoccupied by her work. Only Nanna, laying out the things and pouring out the tea for Grandma, seemed to have a feeling for the occasion. She joked with me and nudged me to hand round the sandwiches. But Grandma frowned at these asides and she relapsed into silence. In the middle of all this Mr Evans appeared on the Red room steps with a large camera and unseen by everyone but Nanna and myself, took a photograph. The parlour-maid gave a sort of yelp when she realised she had been taken and hurried off to hide her indiscretion.

At last it was time to cut the cake. In the stillness of the afternoon it was possible, without difficulty, to light the candles. Everybody stood round as I drew back to blow them out with one breath. I was poised to do so when a little eddy of wind unexpectedly blew across the lawn and did my work for me.

'Oh, how unlucky!' Eva Brailes exclaimed. 'You should have blown them out yourself, David!'

I glanced round to see how the others had taken this omen. Nanna looked scared. George was faintly smiling and Grandma did not seem to have noticed.

'Oh, nonsense, dearest,' Mr Brailes said in the silence that followed, with a little, derisive laugh, 'it's luckier to have it blown out by the wind than to have to do it yourself. Certainly it is.'

Before any more could be said he thrust the knife into my hand and I was cutting the cake.

Perhaps because of this mishap, or perhaps because there was at that moment a rustling of wind in the trees, we did not hear the doorbell ring. When at last we did, the parlour-maid was too flustered to go and answer it. She simply lifted and put down the teapot and heaved her huge bosom. Nanna, who loved a crisis, ran forward to the Red room. She disappeared for a moment and returned with a smartly dressed woman leading a spaniel puppy on a lead.

The new arrival was dressed in a simple light brown frock and wore no hat or gloves. Her complexion was creamy, slightly tanned, healthy. Thin golden bracelets jangled at her wrists. She stood at the top of the Red room steps and surveyed us with a little smile, assured and poised. Sunlight glinted in her short, straight, dark hair. She might have been a model, the sort of person who had never stepped across the threshold of The Firs before.

'Madam,' Nanna called across the lawn, excited and incoherent, 'it's young Mrs Porteous.'

And then I knew it was Mother. I had not seen her often, not for two years. She was only a vision. But even in that brief moment, as she stood there, I had known her. I had recognised her by instinct.

I leapt from the rug, ran to her, seized her as she bent down to kiss me.

'Davey!' she exclaimed and her voice was calm and warm, 'How you've grown! You're quite a big boy.' There was just the trace of an accent, or was it that she spoke with more precision than a native born English woman? Somehow it gave her an air of command, as if she had thought out everything she was doing in advance.

I kissed her on the cheek and she kissed me on the forehead. As she straightened up she patted her hair to make sure that it had not been disarranged. The bracelets on her wrists jangled musically. I hung on to her left hand as she went round greeting everybody. It impeded her but she only smiled at me. I was a nuisance, her eyes seemed to say, but a darling nuisance. I was classed with the puppy with whom I kept getting entangled.

Everyone rose to their feet in an embarrassed way. Grandma stood very upright. She pecked Mother on the cheek and

Mother pecked her in the same way, murmuring as she did so, an excuse for her unexpected arrival. To this there was no reply.

'Mother,' I cried, 'look, your dog has got loose and is gobbling everybody's food.' Everyone had put their plates of birthday cake on the lawn when they got up and the dog with systematic and uninhibited greed was going round them. His ears flopped charmingly in the crumbs.

'It seems a very hungry dog,' Mr Brailes observed, trying but failing to snatch his plate away in time.

'He's so thorough,' his wife said with a little laugh.

Only George seemed to appreciate the dog's qualities. He whipped him up onto his lap, turned him on his back, and stroked the wriggling creature's hairless stomach. 'You're a naughty, greedy, ill-bred dog,' he whispered into the great ears, glancing up at Mother between caresses. The dog squirmed and smiled and licked its chops.

'But Davey,' Mother cried, 'it's not my dog. I forgot to tell you. He's your birthday present.'

I embraced Mother again. 'He's just what I would have wanted, absolutely.'

Everybody laughed at my pleasure. George let the dog go and it pursued its exploration of the lawn occasionally squatting down on its back legs to squirt surprisingly large puddles of clear, golden urine.

'He's called Buzz,' Mother pronounced.

'It suits him,' I said after thinking about it.

Everybody agreed.

'How large will he get?' Grandma asked a little frostily.

'He's a cocker,' George said reassuringly, 'so he won't get any bigger than mine.'

This made me think that George had never brought his dog to the house. Was it that Grandma did not want a dog?

'Grandma,' I asked, feeling the ground, 'do you like Buzz?'

Grandma sniffed before she answered and I noticed Mother watching her. 'I've always loved dogs,' she said at last, 'but

I'm thinking of the extra work for the maids. You will look after it, won't you, Davey?'

'Of course.'

'I'm sure you will,' Mother said with a little smile at Grandma and with something proprietary in her voice, 'I'm sure he will. Animals are so good for children.' She watched me as I dragged the dog between my legs and held it there.

'Why?' I asked.

Mother laughed gaily as if I had made a good joke. 'Of course they are, Davey. What a silly question. Children get confidence and responsibility from really looking after their pets.'

'We could train Buzz for shooting later on,' George remarked, taking the pipe from his mouth and watching a thin curl of smoke twist away into the air. He turned to Mother with a smile, as if he were asking her to help with the dog's training. He eyed her with keen appraisal and admiration.

'You will,' Mother said, turning from George to Grandma, but at the same time expressing I don't know how, that she was interested in everything he had to say. 'You will let him keep the animal?' The question seemed like a test.

Grandma sniffed slightly and pinched the bridge of her nose. 'Oh yes,' she replied with an indifference I had never noticed in her before, 'oh yes, if he learns to look after it.'

'That's all right then,' and Mother turned back to George, her bracelets jangling as she did so. She had sat down on a vacant chair and now Nanna came bustling up with a piece of cake and a cup of tea. 'Thank you so much,' Mother said with a dazzling smile. 'You must, of course be Nanna. I've heard in letters so much about you. In fact we have met before, haven't we?'

'Oh yes, madam,' Nanna said, well pleased, 'I could not forget you.'

'It's a long time ago now,' and the smile vanished from her face, 'I think Davey had forgotten me.'

'I hadn't,' I said stoutly, still playing with the dog.

'He remembers you every night in his prayers,' Nanna said.

Mother looked at me thoughtfully and then smiled in a reminiscent way. She gave Nanna a little sideways nod of her head which seemed to betoken dismissal and a sort of complicity.

For the next half hour I was too preoccupied with Buzz to notice much about the grown-ups. Buzz had the slightly puzzled expression of an animal whom the life-force had called into being without explanation. This had caused a melancholy, expressed by his drooping mouth, to settle on his friendly face, and there was a distant look of sadness in his brown eyes. Nevertheless he did not regard the situation as hopeless, for he consoled himself with pieces of birthday cake.

'We'll have great fun, you and I, won't we?' I whispered into his shaggy ear.

He gave me a quizzical look and went on with his eating.

The Brailes were the first to leave. Then George got up and bent over Mother's chair with what I can only describe as a courtly expression on his face. I thought for a moment he was going to kiss her hand, but if he ever had had the intention, he did not do it. Instead he made a few jocular remarks to me and went off down the wood with the Brailes.

Grandma and Mother were left seated side by side. The tea things and the rest of the chairs were cleared away. I lay on the rug and played with Buzz who had now recovered enough to bite my fingers with his sharp little teeth.

Grandma sat severely upright in her chair. Mother lay back in hers, crossed her legs, and lit a cigarette. She blew little rings of smoke into the air. The silence between the two women became oppressive. And then Mother said suddenly, as if on an impulse: 'Davey, I was wondering if you'd like to go for a holiday by the sea?'

'By the sea!' I exclaimed excitedly. I had never been to the sea.

'You and Nanna could come and stay with me for a few weeks. Would you like that?'

'Oh yes.'

Mother turned to Grandma and raised her eyebrows. Grandma sniffed and looked from Mother to me. But she said: 'He's never been to the sea.'

'All the more reason for him to go now, then.' Mother stubbed her cigarette on the ground with a gesture that implied that all was settled.

I anxiously looked at Grandma's face but I could not read what it signified. After a silence Grandma said: 'And where, Marie, are you staying?'

'Now, you mean?' Mother gave a little shrug of her shoulders. 'I came on an impulse. I have a suitcase in the hall. But I can easily find somewhere....'

'You want to stay here?' It was said ungraciously but, then, Mother's remarks had not been gracious either.

'That's just as you like.' The bracelets on Mother's wrists jangled.

'I only asked, because not so long ago you told me you did not want to stay here.'

'You know what the reasons then were.' She gave a faint little smile in Grandma's direction. 'Things have changed. Changed very much. I've been thinking things out. Perhaps it's time....' She paused and looked at me. 'But,' she went on, taking another cigarette and lighting it, 'we ought to have a talk.'

Grandma said nothing but rose to her feet. 'I shall make arrangements for your stay,' she said at last over her shoulder, as she made her way to the house.

When Grandma had gone Mother watched me with an affectionate, hazy interest. 'Leave the dog for a moment, Davey,' she said in a husky voice. 'Leave the dog and give your mother a hug.' She looked at me intently and when I hesitated, uncertain what was expected of me, added: 'After all, I am your mother. Even if I've been a rotten one to you.'

I got up shyly and stood by her chair. She leant forward

and put her arms round me. She kissed me with a sort of reverence on the forehead. She smelt fragrant with some scent – to me it seemed like roses. Then she sat back in her chair and held me at arm's length. 'You mustn't be shy of me, must you?' Her little laugh was infectious and I laughed too. 'Now let me see. Do you look more like your father or like me? Neither,' she said affectionately, 'but you do look like the photographs of Giorgio. Yes, definitely, you do look like Giorgio. Perhaps, who knows, you'll be a poet one day!'

'Don't I,' I stammered, 'look at all like Daddy?'

'Perhaps a little, darling.' Then she added; 'but to be truthful not very much.' Then seeing my disappointment she went on kindly. 'You will grow to be like him. And now tell me about yourself. Sit down on the rug and tell me all.'

I did not know what to say and was silent.

'Well?' she asked with a smile of what might have been disappointment. 'Well, how do you like it here? How have you been getting on with your work? Will you be all right for school?'

'I love it here,' I said simply, 'but you see, I don't know anywhere else. I am,' I went on in a burst of confidence, 'a bit frightened of going to school.'

She nodded her head and looked into my face as if to discover a weakness. 'Haven't you any friends of your own age?'

'Not many.'

'Don't you get lonely?'

'No,' I answered truthfully.

'Oh, but you must be really. It's because you've never had any boys of your own age that you don't miss them. You'll love the boys at school. Think of all the games you'll be able to play together.'

I suddenly felt tense and uncomfortable. 'I don't know,' I said awkwardly.

We went indoors and I helped Mother unpack her dressing case, which I suppose I did clumsily, for she seemed to be irritated with me.

I ran off to the night-nursery to change for the 'attack'. The puppy followed me everywhere, making little puddles wherever we paused. Nanna good-naturedly rolled up the rugs in the night-nursery and put down sheets of newspaper.

'Now, Davey,' she said admonishingly, 'I can't wipe up these messes all the time. You're Buzz's master and you must look after him. Go down to Cook and get him his dinner. That will give Grandma and Mrs Porteous time for a little talk. Don't interrupt, as they'll have lots to say to each other.'

Buzz was given a large meal on the verandah at the back door and left there. I went to the drawing-room impelled by curiosity to know what Grandma and Mother would be saying to each other. I paused, not without a pang of shame, at the door.

'You must understand, Marie,' Grandma was saying, 'that I've no legal rights. You must see this yourself. You are the only one with legal powers of any kind. But if I've no legal rights, I also have no obligations.'

'I see,' Mother replied quietly.

'So,' Grandma continued, her voice unusually strained, 'you may rest assured that I shall not stand in the way of anything you wish to do with the child. But please remember your responsibilities, if you decide to take them on.'

I entered the room and the conversation ended abruptly.

We had a cold supper and walked down to the tent in the field. There was no wind and the air was oppressive. Great masses of white cloud, forming and reforming into majestic shapes floated in melancholy detachment across the sky. Below them, and as if belonging to another universe, a wedge of grey vapour drifted away to the horizon, its edge like a finger spelling out the act of creation.

Outside the bell tent the trestle table had been laid with glasses. At one end on the grass was a crate of lemonade for the women, at the other a crate of beer for the men. The few fireworks were already placed in sand-filled flower pots. We waited in desultory silence. And then we heard the voices of the maids as they came down the drive. They were headed by Cook, her face suffused in a good-natured smile of anticipation. Then men, gardeners and villagers known to the household, also arrived but from the lower lawn, large, awkward, bucolic in their best clothes. George appeared with his gun which was to be used for starting the attack. He was talking to Mr Evans now dressed in his Arab costume. The latter had darkened his thin, Welsh face, and he looked as if he had just stepped out of a bazaar.

By this time the clouds had darkened, and Cook, always practical, whispered to George that he should start the proceedings without delay. Mr Courtenay had strolled up with his wife on his arm. She was dressed, as usual, with the stiffness and majesty of Queen Mary. Mr Courtenay placed her with the rest of the maids and she began to converse in her high pitched stilted voice with the housemaid about the likelihood of rain. Mr Courtenay went over to the fireworks and stood in front of them talking to nobody, his mouth pursed into an expression of importance, as if he were at a military review in charge of a cannon. Mother talked in a low voice, smiling as she did so, to George. Her beautifully regular features and her smooth complexion stood out among the party, as did the way she wore her perfectly fitting frock. Everyone glanced at her, fascinated and curious. This notice pleased rather than embarrassed her. George had his head on one side, intent on her and nothing else. Grandma stood abstracted and melancholy, looking at the scene, as it were from a distance. Nanna and Kitty bustled round filling up the glasses, cracking jokes with the men, under the supervision of Cook's all-seeing eyes.

It grew darker. Mr Evans melted away into the wood. His two sons, awkward lads in their early teens, skulked behind the tent waiting for me. At last George placed the cartridge (from which he had removed the shot) into the breech of his gun. The buzz of conversation died down. Ripples of giggling broke out from the maids as they waited for the report. George raised his gun to the darkening sky and fired. Unexpectedly it made a bang little louder than a pop gun. Mr Evans would never hear it in the wood – where I imagined him leaning against a tree smoking a cigarette. Cook made a sound like 'Pshaw', drew in her lips and wrinkled her forehead.

By this time I was over-excited. I stamped my foot in chagrin and exclaimed in a voice everyone could hear: 'You fool! I told you it wouldn't work, if you took the shot out. He'll never hear it.'

There was complete silence. Grandma looked grave. Nanna seemed horrified at the outburst. Cook shook her head and clicked her teeth. George looked round foolishly, and then at me with a surprised expression on his large face.

At that awkward moment for everyone Mother suddenly laughed. It was a light, silvery, infectious laugh. She looked at me and looked at George and went on laughing. The tension was broken. George smiled and everyone began to laugh as well.

A moment later, on instructions from George, Mr Courtenay sent off a rocket. It shot up into the sky, plumed out into a shower of stars with a loud report. The situation was saved. I ran to George and apologised. He smiled and shook his head. 'Run along quickly,' he said, 'before the Arab takes your stronghold.'

For the next hour or so Mr Evans, his sons and I crept about in the darkening wood, occasionally letting out blood-curdling yells and throwing our paper-bag bombs. It was an inconclusive battle till the end, when Mr Evans scored by hitting me on the head. The contents of the bag fell over my face and hair, momentarily blinding me. Mr Evans crept up, whisked me into his arms and carried me off as a prisoner. One of the sons was already out and the second one shared my fate. The stronghold fell. The attack was over.

We walked slowly through the wood in the direction of the bonfire, sweating profusely and recounting our adventures and mishaps like soldiers. The bonfire was flaring up under a new load of withered greenstuff and we could hear it crackling as we approached. Festivities were in full spate. The beer had loosened everyone's tongues. Cook and Nanna were raking chestnuts out of the fire. Grandma had already gone to bed and Mother was sitting on a chair talking to Mrs Courtenay. I told her everything that had happened as I drank Eiffel Tower lemonade and ate sugar-coated biscuits. She listened as she smoked a cigarette and looked into the gradually failing fire. George watched us both but did not speak, and drew slowly at his pipe with a meditative expression on his face. The firelight accentuated his baldness so that his brow seemed almost Socratic in size. He made a few polite remarks to the maids from time to time, but without much attention. Always his eyes returned to Mother's face and then back to mine. At the other end of the table Mr Evans had been given a chair and was resting his face in his hand. He drank swiftly from a great tankard of beer and chaffed the maids in the way he had done in the servants' hall in the past. As the fire died down he leant across to Catherine, the kitchen-maid, and whispered something in her ear. Her white, heavy face, with its rimless spectacles expressed nothing, but there was a faint smile on her thick lips.

The fireworks were let off with exclamations of 'Ooh' and 'Ah' as they lit the happy faces of the spectators. As the light from the last rocket died away Cook suggested my health which was drunk with shouts of 'Bravo'. Grandma's was then drunk, and finally a voice suggested 'young Mrs Porteous.' Nanna said warmly: 'Yes, yes!' As we finished there was a patter patter of rain on the leaves in the wood. Drops fell with a hiss into the fire. A moment later we were hurrying up the drive to the house.

George took Mother's arm and guided her. Half way up he bent over her. She gave her silvery laugh and shook her head. He paused for a moment remonstrating in a whisper and then they went on up together. They seemed to have forgotten me. But I was too flushed with the glory of the day to mind.

Buzz was asleep in the corner of the night-nursery on an old cushion. I was ashamed I had forgotten him and gave his head a kiss before getting into bed. He wriggled comfortably and feebly wagged his tail. Nanna came in and then I heard her steps on the stairs as she went down for a last chat in the kitchen. A few minutes later the door opened again. It was Mother. She bent over my bed and I was aware again of that fragrant, indefinable scent, the sense of being in the presence of beauty.

'You're not asleep then,' she whispered. 'Goodnight darling Davey. I'm glad you've had a happy day. Before long we shall be together by the sea.'

And then she seemed to float out of the room like a shadow cast by the night light. I dreamt quietly of the ceaseless ebb and flow of the tide breaking again and again softly on the silver sand, making an eternal rhythm.

CHAPTER FIFTEEN

Next morning I woke to a grey, lagging sky. A restless wind lashed at the flowers round the house, scattering their petals into whirling heaps on the lawn. Gusts of rain whipped at the windows with pointless ferocity, and trickled down the panes. Mother had breakfast in bed, so Grandma and I stood, as usual, by the dining-room window at breakfast time and looked out at the dismal scene. A little chestnut, newly planted, near the laurels, swayed to and fro, stripped of many of its leaves in an ecstatic struggle with the wind. It seemed determined to survive what the great pines behind it had resisted. They moved slowly, plaintively with rhythmic motion, their dark branches and needles creating a seething music of their own.

Grandma watched the scene as usual, but that day she did

not sigh. There was a hard determination in her look which took in what she saw but was not moved by it. She avoided taking my hand as if, overnight, I had become a stranger.

'Grandma,' I asked, 'why didn't you stay up last night till the "attack" was over?'

She looked down at me with an interested, detached expression. 'Did it go off all right?' This was the only enquiry she made although she knew it was the most important moment of the year to me.

I nodded. But I waited for her to answer my question.

'I did not feel very well,' she replied evasively, pinching the bridge of her nose and looking back out of the window. What she saw seemed to correspond with her thoughts for she added: 'I thought you had your mother and that was enough.' She gave a little shrug of her shoulders and, turning again, looked into my face.

I knew that it had been enough and, perhaps, it should not have been. I did not reply.

And so we stood in silence, watching the wind tear at the little tree as if it wished to destroy it.

The days which followed were overcast. The wind dropped but a grey cloud, warm and ominous, lay over the wood making a prison of it. Mother's presence created a tension which had not existed before. I dimly perceived it within myself – a tension between what was bright, new and enchanting on the one side, and my old loyalties to Grandma on the other. I even began to prefer to hear her step on the stairs to the night-nursery to that of Nanna. She came up late at night when I was half-asleep. She bent over me and whispered a few endearments in my ear. It was enough to send me to sleep. But my dreams were filled with restlessness and confusion. Through them all Mother's figure, like a triumphant shadow, as I had seen her pass the night light on my birthday, glided and floated, desirable, unattainable. Grandma no longer came to the night-nursery with her stories and I did not miss her.

Everyone, or almost everyone, except Grandma, felt as I did. Mother had enchanted us all. Nanna hung on every word she said and quietly stepped aside from being the first person in my life. George was captivated from the start. I saw him in the little dark hall bend over her hand and kiss it. There was an interested look on Mother's face, of surprise and gratification. She did not withdraw her hand. George's great face, as he turned away, expressed intense seriousness, as though he had been moved more than he wished. He seemed on the point of tears. He hurried to the door and slammed it behind him. Mother stood there for a few moments after the door had clanged to. She raised her eyebrows and shrugged her shoulders.

I was resolutely excluded from any conversations there may have been between Grandma and Mother. If I so much as approached the door, they ceased talking. I did not know what, if anything, they were discussing. It all happened within a few days, one might say within a few hours: Mother became the reality and Grandma the shadow in my life.

One evening as I was walking back from my bath along the passage I met Grandma. She stopped me and patted my head. She looked more serene than she had done in the past days.

'You're growing a big boy now, Davey,' she said, slightly ruffling my hair as she did so, 'and I want you to be able to stand on your own feet. All great and good men have been independent. They have fought for what they felt to be right.'

I did not know what to make of these unexpected remarks and did not reply.

'Your Grandfather,' she continued, 'fought his way to the top and that was why he was a great and good man. You must never let things pass you by. Never be just an onlooker. Your Grandfather wasn't. He was a great poet but he had not stood back from life. Every tree and flower fights for its existence. That is the law of life.' She paused, looked down at me thoughtfully, and then beckoned. I followed her into her shadowy bedroom. An almost imperceptible scent always hung

177

about it, faintly resembling that of the blacksmith's forge in the village. This was caused by Grandma's habit of singeing her hair with curling irons in the mornings. The walls were a dark but faded blue covered with reproductions of frescoes from Italian churches. There were several oak bookcases filled with Grandma's favourite authors, the Romantic poets and the poets of the seventeenth century. Grandma had moved from the big South bedroom when Giorgio died. This room, so cold and dark, was a sign of her mourning for him.

She went to a drawer in a chest of drawers and drew out a silver bound notebook which she handed to me.

'Davey, I want you to have this,' she explained, proferring it, and then enclosing the book and my hands in hers, 'it was Giorgio's and it should be yours.' She picked a book from the shelves. 'This is Giorgio's copy of *In Memoriam* with his notes. I want you to have these books so you always remember your grandfather.'

'Are you sure?' I asked, 'you want to give them to me?' I looked into her old face as though at another species of being.

She shut her eyes for a moment. 'Yes I do. I'm growing very old, Davey. These things aren't really mine. I don't need them any more, although I still love them. They should be yours. Some of them at least. When you're as old as I am you want to lighten the burden of possessions. I suppose it is,' she went on slowly, rubbing her forehead with her fingers, 'one wants to go on one's way without too much luggage.' She smiled a little faint, sad smile which I could not interpret.

'I shall look after them very carefully, Grandma,' I said proudly, 'they're my best treasures.'

'That's right,' she said absently as if she had forgotten the previous part of the conversation and expected me to go.

'May I take them to the sea?' I asked.

'Of course. I should like to think that you'll keep them by you all the time, especially after I've gone.'

I kissed her goodnight, thanked her again and went to the door. As I passed out I looked over my shoulder. She was watching me reminiscently, almost as if at a person she had once known, and now would know no longer.

I showed my trophies to Mother in the night-nursery when she came to kiss me goodnight. They lay on the table beside the bed and she idly turned the pages of the notebook.

'I suppose she gave them to you,' she said without much interest in her voice, 'because you're going to the sea. You know we leave the day after tomorrow.'

'The day after tomorrow! No, Grandma said nothing about it.'

'You could use the notebook. There are a lot of blank pages.'

'Are we going by train?' I asked eagerly.

'No, by car with Mr Courtenay.' She paused for a moment and read out in her clear Gallic voice with the slightest touch of mockery: ' "A withered bud upon the bough..." I suppose he couldn't think what to rhyme with bough. But, after all there is "sough" of the wind, and "allow"! "The crimson petals shed one by one. The flower is...." It's all very sad,' she commented petulantly, 'I don't know why poets have to write about melancholy things.'

'I suppose they think things are sad,' I remarked.

She looked at me sharply. 'You shouldn't be worrying yourself about such things at your age. Anyway,' she went on, 'however much poets wail there's nothing to be done about it.' She straightened out the top sheet and smoothed it with her hand. 'There are no solutions.' She bent down and kissed me lightly on the forehead.

I lay awake for a long time as the dusk filtered in at the window, casting faint shadow after shadow, and making the night light shine every minute more brightly. The night light stood at the far and dark end of the room on Nanna's dressing-table. The air was filled with the cool scent of rain. A fly, as if reviving unexpectedly from a deep sleep, buzzed intermittently at the window. A few late birds twittered and fell silent. I thought of the 'withered bud' and the falling petals. Something was dying, but something was being born. Buzz, in his corner, stretched himself and whimpered a little in his dreams.

CHAPTER SIXTEEN

It was a morning of summer serenity when we set out for Bathampton. The old, highly-polished Austin drove up to the door after breakfast. It glinted in the sunlight. Mr Courtenay's gaiters shone almost as brightly as he creaked up to the house for the luggage. There was no wind and you could hear the murmur of bees and flies. High up in the pines the inevitable wood pigeon crooned – perhaps, who knows, of other summer days.

The great old-fashioned trunk was carried out to the rack at the back of the car and carefully tied on, together with my bicycle and half a dozen other 'bits and pieces' as Nanna called them. She pretended that they were items she would need on the journey or on arrival. Actually they were things she had forgotten to put into the trunk or had had second thoughts about.

I said good-bye to everybody as if I was going to the ends of the earth rather than a mere seventy miles. Cook stood at the kitchen window to wave us on our way. Grandma, a little pensive and sad, but not as sad as I expected, stood in the shadow of the porch. She slipped a ten shilling note into my hand as she bent to kiss me and said it was to be spent on a spade and a toy boat.

George, who had decided the night before to accompany us, climbed in at the back with Mother and Nanna. I sat in the front with Buzz. We were about to start and Mr Courtenay had cranked the engine, when there was a rapping on one of the dormer windows. I looked up and saw Fanny, the housemaid, leaning out waving a duster. Behind her I could see the smiling ugly face of Kitty. And then we were off.

It seemed a long journey and Buzz slept all the way. I did not listen to what they were saying at the back but kept my attention on the dashboard, the road ahead and Mr Court-enay's serious face. For the first half of the journey he spoke all the time as he carefully steered the Austin through the green countryside, now and again changing gear with what I thought was marvellous dexterity. He pointed out the boundaries of the counties as if they were national frontiers. This gave me the feeling that I was passing into an alien world, a world in which The Firs would be as distant as the moon.

We passed some workmen laying drainpipes. Mr Courtenay remarked enigmatically: 'I'm glad Mr Oldacre stops at 'ome and goes up to the 'ouse.'

'Why, d'you think Grandma will be lonely while we're away?'

Mr Courtenay paused before replying. 'I was thinking,' he said meditatively, 'of the cesspit tank.'

'Oh?'

'It's one of them new tanks,' Mr Courtenay pronounced, 'and it works by the sewage a-eating of itself.'

'Does it?' I asked, considerably surprised.

'The males eat up the female germs, that's 'ow it works.'

'But what...?' I began.

'It's like this, see, if there isn't a gentleman to use the W.C. it don't work.'

'But what happened before Mr Oldacre came. Was I...?'

Mr Courtenay had his eyes on the road and he did not remove them for a moment to shake his head. 'It didn't work, that was the trouble. That's the long and short on it. It needs,' and he paused thoughtfully, 'an hadult.' He pronounced the last word almost in a whisper, so that those at the back should not hear.

It was years before I discovered by accident that all this was a fantasy.

'I forgot,' I blurted out suddenly, 'to say good-bye to Mr Evans.'

Mr Courtenay considered. 'I suppose you don't see 'im so often nowadays?' He frowned slightly as he waited for my answer.

'I suppose I don't,' I said thoughtfully, 'he doesn't come into the servants' hall now.'

'No,' Mr Courtenay said gloomily.

'All the same that's no reason for not saying good-bye.'

'I shouldn't worry,' he said easily, 'and I can say good-bye for you. Not that I see much of him myself nowadays.'

From behind I could hear the rumble of George's voice. Puffs of smoke from his pipe drifted across to the front seat. He was sitting between the two women and Nanna was squashed by his great bulk into one corner while he talked to Mother.

'Beauty,' I heard him say, 'is all that matters.'

'Surely,' Mother said playfully, as if she was laughing at him, 'there are other things?'

'Other things? You mean truth and goodness? Of course they exist. They are. They are facts. But truth and goodness are as nothing compared to beauty. The whole Universe is created by an artist who loves beauty, and beauty alone. Truth and goodness are mere playthings in comparison, invented by man himself.'

'You may be right,' Mother said vaguely, 'but I sometimes wonder if beauty has any real existence. Perhaps it, too, is an invention of man.'

'No,' George said decisively, 'I can't believe that. You only have to look out of the window to see that I'm right. Look at the green of those trees and the blue haze on the horizon.'

'Oh, Mr Oldacre,' Mother said in an altered tone, 'you've turned round so much you're squashing Nanna. She's hardly got any room at all.'

'I'm so sorry,' he murmured apologetically, shifting about in his seat.

'You're now squashing me,' Mother said with a little silvery laugh.

'I'm all right, sir,' Nanna said almost at the same time, 'you come this way a bit and then you'll give Mrs Porteous more room.'

'I can see we should have had Master Davey at the back. I'm too big.' A moment later he had returned to what he had been saying before. 'Beauty is not the same as prettiness. There's something tragic, providential, godlike in beauty. That's why beautiful women are so dangerous.'

Nanna gave a sort of snort, either because she had once again been pushed into the corner or because she felt bound to protest against this view.

'Yes,' he continued, busy with matches at his pipe and ignoring the interruption, 'it's better for a man to have to deal with a pretty woman rather than a beautiful one. Beauty is elemental and who can stand up to nature?'

'And what,' Mother asked, bored with the subject, 'about handsome men?'

'Handsome men,' George responded, as if he had not thought about it, 'they're like pretty women, I suppose. Men are not elemental like women. Women are nearer to nature. What's this place?' he asked, breaking off.

'Bathampton, sir,' Mr Courtenay said gravely.

'Bathampton?' George considered. 'It's very ugly. I had no idea it was such an ugly place.'

'This is only the outskirts,' Mother said irritably, 'these are rows of cheap boarding houses.'

'I suppose so,' he answered vaguely, continuing to lean forward. 'But, Davey, it won't be such an ugly place where you're going.'

We passed a wide green in front of the sea and stopped in front of a smart terrace of Regency houses.

'There you are,' George said, leaning across Mother and poking his head out of the window, a broad grin on his face, 'charming houses, small and a bit windy, I suppose, but charming. I like the variegated brick and the porches. They're not beautiful,' he commented, putting his head back inside the car and smiling at Mother, 'but they're very pretty.'

'I'm glad you like Bathampton after all,' Mother said dryly.

'Oh, I like it here very much.'

'Well, if you'll open the door . . .'

The sun beat fiercely on the blue-green sea. A smartish breeze flapped at the deck chairs and billowed in the net curtains of the little houses. The sash windows rattled merrily. There was a smell of salt water and fish.

I jumped out of the car with Buzz and was greeted on the steps of the porch by a diminutive maid. She wore a long apron and was dusting her hands as though she had come straight from the kitchen. 'Truth to tell,' she said in a hoarse little voice, running to the car and taking in everything, Nanna, George, Mr Courtenay, and then Buzz and myself, with a few brisk blinks, 'I was in the middle of the suet puddin'. I hope you like that, Davey? You look well, Madam.'

'While we get the things inside,' Mother shouted to me, 'you go on a round of exploration.'

Like the maid, the house was neat and diminutive. The stairs were hung with prints of flower sellers and the curtains were made of gay chintzes. Everything, in fact, was pretty, neat and bright. At the back was a tiny, sunless garden, but the drawing-room on the first floor looked over the Green and on to the sea. There was a dim basement kitchen and a maids' sitting-room behind an area surrounded by ornamental railings. My bicycle leant against these railings, as if I had always lived there. Buzz ran out of the back door and seemed fascinated by the dark garden.

'Oh, he's a very good boy,' I could hear Nanna's voice in the kitchen and the portentous creak of Mr Courtenay's gaiters. Upstairs George had sunk into an armchair and was sipping a glass of sherry. He gave me a vague, benevolent smile as I entered. 'Well, how do you like it here?' he asked in his low, kindly voice, looking vaguely at the little mantelpiece.

I stood at the window and looked through the neat net curtains across the Green to the shining sea. Children in groups, younger than myself and dressed in coloured waders, were making their way across the grass to the houses for lunch. They chatted to each other as they walked along, waving spades and buckets as they did so. Behind them there were nurses in uniform, walking in pairs, deep in conversation, but occasionally shooting sharp glances at their charges. In the distance, by a group of stunted, wind-blown firs, a huddle of donkeys shifted their hooves. The donkey man sat at the foot of a tree and munched a sandwich. A ragged boy led one of the donkeys round in a circle on the grass, a diminutive little girl clutching the saddle. 'Why can't we have lunch in the hut?' a little voice, out of sight, below the window, whined plaintively. 'I've already told you, Susan, we're having lunch in the house today,' a weary adult voice replied. There was the sound of a slight scuffle and the child was dragged wailing indoors. The front door slammed and the wailing ceased abruptly.

'There are donkeys on the green,' I said, turning from the window, as from a spectacle performed by actors, and sat down beside George.

'Are there?' he asked vaguely, thinking of something else. 'After lunch I'll stand you a ride.'

'Thank you very much,' I said and jumped up again to the window to look for the huts. I could see their green roofs against the sea. 'D'you think Mother has a hut?' I asked.

'I expect so, Davey,' he answered and put his large hand on mine reassuringly.

'One thing,' Mother said briskly, coming into the room and taking a cigarette from the mantelpiece, 'there's plenty of children for Davey.'

We could hear their voices as they crossed the road to the houses. They trailed tin spades on the tarmac. The spanking breeze from the sea rattled the sash windows and set the pulley handles dancing.

'They're much younger than me,' I pointed out.

'The ones of your age are at school,' Mother said, looking at me and blowing a cloud of smoke into the air.

'I suppose so,' George ruminated, as if he had only just thought of it.

'Davey!' Mother suddenly exclaimed, 'don't put your dirty shoes on the clean covers.'

I looked guiltily at the newly laundered chintzes. Luckily my shoes were not dirty and had not made a mark.

'Where's Buzz?' I asked suddenly.

'He's very happy in the garden. He can do no harm there. Jessie is giving him a meal.'

A silvery gong sounded from the hall and we made our way down the little staircase to the dining-room. As we did so the maid was disappearing into the basement, having deposited the food on a sideboard. The dining-room was another neat little room furnished with a small round table and spindly little chairs. When George sat down, it looked as if he must crush his chair beneath him. The wallpaper, the curtains and the dinner service were all Willow pattern which created an atmosphere of elegance and uniformity, as if one had entered a carefully stylized doll's house.

'Ah, Willow pattern,' George said, looking round with a smile, 'I did not know you could get wallpaper and curtains. It makes,' he went on, turning to me, 'one feel one is in China.'

Mother did not reply but served the meal from a hot-plate on the sideboard, while Nanna handed it round. Then we all sat down together. From the basement we could hear Mr Courtenay conversing in measured tones. The food was plainer than at The Firs but each dish was prettily dressed.

After the first course Mother tinkled a little bell. The maid appeared from the basement to change the dishes. Nanna sat uncomfortably in her chair till Mother said deftly: 'Jessie, Nanna will collect the plates while you fetch the pudding.' Nanna jumped up and did as she had been told.

'Well,' Mother said as she watched George eat his pudding,

with an amused expression on her face, 'are you still thinking of truth and beauty?'

George looked up and smiled roguishly, his mouth full. 'No, I wasn't,' he admitted, 'the suet pudding is too good. But,' he went on with mock gallantry, 'I am thinking of beauty now.' He stretched out his hand to take hers. But as there was no response, he withdrew it. Mother did not look reproving but continued to watch him with an enigmatic expression. The light from the window fell on her perfectly shaped face. Her skin was the texture of a nectarine. Her lips were parted. She looked cool and poised. This was her world and she was its mistress.

Nanna cleared away the plates. Downstairs there was a clatter as the washing up began. The sea breeze as briskly slapped at the house. The sun poured down outside. George slowly filled his pipe, unaware that he was in a world which did not suit him, where his bulk, his untidy hair, his frayed shirts and the slow train of his rambling thoughts were out of place.

Outside on the pavement there came the sound of a fiddle, followed by a slight tapping sound. A vexed expression crossed Mother's face.

'There's that old fiddler again,' she said, 'I had forgotten it was Thursday.'

He was playing a tune I had never heard and have never heard since. It was curiously incongruous in front of those neat little houses. It was plaintive, melancholy, expressive of the sadness of existence. And yet it had a dance-like, almost jaunty rhythm behind it, as if it had originally been intended to be gay.

'He will play that wailing thing,' Mother exclaimed, 'Davey, will you give him a few pennies and tell him to move on?' She snapped open her handbag which was lying by her chair and I was despatched with the money.

I hesitated for a few moments on the steps under the white porch. The fiddler was an old man with a wooden leg. He was wearing dirty clothes and a cloth cap. He had a blotched red face with an untidy white moustache which drooped over his lips. He had small, dark eyes, sharp and cunning, red-rimmed like a ferret's – all totally at variance with the tune he was scraping from his fiddle. As I approached he stopped playing and put out a scrawny hand, tucking the bow under his arm.

'Yer new 'ere?' he asked in a disagreeable, hoarse voice, giving me an inquisitive look.

I nodded as I handed him the pennies. 'They're from my mother,' I explained.

'To get me to move on?' He shifted the weight from his stump and it made a soft tap-tap on the pavement. He looked me up and down as a weasel might look at a rabbit. 'Mother, eh? I knew she was married but I didn't know she 'ad a son.' He smiled, as if he found it funny and displayed a row of brown, broken teeth. 'I suppose,' he continued, grinning into my face, 'yer'd like to see me unstrap me leg. They always do. But, yer see, I always charge sixpence for that. That's not too much is it for the likes of you?' He began to roll up his trousers, as if he might show me then and there. I suppose I could not hide my disgust, for he suddenly laughed and turned away. He tapped his way up the street without looking round. When I got back to the house, I could hear the plaintive strains of his unearthly tune in the distance.

After coffee in the drawing-room Mother said: 'Now, Davey, you and Mr Oldacre go for a walk along the Promenade. And don't take Buzz till he's more at home. I have some business letters to write.'

George raised his eyebrows. 'Do you do all your business?'

'Who else?' she asked sarcastically.

George watched me have my donkey ride. He leant against a tree and slowly puffed at his pipe. Then we strolled along the yellow-paved promenade towards the jetty. The tide was out and on the long stretches of sand children were digging castles and damming streams. Nurses sat in front of green huts knitting and gossiping. Near the jetty end the beach was less select. Canvas huts flapped in the wind, older members of families sat in the shade of breakwaters and watched games of beach cricket or uncorked thermoses of tea. There was a tall flagstaff on the jetty hung with various weather symbols which neither I nor George understood. Beyond it was the mouth of a swiftly flowing river, green and flecked with white foam. A small fishing smack chugged upstream, leaving behind it a smudge of black smoke and the smell of fish. The green behind the jetty at this part of the town was much wider and was flanked with rows of ugly redbrick boarding houses.

'I suppose,' I said timidly to George, 'I won't see you for a long time.'

George stopped in his tracks and looked down at me. He took the pipe out of his mouth, put it back again, and then held it in his hand. 'I'm thinking of buying a second-hand car. And then I shall come and see you often. Perhaps,' he went on, as if the idea gave him pleasure, 'you'll be able to drive back with me and stay at the cottage, for a night.'

'I should like to do that,' I said but without much conviction. The Firs seemed another world.

'It won't be long before you're home again anyway.' He gave me a long look of curiosity and added: 'It's only a visit.'

'I know.' The word 'home' had come as a cold hand at my heart.

We strolled back along the promenade. I noticed that other strollers eyed George with interest and a little amusement. He was wearing a large brimmed panama hat, the front of which had blown up in the breeze and this made him look incongruously like a deep-sea fisherman. He walked very slowly and unself-consciously smoking his pipe and enjoying everything going on around him.

As for myself I was both self-conscious and ill at ease. The trippers, the wide sands, the shout of the players, the spanking breeze which rattled the doors of the huts, and sent convulsions over the grass on the Green, the cry of a fractious child – all this was contrasted in my mind with the silence and the melancholy peace of The Firs.

'I like,' George said with mock seriousness and staring amusedly at some holiday makers eating ice cream cornets, 'to get away and see a bit of real life. I love the exuberance of it.' And then realising that I would not understand he added: 'The vitality, the enjoyment of it all. You and I, Davey, have been born into the wrong world. That's where the future lies –' he pointed at the cornet eaters – 'not with us. It's the vulgarians who have it everytime. We're like shallow flutes compared to a brass band. Ah well, let's get back to tea.'

After tea it was time for the car to leave. I stood on the porch with Nanna and Mother to wave good-bye. Buzz escaped from the garden and barked at the wind. George put his head out of the window. Suddenly, on an impulse, he blew Mother a kiss. His great face, usually so passive, looked almost tragic. A momentary spasm of irritation seized me.

I had my supper, alone, waited on by Nanna, in the little Willow-patterned dining-room. Mother and Nanna kissed me goodnight in the night-nursery and I fell into a deep sleep.

It had grown almost dark when I awoke with a start. I thought I had heard the old fiddler's music and the stump of his wooden leg on the stairs. The night-nursery was very quiet, filling with shadows as the light ebbed from it like a tide from a forsaken cavern. I sat up in bed startled and lonely. Everything except Nanna's pink dressing gown, hanging behind the door, was unfamiliar. I crept to the window and looked out. I patted Buzz but he turned irritably in his sleep.

Below me was the narrow patch of neglected garden, beyond it at right angles a narrow unmetalled lane. Lights were beginning to go on in the town, bright and comfortless, unlike the paraffin lamps to which I was accustomed. A cat prowled along one of the garden walls and somewhere in the shadows another wailed to it. A gull mewed, as it circled round the chimneys.

CHAPTER SEVENTEEN

And so a new life began. It centred round the neat little house in which Buzz and I seemed to be intruders. But there was also the hut on the beach where we often had picnics. A little table would be set up, chairs arranged, and just at the right moment Jessie would appear with a hamper.

Yet it was not really the house that was at the centre of things but Mother, whose orderliness and practicability it faithfully reflected. The three of us revolved round her like satellites round a moon. We were devoted slaves. A lesser woman might have had qualms in introducing Nanna into the household. There might well have been jealousies. But Nanna had sized Jessie up and, sure enough, she and Jessie became firm friends, united in their desire to please Mother.

Jessie did not make much impression on me. She was not particularly interested in children whom she regarded in a detached way. She had made an unfortunate marriage. Her husband, so I gathered, had beaten her and she had left him. She had an indomitable cockney spirit. She used to hum, and sometimes sing, in her hoarse little voice, music hall tunes. I would hear them rising up from the semi-darkness of her basement. She loved Mother and that was enough for her.

I was a worshipper of Mother, too. I suppose her strong character played a part in my subjection. But, looking back, I think it was also her beauty and her poise. You could not but admire. I had seen much natural beauty, but not before in human form. By comparison Grandma was austere and unattractive. Nanna and the rest were made in a different mould, capable indeed of inspiring affection, but incapable of arousing that feeling of delight which seemed to be Mother's prerogative. Mother was to me like a princess from fairyland.

I was not quite at ease in her presence, but who is before a princess? To stand in her bedroom and look at the glittering dressing-table, with its three-cornered mirror, its hand mirrors, its silver-backed brushes, its combs; to smell the scent of the perfumes and powders, in their boxes, bottles and jars; to watch Mother as she lay in bed, drinking her breakfast coffee – was to be in an unreal world I had not known before.

Perhaps because it was an unreal world, or perhaps for some other reason, I did not feel that I belonged. I did not think, insofar as I thought of it at all, that the little house could become my home, even temporarily, or could be compared in any way to The Firs. But then, I suppose, The Firs was part of me and I was part of The Firs.

Perhaps it was that I was an alien on the beach. I was older than the other children but they did not respect me for that. On the contrary, I was regarded as a freak who should have been, and was not, at school. But I learnt to swim, to dive for plates in the murky, salt water, and later, to ride, after a fashion, on horses from a riding school. But nothing pleased me, or seemed to please me, unless it also pleased Mother. She did everything for me that a mother should do for her son. She arranged my life precisely, in accordance with the way she thought I ought to grow up. She was like a deft gardener faced with a sickly plant who does not shirk using a pruning hook.

'Davey, you must grow into a man.' She would pause, looking into my face as if to see there the man I should be. I made no resistance. I wanted precisely what she wanted. The question was whether I was capable of attaining the image. 'Davey, you must be like your father, a brave soldier. And you must be tidier, Davey, smart, like men should be. Look, your stockings are hanging down and you've scuffed the toes of your shoes. You know you won't have Nanna to look after you always. Swim out further into the sea, Davey. Every day, a little further. And then you'll grow into a strong man. When you're older you must learn to take the tickets at the theatre, to know about wine, to be able to wait on a woman.'

These admonitions were given from time to time when Mother and I were alone. I looked forward to them as an expression of her love for me, but I also dreaded them. I felt I could not attain what she wanted. I, who was awkward and shy, could never be what she expected. She would speak in a low, intense voice as if willing me to do what she wanted. On these occasions I used to notice, with another part of my mind, that her intonation and accent, even some of her phraseology, became more French. If it is true that you can become what you want to be by the willing of it, then I suppose there must have been an inner resistance to her of which I was unaware. But, more likely, there was a force in me which could not be resisted, a force which was determined to express itself as it would, and not as anyone else wished – even as I consciously wished.

And sometimes she would laugh at me. 'You look so funny, Davey, with your hair all over the place,' she would exclaim with a smile. And, 'Really, Davey, you look like an urchin from the street!' And, 'Don't dream so much, Davey. Didn't you hear what I said? You always seem to be thinking of something else.'

One night, after putting aside Grimm's *Fairy Tales*, which she had been reading to me in bed, I said: 'Mother, haven't you got any brothers and sisters?'

She was sitting on the bed and the light from the window fell on her dark hair. She shook her head.

'And your father?'

Again she shook her head. 'He was killed by the Germans during the war.'

'He was my grandfather,' I said, tracing with my forefinger the pattern on the quilt.

'He was,' she explained, 'the mayor of the town. He was taken as a hostage and shot.'

'He was very brave to die like that.'

She shrugged her shoulders slightly. 'Yes,' she said, 'he was brave. But what else was there to do? He was obliged by the circumstances to be brave. That is how it is, Davey, you don't have to choose to be brave. You have to be brave, because there is something round the corner which will force you. I had to be brave, too. After all, I was his daughter.'

'And your mother?'

She shrugged her shoulders more emphatically and made a little grimace. 'Mother,' she said, looking out of the night-nursery window at the waste of roof tops behind the house, 'it was not a tragedy for her. She did not suffer. Perhaps she could not suffer. She was not made like that. She married again. She's living somewhere in the south of France, I think.'

'With her new husband?'

'Oh,' Mother exclaimed, 'he's not as new as all that. This was a long time ago. She took no interest in me. But, then,' she shrugged again, 'I see what I could not see at the time, that life has to go on. Still, I do not want to see her again.'

'She was English?'

'Of course. Otherwise, how should I speak English so well? She was not from a good family, I think – from the north of England, somewhere. She hated Belgium.'

'How did she meet your father, then?'

'I was always told,' she replied with a little sniff, as if the truth did not matter, 'that her father was a business man who came to Belgium on visits and wanted his daughter taught French. And that,' she concluded, 'is how I'm here and how you are, too.' She began pushing me down into bed and tucking up the bedclothes. 'Now go to sleep and think no more about it. The past is over and nothing can be done about it.'

'But tell me again,' I said, playing for time, 'how you met Daddy.'

'No more now Davey. You've heard it all before. We met at a dance in the village when I was very young. He was handsome in his uniform. We were married in the village church very quietly, because Father was dead and Mother didn't much care.'

'And how was he killed?'

'You know quite well, Davey, I've never been able to find out. It was during the last German offensive.'

'And did,' I asked boldly, pressing my head into the pillow, 'Grandma go to the wedding?'

'No,' she replied shortly, 'she didn't, because she didn't know of the marriage till your father was dead.'

I considered this. Her hand was on the door. Before she had time to open it I put another question. 'And when did she know I had been born?'

'Why,' Mother demanded, 'do you ask that?'

'I just wondered.'

'I wrote to her about you and the marriage at the same time.'

'I see.'

Mother was struck by the tone of my voice and paused. 'What do you mean? You're far too young to be raking over these things from the past.'

'I don't know,' I said, 'but it makes me understand Grandma better.'

'It was her idea that you went to The Firs,' she said dryly. 'Once,' she continued, 'she was convinced of the facts.' She paused, looking back at me from the door, and said: 'I was so young. I agreed. I thought it was for the best. I thought I had to start again.'

'Do you think that's why,' I asked, considering the matter seriously, 'Grandma wants to leave The Firs to the nation in memory of Giorgio?'

Mother started. 'What?' she demanded.

'That's what I think she wants and means to do.'

'But what about you?' Mother asked again, her voice quivering.

'Perhaps she feels I don't quite belong to her, not quite.'

'The old b.!' She stopped herself just in time. 'But how,' she asked, 'do you know all this?'

'From what I've heard,' I said evasively, 'and other things too.'

'Have you told anybody?'

'Not exactly, except Cook.'

'And what did she say?' Mother asked shrewdly.

'She pretended not to know about it. But I'm sure she did.'

Mother's hand trembled on the door handle. 'Now you really must settle down,' she said briefly and went out. I heard her make her way to the basement instead of to the drawing-room, as was her usual custom. And then she came up again with Nanna.

Every Thursday at lunch time the old fiddler stumped up to the front of the house and played his haunting lament. And I was always sent out with a few coppers to send him away. I dreaded his coming and yet looked forward to it. It was, I suppose, the one thing of beauty I knew in my life at Bathampton. There were only the few stunted trees on the green. There was no garden, and such flowers as Mother had, were bought at a florist's. The beach was frankly ugly and utilitarian, as was the rest of the town away from our terrace. I seldom visited the river's mouth where the fishing boats sent smudges of smoke the colour of charcoal low over the waves. Our house was prettily symetrical but it lacked the atmosphere of melancholy which I had grown used to. I missed the slow movement and the soughing of the pines, the varied greenery of the little wood, the continuous call of the pigeons in the trees. Even the sky at Bathampton was featureless. It seemed to me to be either bright and empty or a uniform grey. In fact I was already a little homesick.

And then came what, subconsciously, I had been expecting – a letter from Grandma. It described the happenings at The Firs, how a hare had come to the birdbath, how some small owls had fallen down the chimney, how a jay had been shot, nobody knew by whom, at the bottom of the wood. It continued:

You are now growing up, Davey, and I think it time to say

what has been in my mind for a long time. I am growing old and muddly, not the sort of person to look after a growing boy properly. I have come to the conclusion that you ought now to live with your mother who has her life before her and wants to have you. She will be more use to you than a poor old Grandma. It is, after all, only right that you should be at her side, both for your sake and hers. . . .

I received this letter at breakfast and read it over and over again. Mother had not yet come down so I had a long time to think about it. I did not want to be parted from Mother but I also did not want to be parted from The Firs. I did not know what I wanted. I took the letter up to Mother. She was lying in bed, drinking her coffee. She was dressed in a white quilted bed jacket, which admirably displayed the olive colour of her skin. Her black hair, always so short, tidy and smart, was swept back from her face on to the pillow. She gave me a brief smile as I entered, put down her coffee cup and cursorily read the letter.

'I got the same sort of thing myself,' she said, taking up her cup of coffee once more. 'I think,' she continued, looking at me over the cup, 'that she had made up her mind before we left.'

'But . . .'

'Yes?'

'Will I never go back to The Firs?' As I said this I watched the lights play among the bottles and looking-glasses on the dressing-table. The air in the room was faintly scented by a perfume from an open jar. Outside the sun chased across the Green. I could hear the voices of children on the beach, borne on the wind. The bedroom was Mother's citadel, in which her personality, and hers alone, could exist. It was a prison to which, from the fact that I was her child and no-one else's, I belonged. I was as much a part of it, as the brushes on the table.

Mother gave her silvery laugh. 'You shall, if you want to.' There was a little irritation in her voice. Her eyes fell on

Grandma's letter which lay on the blue silk eiderdown. She gave it a slow pensive stare and I realised that she was obscurely jealous of Grandma. I should have felt pleased, but I felt instead that I was being forced into an attitude I did not, and could not, take up. Resentment, like the touch of cold air on a warm day, made me stiffen. It was not me she wanted, but her son, the idea not the reality.

And, yet, how did I know? It was a momentary guess, perceived by its effect on me, but not understood. Even now, looking back, when the affair is like the memory of a scene in a play, the nuances simplified by the passage of time, I do not know the truth, if there is such a thing as truth. Is it likely that Mother, with her realistic attitude to life, could make so elementary a mistake as to confuse a conception with the reality? Perhaps, after all, it was only a misunderstanding, such as happens when people of different languages try to converse. But here there was a barrier not only of kind but of age as well.

'Grandma says in her letter to me that you may pay her visits,' Mother continued after a pause. The stilted phrase 'pay her visits' was due, I think, to her Belgian origins and was not calculated to cause me pain.

'But what about all the people there? Won't I see them for more than a few days at a time?'

'You'll be most of the time at school. And, you know, the holidays are not all that long.'

'And what about George?'

Mother smiled to herself. 'When he has his car, I expect he will come down quite often.'

'I suppose he will,' I said dubiously.

Mother rearranged the folds in her bed-jacket and ran her tapering fingers through her black hair. 'You are fond of him?' she asked curiously with a little sound of interrogation at the end of the sentence which was characteristic of her and which made her questions seem more formidable than they were.

'Yes,' I said uncertainly, never having probed the matter in my mind, 'I think I am. Yes, I think I am.'

'I suppose,' she said dreamily, her eyes fixed on the dressing-table, 'he will go on with his job at The Firs?'

'I think he'll look after the papers when Grandma dies.'

'An extraordinary arrangement,' Mother remarked, looking down at her nails with a slight frown. When she raised her head, it was to scrutinize my face with something like exasperation. 'It's a pity,' she said more to herself than to me, 'that you are so young, so detached, so ...' She could not find the word. She took my hand in hers. 'Davey,' she went on as if she was speaking of an illness, 'you're like someone who stands at the brink of the sea, watches everything going on but never jumps in.'

'Do I seem like that?' I answered uneasily. And then to change the subject: 'And what about Nanna?' I realised as I asked the question how important the answer would be.

'She'll stay on till you go to school.' She shrugged her shoulders slightly.

'But I shall soon be going to school.'

She nodded. 'I can't afford to keep her for ever. When you're at school what would she do?'

I looked at the carpet.

'But, Davey,' she went on, and as I raised my head, looking at me with a quizzical glance, 'you haven't said you're pleased at the arrangement.'

I hesitated a moment. Truth to tell I did not know what to say. Instead I bent over the bed and kissed her. She, in her turn, kissed me rather coldly on the forehead.

From that time I had a recurrence of my illness, or rather it seemed a recurrence rather than something new. I would wake shrieking in the night. I never remembered what the dreams were that frightened me so much. What caused them I do not know. On one occasion when I was awake, staring into the darkness, I heard the old fiddler's tune. It had just commenced and then everything seemed to stop. A moment later

I became conscious of the darkness again and found myself sobbing. After these attacks I would run a slight temperature, be out of sorts, and hang moodily about the house. The doctor was called but was as puzzled as everyone else. He said he thought I would grow out of it. Mother was at first concerned, but later she was irritated by my pale, long face. Her cure for it all was boarding school. But till the attacks ceased, the doctor would not think of it. Reluctantly she once more postponed the date of my entry to St George's.

Instead I was sent to a convent by the day. The nuns were not able to teach me Latin, but they did teach me, with a considerable amount of severity, the other subjects. Every morning after breakfast I trailed drearily down a wide and windy street which led from the Green to a residential part at the back of the town. At lunch time I trudged as wearily home, back to school in the afternoon, home again after tea. I was bought a satchel like the girls' at the school, but which the boys, who were all considerably younger than myself, did not carry. This immediately marked me out as a freak. Moreover, I had to have lessons with the girls which humiliated me. They did not treat me like one of themselves, nor did they treat me as a boy. My position and my character made me fall into an intermediate type. They either ignored me or pinched me during class. I made no friends and learnt to dislike them as much as they disliked me.

There was one older girl in the class above me whom I admired from a distance. She was tall, athletic, extroverted. She moved about with self-conscious grace like a goddess. I followed her trim, tunicked figure down the bleak corridors of the convent with hungry eyes. But her bobbed black hair, her dancing eyes, her smiles and laughs were not for me and I knew it. I never spoke to her and I have no reason to think she ever so much as noticed me.

One afternoon at a weekend in autumn, I was sitting on the stones in front of the hut when she passed by with a group of classmates. The girls went down to the edge of the sea which was murmuring quietly and coming in over the sand in little dimpled rivulets. They threw stones for a while and then stood watching a steamer out to sea. She stood at the edge of the group, very still with her back to me, intent on the horizon. And then, forgetting where she was, she raised her dress and began scratching her knickers. They were dark-blue cotton and hung loosely over her buttocks. This inelegant gesture kindled a passionate desire which almost overwhelmed me. But the nun in charge of the party, her habit flowing in the wind, moved on. It was only a moment but in it I had tasted the sweet forbidden fruit and knew the hopeless unhappiness it induces. When she had gone I sat staring at the sea unable to believe that what had been so intense was now no more.

But I had other and more important things to think about. The girls in my class induced the boys in the lower class to waylay me on my way home. I was taller than they were but they outnumbered me. I was never hurt but I was wounded by their taunts which seemèd to me quite unreasonable. I had always thought of myself as a tough boy and I was certainly as strong as any of my tormentors. But somehow in the crowd I was unable to assert myself. I was as helpless as the shorn Samson.

One evening, after tea, as I walked home to the little Regency terrace, gusts of wind from the sea were blowing down the street. I was thanking heaven that I had not, on that walk seen any of the junior boys. I was looking at the numbers on the doors as I walked along and at the shoe scrapers which were built into the walls. I did not know what they were for and was wondering what the inhabitants of the houses did with them. Suddenly and unexpectedly a bunch of children were all around me. As usual they kept their distance but jeered and taunted: 'Mother's darling. Where's Nanna? Where's Mother?'

At this moment Mother turned the corner from the terrace. She took in at a glance what was happening. She hesitated a moment and then came towards us. One look from her and the children fled. I had feared that this might happen – and now it had. On the other side of the road one of my class-mates, a little girl with freckles and wavy hair, had also witnessed the scene.

Mother walked back with me but did not speak, and nor did I. When we got into the drawing-room I burst into tears.

'I don't know why it is,' I said, choking back my sobs, 'it's not my fault that I can't go to school.'

Mother had turned to the mantelpiece and had taken a cigarette. She lit it slowly, without speaking. Then she said deliberately: 'It's because you're different. You *are* different. I wish you could understand that...' She dropped her hands in despair. She was almost as deeply wounded as myself. 'Your whole life has been different from other children's and perhaps it's my fault. I could have helped, had you been with me. I thought I was acting for the best.' She shrugged her shoulders. 'But there is no point in wishing that things had been different. Things are as they are. Now,' she went on, 'dry your eyes and go and have your supper in the sitting-room. You don't want Nanna to know you've been crying.'

I dried my eyes and said: 'But Nanna knows. I've told her already.'

'I see.' She frowned slightly and there was a faint flush on her cheeks. 'Perhaps,' she said, more to herself than to me, 'I do not understand you.'

There was a gilt Rococco looking-glass over the mantelpiece and, as I went out, I saw her look into it and shrug her shoulders. I began to close the door but she called me back. She held out her arms and I stood beside her, enfolded by them. Then she slowly stroked my hair with a protective gesture.

'You won't say anything to the nuns?' I asked.

'Why not?'

'It would make it worse.'

'Yes, I see that. You must fight your own battles.'

'I shall,' I said, 'if I can.' My voice was a whisper.

She bent down and kissed the top of my head. There was something of despair in it, something of disappointment, perhaps of farewell.

I awkwardly left the room, awkwardly because I was aware that I had witnessed what I should not have understood, but which I did, at least partially.

Nanna saw that I was upset, made a fuss of me at the meal, but when she thought I was not looking, shook her head in bewilderment. Jessie said: 'Got to keep your pecker up, 'aven't we, Davey?' And I was somehow comforted.

Next day as I was setting off home from school the little wavy-haired girl, who had seen what had happened the previous evening, came up to me and said, 'I want to walk back with you.' I dreaded that this would lead to a more humiliating ambush. But, as we walked along together, she said: 'I want to be your friend. When you go to boarding school will you write to me?' She was pretty and trim, as if her clothes had just been ironed. She wore a tortoiseshell slide in her auburn hair and, as she talked I noticed that she had dimples in her cheeks. The freckles made her look friendly. But, then, one of the worst tormentors also had freckles and I distrusted them.

'Yes,' I said cautiously, 'if you would like me to.'

'I've got some invisible ink so no-one will know what we say to each other.'

'No?' I was interested but incredulous.

'I've got two bottles, one for you, and one for me, so we can try it out. The nuns don't know about it. You put the letter in front of the fire and the writing comes out with the heat.'

'But what shall we write?' The idea opened up all sorts of possibilities.

'Secrets,' she said practically.

We walked on in silence and then she said: 'I'd love to write to you.'

'So would I, if you'd let me.'

' "If you'd let me!" ' she mimicked. 'Why don't you hit one of those little boys on the nose? That would stop it.'

'It might make it worse.'

She shook her head definitely.

Then we came to the alley at the side of the street and the little mob of boys ran out. They rushed at me as usual but my companion seized one of them by the hair and gave it a good pull. He went howling down the street followed by the others, abashed and resentful.

And that was the end of the trouble.

We parted at the end of the street.

'What's your name?' I asked.

She laughed. 'Don't you know? Betty, of course.' She waved her satchel and was gone.

Betty was a precocious child and I do not know why she attached herself to me. Perhaps she was attracted by my apparent helplessness. We exchanged letters written in invisible ink containing rude remarks about the nuns. She sometimes came to play with me but Nanna did not approve of her. Nanna hated anything underhand and disliked the invisible ink. Betty's habit of speaking to me in a whisper especially annoyed her. We did indeed speak of sex sometimes, for Betty considered herself an expert on the subject. But our letters and conversations were mostly quite innocent. She gave me a graphic description of the way the king used silk handkerchiefs for lavatory paper and how the Queen used the finest linen.

She loved secrecy and we had a secret game we used to play at weekends. In the little unkempt garden at the back of the house there was a garden shed which had in it the cistern of the outside lavatory below it, at basement level. Betty thought this would make an excellent altar. The shed was approached by a short range of brick steps and this gave it a somewhat ecclesiastical approach. Betty made priestly garments for me which she stitched in the evenings. They were half surplice and half vestment. This reflected her religious position. She was an Anglican but attended Mass at the convent. The main garment was long and white and made of cotton. It was also very tight when I had got it on. Over this I had a sort of miniature cape made of violet material which I wore like a shawl. I was provided with a prayer book, a pair of scissors and a tooth glass. Betty herself wore a black nun's habit from which her freckled face peered like an illustration from Boccaccio.

We would disappear into the shed and dress up in the semi-darkness. I would then stand at the altar which was draped with a piece of red silk. I would recite some prayers and we would sing a hymn in low voices so that we were not over-heard. All this time Betty would be kneeling in front of me with her hands clasped in an attitude of prayer. As the service proceeded she would gradually prostrate herself. Then I would turn to the altar, take off the crimson cloth, lift the cistern lid and fill the tooth glass with water. I would then elaborately replace the lid and the cloth. Turning round I would say: 'Dominus vobiscum' – which I did not understand, as it did not conform to the sort of Latin I had learnt, but which Betty had taught me. Then I would ceremoniously remove part of Betty's veil, clip off a tiny piece of her hair, and pour the water over the shorn particles. After that she would resume her veil, kiss me chastely on each cheek, and the service would be over.

Gradually the service became more elaborate. I would process round the little shed, and, sometimes round and round Betty. Occasionally she played a more active part, sprinkling me with the water and making me kneel before her while she gave me her blessing. Once, but only once, she stripped herself for the ceremonial hair-cutting. On this occasion at the critical moment, as I was cutting her hair with the scissors, Jessie pulled the chain in the lavatory below. The tooth glass fell from the altar with a crash and the ceremony came to an abrupt end. Betty scrambled into her clothes and by the time Jessie appeared at the door to enquire what had happened I was decorously giving my blessing.

'Well, whatever are you up to?' Jessie asked in amazement.

'We're just playing at religions,' Betty said, pulling aside her veil.

'Oh, that's it is it?'

'Yes, but don't tell Nanna,' I interposed.

'Don't tell her what?'

'She might,' Betty said, 'stop it. And it's secret.'

'Oh, is it?' Jessie asked, undecided.

'If you don't tell her, you can come to the next service,' Betty said diplomatically.

Jessie went out and shut the door behind her. We could hear her saying to Nanna, who had come out into the back basement area: 'I was jest see' what thet were up to. They're playing religions.' And they walked back into the house.

We slowly took off our robes. The game was finished. It was no longer secret. It could not be played again. And it never was.

Near the convent, along the street which we passed on our way home, there was a piece of rough ground bordered by a straggling hedge. One evening on our walk homeward she dragged me through the hedge and we lay for a while, hidden from passers-by. It was growing dark and the wind was chilling. In our hide-out we were warm. Betty pressed her body to mine and gave me a wet kiss on the lips which I did not much like. I timidly kissed her back, uncertain what was expected of me. We could hear the footsteps and voices of the children as they walked along the pavement. They sounded as remote as if from another planet. Betty lifted her tunic and pulled down her knickers. She did it unself-consciously, waited for me to make an inspection and then re-arranged her clothes. I was glad of the dusk for my cheeks were burning. I was more aware of the withered grasses and sorrel in the hedge than of Betty's anatomy. I feared that she would want an inspection of my own. This, of course, she did. But she regarded me with such detached and professional interest that I was not as embarrassed as I had expected.

'Isn't this wrong?' I whispered as I tightened the belt of my shorts.

'We're brother and sister now,' she pronounced, 'but there's one more thing. We must rub noses.'

The voices had died away. There were only occasional footsteps, on the other side of the pavement, of people hurrying home to their houses before nightfall. The wind had grown sharper. Some of the gaslights had been lit. We rubbed noses slowly and comfortably. It was a pleasant sensation and we lingered over it. Her snubbed and freckled nose was warm. Then we scrambled to our feet and hurried home.

When we got to the corner she suddenly said:

> 'Caesar did a wheezer
> Right across the street.
> His wife tried to do the same,
> But did it at her feet.'

After that we called ourselves for a time 'Sister' and 'Brother'. But, somehow, Betty was not real to me as other people were real. She came from a world I did not know or understand. I never went to her house, I did not know why. There was some trouble at her home. She talked only occasionally of her mother who was very ill. Of her father, who, I understood was frequently away, not at all. It was as if, when with me, they did not exist. Perhaps I was a mechanism in her life with which she blotted out what she wanted to forget. And that may have been the cause of the unreality which clothed our friendship.

But, then, how real was Bathampton, even Mother? There seemed to be only relics of reality left – Nanna, for example. And she was related to The Firs. The Firs, and The Firs only, was the true reality. When I went to sleep at night I thought of the tall, melancholy trees, and when I woke I seemed to hear their music till it was shattered by the alien cry of a gull or the sound of the wind rattling the sash windows. Nanna had stepped from the reality of The Firs into the neat little world of Bathampton without trouble and had somehow, under the influence of Mother, merged herself into it. She had faded into a background figure, who indeed was always physically present as before, but with whom I had little contact. Buzz, alone, seemed to understand what I inchoately felt. When I returned from school he would greet me with sympathetic wags of his tail. He was now house-trained and growing fast.

CHAPTER EIGHTEEN

Now that my future had been settled Grandma wrote more often. I received a letter with news from The Firs regularly once a week, and once a week I wrote laborious letters back. I found it difficult to find things to say. I did not often mention Mother, and Betty not at all.

Summer had long since gone. Visitors, even the late ones, had departed. Many of the little houses in the terrace were closed. Shelters on the promenade were empty. Cold winds shook the house and rattled through the town. Bathampton was like an evacuated city. Sea horses hissed against the break-waters and in rough weather discharged stones onto the promenade. Gusts of rain swept over the Green and up the street which led to the convent.

I made desolate walks across the Green up to a drinking fountain which had been erected to commemorate Queen Victoria's jubilee. The wind blew back Buzz's ears like a woman's hair and gave him a nautical appearance. He would dutifully cock his leg on the plinth of the fountain – he had now learnt to perform this feat – and turn homewards. We would walk without pausing till we came to the Promenade hotel, the only other building on the Green and the nearest to the sea. It was a low built, Tudor style erection, surrounded by a thicket of trees. Here, after a good deal of fuss, Buzz would again carefully cock his leg on the white gate post. I would look into the swing door and see the pages and the palm trees. It was a sumptuous place with thick, bright carpets, strong lights and little cane tables at which couples sat drinking cocktails. The men were rich and smart, the women elegant and aloof. Often there came from the ballroom the sound of dance music like a murmur of sensuality into an ascetic world. At other times there would be the sound of a waltz, swept to pieces by the wind. I would linger with envy and distrust at the gate till Buzz nudged my leg.

On these walks I used to think with nostalgia of The Firs and the self-contained life that was going on there. I regretted the change in Nanna, which was as much a change in myself. It seemed on these introspective occasions that she had drawn away from me. In fact it was much more like two boats drifting apart. I no longer crept into her bed to feel the warmth of her body on my back. I needed different consolations which she could not give, and which Mother could not give either. Betty was a diversion but no more. I yearned for the stability of manhood and the peace of childhood. What I could not accustom myself to was the world between, dark and comfortless, in which I found myself. Happiness or unhappiness is relative to what has gone before, and in retrospect to what comes after. I was lucky to have been happy. But, of course, I did not understand that. Like all human beings I thought that what I had been would be what I should be. Poor little fool on the windy Green, thinking of these things, when I should have had my head full of school life and hobbies!

One evening when I got home after a walk with Buzz, my face dashed with rain and spray from the sea, I found a letter waiting for me from Grandma.

'Dearest Davey,
I have tragic news to tell you. Mrs Brailes's baby died

only a few hours after its birth. She has been very ill, and is not yet, I am afraid, herself. The disappointment has been too much for her. The poor vicar is distracted. The loss of the baby was quite enough. His wife's illness is almost too much.

The weather here is very dull and as I write the rain is dashing at the windows, spoiling the last of the flowers. I miss you very much, especially at breakfast time. Perhaps when the term is over you will be able to come here for a short time to see how we are all getting on. Everyone here is well and sends their love. Mr Evans looks tired and ill but he says there is nothing wrong with him.

Mr Treet, after all, is to be the new archdeacon. I had hoped for Mr and Mrs Brailes's sake this would not be so. It would have helped Mrs Brailes at this time had there been one little ray of success. But it was not to be. Of course for me it is a comfort to have Mr Brailes in the parish still. I am sure on the other hand Mr Treet will make a very business-like archdeacon.

Mr Oldacre has just come in and sends you his love. He says he has written to your mother to ask whether he can take Mr and Mrs Brailes down in his new motor car to see you for the day.

Your loving Grandma.'

I ran up to the drawing-room pursued by Buzz who had been systematically shaking himself in the hall while I was reading the letter.

'Mother!' I shouted, as I opened the door.

I stopped suddenly for I had caught sight of a dark-clothed man seated in a chair in front of the fire.

'This,' Mother said, getting up, as the stranger rose to greet me, 'is Monsieur Turenne, a cousin of mine.'

I awkwardly shook the man by the hand and he gave mine a shake. He was tall, thin, elegant, about forty. He had rather long grey hair neatly brushed back behind his ears and away from his lined, intelligent face. He was dressed in a smart blue pin-striped suit and wore a pearl in his tie. He had a pale-blue silk handkerchief protruding from his breast pocket. His long, white manicured hand gripped mine briefly and then fell to his side. He murmured something and sat down again. His complexion was sallow and pale, his expression aloof and unfriendly. I was made to feel that I had interrupted him.

Nobody spoke and at last he said slowly and with a marked French accent. 'So this is David.' He addressed the remark to Mother who looked a little put out. 'I suppose,' he continued as slowly as before, 'you are 'ere on a visit?'

I shook my head. 'I live here,' I said.

He raised his eyebrows and glanced at Mother.

'Yes,' Mother said softly, 'Davey lives here now. Monsieur Turenne,' she explained to me, 'has only just arrived and I had not had time to tell him.' She paused. 'I have not seen him for some time. But Davey will soon be going to boarding-school, won't you, Davey?'

I nodded. There was an undercurrent in their conversation I did not understand.

'But, then,' Monsieur Turenne said almost as softly as Mother and with something cruel in his voice, 'there will be the 'olidays?' He smiled at me showing his teeth and then turned to Mother.

There followed a silence during which Buzz suspiciously sniffed at the stranger's shoes. He took no notice and continued to look at me and Mother, from one to the other, with a sardonic expression.

'And what,' Mother asked at last, 'were you rushing in to tell me?'

'George has got his new car, and... ' I paused. Having started with the wrong subject I did not know how to go on.

'Well?' Mr Turenne asked.

'He wants to bring Mr and Mrs Brailes down because their

baby has died.' The information seemed a little tarnished by Monsieur Turenne's presence.

'I know,' Mother said as if my remark was unfortunate.

'Whose baby 'as died?' Monsieur Turenne asked, 'and 'o is this George, Marie?'

'It's only the vicar ... Mr Oldacre is in charge of the papers at The Firs.' She spoke depreciatingly.

Monsieur shrugged his shoulders. 'The *bibliothéquaire*?'

'I suppose you would call him that.'

'I did not know there were so many papers.' He sniffed and took a cigarette from a gold case.

'No?' Mother seemed uninterested.

'Isn't it awful about the Brailes's baby?' I said, but added: 'It's wonderful about George's new car.'

'I'm sure it isn't new,' Mother corrected, 'it's second-hand.'

'Second-hand,' Monsieur Turenne was puzzled.

'*D'occasion*,' Mother explained.

Monsieur Turenne gave a little grunt of recognition and drew at his cigarette.

'And did George tell you about Mr Treet?' I asked Mother.

'But, Davey, who is Mr Treet?' Mother gave her silvery laugh.

I explained at rather too great length what had happened. Monsieur Turenne listened and then turned to Mother with his eyebrows a little raised. '*La politique écclésiastique*?' He looked at me with his hard eyes for a few moments while the cigarette smoke streamed from his nostrils. 'Your 'eart,' he said to me, 'is at The Firs?' He gave a little confirmatory grunt as if answering the question for me.

I stood in front of him and said nothing. Instead I put my hands behind my back. What was I to say?

'You 'ave been for the walk on the Green with this dog?' he asked, looking down on Buzz who seemed to have a great interest in his well-polished black shoes.

'Yes,' I said, still standing and rocking from one foot to the other, 'we always go to the fountain and the Promenade Hotel.'

'Ah,' he responded, 'that is where I stay and where your mother will be dining tonight. Isn't that so, Marie?'

Mother made a little motion of her head of acceptance.

'What cousin,' I asked Monsieur Turenne, 'are you to me?'

'Cousin?' he enquired as if he did not understand what I meant.

'A distant cousin,' Mother said quickly, 'of your Belgian grandfather.' She glanced swiftly at Monsieur Turenne, who made a slight grimace.

'My grandfather, who was shot by the Germans, and was Mayor?' I asked.

'That is so,' Monsieur replied briefly.

'And now,' Mother said, getting up out of her chair, 'Davey, it's time for your supper and Buzz is annoying Monsieur Turenne. As I'm going out, say goodnight to me now.'

I shook Monsieur by the hand and kissed Mother's cheek. I felt a little resentful that I had not been asked out, too. There was also a proprietary air in Monsieur Turenne's manner towards Mother which I did not like. He seemed to presume on a greater degree of intimacy than that which existed between Mother and myself. And yet I had never so much as heard his name before. By sitting so easily in the arm chair at the side of the fireplace he was usurping my position. I loitered on my way to the door.

Monsieur said something in French to Mother. I guessed that it was to the effect that I was thin and pale. Mother replied, also in French, in a tone of annoyance. Hearing her speak for the first time in a foreign language made me feel more than ever that she did not really belong to me.

Downstairs in the little basement sitting-room Nanna and Jessie were sitting in front of a large coal fire which glowed comfortably in the cast-iron grate. The curtains were drawn and the electric light was on. There was an air of intimacy and conspiracy about the room.

'You see if she don't,' Jessie was saying in her hoarse voice.

'Not she,' Nanna replied, intent on her knitting.

213

'Yer don't know 'er as I do.' And Jessie shook her head.

'You may be right after all.' Nanna sighed.

I coughed delicately but as a sign of disapproval.

'Oho!' Jessie exclaimed with a wink at Nanna.

As I ate my supper at the sitting-room table I heard the front door clang. The knocker shook and a moment later I heard Mother's footsteps, firm and precise, followed by those of Monsieur Turenne, slow and almost silent, pass by on the pavement. Jessie peeped out of the curtain.

'She's got 'er fur-collared coat on,' she whispered to Nanna who glanced apprehensively at me, 'and 'e's 'olding 'er arm.'

That evening I could not get to sleep. I was still tossing after Nanna's breathing had become regular. The front door closed quietly. There were steps and a whispered conversation on the stairs. The drawing-room door closed and all was silence.

I waited till I thought I heard a creaking on the stairs and the slight shudder of the front door closing. Mother did not come up and I went down to the drawing-room. Everything was very still. Had she gone out too? If not what could she be doing by herself? Then I softly opened the drawing-room door.

A pink-shaded standard lamp cast a circle of warm light into the near end of the room. The fire was almost out, settling slowly in the hearth. Monsieur Turenne sat with his back to me at one end of the sofa. I could just see the side of his cheek but not his eyes. His hair was ruffled. He was bending over Mother who sat on his knees with her head thrown back against the back of the sofa. She lay limply, with her eyes shut, in an attitude of receptiveness. Her black hair lay about her face and her eyelashes fluttered as he bent forward to kiss her lips. One of his hands was about her waist, the other fumbled at her breasts. Her dress was drawn up above her knees. I could see the fastener of her suspenders and a patch of olive coloured skin.

I closed the door and went back to the night-nursery. I switched out the passage light and crept into bed. The scene I had just witnessed returned again and again to my mind like a picture projected onto a screen. I saw every detail. Mother's gold dress in the golden light, her black, tousled hair, her silk-stockinged leg, her fluttering black lashed lids. There had been a red rose on the arm of the sofa near her black hair. It must have fallen from it. And then there was the picture of those long white fingers round her waist, fumbling at her breasts. Did I imagine it or had he been muttering words of endearment as he pressed his lips against hers?

After what seemed hours, but was in fact about half an hour, I heard whispers on the stairs and the gentle bang of the front door. Mother went into the drawing-room again, switched off the lights and walked slowly upstairs. She paused on the landing as if in thought. Then she softly opened the night-nursery door. Light flooded into the room from the landing on to my bed. I lay still but watched her through half-closed lids, as she stood in the doorway. She looked flushed and happy but as her eyes fell on my bed an expression of disappointment and anxiety crossed her face. A little frown creased her forehead. I thought for a moment she was going to cross the room to kiss me. But she did not do so. Instead she closed the door and went into her bedroom which was next door. I could hear her moving about as she undressed.

I waited five minutes and then crossed the dark landing. Light showed from under her door. I tapped gently. At first she did not hear but at last answered: 'Come in,' in a surprised voice.

She was sitting at the dressing-table and half-turned as I entered. She held her pearls in her hands about to lay them on the dressing-table. She had just unclasped them from her throat. She was in a dead white night dress which showed up the olive colour of her skin.

'What are you doing up at this time of the night, Davey? You were asleep just now.' She spoke in a whisper.

The chintz curtains were drawn. Only the bedside lamp was on and it cast only a suffused light into the room. The satin bedspread had been turned down. It was a quiet warm night. Not a sound disturbed us.

'I woke up,' I said, 'and I can't get to sleep again.' I was still standing in the doorway.

'Well, come in and shut the door and tell me what's the matter.' She turned back to the dressing-table, placed the pearls on its glass surface with a little rattle, and then slowly began to draw the rings off her fingers. She looked at herself in the three cornered glass as she did so.

I shut the door but stood in front of it irresolutely. 'I just can't sleep, that's all.'

'But you were asleep a few minutes ago. I saw you.' She slowly began to brush her hair with a blue enamelled brush.

'I thought I heard voices,' I said.

'You may have done but that is nothing extraordinary in a town. Light the gasfire and sit down.'

I did so and sat on a satin covered chair. The fire gave out a pleasant heat and hissed comfortably.

'Whatever will Nanna think if she finds you gone?'

'She's asleep.' Her remark made me feel that I was in a conspiracy with her.

'Well?' she asked, getting up and bending over me. There was still a flush about her cheeks. She drew me to her so that my face was brushing her night dress.

'I felt very lonely.' I said

'You're not thinking about the school?'

'No. No, that's over now.'

'Because of Betty?'

I nodded.

'You like her?'

'Yes,' I said indifferently.

'Well, what is it?' She ran her fingers through my hair.

I hesitated. 'I want to go back to The Firs,' I said at last.

She paused as she stroked my hair. 'Ah,' she said but without resentment.

'I love you, Mother.'

She recommenced stroking my hair. There was a long silence as the gas hissed in the still room. I heard a few soft patters of rain in the street outside. I glanced up at her. Her face was softer than I had ever seen it. Her eyes were liquid as she gazed into the lights of the dressing-table, but without taking them in. Then she saw I was looking at her and her thoughts returned to me. Her eyes and her expression hardened.

'But it is folly, Davey,' she said kindly, but with her usual realism. 'You have to go to school ... There are reasons why you cannot return to The Firs ... You are already too old to be with your mother. With your grandmother, that is even more stupid. ...'

I gazed into the gas fire and said nothing.

'Would you like a drink of hot milk and a biscuit?'

I shook my head.

'It might send you to sleep again.'

'No, I don't feel hungry, thank you.'

Mother considered. 'You'd better come into my bed.'

I said nothing.

'Well, would you? You can if you want to.'

'All right.'

'You can go back to your own bed.' She turned out the gas.

'No, I'd like to be here.'

I got into the bed and Mother got in at the other side. It was a wide bed and there was plenty of room. The sheets were cold and crisp. Mother put out her hand, switched off the bedside lamp, and slowly stroked my hair. I did not like the sensation and lay very still. Then she turned over with her back to me.

I lay on my back, staring into the darkness, savouring the new sensations. The pillow was soft and had about it the scent of Mother's body. The silk quilt, outside the bed, felt smooth and cold. Mother's body was warm, although she had her back to me. I could not relax. I wanted but dared not speak.

At last I whispered: 'I don't like Monsieur Turenne.'

There was no answer, not even a stir.

I repeated what I had said but Mother was asleep. The soporific warmth of her body made me drowsy. I, too, slept.

But not for very long. I woke up in a sweat of fear. Something awful had happened in my dream. I found myself sobbing. I could remember that I had been crying-out in terror.

Mother switched on the light. 'Well what is it now?' she demanded, wide awake.

'I don't know,' I said, still sobbing and getting out of bed. 'I was dreaming or something.'

'Well, where are you going?' Mother asked exasperated by my incoherence.

'I don't know.'

'I think perhaps you'd better go back to your own bed.'

I nodded tearfully. I felt I had failed myself and her.

She led me into the night-nursery and tucked me up in bed. She kissed me and gave a little sigh of annoyance. Then she crept out and I heard her getting back into bed. Then all was silence except Nanna's rhythmical breathing. I could smell the scent of Nanna's hand cream. It was all familiar. I could not see it, but I knew that her pink dressing gown was hanging behind the door.

And then I slept till the morning.

CHAPTER NINETEEN

A few days later George and the Brailes's arrived. I had seen no more of Monsieur Turenne and presumably he had left Bathampton. George drew up to the door at the wheel of a blunt-nosed Morris with a tattered hood. There was a squealing of brakes and he pumped at his horn to let us know he had arrived. We all ran on to the steps of the porch and Jessie peered through the sitting-room window. George slowly climbed out of the vehicle, dressed in a thick overcoat, buttoned to his chin, and with a motoring-cap on his head. He gave us a boyish grin of pleasure and said: 'We did it but only just!' He began unbuttoning his coat looking around him at the terrace of Regency houses with an appreciative smile.

Mr Brailes got out of the back of the car and held the door open for his wife. His face was pale and distracted. He peered at me through his spectacles and made a gesture of recognition with his hand. He seemed to concentrate on the physical motions of opening the door and helping his wife out, as though it would divert his attention from his own thoughts and the embarrassments of the greeting. Eva Brailes – to my surprise – seemed much the same as before. There was, perhaps, a vaguer expression in her eyes. That was all.

But as soon as she greeted Mother, I saw there was a change. She held out her hand and murmured: 'So very pleased to come!' with a queenly gesture, as if she was conferring an honour on us. She appeared to be seeing us all through a fog, or at a distance. 'Now, Mark,' she continued turning to the car from which her husband was removing a rug, 'aren't you going to say anything to Mrs Porteous?' There was a gleam of malice in her eyes which I had never seen before.

'Of course, of course,' Mark Brailes murmured, shaking Mother by the hand. He nervously peered from one to the other of us while his wife looked on. George was busy lighting his pipe but glanced over the top of it at what was going on.

'As it's such a fine day,' Mother remarked, 'I thought we might have lunch in the hut.'

'Delightful!' Eva exclaimed with a little gesture of loosening her coat. 'One gets so tired of being on one's best behaviour in a village. We have to be, you know.'

It was a fine, windless autumn day. The sun shone with

unusual clarity. The sea, as it retreated down the beach, murmured languidly, expressive of sleep and meditation. From the back of the town a steam-engine shunted energetically as though to protest that life had to go on. A lorry rattled along the road that lay between the beach and the furthest edge of the Green.

As we walked across the Green, Eva Brailes took my hand and drew me aside from the others.

'Ah, David,' she said, 'it is nice to see you again.' She spoke to me as if she was talking to a very young child. 'You look older and taller than you were. And now you're at school, I hear. That's better than a tutor, I suppose.'

'I don't know,' I said evasively.

She laughed dreamily and I had the impression she was not listening to what I was saying.

And then she said, a cloud passing over her face: 'You heard that you're not to be a godfather after all. You know I wanted you to be?' Her face, deprived of its smile, like a landscape of the sun, suddenly looked different. She seemed to have the features of a crude, undeveloped child. It was more the appearance of an unwilling animal in a cage than of an unhappy woman. I thought for a moment she was going to cry but her eyes were dry. 'And, you know, I can't have any more children.'

I nodded as sympathetically as I could.

'But,' she went on more brightly in her pretty childish voice, 'I have had one child. Perhaps that is enough. Marguerite will be praying for you in heaven. It's just the other way round to what we expected, isn't it? She'll be praying for you instead of you praying for her. She will be your guardian angel, a sort of godmother to you. Things don't turn out as you expect. You'll find that.'

I looked up into her eyes but they were expressionless.

'We called her Marguerite after Mary, the Mother,' she remarked as if she was talking of a doll or a living baby. 'She had a grand little funeral and she was all in white. Unlike you and me she couldn't sin. She was so young. Only,' she added, the same blank expression returning to her face, 'a few hours.'

When we got to the hut Eva sat herself at the head of the table. Her husband nudged her and whispered something in her ear.

'Oh dear, how silly of me,' she said to him, 'I get used as the vicar's wife to being head of everything.'

Mark Brailes winced, not, I think, because of his wife's lack of manners but because of the undertone in her remark.

'You see, Mrs Porteous,' she went on, smiling with her vague, china-blue eyes, round the hut, 'you see it's so difficult to forget that one is the most important person present.' She got up but Mother made her sit down again. 'Well,' Eva said in her most simpering voice, 'if you want me to stay here in virtue of my husband's position.' She looked vaguely past him out at the placid sea at the edge of which seagulls were feeding.

Mother had taken in Eva's smartish, but just out of fashion, clothes, the vicar's creased suit and lack of *savoir faire*. I could see she had never met such people and despised them as coming from a lower milieu than herself. She had slightly shrugged her shoulders at Eva's remarks as though saying to herself: 'Well, it's only for an afternoon.' And Monsieur Turenne, I could not help wondering, what would he have thought? I do not know whether she understood there was more to it than a question of background.

'I suppose,' Eva said, 'Bathampton is a very smart place in the season.'

'I wouldn't say that,' Mother remarked dryly, busying herself with unpacking the meal.

'Oh, but what about the Promenade Hotel?' Mark Brailes asked unexpectedly in his thin, detached voice, as though he was talking of a theorem in mathematics.

'I don't know,' Mother replied vaguely. 'If so it's the only smart place in the town.'

'Come,' Mark said banteringly with sudden animation, as if

drawn out of himself by Mother's presence, 'they have an orchestra and a Palm court.'

'And what else do you know about it?' Mother asked, surprised.

'Oh, that it is full of rich people and divorcees.'

'You may be right. I suppose,' Mother continued, 'I should have taken you there for lunch.'

'Too expensive for all of us,' Mark laughed. 'Besides it's much nicer here by the sea.'

'I should like to go to the Promenade Hotel,' I said, 'just to try it out.'

'I think,' Eva said looking vaguely at her husband, 'Mr Brailes would have liked to have had lunch with your mother alone.'

There was an awkward silence. Mark bit his lip and reverted to his remote and nervous manner. Mother gave him a look such as she might have bestowed on a dog walking on its hind legs, a compound of admiration, surprise, and disgust.

'And how,' George asked me, to turn the conversation, 'do you like your convent school?'

I privately made a face at him across the table. He looked sympathetically back at me.

Mother, who was now undoing a little hamper, looked up and said: 'What nonsense, Davey. The nuns,' she continued to everybody present, 'are very pleased with him. And he now has a nice little girl who has become his friend.'

'It's not the nuns,' I confided in George, 'it's the other children.'

George gave me a confidential nod. 'I know all about that,' he said in his rumbling voice, putting his pipe into his pocket, preparatory to lunch.

Mother gave a little 'hem' of vexation.

'It may not be the nuns or the children,' Mark Brailes said with a little, bright smile, recovering himself, 'it may be the work.'

'I don't think, sir,' Nanna said in a low tone as she laid the plates, 'the children are very nice.'

'Are they all Catholics?' Eva asked.

'I suppose,' her husband said in a tone of correction and with a dart of disapproval from behind his spectacles, 'only the boarders are Roman Catholics.'

'Most of the other children are Church of England,' I corroborated.

'Well,' Mark Brailes exclaimed with a sort of brittle heartiness, 'thank God for that!'

'And what sort of punishments,' George enquired, 'do the nuns inflict on their pupils?'

'Oh,' I replied, 'there's lots of them. You have to learn the *Pater noster* by heart. And if you do something very bad you have to kneel on a ruler and recite the creed.'

'And what are the prizes?' Eva asked, not very pleased at my tone.

'Oh, I know that one, Eva,' Mark Brailes said skittishly, 'a rosary or a holy picture.'

'How did you know that?' I asked.

'There are,' he said dryly, 'Church of England convents, too.'

'The nuns,' Mother said, as if to explain it all, 'are mostly peasants from Bretagne.'

'It sounds awful,' George said to me *sotto voce*, his mouth full of veal and ham pie.

'And on Sundays and holy days,' Eva Brailes remarked as if she were describing what she had seen, 'the children plait crowns of thorns taken from the rose bushes.' She looked round the hut, smiling sweetly like a child who has made an intelligent remark.

'And,' Mark Brailes chimed in triumphantly, 'the nuns tell the children that the M on the palm of their hands stands for Mary.'

No-one replied to this and we all became concerned with our food.

After lunch Nanna went back with the dirty dishes to the house. Mother and Eva walked down the deserted promenade. George and Mark Brailes sat in the hut while I sat outside and idly played with the large beach pebbles. They were faintly warm to the touch, rounded and polished by the sea.

George lit his pipe. As he slowly smoked it, he looked complacently out to sea. He did not seem in a conversational mood and did not make much response to Mr Brailes's desultory attempts to get talking. The latter turned a pencil over and over on the table.

At last, as if overcoming some interior obstacle, Mr Brailes said in a rush of confidence: 'You see, Oldacre, how it is?'

George kept his eyes on the horizon. 'Yes,' he grunted.

'It's all so hopeless,' Mark Brailes continued, also looking out to sea over the top of his spectacles with a frowning glance, 'there's nothing you can put your finger on.'

'I wonder,' George said in his rumbling voice and taking the pipe out of his mouth, 'if it wasn't coming on before.'

'Not till the baby was conceived,' Mark replied and looked helplessly at the floor of the hut. 'Before that we were so happy.' He let his hands fall to his side. The pencil fell with a little crash to the floor but he made no effort to pick it up. 'It's as if the only light and warmth in my life has been maliciously trampled on. It's not only the child's life which has gone, it's Eva's and my own as well.'

He paused, raised his spectacles and rubbed his eyes. When he had finished he looked short-sightedly, helplessly around. 'And,' he pursued, a look of haunted fear on his face. 'I did it. It's a temptation not to be content with the happiness one has.'

'Oh no,' George growled into his pipe, 'it was an accident, an illness, nothing to do with you.'

'Ah, but *are* there accidents?' He pinched the bridge of his nose. 'Perhaps it was wrong of me ... I am the one to blame.'

'If you believe that,' George growled in a very low voice so that it was almost inaudible, 'you'd believe anything.'

But Mark Brailes was not listening. 'You see there are degrees of calling. One precludes another. Your way is not my way and my way is not yours. But one must follow the path.'

He paused and cleared his throat. 'I hope you don't mind my talking to you like this.'

George shook his head and made an inaudible remark.

'And what is worse,' Mark Brailes pursued without waiting to hear George's reply, 'this might not have happened, or would have been less bad, if I had had some success. . . . It is a weakness, of course it's a weakness in her. And in me, too. But one might have expected for some little help at this time. And it *would* have been for me a *little* help. It's been,' he went on looking across at George's face, 'it's been like looking out of the window in the early morning to see the dawn. And no dawn has come. Not even a wisp of redness, no sign of light. I may not have been fitted for it. . . . But it might, at least, have helped her.' He put his head into his hands again. 'It would have given her the position she wanted. Silly enough, I know. And now, deep down, she hates me.'

'I don't know about that,' George said uncertainly taking the pipe out of his mouth and holding it for a moment in his hand.

'Oh yes, she does.'

'It's part of the illness, whatever it is.'

'But why? Why? Why should it be?' He seemed to be talking to himself. 'I don't know why I'm telling you. I've not spoken to anyone else. But it does me good to talk it out, especially to someone who doesn't believe.'

'I don't know about that,' George said a trifle offended, 'I have my beliefs, too.'

'What I mean is that they are not mine. You see,' he went on in a rush, 'I've preached the cross and self-sacrifice. And here it is, staring me in the face.'

'Perhaps,' George said gruffly, sucking at his pipe, 'we're given only what we can bear.' He spoke diffidently as of an opinion he did not wholly subscribe to.

'Yes, yes,' Mark Brailes said irritably, 'these saws of the

225

clergy don't ring very true when it comes to the point. How can anyone know who hasn't suffered it whether it can be borne or not? How do you or anyone else know whether I can go on living with the one person who in all the world I loved and trusted – without in the end … ?' He left the sentence unfinished.

'But,' George replied with a certain curiosity in his voice, 'if you believe in the goodness of God, then surely your burden will not be too heavy. I know,' he went on apologetically, 'I'm talking like my old father. But, then, I've never had to bear anything that was intolerable.'

Mark Brailes ran his hands through his thin, fair hair and looked at George. '*Of course,*' he said almost wildly, 'there are things too hard to bear. We only see the survivors. But there are the others in asylums or simply dead. That, Oldacre, is the truth. And as to the goodness of God, I believe it with all my heart. From the depth of my soul I know it. But what is goodness as related to God? God is awful, terrible, dark. Our wretched maimed religion has only shown us one side. All things bright and beautiful!' He let out an unhappy, high-pitched laugh.

There was a long silence. And then, like a man who has not had his say, he resumed again. 'I think I might be able to bear a lot of physical, even mental suffering. What I cannot bear is to learn to hate what I loved. That is the most terrible suffering of all. And then,' he went on, 'I used to think that we should bear one another's sufferings. But who can bear her suffering except myself? And how can I bear it, if I do not love her? There may come a time when there is a cure for her suffering – if it is a disease. But what cure can there be for my suffering?'

'I'm so sorry, Brailes,' George said heavily and put his hand gently on the other's, 'I'd help if I could.'

'I know you would,' Mark Brailes responded, leaving his frail, white hand enclosed in George's. 'I also know that religion is not intended to be only a consolation. But it should be consolatory.' He withdrew his hand and shrugged his shoulders. 'I who stand up in the pulpit week after week have only this to say now: "I have a hope that all will be well in the end." That, and only that, is the message I can now preach.'

They both sat in silence, watching the horizon and the skimming of the gulls over the flotsam at the edge of the tide. The mew of the gulls was like cries from an unknown limbo. They had both long since forgotten my presence on the stones outside the hut, if, indeed, they had noticed it from the start. Truth to tell, although there was much that I did not then understand, nothing had been said that I did not already know.

Mother and Eva Brailes at length returned.

'And what,' Eva enquired of George, 'has he been telling you?' She darted a penetrating glance at her husband which was startling because out of character. 'Oh, I see,' she went on, 'he's been trying to lead you back to the fold – one of his lost sheep.'

'I *am* one of the lost sheep,' George said neatly, getting up and taking his pipe from his mouth, at the same time giving her a bland smile, 'and if anyone could lead me back into the fold, it would be your husband.'

Mark Brailes gave him an uncertain glance, unsure whether he spoke ironically or not.

'I expect,' Mother said, with a little smile which did not hide some anxiety, 'he could do with a talking to.'

'As to that,' Mark Brailes remarked with a return to his old facetiousness, 'who couldn't?' He took off his spectacles and rubbed his eyes with his thumb and forefinger. They looked tired and old.

We walked back to the house for an early tea. Mr and Mrs Brailes were the first to get into the car. As I stood on the porch I saw George making his way down the stairs from the lavatory. He caught Mother's hand as she stood waiting in the hall. He snatched it to his lips and I saw on his face that intent look of serious longing which I had seen twice before.

'Beautiful. Beautiful,' he muttered as he kissed it.

Mother smiled a little, but not kindly. She said: 'Don't be a fool, George. Don't make a fool of yourself.' She pulled her hand away and propelled him to the door.

And then they were gone. George was at the wheel at the further side of the car so I could not see his face. He had simply squeezed my hand and smiled a great kindly smile by way of saying good-bye.

Now that George had his own car he made several more visits. I was always pleased to see him as he seemed, in a way that no-one else was, to be my ally against the world. There was a mixture of amusement, contempt and genuine affection in Mother's attitude to him.

And then came his last visit. I heard his voice in the hall one Sunday morning but I could not make out what he was saying. I was playing by myself in the ante-room behind the dining-room and the door was ajar. He was not expected and I was about to run to the door and call out, when I realised that he was in serious conversation with Mother. They were whispering urgently together. I hesitated. Then I heard her say very deliberately: 'No!' A moment later there was the sound of a slap. Silence followed. Mother ran upstairs. The front door shut with a bang. When I got to the porch he had already started the car and was driving down the street.

CHAPTER TWENTY

I was doing quite well at school, if not brilliantly. I was not actively unhappy. But the nightmares and the mysterious periods of giddiness returned. I ran little temperatures, apparently without cause. I grew paler and thinner. This was accompanied by a sense of failure, at what I did not know. But it oppressed me like a cloud. I was a bad companion and, though Betty did not desert me, she came less frequently to the house. She did not say so but I think she had discovered another friend, an older girl, whom she found more congenial. Mother was depressed that I grew no better, indeed grew worse. Nanna shook her head. I felt isolated, a piece of land slowly and silently surrounded by the sea. I rationalized it by saying to myself that my heart was at The Firs – the very sentiment the hated Monsieur Turenne had expressed.

There was in the town a gang of ragged boys who went about throwing stones, breaking windows, swearing and generally making themselves feared. They startled old ladies, frightened dogs, were said to terrify Nannies and children. Nanna certainly feared that she would come upon them. I met them once or twice when I was out for a walk with Buzz. But they did not molest me. They took no notice of me. I came gradually to admire them as boys who were wild and free. I even imagined, quite falsely, that in not interfering with me, they actually liked me. I dreamed that perhaps I could become one of them.... It seemed to me that if I could only join the gang, I would become like they were. I especially admired their vigorous speech and swearing which I secretly imitated in the privacy of my bed. This was an outward sign that I was really at one with them.

Mother was a very healthy woman and it was her belief that if I could only get out more frequently, even in the colder months, I should grow stronger. She had a great love of picnics, even if it meant no more than eating in the hut.

One fine weekend in autumn she suddenly said: 'Nanna, let's take a picnic to the forest. It will be lovely there and it will do Davey good to get out.'

'At this time of year, Madam?' Nanna demurred.

'It won't be cold at all,' Mother said resolutely, 'we'll take a thermos of coffee with us. In any case it will be warmer than the beach.' Nobody else would have thought of going to the beach but that was beside the point.

We had no car but we caught a bus to a nearby village and

then walked to the forest. The trees had lost their leaves and the path was damp and slippery. But at last we came to what Mother considered to be the right picnic spot. Nanna glanced about apprehensively to see whether there were any cows, or worse still, bulls. Buzz was let off the lead.

'There,' Mother said complacently, looking round at the rural scene in which we found ourselves, and with that complacency in her voice which indicated that she had achieved what she wanted, 'Here we are, after all, in spite of the time of year' – and she glanced at Nanna – 'in Burntwood Forest. How pretty the coloured leaves and bare trees are!' She sat down on the trunk of a fallen tree and gave me a dazzling smile. 'It will put some colour into your cheeks, Davey. Let the sunlight fall on your face.' She leant forward and laid the table cloth on the grass. Nanna unpacked the hamper.

We were in a picturesque clearing in a valley by the edge of the little river Assan which eddied moodily through its reed-covered banks. It passed by with the sound of a slow swish, dimpling now and then on its way in the sunlight. The grass was dull but droplets of crystal sparkled from some of the withered sedges. The slender, bare branches of a willow moved fitfully in the breeze. The clearing was surrounded on three sides by the forest – dark, mysterious, motionless – in front of us across the whispering water, behind us on a steep slope to the horizon, and upstream where the trees came down to the banks and seemed to swallow the river up. On the remaining side, through which we had come, there was an irregular field of tufty grass in which sheep were browsing, but how they had got there was a mystery unless they had been driven through the trees. Clouds, archetypal in their glory, floated above us.

In spite of the scene's beauty I felt ill at ease. There was everything to please me but nothing did. I had a slight headache and, while the things were being set out, I moodily threw sticks into the river. I watched them float away on the current and imagined them, days later, tossing helplessly in the tide race at Bathampton. Buzz, whose first real excursion this was, sniffed at every tuft and poked his head into attractive holes with an air of expertise.

'Davey, you're not eating much,' Mother said critically during the meal.

Nanna gave me a professional glance.

'Yes,' Mother continued, 'you're looking very pale again. D'you feel well?'

I nodded my head without replying and mentally shrugged my shoulders. I sauntered off to the bank again before the meal was ended.

'He's not well,' I heard Nanna say, 'I can tell it from his eyes.'

This enraged me. I did not want my health to be discussed. Mother hated it when I was ill and it seemed as if there was a conspiracy against me. In my mind it was Nanna who had inspired Mother to question me.

'You sullie,' I said bitterly under my breath. This was the word I had heard the gang of youths use to each other and it was invested with a dynamism, invective and sheer rudeness such as was no other word I knew. I picked up a piece of wood and hurled it aimlessly into the river. It fell short but out of sight. To my surprise it was answered by a loud hiss. Round the corner sailed a magnificent swan. His white beauty, akin to that of a ship crowned with canvas, and his black markings, were reflected in the sunlit water. He glided swiftly, vengefully, inevitably, to the spot where I was standing.

Buzz had heard the hiss and began to bark in his puppy-like defiant way. He advanced, his coat on end, to the bank and growled at the swan. The swan sailed majestically towards him, hissing menacingly. Buzz, impelled by some demon of daring, continued barking more defiantly than ever. The swan reached the bank and suddenly rose out of the water onto the reeds like an avenging angel. His long, graceful neck, tense and slightly curved, was outstretched. The cruel beak snapped at the dog's nose. Buzz's tail went down. The swan made a rush at him, wings outstretched, and seemed for a moment to overwhelm him by its height, size, and the intensity of its hatred.

'Buzz, Buzz!' I called. 'Come back!' I ran towards the wood to show him where to go. Buzz needed no encouragement. He let out a squawk of pain and then a howl of terror. With his tail between his legs, as though possessed, he tore to the trees past the picnic site. The swan advanced more slowly and then stopped, gloating over its triumph.

Nanna, who had not seen the cause of Buzz's alarm, ran at him to prevent his getting into the wood. This sudden and unexpected manoeuvre added fresh terrors to the dog's mind. He darted aside to avoid what he took to be a new enemy and bolted into the darkness of the trees.

I was outraged by this piece of well meant stupidity on Nanna's part. 'Yer sullie!' I hurled at her as I raced after the dog into the wood. Out of the corner of my eye I saw the swan lower its wings and return towards the water. I also saw the startled expression on Nanna's face as I rushed by her.

The dog dashed on and I tore after him along little paths, and brakes, up the side of steep banks, among the tall dark trunks of the trees. I called and called but to no purpose. The poor animal did not recognise me in his terror. And then I found myself on a steep bank in a plantation of young pine trees. To one side of it there was a long, sloping field, separated from the wood by tall wire netting. Buzz went straight for this barrier and found he could not get through. He sat down and whimpered dismally. I was now able to pick him up. He was trembling but recognised me. I sat down with him in my arms. We were both panting and out of breath. Buzz licked my face appreciatively.

'Oh, Buzz,' I said reproachfully, 'you shouldn't have been so frightened.'

'Well,' I said for Buzz in a hang-dog voice, 'you would have been frightened, too, if you'd had that great animal rising on top of you. Besides, something else ran after me.'

'It was only Nanna,' I said, rubbing his long ears. 'It was silly of her, wasn't it?'

I remembered what I had said to her with a pang of remorse and wished to justify myself. 'She frightened you, didn't she?'

I looked round and saw that nothing in the place where we were sitting was familiar. 'Buzz,' I asked, 'where are we?' It dawned on me that neither of us knew the answer.

I remembered that the place was called a forest and this conjured up in my mind mile after endless mile of trees. There was no sign of the stream which had flowed into the river and which I could have followed back. The field seemed to indicate that I was near the forest's edge. But beyond it there were more trees and no sign of a house or of cattle even. It was abnormally silent, as if I had got out of reach of a road. Occasionally, far away there was the whirr of a pheasant. But nothing more.

How far had I run? And which was the way back?

I decided that it was best to go downhill as the picnic had been in a valley and I had run uphill after Buzz. We were soon out of the plantation and back among the old trees. The leaves were damp under foot and the place was filled with a brooding silence, made here and there more sinister by clumps of hollies as dark and motionless as night itself. There were no paths and what had seemed like paths trailed away into thickets.

We gradually descended and came upon an escarpment where some trees had been felled. There was a large boulder at the top of it and beside it stood the shivered trunk of a pine, struck in half by I did not know what catastrophe. The little clearing was a tangle of bushes and brambles. It seemed vaguely familiar, but I could not be certain that I had, in fact, seen it before. As I looked around the dog gazed up into my face and wagged his tail sympathetically.

'Silly fool!' I muttered savagely and brushed him aside with my leg. Buzz crouched on the ground, cringing.

We descended further. I hoped to find the river at the bottom. But the way became more difficult through thickets of young hazel. By the time we had reached the valley I was covered in scratches and bruises. There was no river, not even a stream or a marsh. I had long since given up trying to find familiar landmarks and was relying on common sense. This had now failed me. The only thing left was to follow the valley and then ascend the slope I had descended further along. The other side of the valley was as new to me as fairy-land – tracts of conifers stretching to the horizon, dark blue, impassive, uniform.

The sun had lost its power and hung like a blood red ball in the sky, quite high over the horizon but slowly sinking. I quickened my pace as far as I could through the brambles, felled hazel bushes and scrub, becoming every moment more scratched and frightened. Feathery clouds were gathering imperceptibly in the west as though in preparation for the sun to sink amongst them. Gradually I climbed the wooded slope again. I was tired and my stomach ached. Buzz crept behind me as dispirited as I was.

And then – I don't know how it happened – I found myself back at the escarpment. I gazed at it in amazement thinking it must be another. But there was the boulder and there the splintered pine but this time a little more eerie as the after-noon came to an end. Shadows were beginning to creep like enemies through the wood. As I stood there, staring about, listening to the silence, a pheasant whirred from under my feet and disappeared.

It was as startling as a pistol shot and I burst into tears. I was alone in an alien place and I would never become familiar with the landmarks. I was hot and trembling. Beads of sweat trickled down my face, quickly chilled by the evening air. My stomach was queasy and suddenly gave a lurch, followed by a spasm of pain. I pulled down my shorts and squatted in that desolate place. Excrement flowed out of me like water, foul-smelling, repugnant. I had not a scrap of paper, and when I finished I wiped myself, sobbing as I did so, with dead leaves. If only, I thought to myself, I could be found, but not, please God, like this.

And then on a sudden impulse, when I had cleaned myself as best I could, I knelt in front of the splintered pine and recited the Lord's prayer. It was like praying to a shattered hope. In my dereliction and misery I prayed automatically, without expectation of being heard. Buzz watched me with sympathy and slowly, dismally moved his tail.

We set out again. Between sobs I called: 'Nanna, Nanna, Nanna!' I trailed on through the innumerable trees. My face was hot with tears of despair. I had, I saw, the reward for turning against Nanna whom I had loved so much. I needed her now, as I had never needed her before. My hatred of her – or whatever it was I had felt against her – was due to the fact that she had withdrawn herself, effaced herself. She had left me alone with Mother because she felt she ought and I, poor idiot, thought that Mother, because she was my mother, could take her place. There was a glitter, and excitement about being with Mother, but there was no peace, none of the old contentment. All these wild thoughts, like those which are said to be seen by drowning men, flashed through my mind. They flashed through my mind but made, as it were, no impression on it. Because I did not understand them, I made no resolution to alter myself in any way. It was a time of vision but not of understanding. Sparks from a hidden fire blazed up into the sky and vanished. I howled like a baby while Buzz pattered along behind me.

I came to a particularly dark part of the wood composed of tall hollies whose dead leaves rustled under my feet. A little cold wind, prelude to nightfall, swept through them. Strange shapes flitted among the caverns of darkness. The sky above them was darkening to an ever richer and deeper blue. I could see the rim of the new moon on the edge of the horizon surrounded by little attendant clouds. Day was melting into night, and the earth, like a drugged man, unconcerned with me, was falling into sleep. A faint whine came from Buzz as though he distrusted what he saw.

And then I heard it. A fading, almost inaudible cry, borne

on the night breeze. I ran towards it and Buzz pricked his ears. It grew louder. At last I came on Nanna. She was standing in the middle of the trees calling my name at the top of her voice. She looked scared and out of breath. I ran to her and buried my head in her blouse. I was home at last. She lifted up my blubbering face and said: 'Where have you been, you naughty boy?'

'I was fetching Buzz,' I answered tearfully, at first too pleased to resent her remark – the sort of thing in any case she always said on such occasions.

'You shouldn't have gone so far.'

I saw that as a matter of fact I had not gone very far, not far enough to have been so frightened. I began to feel ashamed of myself. 'Buzz wouldn't have run away, if it hadn't been for you,' I said resentfully.

'Oh, you wicked boy. You know it was the swan.' Nanna tossed her head, looked at me again and said no more.

We were soon back at the clearing by the river. A thin, white mist was rising from it into the grey evening air. Tiny puffs of cold wind rustled the rushes. A few, pale stars were now gleaming alongside the crescent moon. I wiped my face with the back of my hand before seeing Mother and shivered. Nanna took me by the hand.

Mother was scarcely visible in the failing light as she leant against the trunk of a tree at the edge of the wood. She was smoking a cigarette unconcernedly and she said nothing as I approached. I should not have known that she saw me but for the faint tinkle of her bracelets and the jangle of the amber chain she was wearing.

'So there you are, Davey,' she said at last as I kissed her cheek, 'We were beginning to wonder what had become of you.'

'If Nanna had not chased Buzz...' I began.

'It was all an accident.' She deliberately stubbed out her cigarette on the trunk of the tree. 'And accidents do happen.'

'I was nearly lost. It was getting dark.'

'You would have been found in the morning anyway.'

'In the morning?' I marvelled and then realised she was angry.

She gave a little cold laugh of derision. 'Worse things have occurred.'

'But I was ill,' I said lamely.

'We shall hear about that when we get home. Now we have missed the bus and will have to get a taxi.'

'I'm sorry, Mother,' I said, 'but if Nanna...' I left the sentence unfinished as she had turned away and was picking up some of the picnic things and handing them to Nanna.

'I didn't see the swan at first,' Nanna said defensively, 'and even if I had...'

'I suppose,' Mother said icily to me, 'you don't realise that you've spoilt everyone else's afternoon. But not a word more. We have to find a taxi. It's quite a long way through these tangles.'

'And,' Nanna said, scrutinising my face in the dim light, 'he's in no state to walk far.' She felt my forehead with the palm of her hand.

Mother shrugged her shoulders.

When we got home I was placed on the sofa in the neat little drawing-room while Nanna fetched me a drink. My head was swimming and I felt alternately hot and cold. Mother watched me critically as she stood in front of the fireplace. Nanna appeared at last, still dressed in her Mackintosh, bearing a tray and a cup of beef tea.

I put the drink to my mouth. It was hot and burnt my lips. As I pushed it away with a gesture of impatience the cup slipped through my fingers and spilt on the clean chintz cover. Mother gave an exclamation of annoyance and Nanna ran forward with her handkerchief.

'It was boiling,' I almost screamed.

'It wasn't hot, madam,' Nanna defended herself, 'not a bit too hot. Oh, these covers and the grease.' She was on her hands and knees wiping at the ruined chintz.

237

'Oh yer sullee!' I screamed, my voice rising to a crescendo.

There was a moment's silence. The little room seemed empty. Then my teeth began to chatter involuntarily and I trembled so violently I was thrown to the floor.

As they both bent over me, I heard Mother say: 'It will pass, it is a childish thing. It's nerves.'

When the attack had passed Nanna led me to bed to await the arrival of the doctor.

I was kept in bed several weeks until the symptoms of fever, trembling and sickness gradually passed away. What the illness was nobody understood and it was generally agreed that Mother's diagnosis was probably the nearest to the truth. At first Mother paid me regular visits but, as time went on, and I seemed to be better but not well, she came less frequently. From time to time I would hear the front door clang and Nanna explained that Monsieur Turenne was again staying at the Promenade Hotel.

'He's a very fine gentleman,' she explained one evening, 'he has a car and chauffeur as well as a valet.'

'But why is he staying at the Promenade Hotel at this time of the year?' I asked.

'To see your mother. And,' she went on, 'he has a lot of business to do in England.'

'He is Mother's cousin,' I said.

'And yours,' Nanna responded.

'But he doesn't come to see me,' I said, lying back on the pillow.

Nor did he during the whole of my illness. I did not catch a sight of him or even hear the sound of his voice.

When at last I was allowed downstairs the doctor suggested that I should have a complete change.

Mother shrugged her shoulders. 'But this,' she said, making a gesture round the room, 'is a complete change for him.'

'Ah well,' the doctor responded, packing his bag, 'if there's nowhere else to go, it can't be done.'

'Why couldn't I go and stay with Monsieur Turenne?' I asked Mother. And for the doctor's benefit added: 'He's my cousin, you know. He has a car and chauffeur. He lives in Belgium.'

Mother bit her lip. 'He's a very busy man,' she said shortly. 'I could ask him but I don't think it would do.'

'He lives in the country in Belgium,' I told the doctor.

The doctor patted me kindly on the shoulder.

Mother said: 'Wouldn't you rather go to The Firs?'

'The Firs?' Somehow, I had thought this would be impossible.

'But wouldn't you?' Mother asked again.

'Oh, yes, of course I would,' I answered eagerly.

'You'd have to go yourself. I couldn't leave the house.'

'Oh that would be all right,' I said with the straight-forwardness of youth.

That evening, as Nanna was saying goodnight to me, I heard the front door bang as usual.

'How long is Monsieur Turenne going to stay?' I asked.

'The chauffeur says another four weeks.'

'What does Mother do when she goes out with Monsieur Turenne?'

'They have dinner and then they dance in the ballroom. It's a lovely room with beautiful shrubs in pots and there's the special dance orchestra. Your mother,' Nanna went on, 'is still young and she ought to enjoy herself while she can.'

I considered all this. 'Monsieur Turenne never comes to see me.'

'He spends a lot of the day in London.'

'Not all the time. Perhaps he doesn't like children.'

'He should do,' Nanna said carelessly, 'he's got children of his own.' She stopped herself quickly.

'Has he? Why doesn't he bring them down here?'

Nanna went to the door, and shifted uneasily on her feet. 'Because,' she said, 'they live with his wife.'

'So Monsieur Turenne lives alone?'

Nanna nodded. 'Now no more,' she said severely. 'Don't think or talk about it any more.'

'Did the chauffeur tell you?'

But Nanna would not answer. 'Nanna,' I went on, changing the subject, 'if we do go to The Firs shall we see Mr Oldacre?'

'Of course.'

'He hasn't been here.'

'You'll be seeing him soon enough I expect.' And with that Nanna closed the night-nursery door.

And so I went back to The Firs as a visitor. I was to stay till just before Christmas and then return with Nanna to Bathampton. Mother told me when we parted that she might be going to Belgium while I was away.

'You need a holiday, Madam,' Jessie had said in her hoarse little voice when the plan had been announced, 'it will do you good.'

Mother had stood on the steps under the porch when we drove away. She was dressed in a grey dress and waved a white handkerchief. I had put my head out of the window and she had blown me a kiss.

'See you for Christmas, Davey,' she had shouted. There had been no messages to Grandma or anyone else.

Nanna had also opened the talc window at the back of the car, waved, and then sunk rather heavily back into her seat. Buzz had given a joyous bark and we had set off.

CHAPTER TWENTY-ONE

Life at The Firs was just the same. I stood at breakfast time with Grandma and looked down into the now leafless wood. Pieces of toast were ranged round the Valor perfection to keep them hot. The oatcakes were brought in wrapped in a napkin, straight from the oven. It was the old life, the old ways.

But there were changes, scarcely to be defined, but percept-ible. Everyone seemed older, as if the machinery was running down. I had grown used to younger people around me. I had been to school, although it was only a day school, and I sup-pose I had grown up. Grandma was restless and *distraite*. She talked more to herself than she had been used to do. The maids were less cheerful, Mr Courtenay more portentous.

But the greatest change was in Mr Evans. Grandma in a letter had mentioned that he was unwell. But I had not ex-pected him to be so altered as he was. He seemed to be con-sumed by a secret illness. He had lost his gaiety and talked to no-one. His thin face was thinner than ever. His eyes had grown dull, deep in their sockets. He now took no interest in his appearance. He went about like an unkempt shadow and he always had a few days' growth of beard on his chin.

What was worse he behaved like a creature which shuns the day. He got up very early and did all his work before the other gardeners arrived. He disappeared for hours on end. Of course he did not want to talk to me any more. Then one day I cornered him in the greenhouse.

'Mr Evans,' I said on the spur of the moment and without thinking, 'some photos of yours were found by Mr Courtenay.'

'What photos?' he demanded rudely.

'I don't know what they were and it was a long time ago,' I replied timidly, 'but I saw him put them in the furnace fire.'

He looked at me for a moment in silence. Then he shrugged his shoulders, as if, after all, it had no significance. If ever man was damned he was. I do not know what prompted me to make this tactless and unnecessary remark.

'He told me about them,' he said between his teeth. Talking seemed repugnant to him. The expression on his face was cruel. His eyes were alien like a wild animal's. I felt that, at last, he had become my enemy. He stared into my face a few moments more and then turned on his heel.

I was shocked and frightened. He had gone mad and I was

241

sure it had something to do with the photographs. A great mystery I did not understand had caught him up and was destroying him. The woman in the photograph seemed like an avenging angel. She had turned him into a savage, from a friend into an enemy.

I confided in Nanna how changed I thought he was. 'It's just that he's worried, that's all,' she said, 'don't take any notice.' But she shook her head sadly. And I knew better. I knew he now hated me.

Soon after this I was sitting in the servants' hall as the maids finished their breakfasts. It was all that it had been, exactly the same, everybody in their appointed places. But there was no gaiety. They were now just a collection of ageing women, rather bored with their lives, and trying to be nice to me. There was a crash at the back door. A door slammed.

'What's that?' I asked.

Cook looked up with a frown on her face. 'That's the vegetables, that's all.' She shot a sharp glance at Nanna. The others vigorously stirred their tea – except Catherine who stared impassively at the chequered tea-cloth. Fanny, the old cracked housemaid, began to cackle like a frightened hen.

As a symbol of my having grown older George suggested that I should have the use of part of the great barn adjourning Mr Evans's house. It was to be a sort of workshop and play-room. It was a great gloomy place but I was overjoyed when Grandma agreed.

I thought of fixing up a bell between the house and the barn. Grandma gave me some money for the wire but it was not sufficient to buy two strands. I therefore hit on the ingenious but not very practical idea of using an iron fence which ran the length of the drive as a substitute for one of the wires. The project failed. The bell would ring at odd hours and would not ring when Nanna pressed the button to get me in to a meal.

I decided I needed advice and waylaid Mr Evans in the potting shed. He was mixing pig food in a bucket. This was propitious. I had in the past been allowed to mix the food and then wear the wooden yoke to take the food to the sty.

'Mr Evans,' I began on rather a higher note than usual because of my anxiety. As I spoke I realised, somehow, what a small, priggish little boy I was. I had never felt this with Mr Evans before. Now I did, acutely. 'I'm in difficulties. I wonder if you would be able to help me?' I told him about the bell. 'I thought,' I ended lamely, 'you would know more about electricity than I do.'

He grunted something into the bucket which I could not catch. Then he walked out to the pump, filled another bucket with water, put the yoke on his shoulder and walked off to the pig sty. It was not so much his rudeness in not speaking which affected me. It was putting on the yoke himself. It had become a recognized thing, long before I went to Bathampton, that I was tall enough and strong enough to use the yoke and I was therefore always given it. I considered wearing it a great feat. Not to give it to me was a bitter snub.

I followed him down the kitchen garden. Neither spoke. Then we reached the place where in happier times he had chased a weasel out of the cabbages, so that I should see what it looked like. Things were now so altered that when we came to that spot I could go no further. I realised now he was completely my enemy. And as I turned back to the potting shed, I hated him.

The visit began to draw to its close. I did not mend the bell. I didn't mind whether it worked or not. And then, in a spirit of nostalgia, I went for a lonely walk in the Big wood.

It was a bright, crisp, winter evening. I walked slowly along the overgrown paths. It was very quiet but for my footfalls on the leaves. From time to time, disturbed wood pigeons exploded into the evening sky. Once above the tree tops they winged their way to the green horizon and disappeared. I reached a clearing and stood for a moment or two at its edge. I had never been there before and had never dreamt of its existence. A great, gaunt, dead oak raised its branches to the sky in an attitude of hopeless supplication. All around were hollies and holm oaks which cast long, dark shadows. The light of the dying sun was coloured by their darkness.

And then I heard quiet footsteps on the dry leaves. I stepped into the shadows. Catherine, the kitchen-maid, entered the clearing. She walked slowly, absorbed in her thoughts. She was wearing over her working-dress a brown overcoat which she had left unfastened. It was tipped at the collar with grey fur. Her carriage was confident and relaxed. There was even something majestic about it, I had to admit reluctantly. As she passed me, I saw her face. Its expression kept me pressed to my hiding place. Plain though I knew her to be, and she was very plain, in that eerie light she looked almost beautiful. A slow, satisfied, triumphant smile played about her lips which frightened me. I felt I had seen something I should not have seen. Her hair, which was always rigidly drawn back from her face, was untidy, as if she had let it down and had not had time to replace it. Her eyes, behind the rimless spectacles, were dreamy.

I waited a long time after she had passed. Then I made my way in the swiftly gathering darkness back to the house.

I spent most of my time in the workshop making a model boat. Mr Evans ceased to have a place in my mind – or, at least, in my conscious mind. I ceased to feel bitter. I had outgrown him. And that was that. I did, indeed, see him about the place. But we took no notice of each other.

And so it was that I was working in the barn one evening before dinner. The barn was a huge, eerie place at night. One end had been partitioned off as a workshop by stretching a piece of canvas from a beam to the floor. The canvas was pierced by a little door. The workshop itself was cosy enough. A paraffin lamp stood on the lathe and cast a warm circle of light. A little coke stove, its stack rising into the shadowy roof glowed comfortably. The chink of falling ash was somehow reassuring too. But outside this area there stretched unfathomable darkness which crept in over the top of the partition

244

and threatened my security. It is true that Mr Evans's cottage adjoined the barn; but the room on the first floor at the intersection was said to be haunted.

The canvas partition shuddered. Nanna had called the ghost stuff and nonsense. But I noticed that she wasn't very keen on the far end of the barn at night. In happier times I had also discussed it with Mr Evans. He was non-committal. 'I shouldn't take any notice of stories like that if I were you,' he had said. But he had added: 'Mind you, there are strange things in the world we'll never understand.'

I heard the wicket door open and then the door into the workshop. It was Mrs Evans. She was dressed in an apron and had the customary handkerchief tied round her head. She glanced about the workshop, as she came in looking for something. That she was agitated I could see even from where she stood in the shadows. She was usually too dispirited to be animated.

'Have you seen Mr Evans?' she asked, trying to hide the anxiety in her voice, and peered at me from the darkness.

I shook my head. 'No, I haven't seen him for days.' Why, I don't know, I also assumed an air of detachment, although her anxiety had communicated itself to me as excitement. 'No,' I continued, 'I have hardly spoken to him since I came back.' This was meant as a reproach to be repeated to Mr Evans. I must have felt it more than I supposed.

'Oh, I see,' she answered in her low, musical voice, 'then I wonder where he is...' She made a despairing gesture with her hands and hesitated at the door. 'I'm not sure....'

'Shall I come and help you look for him?' I volunteered, inquisitiveness conquering detachment.

'No, no, that's all right ... It's just that he's a bit late for his supper and I was thinking he might be in here with you.' She disappeared into the darkness, called 'Thank you' from behind the canvas screen and the wicket door closed behind her.

I tried to work at the boat again. But I was unsettled. Something mysterious had happened. A shiver of excitement possessed me. There was the ring of steel tipped boots on the stone path outside the barn. A man raised his voice and then subdued it.

I ran to the wicket door and looked outside. It was a cloud-less, star-filled night, without a moon. The outline of the great poplar at the end of Mr Evans's garden towered into the frosty sky, majestic, motionless. Little lights were bobbing about in the distance. At first I did not know what they were. Then I realised they were lanterns. They were moving in the direction of the Big wood. Just as I was turning back into the barn to pick up my coat, a light approached. It was Nanna and she was running.

She hurried me back into the barn and I saw by the lamp light that she had a scared expression on her face.

'Now put out the light,' she commanded in a breathless voice, bossy as usual when agitated, 'and come along up to the house with me. I suppose,' she went on, not allowing me to speak, 'the stove will be all right. We don't want the barn burnt down. There's trouble enough.' I could see that and opened my mouth, but she stopped me. 'Now, no arguing. You've got to come along at once.'

'But, Nanna,' I protested, having extinguished the lamp and following her out into the night, 'what has happened to Mr Evans?'

'We think there must have been an accident,' she replied in a breathless voice, too troubled to wonder how I knew. 'He hasn't been home for supper.'

'That can't be all,' I said and glanced at the uncurtained windows of Mr Evans's cottage. Every room was lighted up but there was no sign of life. Yellow lamp-light streamed into the deep blue of the night.

Nanna, too, looked in the direction of the cottage but did not answer me. She seemed unwilling to pass it. 'We'll go this way,' she said, wheeling round to go by the back of the barn through the garden made from the old cattle yard. She

246

clutched me by the arm and a moment later we were opening the heavy oak door into the barn garden.

As the door opened we saw we had made a mistake. A huddle of men stood in front of one of the sheds. The door was open and a very bright acetylene lamp hung from a hook inside. It cast a lurid light. I could see the back of a policeman's helmet. Someone inside was talking in undertones. A man turned and said roughly to Nanna: 'Go round the other way.' He looked meaningfully at me. Nanna gave a little gasp of surprise, seized my arm and dragged me back through the barn-garden door.

We were once more in the world of the pitiless star-lit sky. It was very cold and the stars shimmered in a naked perfection of beauty. Under the great poplar Nanna broke into convulsive sobs. The torch shone jerkily on the path.

I didn't know what to say. I wasn't so much frightened as awed. I thought: But I should be the one most upset. Why Nanna? Then I realised that she had forgiven Mr Evans for his strange behaviour. But I hadn't.

'I know what's happened,' I whispered as if it would comfort her.

'I know you do,' and she pressed me to her side.

I was wondering what he looked like in that shed under the lurid light.

'How did he do it, Nanna?'

'I don't know. I know nothing. He was a good man.'

'If he had shot himself, I would have heard in the barn.'

'It was wickedness that killed him, sheer wickedness.'

'But why?' I demanded, puzzled at the mystery of the thing.

Nanna recovered herself, dried her eyes, and hurried me up to the house. 'It was all wickedness' – she wouldn't say any more.

When I was washing for dinner, I said: 'Nanna, I think he went mad.'

Nanna nodded and dabbed her eyes. She held me a moment to her. 'Yes, it was all madness,' she said in a faraway voice.

247

I darted downstairs to the drawing-room to see if I could get any more information from Grandma. I had reached the screen at the door when I realised that Grandma was not alone.

'Catherine,' a man's voice was saying emphatically as if to hammer home his point.

'Catherine?' she asked uncomprehendingly.

'Catherine, the kitchen-maid.'

'That good girl!'

Of course I now knew everything that was to follow. The walk in the Big Wood, the photographs, everything fell into place. But I waited.

'Yes,' the man said grimly, 'she's going to have a baby.'

I thought Grandma was not going to reply. Then she said: 'But she was such a strict Methodist.' I could hear the man scrape his shoes on the floor. 'And,' Grandma continued, 'he was so fond of his wife. He used to write every week from the front.'

'That was some years ago now, Madam.'

Grandma sighed. 'And how did he do it?'

'Cyanide of potassium which he used for the wasps. He had a shot gun on the bench in front of him in case it didn't work instantly. There was a note for his wife.'

'And where is the girl?' Grandma asked.

The man cleared his throat. He was someone I did not know. 'I took it upon me to get Mr Courtenay to drive her home. The car will be at the back door in a few moments.'

'I see,' said Grandma a little stiffly. And then: 'After all, just as well.'

I wanted to talk to Nanna and ran upstairs again. But she was not anywhere to be found. I hesitated at the end of the passage and looked out of the window. The old, highly-polished Austin stood at the back door bathed in the light of the porch lamp. Its engine was running and Mr Courtenay, as stiff and well-polished as the car, stood in front of it. A large, old-fashioned trunk was strapped to the grid. A few moments passed and then the back door opened. It was Catherine, dressed as I had seen her in the Big wood. Now her brown overcoat was tightly buttoned and the grey fur covered her neck. She carried a small bag. On her head she had a shapeless brown hat fastened with a large pin.

The lamp light fell on her face as she walked to the car. Of course she was plain and the light glinted on her rimless spectacles. She had been crying and her eyes were red. But there was a sort of beauty or attraction in the passivity – yes, composure, even at that moment – of her white, rounded face. I noticed her lips for the first time. They were full and sensual. A little smile of derision played about them. But, then, what had she had to face in the servants' hall? Or was it that I was fancying again the smile I had seen in the Big wood? But the door of the car had been opened very stiffly by Mr Courtenay and she got inside, before I could decide. I could see her upright figure on the back seat as the car moved off.

'Oh, Nanna,' I said, running to her as she appeared at the top of the back stairs, 'I know it all now. Everything. Catherine.' And I clung to her.

'She was a wicked girl. But he was his own worst enemy.' I clung to the white apron as to security itself. I wondered if poor Mr Evans had been his own worst enemy and whether he could have helped himself.

Then I burst into a flood of tears. 'Anyway, Nanna,' I said, trying to dry them with my handkerchief, 'he wasn't my enemy, not really.'

The day of the funeral was chilly and overcast. Rays of thin sunlight gleamed among the bare trees and disappeared. An uneasy wind stirred and died away. Grandma had seen to it that the ordinary religious ceremonies should take place. The reason which she gave for demanding this was that Mr Evans had died as a direct result of his wartime experiences. Otherwise how was his extraordinary death explicable? Mr Brailes and the bishop accepted this merciful explanation.

With the priggishness of youthful inexperience I secretly demurred at their decision. It seemed to me that if the church denied burial to the suicide there should be no exceptions. There was, perhaps, in my feelings still a lurking rancour at Mr Evans's conduct to me. An ordinary burial also tarnished the wonder of the thing I had experienced. That morning the routine of the household was in confusion. Breakfast was at a different hour in order to give the maids time to change for the ceremony. I was not to attend.

When everybody, or almost everybody, had departed for the church, I was left to my own devices. I wandered round the house, looking out of the windows, examining my toys and putting them away, and wondering to myself how it was that I felt at this important moment so very little. Buzz pattered across the parquet floors behind me as if he might lose me and with the air of having been caught up in a catastrophe he did not understand.

And then I came across the letter in the hall. Usually I received what letters I got at breakfast. But that day everything was upside down. It was in Mother's bold handwriting conventionally rounded by her continental education. It could not have been written by an English woman and it made her seem more remote. Moreover the paper was thin and foreign. I picked it up and read it in the shelter, that dark and gloomy retreat under the north studio. I should be able there to read the letter and at the same time hear the tolling of the cemetery bell. It was a long letter, written from the heart and without any concession to my age. I still have it after all these years, now grown yellow with age.

My dearest Davey,

As you will see from the stamp I am writing from Belgium. I have made up my mind to marry Monsieur Turenne. I am afraid this may surprise and upset you. It means that I shall now live in Belgium and that you will not be able to live with me. I have written to your Grandmother and I am sure she will be pleased to have you back at The Firs. She has already said in a letter that she has missed you very much. And you will be back in the place you love.

I always write as I think, directly. What I have told you is the truth. But I must also tell you how much I have suffered in making the decision to marry Monsieur Turenne. I have known him for a long time and I love him. You have been the source of the worry. I thought when I handed you over, little more than a baby, to your Grandmother that I might be making a great mistake, that my own child came before everything else. But it seemed for the best. How could I provide for you adequately without money? My husband and my father were dead. My mother would not help except on terms I could not accept. I was forced into a decision. But all the time I was worried that I had done wrong.

It all came to a head when I realised that Monsieur Turenne wanted to marry me, even at great sacrifice to himself. If I was to marry him, on my side I should have to cut myself off from you for ever. Even though you were little more than a name to me you were my child. I could not face the prospect of a final break. That is why I arrived at your birthday party. I wanted to see how strong affection and blood would be when put to the test. They were strong, very strong. I knew then that I loved you as my son and that I could never have the same affection for any other child. I blamed myself for what I had done. I felt I had violated a natural impulse. I wanted to show that I was not the bad mother I appeared, even to myself to be.

But when you came to me things were not as I supposed. Love, however great, and it was great on my side, cannot heal old wrongs or change past events. You had grown one way and I had grown another. A mother and son should see

251

things in the same way, at least until the son is grown up. You were the product of an environment different from mine. You saw things in a way that I could not see them. You were, in fact, my child only in name. Later on, when you are older, you will see this to be true. I tried to hide the truth from myself and I suppose you hid it from yourself. Now is the time to get rid of pretences. You could not be happy as my son, and, perhaps I could not be happy as your mother.

I want you to keep this letter. You will not, and cannot understand it now. You will understand it later when you are older and perhaps be able to judge less severely than you will at this moment.

God bless you Davey in your life. I have been such a bad mother to you that I know you are bound to think unkindly of me. But, remember later on, I had my difficulties, too. Oh, if only it had not happened as it has, or, that having happened, you were older, so that I could speak to you as I want to speak to you, from one heart to another. It was not from selfishness that I asked you to come to Bathampton. I loved you and wanted to put my love into practice.

It did not turn out as I intended. I should have married Monsieur Turenne without entering your life at all. But what I did I did for the best. Please forgive me. I shall never forget you, even if in the future we only write to each other.

When I came back into your life on your birthday Nanna said that you prayed for me every night. Will you go on doing that? Then I shall know that something of my love is returned to me. Again I say: Keep this letter so that in the future you understand something of how I feel at this time of parting.

Your loving Mother

I read and reread the letter. If I did not understand it all, I received the impression she meant to convey. The mother I had known was all there, the trim, neat, self-possessed woman. I caught again her fragrance, a mixture of the smell of her newly-cleaned frocks and the smell of her scarcely perceptible scent. I saw the beautiful olive-coloured skin, the blackness of her hair. And I also saw her writing the letter, swiftly, thoughtfully, directly, writing as she would perhaps write to Monsieur Turenne, as she put it, 'from the heart'. Would she have sat at some little ormulu mounted writing desk such as I had seen in picture books, far away in a distant place surrounded by strange sounds and smells? It was as if she had written not merely from another country, but from another existence. But then Bathampton was another existence. I looked round and I wondered how real the shelter was. At Bathampton it had seemed as strange, as Bathampton seemed at that moment. I was unable to grasp what true reality was.

And then I reflected that this was a new woman whom I did not know. It was the same voice, the same appearance, but transformed. It was as if I had had an idea which the reality contradicted. There was a warmth of emotion in the letter I had not expected. A door had been opened, as it had been opened when I had looked into the drawing-room that night at Bathampton. I had put the image from my mind. It, like the letter, had been something I had not been meant to see, and did not wish to see. Was it hatred or love or fear I felt? Or was it a combination of the three which neutralised each other? Or did I feel nothing at all?

The idea had been driven out for the moment. But for a moment only. The idea of what should be, and which up to that moment had been, reasserted itself. I remembered the dream I had had when she said she was taking me to Bathampton, of the sea breaking peacefully on the tranquil sand, murmuring as it eddied and flowed like the motion of a sleeping woman's breasts. The cruel vision of what the sea at Bathampton had really been flitted through my mind and was gone, leaving only a sense of disenchantment. Now I thought of her sitting in the drawing-room at a little desk, myself standing in front of her, with my hands behind my back listening to what she said I ought to be, and what I ought to do. The remembrance was sweet, the tutelage and dependence what I desired in the depth of my heart. Grandma and Nanna could not take her place just as an idol cannot take the place of a living goddess. Nature, or whatever it was, had created between us a special bond, which difference of character or attitude could not alter. She was mine and I was hers. Time and custom can forge such a bond, but nature creates it all at once between a mother and her child.

She was right. She had violated nature. And now she was making the violation permanent. It did not matter that the wound had been, and perhaps was being made in good faith. A wound is a wound however it is struck. And a blow that strikes at the springs of life cripples. I knew then, as I know now, perhaps now in a more sophisticated fashion, that I should grow up in some way deformed, different, and that much of my vitality would be consumed in trying to right what had been done to me. I realised, I suppose for the first time, that life did not merely appear cruel but was cruel.

In the shelter it was dark and cold. There were gleams of wintry sunshine in the clouded sky but they scarcely penetrated the thick curtain of evergreens. A dry leaf scuttled across the brick floor impelled by a puff of cold wind. Desolation lay everywhere. There was not a leaf on the deciduous trees. The fields which I could see through a gap, the far side of the lane, were bare plough furrow, the colour of chocolate, gleaming now and then in the fitful light. The poet's laurel seemed to be withering before my eyes. The door to the photographic dark-room looked as if it had not been used for years. But it was there, so short a time ago, Mr Evans had printed his photographs. Everything was very still. There was only the indistinct sound of little footsteps, of rustling and murmuring, that one gets in every wood in winter.

And then, loudly with an ugly peal, the bell of the cemetery chapel began to toll in a regular, remorseless rhythm. Mr Evans was being buried. Buzz sat thoughtfully in the shadows as if waiting for something.

Even as I thought of the inert figure in its coffin being lowered once and for all into the earth with only the faint hope of resurrection, like the scent of rosemary, to soften the harshness of the scene, I thought also of myself. Could I go to Mother in Belgium? No. Could she come here to The Firs? No. Could I go back to Bathampton, after all, do what I had a few hours before, hated the thought of doing? No. What if Grandma did not want me back? She had made up her mind as to the future and that I should live with Mother. What would she say now? I had, I knew it, deserted her and Nanna for Mother. And now.... A sense of isolation, desolation, and insecurity, blew over me like a gust of wind from the wintry sky. I thought of the poor corpse on whose coffin the thuds of earth were now falling, and shivered.

And then, like a boat into whose sail an unexpected breeze suddenly blows, I thought of Christmas. My heart swelled out. Troubles, like storms of rain, might spoil the beauty of one rose, but there were always buds, there was always life. Christmas, after all, would be at The Firs where it ought to be. There would be Grandma and Nanna. There would be the gleam from the fire in the servants' hall on the paper-crowned bust of King Teddy. Cook would take the pudding in its veined china mixing-bowl from the seething saucepan.... There would be George and the usual visit to Mr Courtenay and Gertrude.

There was a pang in my heart for Mother. But she had never fitted into the Christmas picture. Already the thought of her was like that of a death which had occurred long ago. It was a dull ache that mingled with the fear and shock I felt at Mr Evans's burial, an ache that was buried with him. When the ceremony was over, the last clod filled in, hardly any conscious remembrance would remain.

The tolling of the bell ceased, its last peal reverberating in the air as though trying not to fade into oblivion. But slowly it did. I folded the letter and put it in my pocket. I made my way past the photographic studio, glancing at the grimy windows and at the darkness inside. Faces seemed to peer out at me. But they were, as I well knew, only shadows, chained to their places by a spell which would not release them from their non-entity. If the spell was broken, what had been would be one with what was to be and what is. And that, not knowing whether to be comforted or sorry, I knew would never happen.

I had thought of going straight to Grandma. But, as I passed through the Red room, I looked across the hall and saw the car drive up to the front door. Nanna and Cook got out and walked heavily round to the back door talking together in low voices. Then Mr Courtenay helped Grandma to alight. She was dressed entirely in black and wore a veil. She leaned heavily on Mr Courtenay's arm and shuffled into the lobby. She came through into the hall, having drawn aside the veil, slowly took the pins out of her hat, lifted the hat from her head.... She did not see me as I stood in the Red room and exclaimed to herself in a sad, tired voice: 'Ah me! Alas!' It was not the voice of tragedy but of age.

I came up to her and slipped my hand in hers. I looked up into her face trying to read there what it contained. But all she did was to stroke my hand gently with her old dry fingers. She was clearly not thinking of me. Perhaps she was thinking of Mr Evans, but more probably of that greater, more awful funeral, when Giorgio had been buried on the hill beneath a mound of wreaths. Or perhaps she was thinking of her own funeral which could not be long delayed and whose approach would be peopled with haunting fears.

She said not a word about Mother, or of a letter from her, or anything of my future. The fact that I was really only on a holiday to The Firs seemed to have been forgotten. After lunch I asked Nanna if she had heard from Mother and she shook her head. I then told her the news. She nodded her head sadly as if some inevitable catastrophe had happened and wiped a tear from her eyes with the edge of her apron. I did not know whether the tears were for me or for Mother or for herself or, perhaps, at the culmination of a romance she had witnessed. But I do know she had learnt to love Mother. She pressed me to her without saying anything. I did not cling to her, as I would have done a short year before. I now loved her but with a certain detachment.

'Nanna,' I said, breaking away from her arms, 'what will happen to us now?'

'You needn't worry about that. Grandma will tell you soon enough that you're staying to Christmas. We'll make as good a Christmas as we can after all.' There was a tone of lament in her voice. She looked at me once or twice with her big, brown wide-set eyes and I knew she wondered that I had not mentioned the funeral. But then for me the Mr Evans I had known and loved had been buried long since.

Grandma never said a single word to me about Mother. Out of pride or shyness I did not speak of it either. It was tacitly assumed by everyone that I had come back to The Firs to stay. After all, what alternative was there? The trunks were fetched from Bathampton and life went on as if Mother had not so much as crossed my path. Nanna composed a letter for Mother from me which Mother must have realised was not written by me. It was posted and that was the end of it except for an expensive present which arrived punctually for Christmas.

I have often wondered, and still do, whether what Mother said in the letter was true. Grandma did not think so. I overheard her talking to George one evening in the Red room as I lingered in the hall after tea. The sliding doors were ajar. George was sitting under the Aladdin lamp in front of the fire reading a book aloud. Grandma was lying on a sofa in the niche Giorgio used to use.

Suddenly, as was his way, George threw the book on to his

knee and exclaimed: 'I often wonder what happened about Marie's marriage.'

Grandma sniffed, screwing up her nostrils. 'In what way?'

'It was so sudden. Why did she have the boy, if she wanted to get married?'

'She wanted to try out the sensation of being a mother.' And she sniffed again.

'You think so?'

'Yes, she'd known the man for years.' She pronounced the word 'known' significantly. 'Of course he'd had enough of children by his first marriage. She wanted to make sure she wasn't making a mistake in giving up her son – so she put poor little Davey to the test.' She paused. 'She can't tell the truth. She's only out for herself. I never heard of her first marriage to Nick till she produced all the papers and the baby. She brandished them in front of my nose in the drawing-room. She thought there was money in it. As it turned out it was all mine. . . .'

George picked up his spectacles, put them on his nose and placed the book under the circle of light. He sighed a little and began to read, but only a sentence or two. Then he stopped and again threw the book on to his knee.

'But if you foresaw what was going to happen . . .'

'Yes?'

'Was it wise to make such drastic changes, to . . .' He paused.

'I should have foreseen,' she corrected him, 'rather than I did foresee. It makes no difference now. It's easy to be wise after the event.'

'I see.'

George began to read again. Grandma looked up at the gesso ceiling of the niche and frowned with a sort of anguish.

CHAPTER TWENTY-TWO

Strangely enough I remember little of that Christmas I was so much looking forward to. On Christmas Eve I remember lying on the rug in front of the drawing-room fire before the lamp had been brought in, waiting for tea and idly playing with some bricks. Grandma had not come down from her afternoon rest and I was alone in the great, shadowy room. Grey, dim light, reflected from the powdery snow and seemingly almost tangible, filtered through the west window and the skylight over my head, giving the place an eerie, cheerless appearance. But in front of the fire, in an area bordered by the hearth rug and the circle of chairs, it was warm and bright. Lively flames burst from the hissing logs and were reflected in the highly-polished knobs of the fire dogs. As darkness edged in upon the house, like an enemy creeping upon an undefended fortress, the flames were also reflected in the glass panels of *art nouveau* bookcases. From the other end of the house came the muffled rumble of curtains being drawn. Soon the lamps with their pale, yellow light would supplant that of the chill, dying daylight. In the kitchen Cook, I knew, was trussing the great turkey which I had seen carried through the back door, carefully wrapped in sheets of greaseproof paper. Upstairs Nanna was wrapping her presents in the night-nursery. I lay on my stomach and looked into the fire, at the glowing faces of Giorgio, Grandma, Mother, or faces that were like theirs. Trickles of ash fell into the cinder tray with a sparkle and tinkle. The darkening room was scented by the burning pine logs.

For the first time Christmas seemed like any other day. The weather was warm, almost sultry, and the dining-room at lunch time, heated by the Valor perfection stove, was stifling.

Wisps of mist hung about the dripping trees. All I can remember – why, heaven knows – is passing through the dim hall after lunch. Grandma leant heavily on my arm and shuffled her feet on the parquet floor. George wiped his mouth on a coloured handkerchief. Grandma slumped down in one of the claret-coloured armchairs in front of the drawing-room fire and whispered to herself: 'What will happen to this little place?'

The same grey, enervating weather persisted during the days after Christmas. Grandma, fussed and distracted, answered every Christmas card by a letter. She shuffled about in the darkened house with a look of anguish on her face. She would often stop half way across the hall or in the middle of the long passage outside her bedroom and exclaim, as if suddenly recollecting herself: 'Ah me! Alas!'

A new gardener, old, handsome, and past the work, was engaged. A new, unfamiliar face, that of the new kitchen maid, was added to those round the table in the servants' hall. And then a letter came from the headmaster of St George's. It was short and to the point: if I did not arrive for the next term, a place would no longer be kept for me. The days of my old life were numbered. I knew it with foreboding, but I also looked forward to what was to come with a sense of anticipation.

On New Year's day the weather changed. The front lawn was covered with hoar frost and sunlight sparkled on the boughs of the trees in the wood. Ice gleamed on the bird bath.

I was standing in the hall, dark by comparison with the brightness of the south side of the house. I idly held the main post at the foot of the bannisters and swung one foot to and fro, which I had done in moments of boredom from the time I could remember. Grandma shuffled out of the dining-room and asked me what I was going to do. I had been thinking of St George's, of Mother and the little garden at Bathampton, the thoughts trickling through my mind without pattern or purpose. On the spur of the moment I said: 'I was thinking of going down to Kiln Cottage and taking the two dogs up the Sandy Way.'

'Perhaps, Davey,' Grandma said, 'I could come part of the way as far as Kiln Cottage? I want to see Mr Oldacre. I don't feel like going by myself. I am rather shaky on my pins today. But it's such a capital day and I should like to go out.'

I waited for her in the Red room while she fetched her coat and hat. Buzz whined at the glass door. The birds were fighting over the scraps on the lawn. The birdbath was now steaming with hot water placed there by the parlour-maid, whose broad back clad in an old coat, could be seen waddling to the back door. The sun shone out of a blue sky but on the horizon, over the trees, long cloudlets winged with gold and grey were beginning to form.

'I don't think,' Grandma said coming up behind me, 'the weather is going to last. Perhaps that's why I feel so unsteady today.' She sniffed appreciatively, sighed and took my arm. As she walked down the brick steps she held on to me and gripped the wooden rail. She paused on the terrace path, looked around and sighed again. 'I'm glad to have your arm, Davey,' she murmured and smiled into my face. We walked slowly down under the studio window, stopping now and then. 'There's one last red leaf on the American oak,' she observed pointing to the little tree in the middle of the lawn in front of the giant fir. Buzz was scuffling in the frost at its foot where there was a mound on which primroses grew in the spring and where I had sometimes seen hares at play.

We passed the Della Robbia under its wooden canopy. There was a grey wooden seat in front of it at which Giorgio, dressed in his doctoral robes, had posed for his photograph. The face of the Virgin smiled in the sunlight. Grandma paused and looked up at the studio window festooned with its vine to which, even now, there clung a few purple leaves. Grandma pinched my fingers affectionately as we walked on.

We turned the corner into the wood and at that moment met George coming in the opposite direction. He was meditatively smoking his pipe which was almost buried in the thick scarf round his neck. He grinned and took the pipe out of his mouth.

'George,' Grandma said with something defensive in her voice, 'Davey was taking me down to see you. I want,' she continued, disengaging her arm from mine and placing her hand on his in a gesture that was grave and supplicatory, 'I want to speak to you.' There was a look of appeal in her eyes, as she gazed up at him under the brim of her large hat.

'Of course,' George murmured in his deep voice, raising his eyebrows in surprise, 'let's go back to the house. Here, take my arm.'

They turned and walked back to the house forgetting my presence. She leant heavily on his arm and looked up into his face as if asking his forgiveness.

'I'm very anxious,' she began and then broke off. 'I feel,' she continued, 'I've made a great mistake. What will happen to this little place when I've gone?'

'But,' George responded, his heavy face almost as grave as hers, 'surely it's all been settled. There is to be a library built round Giorgio's papers.'

They had reached the Red Room steps and Grandma paused, leaning on the wooden rail. 'But will this little place be kept as it is? Won't it be altered into something different ... vulgar?'

'If there's the money,' George said in a tense, exasperated voice, 'it will be kept as it is.'

'If there is the money ...'

'That was the arrangement you made.'

'It will no longer be a home.'

'In a sense no.'

George propelled her up the steps. 'I think,' he said, as if he was talking to a child, 'we ought to discuss this inside. You're upset and have forgotten what was planned. I shall remind you of it all ...'

'And what,' Grandma asked, her hand on the handle

262

of the glass door, 'what will happen to little Davey? Won't people say that it is his by right?'

'The cost of his education is to be paid for,' George said, pushing open the door.

Grandma turned round so that she faced him. 'But is that enough?' she asked wonderingly. I could see now that she was unwell. Her hands were trembling and there were patches of red on her cheek bones.

'Let's come indoors,' George said coaxingly, and, at last, managed to get her inside.

I could hear their voices for a few more moments and then George returned to close the half-open door.

I walked slowly down to Kiln Cottage, meditatively whistling as I made my way through the wood. But when I got there I wondered if George would like me to take his dog without asking him. She was tied up in a shed at the back of the garden and this, I decided, probably meant that she was on heat. I looked for Mrs Farmer but she was out. I sat down in front of the range and waited. The ash chinked in the grate and George's bitch moaned caressingly from the shed. Buzz sat beside me and cocked his ears excitedly. Occasionally he made for the door and whined.

I waited a long time and then the front door opened and I heard George's footsteps. I got up to make myself known but he walked very quickly through to the dining-room and picked up the receiver of the telephone. I could hear him through the kitchen hatch ask for a London number. I sat down again.

'Is that Mr Bigelow?' I heard him ask. 'Yes George Oldacre. It's about The Firs . . . There's some trouble. I've just seen Mrs Porteous. She wants to alter the will . . . She thinks she's made a mistake . . . I told her that. But the most I could get her to agree to . . . Oh, yes, she wanted to alter the whole thing . . . I know . . . And of course it puts me in a very nasty position . . . Well, yes. You can see how it affects me. I was saying the best I could do was to make her understand that the general lines of the will must stand and that she should make provision for her grandson ... I remember you warned her ... She wants the house and ten thousand settled on him, so that he can keep it going ... No, I suppose it wouldn't be enough. I suppose not.' There was a long pause. 'Well,' George resumed at length, 'if you think that, you'll have to tell her. But in her present state of mind if she doesn't have her way she'll alter the whole thing and that would be worse ... Yes, having made up her mind one way she can't simply go back on it ... Of course she has the right. That's just it. But wouldn't the second idea be a way out? ... Ah, I see. If that's the case I suppose it's impossible ... No, quite honestly she isn't herself at all. She's very worked up ... I see your point. Yes, I see. It could be argued ... A doctor? I don't know what to think ... I had better come and see you. Today? Right.'

I had made my way to the door again only too well aware that I should not have overheard as much as I had. Buzz and I slipped outside.

The weather, as Grandma had foreseen, was no longer clear and bright. Heavy grey clouds were crossing and recrossing the face of the sun. Buzz and I had a melancholy walk up the Sandy Way and then returned to the house.

I sat broodingly by the fire in the drawing-room. What did Grandma really want? The house seemed to brood with me as though about to answer an unasked question. I understood in the way that a child does understand the essential issues at stake. I knew Grandma loved me but I also knew that the house and Giorgio's memory came first. I also knew that George was fond of me. But how fond? I had been struck by the way he had referred to Grandma and myself on the telephone. He had talked of us as if we were strangers. How he could have done otherwise, I did not know. But I did not think of him in the way he thought of me. There was a part of his mind which his fondness for me could not penetrate. Perhaps, I thought, as I looked into the fire, no-one is as fond of another person as one thinks, that there are natural limits

beyond which affection cannot pass. All this I thought inchoately with a sort of depression and melancholy I had never
experienced before. It was a first intuitive glimpse into the
way things are.

And then I noticed for the first time that there was a
noise and bustle going on upstairs. I ran up to the passage to
see what was the matter and almost collided with Fanny.

'Oh there you are, Master Davey. Your Grandma's been
took ill and we're waiting for the doctor.' She looked considerably fussed, but I could see the drama of the situation
pleased her. 'I've got to go to the kitchen for a can of 'ot water.
You can sit by 'er till I come back.'

There was nobody about and I softly opened Grandma's
door. As I still stood with my hand on the handle, I could
hear the murmur of Grandma's voice. At first I thought she
was talking to someone and then I realised there was no-one
else in the room. She was lying in her nightdress in bed. Her
head was thrown back on the pillow. Without her false teeth
she looked old and wizened. Her cheeks fell in and were very
pale. Her hair which looked plentiful enough under her lace
cap, deprived of it, was pathetically thin. Her eyes were closed
and her hands gripped the sheets nervously.

I came over to the bed and sat down. I took one of her
hands but she was unaware of it. The other still plucked at the
bedding. At first I could not hear what she was saying and
then gradually I began to make out the slurred, hurried
sentences.

'I haven't got my cotton gloves. I left them behind. I didn't
think I should need them. No-one told me. No, no, you didn't
Emily. You know you didn't. Don't ring the bell till I've found
them. Do be kind. Do be kind. Let me run back to the carriage
...It's driven away. They're opening the door and I haven't
got my cotton gloves. I haven't got my cotton gloves....' She
ended in a low wail and the words became incoherent. All the
time she spoke her eyelids had been fluttering and with her
right hand she was plucking and plucking at the bedclothes.

265

Her left hand, in mine, moved convulsively like a blind animal in a trap.

She lay quietly for a few moments and then began to whisper again. 'I'll never forgive you, if you tell Mother. Never. I couldn't help it. Nobody's seen. No thank you, I won't have any wine. No wine, thank you. Where have I mislaid my gloves? How charming.... The fire is bright. That's because of the frosty weather....' Her voice trailed away.

I could imagine the scene. I had seen it in albums filled with old, faded photographs. Grandma had often told me of her early life. The girls stood in the frosty air on the steps of the neo-Gothic castle. In the distance were the blue hills and the glimmer of a loch. The great untidy garden, filled with shrubs and conifers, desolated by the Highland winter, lay around them. The clop of hooves as the carriage draws away down the uneven drive. Grandma, then Mary, a pretty girl in her teens stands on the steps. She rubs her hands together nervously in her fur muff waiting for the door to be opened....

In the still, dark room, the gramophone from the past ran on, whispering of long forgotten fears. The old hands trembled on the bedclothes at the thought of her trifling mistake. I shivered at the thought that the past had really invaded the present.

Fanny arrived at the door with the can of water simultaneously with the doctor. I did not know him and he looked round the dark blue walls, the worn books in their shelves, the ceiling darkened over the bed by the flaring of a lamp with detached interest. Fanny took me by the hand and I left her to fuss round the washstand.

I crossed the passage and looked in at the nursery. Nanna was sitting on the low nursing chair some way from the fire, so that the light from the window fell on her sewing. Her eyes were red. She did not look up but put her sewing on the ground beside her. I went over to her, stood beside her and she put her arm round me. I laid my cheek against hers. She

266

did not speak and we looked into the fire, which was spitting and crackling, as if, somehow, it was connected with Grandma's illness. The canary in its cage on the high window-sill hopped about, so that the wires twanged, but it did not sing. I remembered the morning I had talked to Grandma about my father. It had been just such a morning as this.

'You know Grandma's very ill?' Nanna said, breaking the silence.

I nodded. 'She's rambling about the time when she was a child,' I said with a slight shiver of horror which I tried to mitigate by swinging one of my legs to and fro.

Nanna looked up startled. 'Were you in there?'

'I've been sitting with her. Fanny said I could. I didn't make any noise.'

'When you came in, you should have come in here. It isn't right for a child to see such things.'

'What happened?' I asked.

'After Mr Oldacre left Kitty found her on the floor in the drawing-room. I think she's had a fit.'

'A fit?'

Nanna nodded.

'Will she die?' I whispered fearfully.

'I don't know.' And she sighed. 'But you shouldn't have gone in. It isn't for a child to see such things.'

I considered this, swinging my leg backwards and forwards, wondering for how long the mysteries of existence could be hidden from me. A fly resurrected by the heat of the room hissed painfully at the window pane. Buzz lay with his head between his paws, over-awed by the quietness of the house. He blinked his eyes at the grate and then turned enquiringly to the window, twitching his ears in the direction of the fly, as if its hissing irritated him.

There were footsteps in the passage and the doctor entered. He was a thin, unemotional man in a blue suit. Nanna got to her feet.

'Is Mr Oldacre here?' he asked.

I told him I thought he had gone to London.

'I'll telephone to him this evening. In the meantime keep the patient warm and let me know if there's any change.' He still had his hand on the door and he made a motion to open it.

'But how is Mrs Porteous?' Nanna enquired anxiously.

'She's not very well, of course,' he said with a wintery smile, 'but I'm satisfied there's no danger now. A week or so in bed and she'll be herself again. Mrs Porteous is old but she has a strong constitution.'

'I thought . . . ' I began.

He had opened the door but turned back. 'These things often look worse than they are,' he said with the same smile and an air of superiority.

The doctor proved right. After a day of sleep Grandma recovered and when I next saw her was sitting up in bed. What we had thought the fall of the tree was only the creaking of an old branch.

CHAPTER TWENTY-THREE

Time was running out. Nanna, George and I made an excursion to London to buy my school clothes. It was thought that Nanna alone would not be suitable and George alone would be useless. I tried on the thick serge suit, the regulation boater hat and the rest of it in front of a cheval mirror in a large basement of a store in Oxford Street. The room, stuffy and overlit, was filled with other boys on similar excursions. They looked proud, alien, confident, as though, to them, going to boarding-school was an everyday, even a pleasant, experience. I wondered how many of them were due at St George's.

'I suppose,' George said in his easy way to the assistant, his legs apart, revealing a pair of brown plus fours under his overcoat, 'most of these boys have been to school before?'

'Oh, yes, sir,' the man answered, looking George up and down critically in a way which suddenly made me realise that he was wrongly dressed, 'there are very few new boys this term.' He implied that George would not know, as he had not been to a preparatory school.

'Of course,' George said looking round the shop thoughtfully, and taking out his pipe, 'not this term. They seem very self-possessed. Perhaps,' he continued, lighting a match, 'schools aren't as bad as they used to be. Poor little devils!'

'It's a great privilege to be going to St George's,' the assistant murmured, looking at me as I stood awkwardly in front of the glass.

George grunted. And then recollecting the reason for the visit to the shop, took his pipe out of his mouth and smiled blandly. 'I think that will do, won't it Nanna?'

At the word 'Nanna' a boy standing at the next mirror gave me a painfully hard look. His eyes were full of curiosity and derision. I only hoped he was not going to St George's too.

Nanna made a last tick on the clothing list and got up. 'We've everything now, Mr Oldacre.'

When we returned to The Firs we found Mr Bigelow, the family solicitor, had called and was sitting with Grandma in her bedroom. The parlour-maid told us the news as we entered the lobby from the front door. George's eyes narrowed into an alert and scared look. His manner, which had been easy and expansive during the trip to London became remote and thoughtful as he stood in front of the drawing-room fire waiting for the lawyer to come down. I tried to make conversation but it was no good. In any case I had not much relish for it myself. I could not shake off the impression the basement of the store had had on me. Looking round the drawing-room into which the grey outer light was creeping through the west window, I was appalled that it could remain as it always had been when I was about to be changed into something new, a something which jeopardised even my personality. George pulled at his pipe, took it out of his mouth, put it into his pocket, took it out again and relit it. At last he could bear the waiting no longer and went out of the room.

I slowly made my way to the kitchen hoping to have tea in the servants' hall. But I got no further than the lobby. George and the lawyer were talking on the stairs.

'I've had a long talk with her,' the lawyer was saying in a thin but clear, peevish voice, 'and she agrees that any change in the will is out of the question. I told her that the boy could not possibly have the income she mentioned to you without upsetting the whole scheme. She agreed.'

George said something I could not hear.

'Oh, yes, at this stage,' the pedantic voice resumed, 'a change is out of the question. It might be challenged on the grounds of her ill health. Later on is another matter. Generally speaking the longer she waits the less easy it will be to make any major alteration....'

They were still talking in low tones when I slipped across the hall below them and opened the baize door which led into the kitchen quarters.

The day of departure which, I thought, like a condemned prisoner, could never dawn, dawned at last. I came down to breakfast in my new serge suit and long trousers. The material made the back of my legs sore. I had to wear a starched collar which was not only irksome but was also so slippery that I could not keep my tie in position. My new shoes creaked as I made my way down the stairs. When I got to the dining-room I found that Grandma had got up.

'But, Grandma,' I said, breaking, almost without thinking, the rule by which we were always silent before breakfast, 'you shouldn't have got up. You should have stayed in bed.'

'Not today,' Grandma said with a smile that indicated both love and the triumph she had made over her illness. She bent down and kissed me. 'You look,' she remarked, wrinkling her nostrils as she viewed me as if she was examining a work of art, 'very nice and very grown up.' Then she took my hand, as was her custom, and we looked out over the lawn together.

I had been too preoccupied with dressing to notice the weather. But I noticed it now. It was a fresh, windless day. The sun shone with that brightness which seems to be reserved for winter. Everything sparkled with wetness as the hoar frost melted in the sunlight. Even the great melancholy firs seemed to be basking in the beautiful morning. I looked at the largest of the trees in whose branches I had seen, ever since I could remember, patterns of faces, the heads of melancholy old men with beards, patriarchal in their antiquity, or swan-necked Pre-Raphaelite women. That morning I could see no patterns at all. The birds chattered round the bird bath. A great thrush flipped the water around with his wings and made it flash like a rainbow. Grandma absently stroked the back of my hand with one of her fingers. For a while the vividness of the scene in front of us seemed to move her to a heightened perception of its beauty. But a frown passed across her forehead, she sighed deeply and turned away. I saw she was looking at the blackened rose hips which were all, or almost all, that remained of last year's roses.

'Life,' she muttered to herself, 'goes on.'

I looked up into her old face, bent forward towards the leaf of a petunia on the window-sill which she fingered with a gentle motion of her thumb, and thought of her on the bed, with her eyes closed rambling of her long forgotten child-hood in the Highlands. Her expression was now of reminis-cence and enjoyment. She was looking into the past which she could recollect with happiness. The present was slowly but inexorably fading as though a film was growing over her blue eyes. Nature, with unwonted mercy, was softening the pen-ultimate good-byes.

Grandma recited the prayers with unusual solemnity that morning. It was doubly an occasion. She had got up for the first time after her illness and I was off to school. I peeped through my fingers. I could see her hooked nose, her old, tired eyes, her cream and white hair under the little velvet and lace cap, the moving lips which seemed dry and parched. Nanna was praying at a chair on the other side of the table. The repose of her face was a little troubled as she looked down at the seat of the chair. Fanny's hair, as usual, was beginning to fall down her back and she kept patting it in an ineffectual way to get it under her cap. Next to her was the new kitchen maid, a plain uninteresting girl who seemed, I thought without sympathy, to be homesick. I could just see the trim outline of Kitty's shoulder, her black hair almost invisible against the shiny black frock. Her legs, thin but muscular in their black stockings, filled my mind with an uneasy sensuality which I no sooner experienced than repelled. The parlourmaid on one knee in the corner of the room, looked, with all her bows, ribbons and aprons, like a great galleon which had gone aground in full sail.

After breakfast I made a round of farewells. Mrs Farmer gave me an old, bright shilling piece, which, coming from her, seemed to be endowed with magical qualities. Mrs Courtenay bent down to kiss me after admiring my new suit and insisted on giving me a ginger nut wrapped in tissue paper for the journey. On my way back from her cottage I saw Mr Brailes walking very quickly through the wood.

'Ah, David,' he panted as he came up to me, 'I thought I might be too late.' He gazed at me with an oblique glance through his spectacles. 'Off to school,' he murmured and then with a simper like a cat, as though making the remark for the attention of his wife, 'and all dressed up ready for the fray!' He paused and looked through the trees at the pale blue of the sky. 'Mrs Brailes is ill but she sends you her love and wants you to have this little book.' He drew a parcel from his pocket and handed it to me. 'Have a look. Go on. Ah, you see it's got gilt leaves and a gilt cross on the front and back. Yes, it's a prayer book. When you read it in church, you can think of us.'

I thanked him, turning over the rice paper leaves as I did so.

He turned awkwardly away. 'It's nothing.' He gave a little snort of depreciation. 'Nothing at all. It's just a reminder. I hope you have a lovely term. Be a good boy and remember to pray. God bless you.'

He looked for a moment as if he was about to give me his blessing but he turned and walked quickly down the path.

When I got to the kitchen Cook was standing at the table with a chopping knife in her hand. 'There you are, then,' she said cheerfully, wiping her mouth with the back of her hand in anticipation of the kiss I would give her. 'Now, remember, not too many fights. I 'opes you 'ave some good food such as you like.'

'I hope so,' I said gloomily.

' 'Spects you will. We shall miss you.'

She bent down and gave me a wet kiss on the mouth.

Grandma was waiting for me in the drawing-room. She stood in front of the fire with an expression of anxiety and yet of withdrawal on her face. 'Uncle John and Aunt Emma telephoned while you were out. They both say they are writing to St George's.' She turned to the fire with a gesture of embarrassment. 'I wanted Uncle John to have a talk with you before you left.' She raised her eyes from the fire and looked in the direction of the inlaid table for once empty of flowers. 'I know so little about schools,' she went on. 'Do your best – you can't do better than that. I know you will, Davey. Don't forget to say your prayers at night. I shall be thinking a great deal of you and wondering how you are getting on. I shall write to you and I hope you'll have time to tell me how you are getting on.'

I could hear the engine of the car jugging at the door. Mr Courtenay's gaiters creaked as he carried my trunk through the lobby. Nanna began talking to him in an unnaturally loud voice. I kissed Grandma and she pressed my pocket money into my hand. As I walked across the carpet to the screen by the door I had a momentary impression that I was seeing the place for the first time. It did not seem any the lighter, yet it appeared to stand out more brightly. Every detail was present in a flash, from the Japanese daggers on the little table by the window to the swirling sun-washed clouds in a picture on the wall.

Nanna was standing in the lobby holding my overcoat. She helped me into it and gave me a kiss. I hugged her for a moment and she said: 'Be a good boy.' I next clutched Buzz and handed him to Nanna. Then I went out on to the steps where Mr Courtenay was talking of the weather impassively to George who was to accompany me to the school train. As he saw me come out he gave me a beaming smile which was meant to reassure me. But I saw that there was in it a look of deep concern. He knew what I felt, because he had experienced it himself. Mr Courtenay also looked at me, gave a little chuckle which was meant to be a sign of friendship, and got into the car.

I sat next to George in the back seat. Through the window I could see the maids at the window. Old Fanny tapped on a dormer window, as she had done when we set out for Bathampton. Cook waved her handkerchief from the kitchen. Nanna stood forlornly on the steps and when she thought I was no longer looking, wiped her eyes with the corner of her apron. Buzz crouched beside her. By looking through the back window I could see Grandma in the drawing-room waving a little lace handkerchief.

'It won't be long before you're back again,' George said in a voice which was meant to be comforting but which he seemed to find inadequate. He began fumbling in his pockets. At last I asked him what he was doing.

'I can't think what I've done with the toffees I bought you at the Post Office. I know,' he continued, still fumbling among his many pockets and disarranging his scarf and hat as he did so, 'I did have them. Oh, I wonder if I left them on the hall table.... I'll post them to you.'

I was near to tears but I could not help laughing. I saw in the driving mirror that Mr Courtenay was grinning. The

familiar sights were slipping by one by one. We passed along
the overgrown drive, past the great barn and the barn garden
dominated from the outside by the great poplar. Everything
basked in the unexpected radiance of that lovely day. We
were now through the white gate post and climbing the steep
hill on the down. The familiar was gone and now there was
the less familiar. Soon there would come the unknown.

When we got to London we had lunch in a dingy tavern
which George frequented. By this time we both seemed to
have exhausted everything we had to say to each other. We
gloomily ate a slice of mutton soaked in thin, fatty gravy.
And then it was time to be at the platform. We arrived early
and wandered up and down till we were accosted by a heavily
built man of about fifty who told us he was the headmaster.
He had a thin, veined face, deep blue, penetrating eyes and a
long, lean nose which was strangely crooked at the tip. He
was dressed in a new set of grey plus fours without an overcoat which gave him an out of doors, spring-like appearance.
He shook George briefly by the hand, ascertained who he was
and how he came to be seeing me off. Then he turned his
attention to me.

'So here you are Porteous,' he said, looking into my face,
noting, I felt sure, how pale and tear-stained it was, 'we were
beginning to think we'd never see you. Better late than never.
Now come along with me and I'll find you your carriage.
I've already seen to it that somebody will be looking after
you. You're the only new boy.' He pinched me with affectionate impatience on the shoulder and led me down the
train.

He showed me into a reserved carriage and I put my hand
luggage on the rack.

'I think,' the headmaster said curtly to George, 'it would
probably be best if you said good-bye now. It will give the boy
a chance to make friends.'

George nodded as though talking to a surgeon about to

perform an operation on a friend. He stared gloomily at me through the window, gave me a hearty handshake, and then one of his beaming smiles that were, somehow, tragic. As he turned away the smile left his face and his cheeks sagged. A moment later he was gone, his untidy brown overcoat lost in the crowd. The headmaster was called away to see to the luggage and I was left alone.

I looked miserably out of the window at the disorder and dirt of the station. Trains were sending clouds of steam up into the grimy roof, thudding and panting as they did so. Vapour was escaping from under the carriage in furtive hisses, occasionally obliterating the view. Porters hurried by, trundling mounds of newly labelled suitcases.

A few boys began to appear, hanging about in groups on the platform. They talked loudly and sucked toffees. They were all dressed in serge suits, overcoats and boater hats. They looked sleek and confident, especially when they looked into my compartment. They whispered knowingly to each other: 'New boy,' as though I was a different species. I began to wish that my coat looked less new and that my boater did not shine so brightly.

Two boys suddenly slammed open the door, stared at me and got inside. They banged their hand luggage into the racks without a word. They both had thin weasel faces.

'New boy?' one of them asked, throwing his hat down on the seat, and without waiting for me to reply, continued: 'That seat's taken, see? If anyone comes along and we're not here tell them it's for Gregory minor.'

'Thought I hadn't seen him before,' the other said, looking me over.

They crammed toffees into their mouths, threw me one and slouched off. I was left alone again.

A boy dressed in the school uniform, but so big I thought he was grown up, looked into the compartment. 'Ah,' he said appraisingly, 'you're the new boy?'

I got up and nodded. 'Yes,' I said, 'I am.'

The boy's eye fell on the boater hat on the seat. 'Who's hat is that?' he demanded.

I told him what I had been told to say.

He looked annoyed. 'No-one can reserve a seat on the school train. Anyway hats must be worn on the platform. Give it to me.'

I did as he commanded and he disappeared with the hat. The headmaster returned with an olive-skinned boy in a specially neat uniform and a pleasant open expression on his face.

'This is Porteous, then. Look after him.' The headmaster stood outside the window and gave orders to the boys on the now crowded platform. The boy got into the carriage, sat down beside me and offered me a toffee. 'We're allowed to eat them till the train starts,' he explained. 'I'm going to look after you for the first two or three days. If you don't understand anything come to me.' He glanced at the thinning grey hair at the back of the headmaster's head. 'Rough luck being a new boy on an off term. Been ill?'

I was about to explain when the headmaster opened the door for a throng of boys and the carriage was soon crowded. Everybody began to talk at once. The headmaster was by now out of sight. The boy, who had been ordered to look after me, turned from the others, with whom he was making easy conversation, to me.

'You know,' he said suddenly, 'I believe I've seen you before. Were'nt you buying your outfit at the stores?'

I now recognised the boy who had been standing at the next mirror.

'Yes I did,' I said, but I lied. 'I don't think I saw you there.'

'Was that your father with you?'

'No,' I said, getting hot as I realised everyone in the compartment was listening, 'it was a friend.'

'Guardian?'

'Not exactly.'

'Haven't you got a father?' another boy asked impishly.

'No,' I said, blushing.

'You must have. Everybody has a father,' a waggish voice piped up.

'He was killed in the war.'

'Bad luck,' somebody murmured and there was silence for a moment. It seemed to be considered bad taste to continue the conversation further. I tried to make myself as inconspicuous as possible by shrinking into my seat.

But it was not to be. The boy, who had been ordered to look after me, leant forward and asked: 'Was that your mother in the stores?'

I shook my head and bit my lip.

'Who was it then?' the boy pursued, eyeing my discomfort with complacency. Everybody stopped talking to listen.

'My mother lives in Belgium,' I said defensively.

'It was your Nanny, wasn't it?'

There was a roar of laughter as I didn't answer.

A spirit of dejection and misery passed over me. So it was going to happen all over again. 'Yes, it was,' I said doggedly, bright red in the face, 'there was nobody else to get my clothes.'

To my surprise this suddenly turned the scales in my favour. They seemed to think the arrangement appropriate in the circumstances.

'Haven't you got any relations you live with?' one of the older boys asked, compassion mingling with curiosity in his voice.

I was luckily spared the public recital of more revelations about my life by the arrival of the two weasel-faced boys.

'Hey,' one of them said, 'there were three places booked here. And where's my hat?' he asked turning in an accusatory way to me.

'I'm sorry,' I said with a gulp, 'but directly you left a big boy' – there was a titter as I said this – 'took it away.'

'Took it away?' the boy scowled. Everyone in the carriage listened intently.

278

'Yes, he said no-one could book a seat and that everyone had to wear his hat.'

'That's a good beginning to the term,' the other weasel-faced boy commented wryly, 'it was Stanford, I bet.'

'Had he got rather a red face?' a boy in the corner asked with a certain amount of relish.

I nodded and everyone said that it must have been Stanford, the head boy.

The boy who had lost his hat turned on me. 'You silly little new boy, why didn't you hide it or something?'

The accusation was so unfair that the blood rushed to my face again. 'I wasn't to know,' I said in a strangled voice, 'I did what you told me.'

'Of course he couldn't help it,' somebody said, 'it was your own silly fault.'

'Well,' the boy replied sullenly, 'in any case we're coming in here and that means that two of you will have to get out, doesn't it?'

'Oh does it?' a wiry little boy with curly hair exclaimed. He jumped on to the seat and pulled the cases of my two antagonists from the rack.

There was a howl of assent from the carriage. 'You can't book. Stanford said so.' 'You may be in the third but you can't do what you like.' 'Go on, take your luggage with you.' 'Where's Gregory minor, the third person of the Trinity?' 'I should try and get your hat back from Stanford. You're in for it if you don't.'

It looked as if there might be a fight but the last remark went home. The two boys slouched off and could be seen through the window talking to the formidable Stanford who had accosted them.

'Poor old Sliggers,' one of the boys commented, 'he's always in trouble.'

There was the slam of shutting doors and the train began to move. The boys settled in their seats and we were on our way.

279

On arrival at St George's I just had time to catch a glimpse of the sea and streets of seaside lodging houses. Then I shook hands with the matron on the steps and was ushered into the dormitory. Here we unpacked our cases and went down to tea. We had the thickest slabs of bread and butter I had ever seen. It was explained to me that I could only have jam on the third piece. A little bell tinkled, grace was said and we walked in a file to the chapel. At the door there was a portrait of a soldier which the boys saluted. 'Field Marshal Lord Roberts' was written in gold letters across the bottom. At the corners of the picture and under the glass were Flanders poppies. I did not know who Lord Roberts was but I saluted the picture like the others.

I had not had time till I was in the chapel to sort out my impressions. But as the prayers were being said, a talk delivered by the headmaster about the coming term, and especially during the singing of a long hymn, I had for the first time an opportunity to reflect. I thought with nostalgia of the great drawing-room at The Firs with its brightly burning logs under the Pre-Raphaelite mantelpiece. What would Grandma and Nanna be doing? Perhaps Nanna would be sitting alone in the nursery before going to bed doing some sewing. And poor, dejected Buzz, what would he be doing? At the thought of the poor creature lying under my empty bed tears streamed into my eyes and I only just controlled myself.

The dormitory was a very long room furnished with two rows of ten beds covered with scarlet blankets. At the foot of each bed there was a wicker basket into which the boys carefully placed their clothes for nightly inspection. Between the beds were small chairs on which were set out each boy's photographs, invariably of the mother and sometimes of the father as well. There were no carpets on the well-polished floors and at one end of the room there were rows of ewers and basins for washing. There were no curtains to the big windows and the place was icily cold. Each pyjamaed boy knelt for a moment at his bedside to say his night prayers, before jumping into the cold sheets. There were a few minutes of whispered conversation and then the formidable Stanford inspected our clothes. After he had gone, the lights went out.

I had expected to be left in darkness. On the contrary bright moonlight poured through the curtainless windows making the unfamiliar room more strange than ever. There were a few subdued whispers and then silence except for the sound of even breathing. I could hear voices from the matron's room, the sound of someone moving to and fro, the clinking of bottles. Then the light which shone from under the door was suddenly switched off, the footsteps disappeared down the stairs. I raised myself on my elbow for a moment and glanced round the room. Moonlight was reflected on some of the photographs by the boys' beds and on the row of jugs. The boy next to me shifted in his bed and I could hear very faintly from under the clothes the sound of weeping. I had noticed he was a dark-haired, sensitive-looking boy but he had not spoken to me. I did not even know his name.

I lay still in case he should think I had heard him. Then he sat up and I could see that he was shuddering as he cried. He looked wildly round the room, lay back and began to cry again. I shifted as cautiously as I could but he heard me.

'You're the new boy aren't you?' he asked and I could just make out in the semi-darkness that he was wiping his eyes on the sleeve of his pyjama coat.

'Yes,' I whispered back.

'Can't you sleep?'

'No.'

'Are you homesick?'

'Yes.'

There was a pause. Then he said: 'So am I.'

'Is this your second term?'

'No. My third. But I'm always homesick.'

'I thought perhaps it would be better after the first time.'

'It isn't with me.' He paused as if considering what he had

281

said. 'You won't tell anyone will you? They wouldn't understand.'

'Of course not,' I answered fervently.

'Perhaps we'll be friends,' he said and stretched out his
hand. It was sticky and warm. I grasped it and he left it
lying out of the bed clothes. A few moments later he was
breathing regularly. He was asleep.

But sleep would not come to me. I tossed and turned, my
mind filled with a kaleidoscope of impressions. They came
like photographs on a screen, vivid, involuntary. Grandma's
drawn white face on the pillow. Nanna's scared look as she
hurried me out of the barn on the night of Mr Evans's death.
The outhouse lighted by the acetylene lamp. George in the
lobby turning away from Mother with a tragic, moved expression on his face. Catherine seated at the back of the car
as she was driven off by the impassive Mr Courtenay. The
eyes of the condemned pig as he came out of his sty into the
darkening evening. The flames, after the death, streaming
up into the star-filled sky. Mr Range standing in front of the
studio fireplace, smoothing his black, curly hair, something
haunting his keen, brown eyes. Mother bending over me in
the darkened night-nursery at The Firs. Mr Brailes in the
pulpit preaching of suffering.

These pictures, jumbled and out of sequence, were not only
involuntary, but they passed in front of my eyes without
making any lasting impression on my mind. I could stand
them no longer and crept to the window.

The school garden lay below me bathed in the cold,
impersonal light of the full moon. To the right and in front
of me there was a jumble of buildings, doubtless classrooms,
to the left a lawn with stone steps leading to a path and
border. Beyond were the playing fields surrounded by ugly
seaside houses. There was no sound, not even a whisper. It
was as if the moonlight had petrified the scene. I listened for
the sea, which I knew was on the other side of the buildings,
but I could not hear it.

Everything, it seemed to me, was in the grip of a force incomprehensible, either as to its laws, if it had any, or as to its motives, if it was personal. It was all drawn into being by the glittering light of life. Both in the light and the darkness there was nothing to be done save accept. In the glare of the awful moonlight, down there, was life. In the black shadows, cast by the school buildings, nonentity.

There came into my mind the thought that life was not worth the candle, a tragic episode between nothingness and oblivion. I could not have put it into words, of course. But I understood the meaning of it. Nor did I ask myself whether it was true or not. In such circumstances who does?

But even as the thought passed through my mind it was followed by another. The sense of personal loss and disquiet had passed away. My predicament was, after all, the common predicament of all. The brittle leaf scattered by the cold wind: a tiny, resilient bud took its place. There was the future with its thousand possibilities. Hope, surly determination – joy, the delusive flame of life, call it what you like – came to my rescue.

I shuddered in the cold, turned from the window and crept between the cold sheets. For a few minutes I hugged myself to keep warm. Then I fell into a quiet, refreshing sleep.